Praise for *Heirs of Yesterday*

"This book returns to print a revealing novel by the foremost American Jewish woman novelist of her time, Emma Wolf. In their remarkable introduction, Cantalupo and Harrison-Kahan disclose new details concerning Wolf's life and career in turn-of-the-century San Francisco, her creative circle of Jewish women friends, the subtle antisemitism that she experienced, and her complicated relationship with the men of the Jewish Publication Society. A wondrous contribution to early American Jewish literature."

—Jonathan D. Sarna, University Professor and Joseph H. & Belle R. Braun Professor of American Jewish History, Brandeis University

"Cantalupo and Harrison-Kahan have crafted an impressive volume on the work and import of Emma Wolf. More than just an excellent description of Wolf's contributions to literature, *Heirs of Yesterday* shows us the important intersections between gender, region, and history. Only a woman such as Emma Wolf, writing as she did during San Francisco's early history, can offer us perspectives and understandings all too often missed in scholarly writing. The footnotes themselves offer an extraordinary tutorial for those interested in a nuanced understanding of Wolf's extraordinary work."

—Marc Dollinger, professor at San Francisco State University and author of *Black Power, Jewish Politics: Reinventing the Alliance in the 1960s*

"A powerful corrective to common historical narratives of Jewish American identity and prevailing conceptions of turn-of-the-century Jewish fiction, this beautiful edition is also a substantial work of scholarly recovery. The thorough and rigorous introduction is a valuable resource, giving Emma Wolf the attention she richly deserves."

—Jennifer S. Tuttle, Dorothy M. Healy Professor of Literature and Health, University of New England

HEIRS OF
YESTERDAY

Emma Wolf

Courtesy of Donald Auslen

HEIRS OF YESTERDAY

Emma Wolf

EDITED WITH AN INTRODUCTION BY
BARBARA CANTALUPO AND
LORI HARRISON-KAHAN

Wayne State University Press
Detroit

ISBN 978-0-8143-4668-6 (paperback);
ISBN 978-0-8143-4667-9 (hardback);
ISBN 978-0-8143-4669-3 (ebook)

Library of Congress Control Number: 2019948586

Wayne State University Press
Leonard N. Simons Building
4809 Woodward Avenue
Detroit, Michigan 48201–1309

Visit us online at wsupress.wayne.edu

CONTENTS

ILLUSTRATIONS

ACKNOWLEDGMENTS

The late Donald Auslen (1932–2018), great-nephew of Emma Wolf, shared Wolf family history and photographs, and we are very grateful for his generosity. We were helped in our research by Tim Wilson, librarian, San Francisco History Center, San Francisco Public Library; Jeff Thomas, San Francisco Public Library; Rachel Misrati, archivist, National Library of Israel; Meri-Jane Rochelson, professor of English, Florida International University; Susan Bernstein, research professor, Boston University; Jennifer Tuttle, professor of English, University of New England; Lucas Dietrich, adjunct professor of humanities, Lesley University; Kimberly Chabot Davis, professor of English, Bridgewater State University; Elif Armbruster, associate professor of English, Suffolk University; Carmen Cisneros, office manager, Home of Peace Cemetery; Jessica Lydon, associate archivist, Special Collections Research Center, Temple University; and the Boston College Interlibrary Loan staff, especially Anne Kenny and Shannon McDowell. Thanks go to Doug Hochstetler, director of academic affairs at Penn State Lehigh Valley, for his support of the project. For their help in transcribing the novel, we thank Maggie McQuade, undergraduate research fellow, Boston College; Sara Roth, administrative assistant, Penn State Lehigh Valley; and Liu Tingu, student, Penn State Lehigh Valley. We also thank Anne Taylor for her careful copyediting of the manuscript and Sophia Pandelidis for double-checking the transcription. We are grateful for the translation expertise of Jessica Kirzane, who assisted with footnotes and offered feedback on the introduction. Finally, we thank Kathy Wildfong, Annie Martin,

Kristin Harpster, Kristina Stonehill, Emily Nowak, Jamie Jones, and the rest of the staff at Wayne State University Press for their commitment to publishing works by Emma Wolf and other Jewish women writers.

PREFACE

My work on Emma Wolf began in 1992, when I was asked to write an entry for Ann Shapiro's proposed book on Jewish American women writers. Of the two nineteenth-century writers on Shapiro's list, I chose to write about Emma Wolf rather than Emma Lazarus since I had never heard of Wolf, and I wanted the experience of discovery. Having been trained in a theory-based PhD at SUNY Buffalo, I had no idea what I would be tackling. Naively, I thought it would be an easy enough task: I would simply read what had been written about Wolf and then compose my essay. However, it turned out that only short encyclopedia entries on Wolf and her work existed; all I learned from them was that she had written five novels, she was from San Francisco, and her father's name was Simon Wolf. That was enough to take me to the Bay Area, where I began to piece together what became a short biobibliographical essay for Shapiro's book.[1]

As the years went by, I kept discovering more and more about Wolf, helped especially by two of her relatives, her great-nephew Donald Auslen and her great-niece Barbara Goldman Aaron. I had just missed meeting Barbara's father, Robert Goldman, who had passed away two years before I contacted the family. Both Robert Goldman and his father, Louis Goldman, Emma's brother-in-law, held her work in high regard. In an effort to preserve his aunt's legacy, Robert had, in fact, compiled letters from Israel Zangwill to Wolf, which his daughter generously shared with me.[2] Had I been able to speak with Robert, I might have found out even more about Emma than what his daughter knew. My research on Wolf had many such misses. For example, the relevant records at San Francisco's Temple Emanu-El, the synagogue to which her family belonged, had been destroyed in the great earthquake and fire of 1906. And, recently, the seemingly straightforward task of finding her gravesite almost proved to be a miss as well.

In 2015 I visited the Home of Peace Cemetery in Colma, California, where members of San Francisco's Congregation Emanu-El were buried after 1888.[3] Before traveling to California, I had written to Carmen Cisneros, the office manager at the cemetery, and she had confirmed that Emma Wolf was buried there. When I arrived at the office that afternoon in March, the rabbi affiliated with the cemetery happened to be present. As I told him a bit about Wolf, her literary career, and her life in San Francisco, he was particularly interested because the cemetery offers guided tours for school groups that point out prominent people who are buried at Home of Peace Cemetery— including, for example, Wyatt Earp, the famous gunfighter who is buried beside his Jewish wife, Josephine Sarah Marcus Earp;[4] Levi Strauss, the originator of the blue jean;[5] and Adolph Sutro, San Francisco's first Jewish mayor, who served from 1895 to 1897.[6] I was pleased to hear the rabbi say he would include Wolf on the tour list. After our conversation, I set off to find Emma's plot, armed with a map of the grounds and the set of coordinates I had been sent.

But when I got to Plot G, Section 8, Lot 1, there was no Emma Wolf. Instead, I found monuments to a Wolfe family who were not related to the Wolfs. Dismayed, I returned to the office, and at first Ms. Cisneros was sure that she had given me the correct coordinates. However, she decided to recheck the big, bound book for 1932 under "W." She opened to the relevant pages and drew her finger across the line from Emma Wolf's name on the left-hand page to the line with the plot designation on the right-hand page. Sure enough, it read Plot G, Section 8, Lot 1. Puzzled but determined, she tried another strategy. She counted down the lines from the top of the left-hand page to Emma's name and then from the top of the right-hand page to the same line. It was then that she realized the stitching on the binding had loosened over time, and when she straightened the pages out, the line connecting Emma Wolf's name to her plot actually was G-3, not G-8. So, I set off again.

EMMA WOLF'S PARENTS' GRAVESTONE.
Photo by Barbara Cantalupo.

As I approached the G-3 area of the graveyard, I was happy to see from a distance a large stone marker with "WOLF" on it. However, when I got closer, it became clear that this was not Emma's gravesite. Instead, it belonged to her parents: Simon Wolf (1822–78) and Annette (Levy) Wolf (1838–1929). No Emma in sight. Discouraged and preparing to leave, I happened to notice nearby a large, rectangular, raised stone about a foot high from the ground with the name "Goldman" in large letters. I knew that Isabel Wolf, one of Emma's sisters, had married Louis Goldman, so I decided to stop and look at the Goldman stone. At the top, I saw the names of Louis Goldman (1868–1921), Isabel Goldman (1870–1943), and Georgiana Howard (1911–58). About two feet below these inscriptions, to my surprise, I discovered what I was looking for: Emma Wolf (1864 [sic]–1932). Yet, even here, there was an unsettling oversight from years ago: Emma Wolf was born in 1865, not 1864. Her date of birth had been

EMMA WOLF'S GRAVESTONE.
Photo by Barbara Cantalupo.

incorrectly engraved, just as it had been incorrectly noted on her death certificate. Even more striking is that her death certificate lists her "trade, profession or kind of work" as "housewife" although Wolf was a well-regarded, unmarried author when she died.

Just as Wolf's work had been overlooked for decades, I had almost overlooked her place of rest. Nonetheless, despite near misses and after more than twenty years of research, I was gratified to have found not only her place of rest but more and more about Wolf's writing life.

Barbara Cantalupo

NOTES

1. See Barbara Cantalupo, "Emma Wolf," in *Jewish American Women Writers*, ed. Ann Shapiro (Westport, CT: Greenwood, 1994), 465–72. As my continuing research revealed, some assumptions I made in this initial effort proved untrue, such as the belief that Wolf spent her last fifteen years at Dante Sanitarium. For further discussion of my efforts to recover Wolf and her work, see Barbara Cantalupo, "Discovering Emma Wolf—San Francisco Author," *CCAR Journal* (Winter 2004): 77–84.

2. See Barbara Cantalupo, "The Letters of Israel Zangwill to Emma Wolf: Transatlantic Mentoring in the 1890s," *Resources for American Literary Study* 28 (2002): 121–38.

3. "Shortly after the first Jewish settlers joined in San Francisco's Gold Rush era, they purchased land for a cemetery on Vallejo Street. In 1860, Congregation Emanu-El dedicated its second cemetery in the area that is now Dolores Park. When San Francisco's booming growth encouraged relocation outside the city, Congregation Emanu-El dedicated Home of Peace Cemetery in Colma in January 1889." "Home of Peace Cemetery," Jewish Cemeteries of San Francisco, https://www.jewishcemeteries-sf.org/contact-us/home-of-peace-cemetery.

4. On Josephine Marcus, see Ann Kirshner, *Lady at the O.K. Corral: The True Story of Josephine Marcus Earp* (New York: Harper, 2013). According to Harriet Rochlin, Josephine Sarah Marcus was the daughter of German-Jewish immigrants who moved to San Francisco when Josephine was seven. She met Wyatt Earp in Arizona, and they lived together, traveling throughout the various "boom towns" of the West until settling in San Francisco. As Rochlin writes, "Josephine Sarah Marcus Earp died in 1944, and her remains now rest with his. But the collision of Jewish and cowboy cultures that epitomized their union goes on. Wyatt Earp enthusiasts have made the gravesite the most visited in that Jewish cemetery and once even stole the tombstone." Harriet

Rochlin, "Josephine Sarah Marcus Earp, 1861–1944," in *Encyclopedia of Jewish Women*, Jewish Women's Archive, https://jwa.org/encyclopedia/article/earp-josephine-sarah-marcus.

5. See Lynn Downey, *Levi Strauss: The Man Who Gave Blue Jeans to the World* (Amherst: University of Massachusetts Press, 2016).

6. See Eugenia Kellogg Holmes, *Adolph Sutro: A Brief Story of a Brilliant Life* (San Francisco: Press of San Francisco Photo-Engraving Co., 1895), which is available at the "Virtual Museum of the City of San Francisco," http://www.sfmuseum.net/sutro/bio.html.

INTRODUCTION

Barbara Cantalupo and Lori Harrison-Kahan

My purpose in writing . . . is to give genuine pleasure to my readers. But one must not place heart before art. I try to paint the subject as truthfully as possible in the colors in which I see it myself mentally. Truth-telling should be an author's religion. It is mine, and because of it I have caused considerable discussion among my own people. But all that I have written has been said in the spirit of love—the love that has the courage to point out a fault in its object.

—Emma Wolf, 1901

Making available an important and influential novel by Emma Wolf (1865–1932), this edition of *Heirs of Yesterday* (1900) fills a significant gap in American literary studies, Jewish studies, and women's writing. Although Wolf has received little notice by literary scholars and historians, the Jewish press in her time bestowed attention and praise on the work of this San Francisco writer, who, in 1900 at age 35, was publishing her fourth novel.[1] In its front-page review of *Heirs of Yesterday*, the *Jewish Messenger* labeled Wolf "one of the rare exceptions to the general rule" in the recent explosion of Jewish fiction. "She is expressly omitted from the category of Jewish novelists who exploit their religion and special class of people and call the result literature," the reviewer stated.[2] During the late nineteenth to early twentieth century, a period of Jewish American literary history dominated by the genre of the New York–centric ghetto tale and by Yiddish-speaking, Eastern European immigrant writers, Wolf's *Heirs of Yesterday* offered a very different representation of Jewish life in the United States. Set far from the sweatshops and tenements of the New York ghetto, the novel takes place in the Reform Jewish community of San Francisco's Pacific Heights. Its central characters, physician Philip May and pianist Jean Willard, are not striving immigrants in the process of learning English and becoming American. Instead, they are cultured, middle-class, native-born Americans who interact socially and professionally with their gentile peers. Overturning readers' expectations of Jewish American identity and Jewish fiction, as well as complicating well-engrained narratives about US immigration and religious minorities, this edition of *Heirs of Yesterday* brings a forgotten novel to the attention of twenty-first century readers and scholars. Our introduction expands upon the current scholarship on Wolf, offering biographical background based on new research findings. It also explores key literary, historical, and religious contexts for *Heirs of Yesterday*, thereby opening avenues for further research on a writer who has been called the "mother of American Jewish fiction."[3]

"A JEWISH GIRLHOOD IN OLD SAN FRANCISCO": EMMA WOLF'S LIFE AND TIMES

On June 15, 1865, Simon and Annette (Levy) Wolf, Jewish immigrants from Alsace who had settled in the San Francisco Bay Area, welcomed a new daughter. The fourth of eleven children, Emma was to grow up in a family dominated by girls. The Wolfs' first child was a son, Morris, who was born in 1858 when Annette was twenty years old but died at age four, before Emma was born. Emma joined her older sisters, Florence and Celestine, who were born in 1861 and 1862, respectively. A year after Emma's birth, in May 1866, another son, Julius, arrived. He was followed by six more girls: Alice in 1869, Isabel in 1870, Mildred in 1873, May in 1875, Estelle in 1876, and Esther in 1879. On September 12, 1878, while Annette was pregnant with Esther, Simon Wolf died unexpectedly on the way home from a routine business trip, leaving his wife to raise ten children on her own. Thirteen-year-old Emma was profoundly affected by the sudden loss of her father; as an adult, she continued to revisit this loss in her fiction (including in *Heirs of Yesterday*), where the death of a loving paternal figure bears symbolic weight and marks a turn in her protagonists' fates.

Simon Wolf's financial success as a businessman meant that the family, with some economizing and despite its size, had the resources to maintain a comfortable middle-class lifestyle. But

SIMON WOLF, EMMA'S FATHER.
Courtesy of Donald Auslen.

at a time when most women of their class would not have sought employment, even prior to marriage, their father's early death impelled Emma and several of her sisters to work, albeit in suitable jobs for women of their social standing. Two of Emma's sisters, Isabel and May, were employed as schoolteachers, while Alice found work as a private secretary. Like Emma, Alice was also a writer, publishing short stories as well as one novel, *A House of Cards*, in 1896. Most of the Wolf sisters married out of the wage-earning labor force. Alice, for instance, discontinued her writing career following her marriage to her employer, Colonel William MacDonald, in 1898. Emma, however, remained single, due in part to a congenital physical disability, possibly exacerbated by polio.

Emma's status as a single woman and her limited mobility freed her from domestic duties and allowed her to devote her time and energy to writing. While remaining involved in the lives of her siblings and their children, Emma continued her lucrative career as a writer until age fifty-one, publishing her last and longest novel, *Fulfillment: A California Novel*, with New York publisher Henry Holt and Company in 1916. As a review of *Fulfillment* in the *Overland Monthly* makes clear, Wolf's fiction had not faltered in style or content: "In the locale, San Francisco, where she lives in real life, the author has woven a web of interesting temperaments in such a manner that the ensuing developments grips [sic] the reader to the last page. . . . the story is told crisply and with artistic restraint."[4] Given such praise from reviewers for the quality of her late work, it is likely that Wolf's retirement from writing and public life was driven by ill health. When she died in 1932, her obituary in the *San Francisco Chronicle* noted that she had spent the last fifteen years of her life "virtually confined to her room."[5]

Emma Wolf was born at a moment in US history when the Civil War had just come to an end, ushering in a new order with the abolition of slavery in the Southern states. Like the rest of the nation, which was undergoing industrialization and modernization, the West was experiencing rapid development, and Wolf's hometown of San Francisco was well on its way to becoming a cosmopolitan city, a destination for migrants from around the world. The seeds of the coming era's progressive reforms were beginning to have an impact upon women, many of whom were demanding rights of citizenship and seeking alternatives to conventional lives of marriage and domesticity. The end of the nineteenth century would prove an especially fertile period for women writers, with the expanded growth of periodical culture and an ever-increasing audience of middle-class female readers. By the time Emma reached adulthood, American Jewish life was also undergoing radical change, as the Reform movement took hold in cities across the nation and middle-class Jewish women formed communal organizations at the local and national levels. The influx of new immigrants led to a dramatic increase in the country's Jewish population. Hailing from Eastern European countries such as Russia, Austria-Hungary, and Romania, these new immigrants changed the face of American Jewry, reshaping and supplanting religious and secular forms of Jewishness established by previous immigrants from

France and Germany and by Sephardic Jews who dated their lineage in the United States back to the colonial era.

Part of a wave of Jewish immigration from Western and central Europe, Wolf's parents immigrated to the United States in the mid-nineteenth century, fleeing religious prejudice in Alsace-Lorraine, a French territory bordering on Germany. Although the French Revolution had officially "emancipated" Jews in France in the late eighteenth century, promising equality and opportunity for all, "the situation of the Jews in Alsace was by no means comfortable." As historian Paula Hyman has documented, "Anti-Jewish hostility," including "anti-Jewish remarks by government officials or in public courtroom proceedings[,] . . . remained a regular feature of Alsatian life into the 1860s."[6] Reports from the Bay Area informed Alsace's marginalized Jewish population that Jews were an integral part of San Francisco's cultural and business communities and that economic opportunities would be available upon their arrival in California. Ava Kahn describes Jewish immigration to the West Coast "as part of a chain or family migration [in which] families and friends from the same homelands settled together in the Golden State."[7] For Alsatian Jewish immigrants like the Wolfs, settling with friends and families meant they could live in proximity to other Jews; just as importantly, however, it allowed them to be part of a community in which they could continue to speak French and celebrate their French culture.[8]

Jews were among the pioneering settlers in the Bay Area during the Gold Rush, and their businesses helped grow and sustain the city of San Francisco. What began as a "population of 462 people 'living in tents, shanties and adobe huts' in 1847" became, in three years' time, a city of 21,000 people.[9] Marc Dollinger describes the historical conditions that enabled Jewish integration into the life of the developing city: "The rapid population growth, lack of preexisting Anglo power structure, and trade skills enjoyed by Jewish arrivals combined to create unprecedented Jewish social mobility. . . . San Francisco Jews counted the 'City by the Bay' as one of this nation's most friendly. Jewish residents tended to resist the temptation to live in cloistered Jewish enclaves, enjoying instead the opportunity to live and socialize among the larger non-Jewish community."[10] A firsthand account by Daniel Levy, a friend of the Wolf family and a lay leader at Congregation Emanu-El, confirms Dollinger's description. In a letter to the editor of the French journal *Archives Israélites*, dated October 30, 1855, Levy relates: "Among all the areas of the world, California is possibly the one in which the Jews are most widely dispersed. . . . [In San Francisco] the French, for the most part from Alsace or Lorraine, do not actually form a real group and are integrated into the mass of their nearest European neighbors. . . . [Jews] of San Francisco are estimated at more than three thousand. There may be as many as that scattered about in the interior."[11] This number represented about 9 percent of the population at that time, yet despite that small percentage, Jews had a strong influence on the city's commercial well-being. For example, in 1858 when the much-awaited day that marked the arrival of steamships bringing goods to San Francisco Bay fell on Yom Kippur, the city postponed "Steamer Day" so that "Jews were not forced to choose between commerce and their faith."[12] As San Francisco historians have noted, the "first generation of Jews in the Bay City" were granted such regard because they were "twice as likely as non-Jews to remain in the area permanently . . . [and] were a stabilizing, civilizing influence."[13]

In the mid-nineteenth century, Jews began to establish secular and religious roots in the Bay Area, founding philanthropic organizations like the First Hebrew Benevolent Society and the Eureka Benevolent Society and congregations such as Emanu-El and Sherith Israel. As early as 1856, two Jews were nominated for public office in San Francisco and a Jewish judge held a seat on the California Supreme Court.[14] Wolf herself described how Bay Area society was relatively free of caste distinctions in a profile of San Francisco that appeared as part of the series "Social Life in American Cities" in *The Delineator*:

> For many years a common hazard and uncertainty of fortune threw down any possible social barriers and prevented the formation of anything suggesting caste. It was in these young days that the seed was sown for that free-and-easy, hail-fellow well-met spirit which characterizes the San Franciscan of to-day. The zest of adventure or the necessity of venture had brought

with it a heterogenous agglomeration of all sorts and conditions of men, which accounts for a certain Bohemian tone and mellow worldliness not generally possessed by cities of such recent growth.[15]

The acceptance that Jews found in San Francisco during Wolf's lifetime was clearly evident with the election in 1895 of Adolph Sutro, a German American Jew, as mayor. As Edward Zerin explains, "Because Jews were pioneers among pioneers [in the West,] there was little overt anti-Semitism. . . . [T]hey were welcomed into the social life of the community, winning the respect of their fellow citizens."[16]

Yet Wolf acknowledged the tentative nature of such social acceptance. In her article in *The Delineator*, she went on to observe that as "order slowly grew out of chaos . . . society began to evolve with the usual demarcations and distinctions of latter-day living."[17] *Heirs of Yesterday* similarly reveals how ethno-racial and religious prejudices undergirded the city's social hierarchy by the late nineteenth century. While Wolf depicts Gilded Age San Francisco as a fairly inclusive environment, she does not shy away from exposing some of the subtler effects of individual and institutional anti-Semitism. In alluding to the differences between Philip May's experiences in New England and on the West Coast, however, the novel suggests that San Francisco was, comparatively, a haven for members of the minority religion, a place where they could be integrated into the social, economic, political, and cultural life of the city while openly identifying as Jews.

Although New York has now eclipsed all other cities as the locus of Jewish life in the United States, in the nineteenth century, San Francisco was well on its way to becoming the Jewish diaspora's West Coast counterpart. In her introduction to *Jewish Voices from the Gold Rush: A Documentary History, 1849–1880*, Ava Kahn details the vibrancy of Jewish life in San Francisco:

San Francisco became the center of Jewish life, as it did of California life. By the 1870s, a distant, drowsy California outpost had become "the City," a center of Jewish journalism and publication second only to New York City, as well as home to debate and literary societies, clubs, libraries, an orphan home, and a host of fraternal and benevolent organizations. . . . [S]ynagogue leaders in California became more independent than their eastern counterparts and had no inhibitions about speaking up or standing out. At times the community was nonconformist in its practices. Such anomalies as the recitation of the Kaddish, or mourner's prayer, in tribute to the memory of an admired non-Jew reflected an ability to synthesize Jewish traditions with a new, American way of life. . . . They joined with coreligionists to form the Concordia and other social clubs, to found literary and debating societies, and to establish B'nai B'rith and Kesher Shel Barzel lodges, among other fraternal organizations. In these associations, small merchants could meet independent of the religious and family constraints of the synagogue.[18]

Kahn's description affirms a vision of San Francisco not only as a welcoming environment for Jews but also as a place of "nonconformist" innovation where a synthesis between American and Jewish life could be forged, opening the way for new formulations of American Jewishness as a distinct cultural and religious identity. Wolf's congregation, Emanu-El, founded as an Orthodox synagogue in 1850, soon changed course and "endorsed . . . resolutions" spearheaded by leading Reform rabbi Isaac Mayer Wise, who initiated the creation of a uniquely American prayer book, *Minhag America*, at the Cleveland Conference of 1855; Wise's goal was to unify American Jews, who adhered to different religious customs due to their diverse national backgrounds.[19] In his role as leader and teacher at Emanu-El, Daniel Levy "favored sweeping reforms for the Jews of the West [and concluded that] 'the future belongs to Reform'" Judaism—a vision espoused by the characters of Jean and Daniel Willard in *Heirs of Yesterday*.[20] As Shari Rabin asserts, Jews on the frontier created flexible and adaptive versions of Judaism and Jewishness in which religion became "a mobile assemblage of resources for living."[21]

Scholars of California Jewish history have emphasized the symbolic nature of the West Coast in American Jewish life of the period. Moses Rischin characterizes California as a place that "more than any other appeared from the outset to project—as seen from a Jewish perspective—a sense of America at its most promising, open, and refreshing."[22] The city of San Francisco embodied this openness, allowing "Jews of all origins and persuasions . . . to enjoy the freedom to pursue varied opportunities and lead vibrant lives, to assimilate the best of modern America and the modern world, and to satisfy their special needs as Jews."[23] The majestic Emanu-El, which originated as a small congregation of traders and merchants during the Gold Rush of 1849, stood as a visible testament to all that San Francisco represented for the Jewish residents who had claimed the West Coast city as home. "Like no other building in the nation, the region's cathedral synagogue dramatically came to symbolize the freedom, equality, openness, and fraternity of America and of the West for Jews and others," Rischin observes of the centrally located temple whose twin domed towers were a visible feature of the city's skyline.[24] Temple Emanu-El projected a vision of San Francisco Jewry as "progressive" and "open-minded," according to Judith Pinnolis; as early as the 1880s, for instance, the congregation invited a woman vocalist to serve as cantor.[25] If Temple Emanu-El signaled the emergence of modern, urban Jewish society in the new West, the building's destruction in the 1906 earthquake and fire was a shock and temporary setback for the community, although the temple was subsequently rebuilt and remains an important landmark today. Along with Harriet Lane Levy's memoir *920 O'Farrell Street: A Jewish Girlhood in Old San Francisco* (1947), Wolf's *Heirs of Yesterday* is the rare creative work that captures the vitality of Jewish life in Gilded Age San Francisco. Published six years before the earthquake, *Heirs of Yesterday* stands as a lasting monument to a time and place in American Jewish history that are often overlooked.

As members of Emanu-El, the Wolfs were at the center of cosmopolitan Jewish life in Old San Francisco. But when Annette Levy and Simon Wolf first made their separate ways to the Bay Area, San Francisco was still a rough and rowdy Gold Rush town with a small Jewish population. Born in 1838 in Alsace-Lorraine, Annette grew up in San Francisco, arriving in the city at the age of five with her parents, Jonas and Amelie Levy. Simon Wolf, sixteen years Annette's senior, was also born in Alsace, in 1822, and spent his childhood and early adulthood there before immigrating to the United States. He arrived in New York on January 9, 1851, at the age of twenty-nine, before migrating westward. Several years later, Simon was followed by his sister, Clemence Wolf (1839–1924), who landed in New York before moving to San Francisco to be near her brother. By then, Simon and Annette were married, and Simon arranged for his sister to live with his in-laws. Although the exact story of how Annette and Simon met is not known, Emma's parents were part of a tight-knit French-Jewish immigrant community where marriages remained endogamous. For the next generation, however, that practice was to change, as evidenced by their daughter Alice's marriage to the gentile Colonel MacDonald in 1898. Though Emma did not wed, her fiction suggests that she was a careful observer of the courtships and marriages that took place around her. In all of her novels, including *Heirs of Yesterday*, Wolf makes symbolic use of the marriage plot, with debates over interfaith unions providing the subject matter for her first novel, *Other Things Being Equal*, in 1892.

In addition to marrying those who shared their faith and background, pioneers like Simon Wolf formed business partnerships with fellow Jews, and these familial and professional worlds often intersected. Simon established a number of general merchandise stores throughout Contra Costa County, working with Jewish partners, including his brother-in-law, Mark Kline (1835–1900), another Alsatian immigrant, who married his sister, Clemence, in 1862. In 1865, the year of Emma's birth, the brothers-in-law opened a store called Wolf & Kline Merchandise in the mining town of Somersville, now one of many unpopulated ghost towns, remnants of the Gold Rush past. With other businesses in Alamo, Danville, Antioch, Point of Timber, and Brentwood, Simon spent his week traveling from store to store to visit his partners, relying on three modes of transportation (ferry, train, and horse and buggy) and returning to his family in San Francisco on the weekends. In the mid-1860s, he also owned and operated a cigar and tobacco shop in the Russ House in San Francisco, the city's first three-story grand hotel. By the 1870s he had opened an office for the operation of his Contra Costa stores in San Francisco—an indication that his various business ventures were consistently profitable.[26]

As part of a Jewish mercantile class that profited from California's mining boom, the Wolfs lived a comfortable middle-class existence in San Francisco's fashionable neighborhoods. They employed servants, Irish immigrant women and a Chinese cook, to help care for the large family, including Annette's parents, who lived with the Wolfs during Emma's childhood. The deaths of Emma's maternal grandparents—Amelie passed away when Emma was seven and Jonas when she was eleven—were followed by the unexpected death of her father at age fifty-six. Simon Wolf's death was also a loss for the larger Bay Area community. "Mr. WOLF during 20 odd years that he was engaged in business in our county, and at times doing a large trade, proved himself an honest, conscientious, upright man and citizen," read the notice of his death in the *Weekly Antioch Ledger*. "Always kind and obliging, he had the respect and esteem of an extended circle of friends and acquaintances. To his family he was always kind and affectionate."[27] This description could easily be applied to the Jewish paternal figures in Wolf's novels, self-made family men like Jules Levice in *Other Things Being Equal* and Joseph May in *Heirs of Yesterday*, whose sacrifices and hard work eased the way for their children.

Following her husband's death, Annette did not remarry and raised her ten children with the help of live-in servants. Although relatively secure due to Simon's business investments, the family did experience the constraints of a limited income and the fear of economic vulnerability, especially during the panic of 1893 and the subsequent depression. In Wolf's fiction, monetary concerns emerge even among members of the upper class and upper-middle class, and her bourgeois female characters remain aware of the way their economic circumstances confer a privileged status. After Simon's death, the Wolf family moved often, partly to accommodate changes in the family's size and partly due to financial needs. Nonetheless, most of their homes were in what are now known as the Pacific Heights, Presidio Heights, and Laurel Heights neighborhoods of San Francisco—all beautiful locales overlooking the San Francisco Bay. As an adult and a successful author, Emma contributed to the family income and continued to live with her mother and some of her siblings. In 1898, for instance, 2105 Pine Street in Pacific Heights was

WOLF FAMILY PORTRAIT.
Courtesy of Donald Auslen.

home to Emma, her mother, three of her unmarried sisters, and her brother, Julius (1866–1923), a businessman who became president of the San Francisco Grain Exchange. In 1901, the family moved to Presidio Heights, today still one of the most prosperous neighborhoods in the city. The Wolf sisters also vacationed at summer resorts, such as the Hotel Ben Lomond in the Santa Cruz mountains, likely the inspiration for some of the natural settings in which Wolf's characters take temporary reprieve from urban living.[28]

Emma and her sisters attended the California public schools, completing their education at San Francisco Girls' High School, which was founded in 1864. In 1882, at the age of seventeen, Emma graduated from Girls' High School, which meant that her time there coincided with the principalship of John Swett, an educational reformer who has been described as the "Horace Mann of California."[29] As principal of the school from 1876 to 1889, Swett imposed high standards upon the curriculum with the goal of professionalizing teaching for the current instructors and for the female graduates, more than half of whom would end up in charge of their own class-rooms. By graduation, the girls would have obtained

> the ability to read and spell well; a fair knowledge of English grammar; some knowledge of the meaning and use of words, of etymology and synonyms; a fair knowledge of algebra and geometry; some knowledge of physical and political geography; a general outline of the history of the world; some knowledge of what to read in English literature, and how to read it; the ability to express their thoughts in correct English, gained by actual practice in composition, rather than by study of technical text-books on rhetoric; an elementary knowledge of physics, botany, and zoology; some knowledge of physiology and of the laws of health; some training in vocal culture and vocal music; [and] a course, for those who desired it, of Latin, French, or German.[30]

Believing in a strong link between reading and morality, Swett held particular views about how to promote literacy among youth, includ-ing limiting homework for high school girls in order to allow them time to read for pleasure. "From ten to sixteen is the golden period for the reading of good books," he wrote, "and any course of school-work that deprives pupils of time to read by keeping them all the time at the drudgery of text-book lessons is a mental wrong and a physical sin."[31] He also had particular ideas about the kinds of books that would en-rich the minds and moral characters of young people. Recommending writers such as Thomas Carlyle, Ralph Waldo Emerson, and—espe-cially influential for Wolf—Louisa May Alcott, he advised teachers to "see to it that [their pupils] do not poison themselves with sensational and trashy stories and novels," such as "the sentimental love-stories devoured by too many girls."[32] Harriet Lane Levy, valedictorian of Emma's class at Girls' High School and one of the few graduates to continue her education at the University of California Berkeley, de-scribed in her memoir how the girls began the school day by reciting lines of verse they had selected, with poets ranging from Shakespeare to Henry Wadsworth Longfellow and William Cullen Bryant. When she became a famous writer, Wolf credited the education she received in the San Francisco public schools. In a 1901 interview in the *San*

Francisco Examiner, for instance, she recalled "a valuable lesson" that she learned in grammar school when a teacher "corrected a tendency to the use of superfluous language in my composition. 'Emma,' said she, 'your balconies are bigger than your houses.' Ever since," Wolf concluded, "I have tried to avoid verbiage."[33]

Wolf's education thus lay rich ground for her career as a writer, even as her experiences at Girls' High School reinforced traditional ideas about gender. Among his sample composition assignments, Swett specified that the prompts "A Fairy Tale" and "How to Make Bread" were for girls and the prompt "Going a-Fishing" was for boys, while sample grammar exercises asked students to identify parts of speech in sentences such as "The boys read well, and the girls sing sweetly."[34] If the school's educational philosophy reinforced gender divisions, Swett's experience teaching in the San Francisco public school system, with its large number of Jewish and Catholic students, made him a strong advocate for religious liberty and the separation of church and state. Explicitly defending the rights of his Jewish students, he eliminated the practice of devotional prayers and the use of the Bible in daily reading exercises. Levy's reminiscences of her high school years confirm that the school's Jewish students would not have experienced significant ostracism due to religious difference. Instead, as Levy relates, social hierarchies were based on the conflation of class and national origin. Levy, whose parents were Polish immigrants, "pretended to be of German origin in school to avoid being considered lower class."[35] As descendants of French-Alsatian immigrants with Germanic backgrounds, the Wolf sisters would have been secure in their social status, although it is unclear whether and to what extent Emma would have been stigmatized for her physical disability. Her friendships with girls of Eastern European descent, including Levy, indicate that she was admired for her studiousness and that she was immune to the snobbery that infected some of her classmates, instead seeking out like-minded peers who shared her intellectual proclivities.

At Girls' High School, Emma developed a close friendship with a fellow Jewish student, Rebekah Bettelheim (1864–1951), a Hungarian immigrant who arrived in San Francisco from the East Coast at age ten. The daughter of Aaron Bettelheim, a progressive rabbi who left Hungary in protest over some of his colleagues' religious fanaticism, Rebekah would go on to marry Rabbi Alexander Kohut and become a leader in the American Jewish community in her own right, publishing two autobiographies that document her life experiences on both coasts. Writing in 1925 of her childhood friend, by then a "brilliant authoress," Kohut remembered Wolf as a strong student. She "was handicapped from birth by a useless arm, but there was no defect in her mentality," Kohut wrote admiringly. "Her memory was the most remarkable I have ever encountered. She could quote with equal facility the texts of long poems or the fatality statistics of each of the world's great battles." Kohut described Wolf as serious and sensitive, a lover of natural beauty. During botany excursions in the California sandhills, the two girls collected "new specimens of flowers" to mount and display at home, "v[ying] with each other . . . to get . . . the largest and best collections."[36]

These walks also provided the girls with opportunities to discuss their shared religious background. Like most thoughtful adolescents, they struggled to define their still-forming identities, openly debating whether it was better to identify as Jewish or to assimilate fully. Their conversations continued to have a profound influence on the two friends, even as they ended up on diverging paths. From her adult standpoint as a distinguished communal leader, having married a widowed rabbi with eight children and devoted herself to the cause of Jewish education, especially for women, Kohut reflected on her conversations with Wolf in her 1925 memoir, My Portion:

> But what meant most of all to me, perhaps, in those impressionable days of adolescence, was the exchange of innermost thoughts with my classmate. I had begun to doubt the worthwhileness of all the sacrifices it seemed to me that my father and his family were making for Judaism. What was the use of it all, I questioned. Why make a stand for separate Jewish ideals? Why not choose the easier way and be like all the rest? The struggle was too hard, too bitter. Emma Wolf was undergoing much the same inner conflict. It meant real suffering to both of us. The spiritual growing pains of adolescence are hard to bear. They cannot be laughed out of existence.[37]

Despite claims from historians that the Golden State removed the restrictions that Jews faced in Europe and on the East Coast, Kohut's declaration makes clear that prejudice against Jews did exist in California. The effects of anti-Semitism may have been minor compared to those experienced by Jews in other regions; nonetheless, these two young Jewish women struggled with, and were shaped by, their sense of difference. Here, Kohut notes the "sacrifices" her father made for Judaism. Elsewhere in her memoirs, she discusses Rabbi Bettelheim's efforts to forge alliances across religious lines and befriend clergymen of various faiths. Kohut inherited her father's "desire for the understanding and amity of those outside the family, the tribe, the religion, the nation," writing that "my father's attitude about people outside the creed is also my attitude."[38]

Judging by Wolf's fiction, these conversations with Kohut about religion left a long-lasting impression on her heart and mind as well. In *Other Things Being Equal*, for example, Wolf's Jewish heroine, Ruth Levice, learns from her father that friendships between Jews and Christians are natural outgrowths of "fellow-feeling," echoing the worldview that Kohut inherited from Rabbi Bettelheim. "I've always been led to believe that a broad-minded man of whatever sect will recognize and honor the same quality in any other man," states Ruth, asking, "Why shouldn't I move on an equality with my Christian friends?"[39] The tension between "mak[ing] a stand for separate Jewish ideals" and being "like all the rest" is also at the center of *Heirs of Yesterday*. While Philip May takes assimilation to the extreme, going so far as to pass as Unitarian, most of the other Jewish characters, including the heroine, Jean Willard, find ways to maintain their Jewishness without significantly jeopardizing their place in mainstream American society. Importantly, it is the institution of Reform Judaism that allows Wolf's Jewish-identified characters to negotiate a middle ground and, by the novel's end, to begin bringing Philip back into the fold.

Wolf and her family made similar negotiations. As early members of Temple Emanu-El, they were at the vanguard of significant changes in American Judaism, with a new generation of spiritual and lay leaders pushing to modernize a religion that was associated with stagnant Old World values. In 1885, a group of rabbis, led by

Kaufman Kohler and Isaac M. Wise, convened a conference in Pittsburgh, where they adopted a set of principles that became the basis of Reform Judaism until 1937, when the Central Conference of
American Rabbis implemented revisions. Known as the Pittsburgh
Platform, the 1885 document held that Jews are "no longer a nation, but a religious community"; that "the modern discoveries of
scientific researches in the domains of nature and history are not
antagonistic to the doctrines of Judaism"; and that "Judaism [is] a
progressive religion, ever striving to be in accord with the postulates
of reason." The articles also addressed the outdatedness of "Mosaic
and religious laws [that] regulate diet, priestly purity, and dress," noting that such rigid observance "is apt rather to obstruct than to further modern spiritual elevation."[40] As one of the earliest American
novels to engage with Reform theology and practice, *Heirs of Yesterday* can be read productively alongside religious documents like the
Pittsburgh Platform as well as subsequent literary works depicting
America's Reform Jewish community, such as Sidney Nyburg's *The
Chosen People* (1917), whose protagonist, Philip Graetz, is a Reform
rabbi of a Baltimore congregation.[41]

In the late nineteenth century, Wolf's congregation, Emanu-El,
became one of the nation's leading Reform synagogues. Under the
leadership of Rabbis Elkan Cohn and Jacob Voorsanger, it initiated
looser interpretations of religious law in order "to remake the Jewish liturgy, ritual, and credo to suit the values of the New World."[42]
For instance, in an egalitarian attempt to "remed[y]" "the evil" that
"excluded women from . . . many privileges to which they are justly
entitled," all congregants were seated together during services,
whereas traditionally women were relegated to a separate gallery.[43]
Emanu-El was one of the first synagogues in the country to priori-
tize Friday evening services above Saturday morning, thus leaving
Saturday open for business or leisure. As Marc Lee Raphael has
demonstrated, Voorsanger, who was appointed rabbi of Emanu-El in
1886, one year after the Pittsburgh conference, strongly emphasized
the progressive potential of Reform Judaism by drawing links to the
American belief in "manifest destiny" and its implied assumption
of white superiority. A proponent of assimilation in all matters but
religion, Voorsanger was concerned that the influx of newly arrived

Eastern co-religionists with their "'meaningless, Oriental rites'" would "chain Jews to the ghetto," going so far as to support immigration restrictions to ensure that Jews who were already settled in the United States would not be deemed backward and racially inferior by association. According to Raphael, Voorsanger's convictions resulted in a "general rejection of all which stood between Judaism and the non-Jewish world" for many Emanu-El members.[44] Thus, in accordance with the Pittsburgh Platform, practices that would have interfered in Jews' ability to socialize and conduct business with their gentile counterparts, such as kosher dietary laws or strict Sabbath observance, were largely abandoned.

While these reforms created a version of Judaism that more closely resembled the practices of their Christian neighbors, many late nineteenth-century Jewish families in San Francisco went a step further, nominally observing holidays like Christmas and Easter to better fit in with the nation's religious majority. Though these holidays primarily served as yearly occasions to bring family together, rituals like gift giving, Christmas tree decorating, and Easter egg hunts were adopted as part of the festivities, though stripped of their religious significance. In her memoir, *The Haas Sisters of Franklin Street*, Frances Bransten Rothmann recalls how her German Jewish grandparents "assimilated the customs and rituals of Christian Americans" after immigrating to San Francisco in the nineteenth century.[45] At Christmas, the Haas family's opulent Queen Anne home (today one of the only Victorian mansions in San Francisco that functions as a tourist attraction) was transformed into a "winter wonderland," complete with a "centerpiece [that] featured a plump suckling pig with a shining red apple protruding from its open snout" and a "ceiling-high tree [that] shone as it revolved slowly on a music stand."[46]

The Wolfs appear to have incorporated aspects of Christmas into their practice as well, especially as the family expanded through intermarriage to include gentile spouses and children who were not raised as Jewish. One of the rare mementos of Emma saved by her descendants is a rhyming poem that she composed for a niece as part of a Christmas celebration. In the twenty-four-line poem, "a little girl" laments that her friend does not have a "blue wrapper" like her own. Instead of going to a "plain everyday store" to purchase "a plain

EMMA WOLF'S
HANDWRITTEN POEM TO HER NIECE.
Courtesy of Donald Auslen.

everyday wrapper / just like plain everyday people wore," the girl finds
a solution by running "to the phone on tiptoe" and putting in a call
to Santa: " 'Hello,' she said, 'Santa! That you? / There's something I
want for my Sweetheart: / Just a wrapper, please—warm and blue.' "[47]
As sweet and simple as it is, the poem betrays a deeper meaning that
resonates with Wolf's symbolic use of the intermarriage plot in *Other
Things Being Equal*: it suggests an ideal of equality ("two little girls in
blue"), but, notably, outward sameness is achieved through the ac-
cumulation of luxury goods, available not to "plain everyday people"

but to those for whom material means can override other obstacles of difference. In *Other Things Being Equal*, Wolf uses class signifiers—including fashionable clothing, elegant decor, educated speech, and cultured mannerisms—to indicate "that religion is the sole factor differentiating" Jews from their gentile neighbors; the 1892 novel employs "genteel realism" to "create believable upper-middle-class [Jewish] characters and to convince . . . readers that an interfaith union based on the principle of sameness—'other things' . . . 'being equal'—is realistic as well."[48]

In explaining the often radical reinvention of religious and familial traditions on the Western frontier, historian Ava Kahn notes that San Francisco Jews were "able to participate more effectively in the development of [the city's] Jewish communities" because they did not have "to accommodate themselves to a preexisting Jewish social and religious structure" as Jewish immigrants did in the East. As Kahn writes, "In the Pacific West, all was their own creation."[49] This proved especially true for the elite group of entrepreneurs who had built wholesale empires and whose children became the scions of Jewish high society in the Gilded Age. In addition to witnessing the formation of Jewish religious institutions like synagogues, nineteenth-century San Francisco saw the creation of Jewish secular institutions, including social clubs modeled on the gentile club system. Emma's brother, Julius, for instance, was a member of the all-male Concordia Club, which was founded in 1864 by denim manufacturer Levi Strauss and other German American Jewish merchants.[50] To maintain the clubs' exclusive status, initiates were nominated and voted on by existing members.

In *Heirs of Yesterday*, Philip May rejects his father's suggestion that he try to get into a Jewish club like the Concordia or the Verein, another fraternal club, which originated as a paramilitary group to safeguard the German Jewish community in the aftermath of the Gold Rush. Instead, Philip believes that a Christian club "will prove more congenial than would a club composed entirely of Jews, from whom I have become estranged both socially and sympathetically" (101).[51] That Philip ends up blackballed from the Christian club by an anti-Semitic member proves that economic and professional status still could not trump prejudice, serving as an important reminder that Jews created their institutions not only out of a sense of ethno-religious camaraderie and separatism but also because of gentile society's exclusionary practices. Interestingly, Wolf not only reflects on how anti-Semitism restricts participation in the city's social life but also shows that blackballing can occur within the ranks; in a turning point of the novel, Philip is rejected from his father's club as well. By including both instances of rejection, Wolf demonstrates her unwillingness to settle for an easy critique. Whether she is writing about religious exclusivity or changing gender roles, she maintains a nuanced ideological stance and examines sociopolitical issues from multiple angles.

With the formation of the National Council of Jewish Women (NCJW) in 1893, the late nineteenth century also became an especially active period for Jewish women's organizations around the nation, and San Francisco was no exception. As a member of the Philomath Club, the Bay Area's first secular organization exclusively for Jewish women, Wolf was part of an emergent San Francisco literary scene that coincided with the rise of the women's club movement in the 1890s. Founded by Bettie Lowenberg, a prominent member of Temple Emanu-El, the Philomath Club drew upon the synagogue's sisterhood for its membership, gathering together intellectually minded, affluent women who were interested in "literary and educational pursuits and [the promotion of] civic ideals."[52] Lowenberg was a socialite and philanthropist who later became a published author—her first novel, *The Irresistible Current* (1908), like Wolf's *Other Things Being Equal*, took on the subject of Christian-Jewish intermarriage—and under her leadership, the Philomath Club had a strong literary bent. True to its name, the club's primary mission was study and learning. But through members' specific choices of "literary and educational pursuits," coupled with a collaborative enactment of upper-class mores, the club accomplished a secondary mission: it made Jewish women an integral and visible part of San Francisco's secular, bourgeois culture.

Despite the shared ethno-religious background of their club's membership, the Philomath women rarely addressed Jewish texts and topics. Instead, they undertook a course of study that "foster[ed] the neo-colonialism of Anglo-Saxonism," in Anne Ruggles Gere's words.[53] English literature was a frequent topic in the Philomath's early years, with lectures on writers such as Tennyson and Carlyle. In addition, the women studied topics such as the German legend of Faust, American history, and transcendental philosophy. In the refined comfort of the club's meeting space at the luxurious Palace Hotel, Wolf was thus able to extend her high school education, engaging in discussion with Jewish women of various ages, attending lectures by professors from nearby Stanford University, and delivering papers herself. Both Wolf and her former classmate Harriet Lane Levy were listed on the program for the Philomath's first open meeting on January 14, 1895, which featured musical and oratorical performances by club members. As the *San Francisco Chronicle* reported of the event, "There was a large and distinguished audience present. . . . Miss Emma Wolf's essay, 'The Passing of the Ideal,' a protest against the masculine woman, Miss Harriet Levy's satire and Miss Florence Prag's paper showing that intellect is always appreciated by great minds, irrespective of nationality or religion, were all heartily applauded."[54]

Like women's clubs around the nation, the Philomath fostered an environment in which women flourished, creating opportunities for members to display their artistic and intellectual talents. While some outside commentators at the time viewed women's clubs as covers for suffrage activism, historians have shown that the club movement was largely a conservative force, especially among upper-class and upper middle-class women. Wolf's presentation, which voiced fears about the "passing" of feminine ideals, demonstrates that the club was devoted to the maintenance of women's domestic sphere and the cult of true womanhood. In deference to Lowenberg's beliefs that direct participation in government would corrupt women, the Philomath Club took an anti-suffrage stance, avoiding the topic of the woman's vote at club meetings.[55]

Still, by participating in the city's cultural and intellectual life in a public setting, the Philomath women were contributing to a shift in gender norms. Karen Blair has argued that club activities can be understood in terms of "domestic feminism"—the notion that the woman's sphere of the home could be extended further to have a positive moral influence on public affairs.[56] The Philomath Club supported and nurtured its members' efforts to enter public life, as suggested by the paths of the three women whose presentations at the first open meeting were singled out by the *Chronicle*. Florence Prag (1866–1948), who was one year behind Wolf and Levy at Girls' High School and whose mother was a beloved teacher at the school, would go on to break gender and religious barriers in national politics, making history as the first Jewish congresswoman when she replaced her deceased husband, Julius Kahn, as one of California's representatives to the House of Representatives in 1925. (By then, with the passage of the Nineteenth Amendment, even the club's staunchest anti-suffragists had conceded the value of women taking more active roles in public affairs.)

Though Prag's fame would come later, by the time of the 1895 meeting, Wolf and Levy were already rising literary stars. Having earned a bachelor's degree in philosophy at the University of California Berkeley, Levy wrote regularly for *The Wave*, where her short stories, society pieces, and dramatic criticism made her one of the San Francisco journal's most promising young writers.[57] Wolf, too, had published in *The Wave*. One of her earliest short stories, "Brissac's Little Debt," appeared in the journal in February 1892. In the same year, Wolf published her first novel, *Other Things Being Equal*, with A. C. McClurg to critical acclaim. Due in part to its controversial intermarriage plot, the book became a popular success. It continued to be read and discussed, including by other women's clubs, well into the twentieth century and was published in a revised edition in 1916. As evidence of Wolf's national reputation, the *American Jewess*, the journal founded by editor Rosa Sonneschein to serve as an unofficial promotional organ for the NCJW, profiled her in 1895, noting that *Other Things Being Equal* "had already reached the third edition and is read by Jews and gentiles with equal interest."[58]

It is no accident that Wolf's most prolific period as a writer occurred in tandem with the golden age of the women's club movement and during a formative period for women's rights in the United States. Against the backdrop of shifting gender ideologies, Wolf published five novels between 1892 and 1916, as well as short stories and poems in magazines such as the *American Jewess*, the *Smart Set*, and *Century*. The terms of gender, class, and religion that Wolf

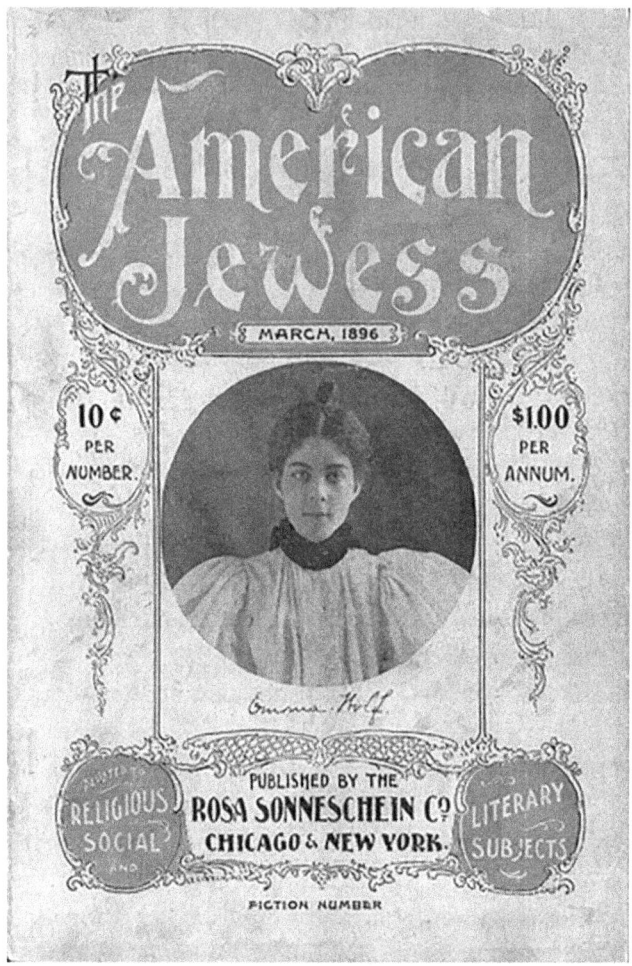

EMMA WOLF ON THE COVER OF
THE *AMERICAN JEWESS* (MARCH 1896).

negotiated in her own life also played out in the pages of her fiction. These negotiations are further evident in the permutations of her literary career; expanding her oeuvre to include works absent of Jewish characters and themes, Wolf explored a writerly persona unconstrained by ethno-racial difference. But if Wolf's representation of middle-class Jewish life on the Western frontier in her first book, *Other Things Being Equal*, made her one of the earliest Jewish women novelists in the United States, her fourth novel, *Heirs of Yesterday*—with its nuanced treatment of religious, cultural, and familial identity—solidified her status as one of the mothers of American Jewish fiction and positioned her as a pioneering figure in women's writing and American literary history.

A "MOTHER OF AMERICAN JEWISH FICTION": EMMA WOLF'S WRITING

In an article that appeared in the *San Francisco News* in the "Who's Who in San Francisco" column in 1930, two years before her death, Wolf recalled having her first short story published when she was twelve years old. "There was no joy in the experience. I cried bitterly over the affair," Wolf told reporter Helen Piper, explaining that the piece of juvenilia was not published under her own free will. Instead, "a daring cousin," thinking "the tale a work of art" and "prompted by the noble purpose of presenting [her] to the literary world[,] . . . stole the manuscript and gave it to the village paper." The story's publication proved a source of humiliation for Wolf. "Too ashamed to face anyone," she "imagined that all the townsfolk were laughing at" her "little love story."[59] The anecdote may not seem like the auspicious beginnings for a literary career, but years later Wolf made an even more dramatic—and this time voluntary—literary debut. In 1892, she published her first novel, *Other Things Being Equal*, with A. C. McClurg, as well as the short story "Brissac's Little Debt" in *The Wave*.

Together, these two publications establish cultural identity as a central theme for Wolf and indicate that her material was often based on astute observations of real people, places, and events. While *Other Things Being Equal* tells the story of Ruth Levice, the daughter of middle-class Jewish immigrants from France now living in San Francisco, Wolf drew primarily upon her French heritage for "Brissac's Little Debt." Demonstrating her connections to her birthland in the American West and to her parents' homeland of Alsace-Lorraine, the frame narrative of the story is set at the Cercle Français, a private men's club for French merchants founded in San Francisco in the 1880s and to which Wolf's brother, Julius,

belonged. Arriving late to a reception at the club after a tiring journey, the story's main character, Josef Brissac, interrupts his friends
at a game of cards to tell them of a "little adventure" that "began
about twenty years ago and ended last week." Brissac begins his tale
by recalling a traumatic event that occurred in France when he was
seventeen years old: his witnessing of the sexual assault and violent death of his mother at the hands of German soldiers during the
Franco-Prussian War. He explains to the men that, just the week before, while "riding alone across the plain" in Arizona, he finally had
the opportunity to avenge his mother's murder when he came upon
a wounded German in the "scorching" desert. Instead of offering the
parched man a drink from his full canteen, Brissac "laughed gayly"
and "slowly, very slowly . . . poured the water, drop by drop, upon the
blistering sand." The story's ending returns to the frame narrative,
where Brissac elicits his friends' responses to his actions, "curious
to have [their] verdict of the means [he] took of discharging" the
"debt." The group of friends—which includes a fierce French patriot
named Little Chalmont, who had also seen the horrors of war up
close—does not respond with words. Instead, Wolf writes, "There
came a sound not often heard in the gathering of men," and she
concludes the story with this line: "Little Chalmont was crying."[60]

In this provocative treatment of masculinity that captures the
deep and lingering emotional effects of war, the brutal death of
Brissac's mother stands in for the men's loss of and distance from
their motherland—a loss that they continue to mourn, even as immigrants in a new land. In this respect, "Brissac's Little Debt" shares
with Wolf's Jewish-themed novels, *Other Things Being Equal* and
Heirs of Yesterday, an interest in exploring the relationship between
familial ties and cultural heritage. But, in other ways, the 1892 short
story is atypical for Wolf. "Brissac's Little Debt" is her rare work of
prose without female characters at the center.

Wolf's five novels and most of her short stories are works of domestic fiction, focusing on young, white, middle-class women whose
lives are typically moving in the direction of marriage. Wolf's reference to her youthful publication as a "little love story" indicates her
long-standing inclination toward plots that center around courtship
and marriage. As literary critics such as Nina Baym have shown, most

nineteenth-century American fiction written by women and for female audiences relied on domestic plots. A novel that ends happily with a Jewish-Christian couple overcoming their religious differences in order to marry, *Other Things Being Equal* might be labeled a "love story," though it could hardly be described with the diminutive "little." Rather, *Other Things Being Equal* uses its intermarriage plot to tackle big questions about class and gender, faith and secularism, modernity and assimilation, religious pluralism and bigotry, charity and familial obligations—not to mention its more straightforward but equally weighty probing of why people from different backgrounds fall in love and what makes for a successful union.[61]

If Wolf experienced embarrassment about the publication of her first story, she appears to have grown a thicker skin by the time her first novel was published. Certainly, it would be difficult to imagine anyone laughing at *Other Things Being Equal*. This accomplished debut, which reads as a work by a mature writer, garnered almost universal praise for its style.[62] However, in her willingness to challenge cultural and religious norms through a favorable portrayal of intermarriage, Wolf risked a different kind of negative response. Not surprisingly, her work was a frequent target of criticism within the Jewish community, and the novel continued to be a source of controversy and debate more than a decade after its initial publication. A 1904 article in the *Los Angeles Herald*, for instance, reported that Rabbi Sigmund Hecht of Congregation B'nai B'rith in Los Angeles opened a talk on intermarriage and apostasy by discussing the "mild sensation" caused by Wolf's novel. Counterintuitively trying to downplay the impact of Wolf's novel with the word "mild" and the false claim that her book was now gathering dust "upon the topmost shelves" of libraries (a claim that his own invocation of the text as a means of connecting to his audience immediately belies), Hecht summarized the controversy: "There were those among the readers of her book who roundly denounced the spirit in which it was conceived and written and declared that the author had broken with her ancestral religion and was trying to undermine the faith of her co-religionists," while "others . . . hailed the sentiments expressed in that book as the powerful manifestation of the progressive spirit of Judaism."[63] Despite the controversy, Wolf did not appear to experience shame about her religious beliefs or regret about her positive representation of intermarriage. When *Other Things Being Equal* was republished in a slightly revised edition in 1916, she doubled down on the importance of her theme, writing in a new foreword: "In presenting this revised edition to a new generation, the author feels that the element of change has touched very lightly the romantic potentialities obtaining at the time of the original writing. . . . Christian youth still chances upon Jewish youth, and with the same difference of historic background, the same social barriers and prejudices—the same possibilities of mutual attraction. The humanest love knows no sect. . . . It is the story of that beauty, which the author, in this revised edition, for a new generation, has not cared to revise."[64]

The existence of the revised edition of *Other Things Being Equal* further disproves Rabbi Hecht's assertion that the novel had "seen its day." If this had been the case, Wolf's publisher, A. C. McClurg, would not have continued publishing editions of the novel. Yet Hecht's critique of Wolf is worth serious consideration. It speaks to the ways that the male-dominated American Jewish establishment subtly suppressed the influence of a Jewish woman writer whose progressive ideas, and means of conveying them, were likely to reach a broad audience and have popular appeal.

Even when she was not writing about intermarriage, Wolf's adherence to a "progressive spirit of Judaism" would continue to dog her throughout her career. The larger questions of how to define Jewishness and whether to maintain orthodoxy or modernize religious practice would shape the works she wrote and determine the stories she chose not to tell. These questions would also dictate which of her writings were published and by whom—and, in turn, who her readers were. The story of how Wolf came to write and publish *Heirs of Yesterday*—her only extant work with explicitly Jewish content besides *Other Things Being Equal*—is also a story about the cultural institution of publishing and the gatekeeping role played by the Jewish publishing industry in shaping mainstream representations of Jewishness. The novel's publication history and reception—from initial responses to its decades of obscurity and up to its recovery today—have much to tell us about which, and whose, versions of Jewish identity hold the greatest weight. In contrast to works by writers like Abraham Cahan and Anzia Yezierska, which have dominated university syllabi and scholarship over the past fifty years, *Heirs of Yesterday* has remained out of print in part because of the way it challenges conventional understandings of turn-of-the-twentieth-century Jewish identity, ethnicity, and Jewish American fiction. As a novel set in San Francisco that grapples with secularism, Reform theology, and genteel anti-Semitism, *Heirs of Yesterday* moves us beyond fairly narrow and geographically confined notions of American Jewish identity.

In the years after publishing *Other Things Being Equal*, Wolf continued to dedicate herself to fiction writing. Previous research has suggested that Wolf turned away from Jewish themes with novels like *A Prodigal in Love* (1894) and *The Joy of Life* (1896), both of which revolve around characters who are siblings. Inspired by Wolf's own large, female-dominated household, as well as by classic works about sisterly relations like Jane Austen's *Sense and Sensibility* and Louisa May Alcott's *Little Women*, the family in *A Prodigal in Love* consists of six girls, while *The Joy of Life* uses two brothers—and the women who enter their lives—to, in Wolf's own words, "contrast the materialist with the idealist."[65] Even the short story that Wolf published in the *American Jewess*, "One-Eye, Two-Eye, Three-Eye" (1896), is absent of Jewish themes, with Wolf again using the contrasting experiences of three sisters to offer a critique of marriage. On the surface, then, the body of work that Wolf published in the 1890s suggests that she left behind the themes of cultural and religious heritage to center on class, gender, and family dynamics. But new research informs us that there is more to the story.

During the period of the 1890s that saw the rising popularity of the ghetto tale, heralded by the Jewish Publication Society's (JPS) release of British Jewish writer Israel Zangwill's *Children of the Ghetto* in 1892, Wolf was actively writing Jewish fiction. The records of the JPS, now housed at Temple University, reveal that they rejected three works by Wolf between 1894 and 1900: a lost manuscript titled *A Dreamer of Dreams*; a children's story, "Little Jaffa," which she submitted for a literary contest; and a manuscript that became the novel *Heirs of Yesterday*. It is not that Wolf took a hiatus from Jewish content; rather, it appears that she was having more difficulty getting her Jewish-themed material into print. When *Heirs of Yesterday* finally appeared in 1900, it was published by A. C. McClurg, the Chicago-based firm that had previously taken a chance on Wolf with *Other Things Being Equal* and subsequently published *The Joy of Life*.[66]

The idea to publish her work with the JPS, the nation's first Jewish publisher, did not originate with Wolf herself. In 1893, the society, in search of "native talent" and aware of the popularity of *Other Things Being Equal*, contacted Wolf to inquire whether she had a manuscript for their consideration.[67] She did. Wolf was working on *A Dreamer of Dreams*, a novel whose title, taken from a line in Deuteronomy, signaled a theme of spiritual struggle: "If a prophet or a dreamer of dreams arises among you and gives you a sign or a wonder, and the sign or wonder that he tells you comes to pass, and if he says, 'Let us go after other gods,' which you have not known, 'and let us serve them,' you shall not listen to the words of that prophet or that dreamer of dreams."[68]

With the original manuscript now lost, the little we know about *A Dreamer of Dreams* comes from JPS records, including letters Wolf exchanged with JPS chairman Judge Mayer Sulzberger and the minutes from meetings in which the publication committee discussed and evaluated her manuscript. Based on Wolf's correspondence, her interactions with the JPS's leadership appear at times fraught, and her ability to work with them was perhaps doomed from the outset. A letter from Wolf to Sulzberger dated May 8, 1893, though respectful, contains hints of her frustration. "As my two last letters to you have received no response, I am in a somewhat unsettled frame of mind in regard to the work upon which we have been corresponding," she begins, explaining that she was waiting for Sulzberger to confirm that he wanted the book by October in order to "apply myself as I must" to meet the deadline. If the letter begins with a complaint, going so far as to evoke Sulzberger's guilt for failing to respond in a timely manner, it concludes with a politely worded demand: "Now, would it be too pressing to ask you to answer this question <u>by return mail</u> in some manner? At any rate it is asked and I trust you will be as kind as heretofore and set me right."[69] Even if lightened at the end by a mild compliment (i.e., noting Sulzberger's previous kindness),

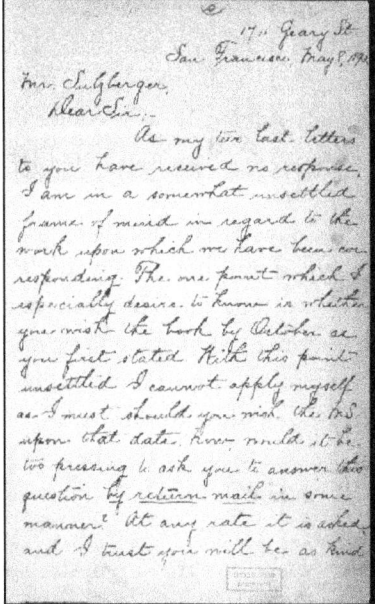

EMMA WOLF'S LETTER TO JUDGE MAYER SULZBERGER, CHAIRMAN OF THE JEWISH PUBLICATION SOCIETY (MAY 8, 1893).

Courtesy of the Abraham Schwadron Collection at the National Library of Israel.

the letter reveals an impatient and assertive side to Wolf's personality. Although others who knew Wolf have portrayed her as retiring, gentle, and even "saintly," she was not simply a passive and compliant woman.[70] Her tone in this letter helps contextualize choices she made throughout her career. These are the words of a dedicated and ambitious writer who was willing to stand by her convictions and ruffle feathers rather than readily comply with the literary establishment's expectations for her.

Subsequent letters from Wolf show that she did finally receive the requested response from Sulzberger, and on November 14, 1893, Wolf mailed the JPS a copy of her manuscript. "I herewith submit for your kind consideration, the MS. entitled 'A Dreamer of Dreams,' sincerely trusting it will meet your requirements and approval," Wolf wrote to Sulzberger. "Should you find any objections upon points which you think I could remedy, I trust you will not hesitate to mention them."[71] Though more deferential in tone than her previous correspondence, this confidently worded letter indicates that Wolf viewed Sulzberger as a professional equal; in requesting his feedback and expressing her willingness to revise the manuscript, she also shows that she saw book publishing as a cooperative venture between writer and publisher. From Wolf's reference to "objections upon points," we may further infer that she anticipated pushback. Given the response to *Other Things Being Equal*, Wolf was well aware that her own religious principles would meet with opposition from others in the Jewish community, especially from an institution like the JPS, which toed the line between orthodoxy and reform to maximize its audience in the interest of revitalizing Jewish American culture.

The JPS's deliberations on her manuscript confirm its desire to steer clear of overly controversial material, as the "objections" were entirely focused on content rather than style or aesthetic value. Soon after receiving Wolf's manuscript on November 24, 1893, the society sent it out to a series of readers: Dr. Marcus Jastrow on November 27; Rev. Dr. Joseph Krauskopf on December 11; Mr. Simon A. Stern on January 8; Mr. A. L. Isaacs on January 15; and finally, on February 7, Dr. Cyrus Adler, a leading Jewish scholar and editor who was one of the founders of the press as well as of the American Jewish Historical Society.[72] On February 28, 1894, the publication committee met to discuss Wolf's novel among other agenda items. The minutes reveal that they were unable to arrive at a decision due in part to "slim attendance" at the meeting. According to the minutes, Isaacs's "favorable report" met with strong opposition from Adler: "Dr. Adler agreed with Dr. Isaacs in thinking the story good from a story-teller's point of view, but considered some of the characters immoral, and the Rabbi hero impossible. In his opinion, the fact that whenever a traditional Jewish custom is discussed in the book, the Rabbi declares himself conscientiously unable to observe it, ought to suffice to prevent the publishing of the book by the Society." Isaacs, in turn, "thought that the Society would be missing a fine opportunity to make itself popular . . . and that the Committee ought to avoid judging" Wolf's manuscript "from any but the literary point of view."[73]

The minutes offer only a tantalizing glimpse of Wolf's lost manuscript. Like *Heirs of Yesterday*, the book appears to deal with the modernization of American Judaism. But unlike Wolf's other fiction, in which none of her Jewish characters are clergymen, *Dreamer* apparently featured a rabbi as its main character. From the sound of it, Wolf was using fiction—one of the few public forums available to women in the nineteenth century—as a means of grappling with the important theological questions of the day. That her "rabbi hero" chooses to forego traditional observance implies that the book was written in a "progressive spirit" and was sympathetic to Reform Judaism, with its initiative to modernize Jewish religious practice as an "alternative to assimilation."[74] Although the brief summary of the meeting offers no details about the style of *Dreamer*, its high literary quality was undisputed. The writing was likely artful and accessible, drawing upon the principles of realism as her other novels did. In Isaacs's opinion, the work would attract a popular audience, perhaps even because of its controversial subject matter; the popularity of a work of fiction by a homegrown American author would be a real boon to the JPS, whose reputation at that point rested largely on historical texts, with the exception of Zangwill's book about Jewish life in the London slums, *Children of the Ghetto*.

If the minutes are too spare to shed substantive light on Wolf's manuscript, they do succinctly capture the competing demands on the JPS and the factors that went into the production of Jewish American fiction at the turn of the twentieth century. Even as the society was committed to publishing works of high quality, artistic value was not the dominant criteria for all of its board members. Many believed the publications should serve political and didactic functions. Given its mission of unifying the Jewish people through shared culture, the press feared alienating readers. Adler's concerns about immorality and the "impossible" rabbi character stem from the press's commitment to "Jewish pluralism and doctrinal neutrality."[75] Most, but not all, of the publication committee may have taken issue with Wolf because they opposed radical Reform Judaism, but their objections were born less from personal ideologies and more from pragmatism. On the one hand, for Isaacs, the controversial nature of the work that bothered Adler would boost the book's popularity. On the other hand, Adler felt that the work would prove too divisive; like *Other Things Being Equal*, it would highlight ruptures within the Jewish community.

Although the committee adjourned the initial meeting, deferring the decision about Wolf's manuscript so that more members could be present for the discussion, Adler's argument was ultimately to win out. On March 28, 1894, a special meeting was convened at the JPS office in Philadelphia with two objectives: to arrive at a final decision about whether to publish Wolf's novel and to consider the report of the Bible translation committee. The minutes of the meeting, again, reveal a mixed response to *A Dreamer of Dreams*. On one side, Jastrow and Stern advised against publication. On the other, Isaacs was joined in his support for publication by Reform rabbi Joseph Krauskopf. Krauskopf's support for Wolf's novel is not surprising; as leader of the Philadelphia synagogue Keneseth Israel and champion of Reform innovator Isaac Mayer Wise, Krauskopf had openly expressed his concern that the JPS held an anti-Reform bias.[76] It was Adler who broke the tie, "mov[ing] that it is not expedient to publish the novel 'Dreamer of Dreams.'"[77] Since the JPS was a subscription service, with all members automatically receiving copies of the society's published works, Adler was not simply motivated by marketability in making his tie-breaking decision. Unlike Isaacs, who insisted that the JPS would benefit from Wolf's popularity even if readers did not need to be enticed to purchase the book, Adler feared that the novel would tarnish the JPS's reputation. While the brief minutes intimate that some members of the committee may have been offended by Wolf's novel, Adler's use of the word "expedient" presents us with an incontrovertible fact: despite the quality of Wolf's writing and her skill as a popular storyteller, a significant portion of the JPS's readers would have found the novel's liberal stance offensive and held the society, not just the author, accountable.

However Wolf responded to the news, the JPS's rejection of *A Dreamer of Dreams* did not affect her productivity or dampen her aspirations to further her career as a writer. Her second published novel, *A Prodigal in Love*, appeared in 1894 with New York publisher

Harper & Bros. Especially productive throughout the 1890s, the decade that saw the publication of four of her five novels, Wolf attributed her success to hard work and determination. "Inspiration," she explained, "was an illusion that I once believed in, in common with most younger beginners. Perspiration has much more to do with it."[78] Nor did the JPS's rejection deter Wolf from trying to publish with them again. Fewer than three years after they passed on *A Dreamer of Dreams*, Wolf entered her story "Little Jaffa" in a literary contest sponsored by the JPS. In an effort to reach the youngest generation of American Jews, the JPS promised a prize of one thousand dollars, a large sum for 1896, to the writer who submitted the best children's story.[79] In this case, we have even less information about the content of Wolf's manuscript and the prize committee's deliberations, but it is clear that the debate was contentious and that some of the contention was sparked by Wolf's writing.

Among the twenty-seven manuscripts received by the JPS, Wolf's story was preferred by one vote to the other top-rated story, Louis Pendleton's *Lost Prince Almon*. Wolf again had won the support of Rabbi Krauskopf, as well as Simon Stern, a Reform lay leader who had opposed publication of *A Dreamer of Dreams*. According to Jonathan Sarna, when the committee reached an impasse in its deliberations, they decided to follow "the Solomonic suggestion" of one of the members that it was best not to award a prize if they could not arrive at a consensus.[80] The contestants were subsequently notified of the JPS's decision to refrain from selecting a winner. Wolf never knew that her story was one of two considered the best of the twenty-seven submissions, nor did she know that the vote was so close. She received the same form letter as all of the contestants, informing her that the committee decided not to award a prize because "no story of Jewish interest suited to young readers and satisfactory to the Judges" was "offered." The letter complimented the "competitors on the ability and taste displayed in many of the stories submitted" and "expresse[d] the hope that works from their pens may someday be added to the Society's list"—words that may have given Wolf partial encouragement to submit one more manuscript, *Heirs of Yesterday*, to the JPS soon after.[81]

The content of "Little Jaffa" remains a mystery, and events that transpired after the contest at once heighten the mystery and offer potential clues about Wolf's lost work. Eager to bring out quality children's literature, the JPS decided to publish two of the works submitted for the contest. One was Sara Miller's *Under the Eagle's Wing* (1899), a piece of historical fiction-cum-adventure story about a teenage boy who becomes a disciple to Moses Maimonides in Egypt during the Middle Ages. The other, Louis Pendleton's *Lost Prince Almon* (1898), turned out to be the story that deadlocked the committee, rivaling Wolf's "Little Jaffa" as a top contender for the literary prize. What makes the decision to publish *Lost Prince Almon* and not Wolf's story especially curious is its author background. Despite the JPS's mission to publish and promote Jewish writers, Pendleton was not Jewish. He was a Southerner whose previous works for children included a Civil War adventure, *In the Okefenokee: A Story of War Time and the Great Georgia Swamp* (1895), and a story of postbellum race relations, *The Sons of Ham: A Tale of the New South* (1896). Marketed by the JPS as an illustrated gift book for Jewish children, *Lost Prince Almon* follows the adventures of a young Prince Jehoash, later to become king of Judah, and was drawn from the Old Testament. Combining religious and historical content with the exotic veneer of Orientalism, Miller's and Pendleton's stories share the didacticism common to nineteenth-century children's literature. Based on the JPS's decision not to publish "Little Jaffa," despite the fact that more than half of the members of the prize committee saw value in it, we can assume that the text defied expectations for religious children's literature of the time. Given the committee's responses to this and other works by Wolf, it is exceedingly unlikely that the decision reflected on her capabilities as a writer.

Thus, a published work of Jewish children's literature from Emma Wolf was never to be. Interestingly, however, her story "One-Eye, Two-Eye, Three-Eye," which appeared in the *American Jewess* in 1896, engages with the tradition of didactic children's literature, especially its effect on girls; the story takes its title from a Grimm brothers' fairy tale to offer a critique of gender relations and the institution of marriage. The year 1896 was to prove an important one for Wolf. In addition to seeing this story and her poem "Eschscholtzia (California Poppy)" printed in the *American Jewess*, she published *The Joy of Life* with A. C. McClurg and began a correspondence with

Zangwill, the JPS's star author of Jewish fiction, which would last for four years and have a strong influence on both their careers.[82]

Wolf initiated the correspondence with Zangwill when she sent him a copy of *The Joy of Life*. The act of reaching out to "a fellow Jewish writer, the best-known in the Anglo-Jewish world," indicates that Wolf "saw herself and her writing as part of a Jewish literary tradition."[83] Zangwill became an important supporter of Wolf's writing, praising it in his letters and in published reviews. In his review of *The Joy of Life*, for example, he wrote that her work "stands out luminous and arrestive amid the thousand-and-one tales of our overproductive generation."[84] Privately, he called her "the most promising Jewish writer of the younger generation" and "the best product of American Judaism since Emma Lazarus."[85] Although only Zangwill's letters to Wolf survive, it is likely that she shared with him her aspiration to continue publishing Jewish fiction, if seemingly without mentioning the fact that the JPS had rejected her work. In a February 1897 letter to Wolf, Zangwill encouraged her to write "the Jewish story which is stirring in your subconscious" and to submit it to the JPS; he later stated that he "had been in correspondence with Judge Sulzberger of Philadelphia about you."[86] Zangwill believed that his recommendation would hold sway with the publication committee based on their regard for him and the popularity of *Children of the Ghetto*, a work that the JPS had commissioned him to write. Zangwill's endorsement of the JPS as a suitable publisher for Wolf's writing was not unequivocal. As Edna Nahshon explains, Zangwill had questioned the JPS's position when they offered him a contract to write the work that became *Children of the Ghetto*, "fear[ing] that by taking the commission he could be subject to pressure that might compromise his artistic freedom." Zangwill's hesitation, it turns out, was justified, as his "correspondence with Sulzberger reveals that the Americans were pressing for validation of their ideals and sensibilities."[87] In his letter to Wolf advising her to send a "Jewish story" to the JPS, he allowed that the publisher's imprimatur might "cramp" her and urged her not to compromise her principles. "You must say exactly what you think about Jews & Judaism," he wrote.[88]

Wolf ended up taking Zangwill's advice, despite his cautionary note. In 1897, she submitted *Heirs of Yesterday* to the JPS. Zangwill's

influence, however, was to prove slight. The JPS publication committee rejected Wolf's work for the third time. The minutes read,
"Messrs. Stern, Adler, and Berkowitz reported concerning 'The
Heirs of Yesterday,' by Miss Emma Wolf, that it was an admirable
piece of work from a literary point of view. But Drs. Adler and Berkowitz thought it inadvisable for the Society to publish the novel
as submitted on account of the treatment of its subject. Discussion
showed that in view of the division existing in the Committee, the
publication of Miss Wolf's novel was impracticable."[89] Once again,
the committee praised Wolf's artistry while questioning whether the
content of her novel fulfilled the JPS's mission. Adler was this time
joined in his opposition by Henry Berkowitz, a Philadelphia Reform
rabbi who had replaced Krauskopf after he resigned from the society
due to theological disagreements. Though the committee now used
the descriptors "inadvisable" and "impracticable" rather than "not
expedient," the reasons are similar to those behind the rejection of
A Dreamer of Dreams. The division within the publication committee that led to the decision not to publish *Heirs of Yesterday* reflected
larger schisms in the Jewish community. The JPS was apprehen-
sive that Wolf's subject matter would stoke that divisiveness rather
than bring American Jews together through common culture and
tradition.

Despite the vagueness of the JPS records, the published text of
Heirs of Yesterday, in conjunction with Sarna's overview of the "fiction debate" in his history of the JPS, illuminates the ways in which
Wolf's writing troubled expectations for Jewish American literature.
In addition to debating whether "standards for selection be primarily artistic or didactic," JPS publication committee members asked
questions such as, "Should authors be encouraged to strive for reality,
even if sordid, or should they be encouraged to idealize Jewish life
by putting the best possible face on it, in the hope that one day that
would *become* reality?"[90] Given that realism was the prevailing literary movement of the time, this question proved especially trenchant.
The work of ghetto writers like Abraham Cahan was praised for its
gritty realism, yet many believed it imprudent to depict Jewish "low
life" in such a manner, fearing that such representations would have
a negative effect on Jews, potentially fueling anti-Semitism. A review

in the *Bookman,* for instance, conceded that Cahan's *Yekl: A Tale of the New York Ghetto* (1896) may be "realism in the narrowest sense of the term," but questioned "the work's realism in a wider sense," asking, "Does Mr. Cahan wish us to believe that the types and phases of the life of the Ghetto thus presented by him are truly representative of his race? That it is as sordid, selfish, as mean, as cruel, as degraded as he has here shown it to be? . . . It is a hideous showing, and repels the reader, who misses . . . that dignity of faith which compels respect from Christians. . . . If, then, these likenesses and these views are reproduced from life, was it wise to develop the pictures?"[91] Cahan himself decided against publishing with the JPS due to "Sulzberger's injunction against . . . 'ugliness as an ideal.'" When the press offered him a contract following the success of his early ghetto fiction, he, like Zangwill, was wary of compromises to his artistic freedom, writing to Sulzberger that "the gulf between the tastes and views of your organization and my own seems to be impassable."[92]

In view of such concerns about realistic representations of Jewish immigrant life in the New York ghetto, we might think that Wolf's genteel realism and portrayal of the middle-class Jewish community in San Francisco would win preference as an alternative. But if Wolf's portrayal of reality was not "sordid," neither did her works uncritically idealize Jewish characters and traditions. In the quotation that serves as the epigraph to this introduction, Wolf stated her philosophy as a writer: "One must not place heart before art. I try to paint the subject as truthfully as possible. . . . Truth-telling should be an author's religion. It is mine, and because of it I have caused considerable discussion among my own people." Acknowledging the controversial nature of her work among her fellow Jews, Wolf claims "truth-telling" as her religion, professing an allegiance to the realism of her art above her faith. Her resistance to idealizing Jewish life is evident, for example, in *Heirs of Yesterday,* and particularly in the character of Philip May, who is repelled by traditional religious practice and believes Judaism to be "a dead letter, a monument to the past" (101–2). Adler's comments on the "immoral" characters and "impossible" rabbi in *A Dreamer of Dreams* hint at his possible objections to *Heirs of Yesterday.* The JPS may have been uneasy with the moral conundrums presented by Wolf's text. Philip, for example, could be read as an "immoral" character, in part because of his attitude toward Judaism but even more so because his dismissal of Judaism translates into disrespect for, and estrangement from, his elderly father, Joseph. Even though Philip and his father eventually reconcile, the prodigal son continues to face the repercussions of his callous actions. He is most severely punished by the loss of his father; when Joseph hears that his own Jewish social club has rejected Philip, whose reputation was tarnished in the Jewish community when others learned of his attempt to erase his Jewish background, Joseph resigns his membership on the spot, but his anger proves too much for him to bear, and he dies of a heart attack. In addition to raising questions about the morality of Philip's repudiation of his heritage, the novel also asks readers to consider what it means that father and son reconcile even before Philip begins to reclaim his Jewishness.

Heirs of Yesterday is not a didactic text—in fact, its ambiguities are what make it so rich for readers today—yet it does hold Philip accountable for his actions and offers a solution to the dilemma of tradition versus full assimilation via a revitalized Judaism. Again, we might think this message would appeal to the JPS's desire to represent the dignity of Jewish life rather than its sordidness. Furthermore, Philip's willingness to sacrifice family ties in his selfish desire to get ahead finds a foil in the admirable character of Jean Willard with her strong sense of morality and familial loyalty. Although Jean's commitment to religious practice is minimal at first, her loyalty to her heritage grows as she is confronted with Philip's outright rejection of his Jewishness. Jean's pride in her Jewish identity and belief in the "progressive spirit of Judaism" force Philip to reconsider his position. But the means of revitalizing Judaism and bringing Philip back into the fold must have proved problematic for the JPS and especially for a historian like Adler. In the willingness of Wolf's characters to forego tradition in order to reinvent their religion as ever evolving, free of "provincialisms and anachronisms" (212), they embrace radical reforms that sever Judaism from the past, and the Jewish past was a key component of the JPS's vision, as evidenced by its many publications on Jewish history.

Indeed, the JPS seemed more comfortable with fictional texts set in the past. As Sarna notes, in addition to "immigrant uplift," one of the key themes emphasized in JPS fiction was "the beauties and terrors of Jewish life in the Old World, with special emphasis on the charms of Jewish tradition and the horrors of anti-Jewish attacks."[93] By setting works in the past, Jewish fiction writers could negotiate the JPS's seemingly competing demands, simultaneously portraying the real horrors and violence of anti-Semitism and idealizing Jewish people and customs by presenting them as quaint and charming. Thus, the fiction that the JPS published at this time may tell us something about the content of Wolf's lost writings and why publishing *Heirs of Yesterday* was seen as "inadvisable." In preferring ghetto fiction set in Europe—either in Victorian-era London (like Zangwill's) or in bygone eras—rather than in America, the JPS aimed to forge ancestral spiritual ties that transcended the geography of the diaspora. This objective is evident, for instance, in the work of another Jewish American woman writer and JPS author, Martha Wolfenstein. Prior to her untimely death in 1906, Wolfenstein published two books with the JPS, including the novel *Idyls of the Gass* (1901), which, interestingly, was reviewed by Wolf. According to Sarna, Wolfenstein's work pleased the JPS publication committee because it successfully negotiated the terms of the "fiction debate," offering a "brighter picture" of Jewish life in the Old World, "full of obvious sympathy for ghetto folk and their traditional, highly ethical way of life."[94]

Wolf's ambivalence about Wolfenstein's work is evident in her 1901 review of *Idyls of the Gass*, which was published in the *Jewish Comment*, a Baltimore weekly. With measured praise, Wolf calls Wolfenstein an "aspirant for Jewish literary honors." She criticizes her "ubiquitous use of the question-mark and the familiar 'I,'" while suggesting that despite these flaws Wolfenstein's work "bears none of the ear-marks of the novice." Through the deft placement of positive regard in a nonrestrictive clause in her next sentence, Wolf continues her critique: "They are simple tales, told with a simplicity appropriate to the material, which is art."[95] In other words, they are simple tales written in a simple style devoid of nuance. The rest of the review reveals similar sleights that can be read as either praise or criticism. Wolf subtly implies, then, that *Idyls of the Gass* is the work of a novice. The review may reflect not only Wolf's evaluation of the book but also her critique of the JPS's publication committee and its prioritizing of content over style. Given what we now know of Wolf's own attempts to publish with the JPS, at the back of her mind in reviewing *Idyls of the Gass* must have been the niggling question of why Wolfenstein's work was accepted and her own was rejected.

The lukewarm review of *Idyls of the Gass* may be Wolf's means of questioning the narrowness of ghetto representations and what it would mean for Jewish fiction if all writers continued to work in this mode. Wolf's admiration for Zangwill's work indicates that she did not necessarily object to ghetto fiction as a genre, but her review of Wolfenstein contains an interesting subtext: the suggestion that she saw Wolfenstein as derivative of Zangwill. Wolf mentions Zangwill's work several times in the review, comparing him favorably to Wolfenstein in this sentence: "Like her famous contemporary, Israel Zangwill, she has found the poetry that lurks in a mean street, but unlike him, she has failed to observe, or chosen to pass by, all that is ugly and sordid therein, thereby illustrating again the idealizing, eternal feminine as distinguished from the more robust masculine instinct."[96] The line offers a critique not just of Wolfenstein but of other women writers for their tendency to idealize; it alludes to Wolf's own attempts to counter such idealization via a genteel realism that aligns her work with contemporaries like Edith Wharton.

In the age of the ghetto tale, a genre that would continue to dominate Jewish American literature for many years to come, Wolf's writing stands out for its originality. This originality is due in part to her circumvention of the ghetto and her offering of San Francisco as an alternative site of Jewish American culture. Interestingly, Wolf was not the only San Francisco author whose work was rejected by the JPS. In 1935, Wolf's former Girls' High School classmate Harriet Lane Levy submitted *920 O'Farrell Street*, a memoir about growing up Jewish in San Francisco before the 1906 earthquake, for an award named in honor of Edwin Wolf, the JPS's president from 1903 to 1913. Perhaps because Levy's work was autobiographical when the JPS was soliciting "novel[s] of Jewish interest" for the prize, *920 O'Farrell Street* was not chosen, losing to Beatrice Bisno's labor novel, *Tomorrow's Bread*.[97] When Levy's memoir was finally published in 1947 by Doubleday, Allen Lesser's review in the *Menorah Journal* praised it for avoiding the "stereotypes of conventional post-Ellis Island stories." He concluded that "the many publishers—including the Jewish Publication Society of America—to whom it was submitted during the last decade, and who rejected it, might well profit by a few moments' reflection on the reasons why they missed up on a best-seller."[98] The JPS's rejections of San Francisco–based works by writers like Wolf and Levy beg the question of what "counted" as Jewish American literature in the early twentieth century. Works with middle-class San Francisco settings were deemed "impracticable" by the JPS because they did not comply with the society's notion of literary Jewishness, which, at the time, was defined primarily as lower class and Eastern European. In rejecting Wolf's work, then, the JPS may have missed an opportunity to expand the regional parameters of Jewish fiction and to contribute to a pluralistic Jewish culture that extended beyond the ghetto, in this case to the West Coast.

In other ways, too, the JPS seems to have missed an opportunity when they rejected Wolf's work. Sarna's history reveals that the JPS was actively courting a female audience, since women made up a significant base of novel readers in the nineteenth century. As domestic fiction, Wolf's work held particular appeal for women. If her "progressive spirit of Judaism" proved alienating to some, her representations of women occupied an ideological middle ground that captured a broad range of women readers. Female characters like Jean Willard and Laura Brookman in *Heirs of Yesterday* are intellectual and independent-minded, but they are not radical. They are characterized by their middle-class refinement and engagement with art and culture. Wolf's Jewish female characters were a source of identification for an important group of readers and book buyers at the time: middle- and upper-class members of Jewish women's clubs, like Wolf's own Philomath in San Francisco. As we know from Anne Ruggles Gere's research on the literacy practices of turn-of-the-twentieth-century clubwomen, Wolf's *Other Things Being Equal* was read and discussed by Jewish women's clubs around the country.[99]

The JPS's inability to capitalize successfully on the potential of Jewish women as readers of fiction was due to the gender makeup of its publication committee. Although the secretary who kept the minutes at the meeting was Henrietta Szold, who played a key editorial role at the press before moving on to found Hadassah, the Women's Zionist Organization of America, her own opinions were not recorded, and the decisions appear to be made solely by men. The little we can glean about Wolf's lost works hints at an unstated gender bias behind the JPS's decisions. From the title of "Little Jaffa," for instance, we can infer that the story featured a female protagonist; "Jaffa," which means "beauty" in Hebrew, was probably being used here as a girl's name, a reference to a main character. Meanwhile, the children's stories that the JPS published—including the one written by a woman, Sara Miller's *Under the Eagle's Wing*—featured boys. Given that all of Wolf's novels contain significant female characters, we can safely assume that *A Dreamer of Dreams* did too. But the only character in *Dreamer* mentioned in the JPS publication committee's discussion is a man (the "impossible" rabbi hero), which speaks to the implicit biases of the all-male committee, for whom women and gender issues were incidental.

Ultimately, the loss for Jewish fiction was not that the JPS failed to publish Wolf's work; as Zangwill warned, a contract with the JPS would have undoubtedly "cramped" her style. Instead, the loss is that two works by Wolf—clearly well written and provocative in content—were not published elsewhere. Fortunately, Wolf persevered in placing *Heirs of Yesterday* with another press, and in 1900 the novel was published by the prominent Chicago-based firm A. C. McClurg. Wolf was far from the only writer to find her work welcomed by other publishers after being rejected by the JPS. As Sarna notes, many of these authors had difficulty "understand[ing] why their work met with a warmer reception from Gentiles than from their own fellow Jews."[100]

That *Heirs of Yesterday* was ultimately published by McClurg is notable in light of Lucas Dietrich's recent scholarship on the publishing house, whose list included groundbreaking works of ethnic American literature such as W. E. B. Du Bois's *The Souls of Black Folk* (1903) and Sui Sin Far's *Mrs. Spring Fragrance* (1912), the first collection of fiction by an Asian American writer. According to Dietrich, McClurg developed a track record for its ability "to mediate between an ethnic author and a mainstream, predominantly white literary readership," positioning these works so that they simultaneously "express[ed] interracial sympathy and sentiment in an effort to bridge cultural divisions" and "reinscribe[d] existing social hierarchies."[101] The first edition of *Heirs of Yesterday* bears evidence of such mediation. On the book's cover, the title and author appear at the top in black lettering against a greyish green background. Below Wolf's name, and taking up more than half the cover, is an abstract floral design, vaguely reminiscent of Orientalist arabesques, bordered in black. One of the vine-like flowers, however, bleeds over the border into the top section

COVER OF *HEIRS OF YESTERDAY*.
Photo by Barbara Cantalupo.

of the cover, coming in close proximity to the name "Wolf." With the lone flower creating a bridge between the staid upper half of the cover and the lusher, more exotic imagery below, the design at once signals containment and crossover.

Based on the cover alone, there is nothing to mark *Heirs of Yesterday* as an explicitly Jewish book. Even Wolf's name does not identify her as a Jewish author, and the book's title and cover presentation hint only obliquely at the book's themes. Inside, however, the book's initial paratexts disclose what is obscured by the cover, establishing the novel's Jewish content. The epigraph is a quotation from Zangwill's *Dreamers of the Ghetto*, a book that was published by the JPS in partnership with Harper & Bros. in 1898 and that Wolf reviewed for the *American Jewess*. The epigraph, which is attributed simply to "Zangwill," reads, "For something larger had come into his life, a sense of a vaster universe without, and its spaciousness and strangeness filled his soul with a nameless trouble and a vague unrest. He was no longer a child of the Ghetto."[102] With that quote, the cover design takes on new meaning; the flower that intrudes upon the upper half of the cover symbolizes the characters' transcending the borders of the ghetto, its proximity to Wolf's name suggesting her own transcendence of the confining genre of ghetto fiction. The page with the epigraph is followed by a short, single-page foreword, which contains the first explicit reference to Jewishness. The foreword sets the scene as upper-class San Francisco, where "the tide of Jewish social culture runs its mimic parallel alongside" gentile social culture, "mounting hill for hill, matching inadequacy with inadequacy." The foreword also introduces one of the main characters, Philip May, with his "contemptuous" cry of denial: "Bah! . . . What have I to do with Ghettoes!" (85). Through these paratexts, *Heirs of Yesterday* is placed in dialogue with Zangwill and ghetto literature—and, by extension, with the kind of literature published by the JPS. In this introductory moment, Philip may even be said to represent Wolf herself. If Wolf's character rejects the idea that anyone born a Jew must be defined by the ghetto, Wolf is rejecting the idea that Jewish fiction needs to be circumscribed by the ghetto genre. Thus, the text mediates between Wolf as a Jewish author and gentile readers via references to more familiar representations of Jewish identity. But the main narrative itself overturns Zangwillian representations of Jews as a "peculiar people" through its representation of Jewish characters as well-off, cultured Americans who are, in most ways, indistinguishable from their gentile counterparts.

As Dietrich demonstrates, when McClurg published *The Souls of Black Folk*, the book's paratexts "reappropriated white fascinations with the racial other."[103] As a result, the text was often misread by its white audiences, who saw in it a confirmation of accepted racial ideologies. *Heirs of Yesterday* was subject to similar misreadings. One reviewer, for example, came away with the perception that "the Jews are in a very special sense Heirs of Yesterday, inasmuch as they have retained their racial characteristics almost unimpaired, and even in the United States, with its enormous power of assimilating all peoples and races, remain what they have always been—'a peculiar people.'"[104] The review is not unsympathetic to Wolf's Jewish characters and praises Wolf's literary skill, describing her style as "clean, strong and fervent," yet somehow it finds previous ideas about Jews confirmed rather than challenged.[105]

Other reviewers of *Heirs of Yesterday* offer a more accurate view, describing Wolf's work as a "picture of modern Jewish life" and her Jewish characters as "people of wealth and culture."[106] A piece on Wolf in the *Mechanics' Institute Library Bulletin* similarly identified her central theme as "modern Jewish life . . . especially the relations of Jew and Christian developed by modern quality of intercourse." The reception of Wolf's novels tends to be mixed, neither raves nor pans. Several identify Wolf as a writer of great promise, imagining the heights she might achieve in future work. The piece in the *Mechanics' Institute Library Bulletin*, for instance, concludes: "There is nothing to be gained by asserting that these books prove Miss Emma Wolf to be one of the world's great novelists, but those who care for sincerity, dignity and human insight will appreciate her work and look forward with keen interest to the further development of her undoubted genius."[107]

Jewish readers were more attuned to the ways Wolf's work negotiated debates about representation in Jewish fiction. As the front-page review in the *Jewish Messenger* stated, Wolf did not "exploit [her] religion and special class of people," further noting that "her delicacy, spirituality, [and] intellectuality are not restricted to Jewish subjects."[108] This reviewer and others saw Wolf's work as an important counterpoint to ghetto fiction. In 1902, for instance, the "Library Table" section of *The Menorah*, the organ of the Jewish Chautauqua Society, responded to an article titled "The Attitude of the Jews Toward Jewish Fiction" by Bernard G. Richards in *The Reader*. Observing that Richards restricted his analysis largely to ghetto writers, *The Menorah* chided him for "shut[ting] out of his purview the novels of Emma Wolf, which, in our opinion, rank high, if not in present value, at least as evidence of a *tendenz*."[109] Similarly, in the *American Hebrew and Jewish Messenger*, Joseph Lebowich singled out Wolf as the rare case who does not suffer from "that fatal disease known as Zangwillitis," referring to the tendency among Jewish writers to imitate Zangwill's style and perseverance on the ghetto. Even so, Lebowich, exposing his own gender bias with his use of the word "virility," compares Wolf unfavorably to Cahan. "Although lacking the virility of Mr. Cahan's work," Wolf's novels, he writes, "are polished and more carefully thought out" than those of Zangwill's imitators.[110]

The literary relationship between Zangwill and Wolf was based on dialogue and reciprocity, not imitation. Despite some reservations about the ambiguous ending of *Heirs of Yesterday*, Zangwill saw the work as an important step forward from her previous Jewish-themed novel. In a letter dated December 12, 1900, he wrote to Wolf that he had read her new book "with much pleasure, not only on account of its art but of its information. . . . There is a great tragic-comic mine for you in the States, & you are sinking your shaft much deeper than in 'Other Things Being Equal.'"[111] If Zangwill provided inspiration for and helped promote Wolf's fiction, she played a similar role for him. The influence of *Other Things Being Equal* and *Heirs of Yesterday* can be traced to Zangwill's 1908 play about intermarriage and Americanization, *The Melting Pot*. In this play, which popularized the concept of the "melting pot" as an enduring metaphor for American identity, Zangwill used an interfaith union to represent America as a "fusion" of different races. Wolf's Jewish-themed works helped stir the pot that produced that potent metaphor.[112]

After *Heirs of Yesterday*, Wolf wrote only one more novel, *Fulfillment*, which was published by Henry Holt in 1916. She also published two novellas and a number of short stories, most of them in the *Smart Set*, a popular magazine with high literary standards commonly considered a precursor to the *New Yorker*.[113] None of these works contain Jewish characters or content. The introduction to *Emma Wolf's Short Stories in "The Smart Set"* notes how the magazine stories demonstrate that Wolf was "operating outside the commonly-held paradigm that early twentieth-century Jewish American women writers were concerned primarily with poverty, politics, class struggle, and ardent discrimination." Instead, these stories, written for an educated, professional, and affluent audience, "address the intimate struggles of upper-class life."[114]

Still, Wolf continued to be associated with Jewish literature. From 1903 to 1911, *Heirs of Yesterday* was included as "required reading" for the Jewish Chautauqua Society's course called Jewish

Characters in Fiction, alongside works such as Shakespeare's *The Merchant of Venice*, Charles Dickens's *Oliver Twist*, George Eliot's *Daniel Deronda*, and Zangwill's *Children of the Ghetto*. For the author of the list, Rabbi Harry Levi, the value of Wolf's novel lay in her treatment of aspects of the Jewish American community absent from narratives of "ghetto life."[115] In his supplementary list of "recommended reading," Levi included not only *Other Things Being Equal* but also Wolf's works without Jewish themes, as if to emphasize her ability to branch out beyond the narrow parameters that tended to circumscribe the literary careers of minority writers.

Non-Jewish readers also appreciated Wolf's writing and her range. In a full-page profile in the *San Francisco Examiner*, reporter Lillian Ferguson noted that Wolf's novels, including the two that "deal with Jewry, present . . . powerful studies that appeal with almost equal force to Gentile and Jew." Describing Wolf as "that uncommon production among novelists, a woman of sound, sane, purposeful thinking—a philosopher," Ferguson admiringly observes that her interviewee has gained "literary recognition on two continents without stirring from her own fireside." Wolf's literary reputation both at home and in London, Ferguson asserts, was earned by her work not through self-promotion: "She has not elected to pave her way to popularity by the mercenary means that others with better business acumen and less ability have employed." Ferguson further alludes to Wolf's reclusiveness when she states that "[n]o woman novelist in California has kept herself so closely in the shadow of retirement as Miss Wolf."[116]

By circumstance and nature a private person, Wolf may have become more reclusive with time. Yet there is evidence that she maintained her connection to Jewish life and culture. In 1920 she presented on the topic of literature at the Western Assembly of the Jewish Chautauqua Society, and as late as 1922 she continued to be listed as an associate member of the Philomath Club.[117] As noted in the preface, when Wolf died in 1932, she was buried in Home of Peace Cemetery in Colma, California, originally established by Congregation Emanu-El. Like her grave marker, Wolf's fiction has long been hidden from sight. This edition of *Heirs of Yesterday* helps her assume her rightful place in Jewish American literary history. The story of how Wolf came to publish the novel has much to tell us about the interplay between Jewishness, class, gender, and region, demonstrating that the agenda of the male-dominated, East Coast–based Jewish book publishing industry was often at cross-purposes with the artistic and social ideals of Western, middle-class Jewish American women writers.[118] Especially when read with attention to its varied historical, literary, and religious contexts, *Heirs of Yesterday* broadens and complicates existing narratives about Jews, immigration, religious minorities, and Jewish American culture at the turn of the twentieth century.

COUNTERING JEWISH STEREOTYPES: ANTI-SEMITISM IN NINETEENTH-CENTURY AMERICAN CULTURE

As previously discussed, historians agree that anti-Semitism was much less a factor in San Francisco compared to other parts of the country. Peter Decker, for example, argues that the city's Jewish merchants and businessmen translated their wealth and financial security into social capital that extended to fellow Jews who were not part of the mercantile class. "Led by their respected merchants, the Jews of San Francisco probably faced less prejudice and carried forth into future decades the memory of fewer unpleasant experiences than the Jews of any city in the nation at midcentury," he hypothesizes.[119] Still, significant undercurrents of prejudice remained. Precisely because so many Jews were successful in business in San Francisco, prejudice often manifested in terms of economic stereotypes that depicted money-hungry Jews as untrustworthy in their financial dealings and especially eager to take advantage of Christians. In one instance cited by Decker, "A credit report on two German Jews who owned rather substantial assets warned: 'They are Hebrews. May be good [for credit] *if well watched*; they are *tricky.*'"[120]

In American history, anti-Semitism has fluctuated with the times, its rise corresponding with increases in anti-immigrant sentiment, nativism, and white nationalism. Just as anti-Semitism has become more noticeable since the 2016 US presidential election (from so-called dog whistles and subtle uses of imagery to vandalism of Jewish sites and violent acts of hate), historians documented a significant uptick in anti-Semitism across the nation by the end of the nineteenth century. Late nineteenth-century anti-Semitism coincided with the mass migration of Eastern European Jews to the United States and with calls for more restrictive immigration policies. The general rise in anti-immigrant rhetoric revived old racial and religious stereotypes that portrayed Jews as dirty, alien, and biologically inferior to Anglo-Saxons. San Francisco was not immune, especially because anti-Semitism insinuated itself into so many aspects of the national culture. Jewish caricatures and stock characters were ubiquitous in the theater, for instance. From British imports like Shakespeare's *The Merchant of Venice* with its portrayal of the notorious usurer Shylock to the distinctly American dialect comedy that was a centerpiece of vaudeville, the stage Jew, whose hooked nose portended the evils of unchecked materialism, was easily recognizable to American audiences.[121]

Anti-Semitic representations were also pervasive in print culture. Popular periodicals regularly published dialect stories and ghetto tales in which Jews appeared as one-dimensional caricatures, as well as cartoons and jokes whose punchlines depended on the audience's knowledge of Jewish stereotypes. While some gentile American writers voiced respect and sympathy for Jews, leading at times to complex literary portrayals, scholars such as Donald Pizer have exposed the extent of anti-Semitic representation in the work of canonical turn-of-the-twentieth-century writers—including, notably, San Francisco's own Frank Norris.[122] In his 1899 novel, *McTeague: A Story of San Francisco*, Norris describes the character of Zerkow, a Polish Jewish junk dealer, in demonic and animalistic terms: "a dry, shriveled old man" with satanically red hair; "eager, catlike lips of the covetous; eyes that had grown keen as those of a lynx from long searching amid muck and debris; and clawlike, prehensile fingers—the fingers of a man who accumulates, but never disburses." Zerkow's "inordinate, insatiable greed" leads him to marry a poor Mexican charwoman, Maria, in order to get his hands on a set of gold dishes that her family once purportedly owned.[123] By the end of the novel, Zerkow's lust for gold turns murderous, and he kills his wife in pursuit of the illusory dishes. As Elisa New writes, "Norris' depiction of the greedy Jew reflects a particularly American anti-Semitism that was very much of the 1890s and was shared by other naturalist writers."[124]

Throughout *Heirs of Yesterday*, Wolf refers to common Jewish stereotypes in an effort to counter them, and she fully develops her Jewish characters as individuals in response to depictions that appeared in the work of her contemporaries. Whereas anti-Semitic discourse relayed Jewishness through a character's outward appearance, Wolf's Philip May is visually indistinguishable from his gentile counterparts; he is able to pass as non-Jewish because his "features are . . . silent" (99). When the novel states that Jean Willard's "religion had always lain lightly upon her," it refers at once to her relationship to spirituality and the fact that she is not readily identifiable as Jewish based on her appearance (117). Wolf's attention to the visual signifiers of Jewishness is especially evident in the plotline involving Jean's refusal to model for the anti-Semitic painter Stephen Forrest, who is enamored with her "shadowy dark" beauty (90). Although Forrest attempts to reassure Jean that her "sex unsects" her when she reminds him of her Jewish background, his view remains circumscribed by the archetype of *la belle juive*, or the beautiful Jewess, an image of erotic fascination for Christian men (114). The beautiful Jewess's Orientalized femininity serves to render the Jewish woman as exotic and different, while also bringing into relief the repulsive physical features that marked Jewish male difference in anti-Semitic representations.

That Jewish men bore the brunt of anti-Semitic stereotyping in the late nineteenth century helps explain why Philip, the male protagonist of *Heirs of Yesterday*, is the one who decides to disassociate from his Jewish background and pass for gentile. In his analysis of cartoons that appeared in the American press between 1877 and 1935, Matthew Baigell observes that Jewish men are depicted as "money-hungry Shylocks and thieving Fagins, social climbers, arsonists ready to claim insurance for property loss, and disagreeable, scheming parvenus who would take advantage of any situation in which they found themselves."[125] Among the periodicals that Baigell analyzes is the popular humor magazine *Puck*, which is specifically referenced in *Heirs of Yesterday*. In a conversation with friends about whether Philip deserves condemnation for his decision to distance himself from the Jewish community, Jean quietly rises to his defense, wondering about the effect of "those diverting Jewish stories in Puck and other witty periodicals" (137).

In the 1890s, Jewish stereotypes and caricatures were a regular textual and visual feature of *Puck*. Throughout the pages of the magazine, men with overdetermined Jewish names like Isaacstein and Cohenstein spoke in English-language-mangling dialect; intended to suggest a Yiddish accent, the improper speech reminded readers of the immigrant's inability to master the national language and thus his unassimilable foreignness. If an illustration accompanied the joke, the cartoonist drew the men as corpulent to signify their greed. Most of the humor was associated with "peezness," *Puck's* Yiddish-inflected bastardization of the word "business," reinforcing assumptions about Jews' miserly unscrupulousness in dealing with gentiles. In a dialogue sketch titled "No Means of Support," for instance, a boy asks his parent if there are any Christians in Jerusalem; when the parent replies in the negative, the boy wonders "what the Hebrews" will "live on" when they move there.[126] As indicated by the dual meaning of "live on" to suggest both exploiting for financial gain and consuming, *Puck* often pushed the stereotype beyond economic threats to evoke and stoke religious fears—in this case, the long-standing myth of the blood libel, the belief that Jews ritually murdered Christian children and used their blood for ceremonial purposes. Reminded by a "prospective victim" that "you boarded at my house when you attended the World's Fair," a cannibal in a joke titled "Unprejudiced" assures his former host that he will not eat him, asking "in some surprise; 'you don't take me for a Hebrew, do you?'"[127] At other times, Jewish religious practice such as kosher dietary laws became a source of mockery. In "Strictly Orthodox," for example, two Jews, Rosenbaum and Epstein, gossip about a third, Ikey Jacobs, who is "such a strict Hebrew dot he von't efen blay football" to avoid "chasing der pigskin."[128]

As the last example suggests, Jews themselves were sometimes in on the joke. (*Puck's* first editor, Sydney Rosenfeld, was himself Jewish, and the magazine sardonically referred to Jews as "Our Hebrew Friends.") In *Heirs of Yesterday*, the character of Paul Stein admits to laughing "over the wit of Puck's stories when our shrewdness, or features, or mannerisms are the point of ridicule," viewing his "good-natured" response as superior to that of "the cultured Irish-man who sets his teeth at the sight of printed brogue" (140). Unlike in the twentieth and twenty-first centuries, when organizations such as the Anti-Defamation League would take action to defend Jews against attacks in the press, many nineteenth-century Jewish Amer-icans, including religious leaders, believed it best not to protest anti-Semitic humor and caricature; they feared that a direct response could draw more attention to the offensive representation and lead to accusations of oversensitivity. In the case of *Puck*, when any mi-nority group objected to being lampooned in the magazine's pages, the editors "invariably responded with: 'Can't you take a joke?'"[129]

In the absence of direct, organized protest against cultural anti-Semitism, Wolf's fiction takes on even greater potency. *Heirs of Yes-terday* can be read as an indirect response to anti-Semitic stereotypes in American culture and their increasing virulence at the end of the nineteenth century. Wolf strategically deploys literary realism as well as narrative conventions of plot and character development to create counter-representations. In an interview in the *San Francisco Examiner* that appeared shortly after the publication of her fourth novel, Wolf explained her approach to realism (what she calls "truth-telling") when it came to crafting her characters. "To me there is a fascination in character development—the gradual unfolding of an individuality until it has attained its full mental and moral growth. No character is complete without both the spiritual and material el-ements," she stated.[130] Wolf's skill at character development allowed her to defy Jewish stereotypes and caricature, producing an array of cultured, refined, individualized, middle-class characters. They are, as Wolf writes in *Heirs of Yesterday*, "a representative group whose blended characteristics would scarcely have produced that legendary composite—the 'typical' Jew" (161).[131]

Even a cursory overview of nineteenth-century Jewish stereo-types helps readers contextualize Wolf's approach to anti-Semitism in *Heirs of Yesterday*. Philip's decision to pass as gentile cannot sim-ply be understood as an act of Jewish self-hatred or a selfish attempt at social climbing. Instead, readers are asked to connect the dots between anti-Semitic thought as manifest in Jewish stereotypes and real-world consequences. Explaining his decision to pass as gentile,

Philip begins by narrating a formative incident from his childhood when he was taunted at school with the slur "Christ-killer" (99, 174). In addition to resisting long-held religious stereotypes charging Jews with deicide, Philip also refuses to allow social, economic, and racial stereotypes to define him personally and professionally. "To be a Jew," he asserts, "is to be socially handicapped for life" (101). Although Jean does not condone Philip's decision to pass as gentile, especially given the emotional pain it causes his father, she does understand what would drive someone to make this choice, recognizing that Philip's actions are rooted in the anti-Semitism responsible for creating social handicaps and fostering Jewish shame and self-loathing. By incorporating anti-Semitism into the novel in this way, Wolf conveys an understated but powerful message about the harmfulness of stereotypes to individuals and to the future of the Jewish community.

COMPLICATING THE COUPLING CONVENTION: EMMA WOLF AND WOMEN'S LITERATURE

In the introduction to a special issue of *MELUS* entitled "The Future of Jewish American Literary Studies," the editors note that scholars of Jewish American literature have overlooked Wolf's work, favoring instead the fiction of Anzia Yezierska (1880–1970), who has become one of the field's token women writers. "Because her work speaks simultaneously to the politics of immigration, feminism, and labor," they write, "a writer such as Yezierska has become the subject of near-constant scholarly scrutiny, but the works of equally interesting Jewish women writers such as Emma Wolf, Fannie Hurst, and Vera Caspary remain largely unknown even to many specialists in the field."[132] As we have thus far shown in this introduction, commentators in Wolf's own time noted a similar tendency, among both publishers and critics, to "center . . . their attention on the poor or the unassimilated," thus "shut[ting] out of . . . purview" writers such as Wolf.[133]

Jewish literary studies is not the only field to neglect Wolf's contributions, however. She has also been overlooked by scholars of

American women's writing. In the last few decades of the twentieth century, when women's literature became a distinct area of study at universities, including in courses devoted solely to women's writing, literary academicians gravitated toward late nineteenth- and early twentieth-century women authors like Kate Chopin (1850–1904) and Charlotte Perkins Gilman (1860–1935), whose radical critiques of marriage and gender roles fit with the ideological stance of the second-wave women's movement. Unlike Gilman's explicitly activist writings or Chopin's provocative depictions of women struggling to free themselves from patriarchal oppression in texts like *The Awakening* (1899), Wolf's domestic fiction does not read as a call to feminist action. She does not level a wholesale attack on patriarchy or unequivocally advocate New Womanhood as a form of liberation from the constraints of traditional femininity. Instead, her fiction gently probes notions of gender equality and questions about whether marriage and motherhood need be the only options for middle-class women. That Wolf's work often adheres to bourgeois values does not make it less worthy of study. Instead, heroines such as Jean in *Heirs of Yesterday*—described in the text as "one of those modern anachronisms, a woman with ideals"—add to and complicate literary portraits of women from the era (112). In the final section of this introduction, we consider how *Heirs of Yesterday* can be read in relation to various traditions of women's literature, situating Wolf's work in the context of domestic fiction and the marriage plot; turn-of-the-twentieth-century movements such as realism and regionalism; and transatlantic, cross-cultural, and comparative ethnic networks.

In employing the underlying structure of the marriage plot, Wolf participated in one of the longest-standing conventions of the Anglophone novel, one that was profoundly shaped by the contributions of Victorian women writers such as George Eliot, Jane Austen, and the Brontë sisters. In nineteenth-century American literature, the marriage plot was also closely associated with women writers whose popular novels were often derided by their male counterparts for their sentimentalism. On the surface, Wolf's reliance on the timeworn tradition of the marriage plot marks her as a fairly conventional writer, but a closer look indicates her careful displacement of earlier romantic conventions with depictions of love and marriage grounded in realism. Her short story "One-Eye, Two-Eye, Three-Eye," for example, acknowledges and then rejects the fairy tale on which it is based in order to circumvent the idealized love of the happily-ever-after ending. "Fairy tales are impossible nowadays," the story begins. "Fact is quite interesting enough at this epoch. . . . Formerly we saw as through a glass darkly, now face to face."[134] In addition to placing her within a long tradition of women's literature, Wolf's use of the marriage plot also helps to situate her among women writers of her era (most famously, Edith Wharton) who used realism—or, seeing "face to face"—to hold the marriage market and the bonds of matrimony up to scrutiny.[135] As scholars such as Clare Eby have observed, the marriage plot did not become passé at the end of the nineteenth century; instead, it continued to have relevance for Gilded Age and Progressive Era writers, many of whom used it to explore gender and class politics, to mark the breakdown of separate spheres ideology, and to agitate for marital reform.[136]

Wolf's symbolic deployment of marriage as a consensual union between equals in her Jewish-themed novels, *Other Things Being Equal* and *Heirs of Yesterday*, and the influence of these novels on theories and representations of ethnic American identity such as Israel Zangwill's *The Melting Pot* (1908) have received in-depth treatment elsewhere.[137] But Wolf's Jewish twist on the marriage trope becomes even more intriguing when considered as part of a broader transatlantic tradition of women's literature in the long nineteenth century. As exemplified by George Eliot's *Daniel Deronda* (1876) and Wharton's *The House of Mirth* (1904), both British and American gentile women writers similarly introduced Jewish difference as a complicating factor in the marriage plot. These examples further demonstrate that Anglophone texts traditionally foreclosed the possibility of interfaith union between gentile women and Jewish men, whether it be the case of a noble character like Deronda or an opportunistic one like Simon Rosedale, Lily Bart's nouveau riche Jewish suitor in *The House of Mirth*. As Elizabeth Ammons succinctly described the plot of Wharton's novel, "The book is about the snow-white heroine, the flower of Anglo-Saxon womanhood, not ending up married to the invading Jew."[138] Novels such as Eliot's and Wharton's can be read productively alongside Wolf's work. Her first book, *Other*

Things Being Equal, for example, stands out for its positive portrayal of intermarriage; in it, Wolf's Jewish-Christian couple successfully overcomes the obstacle of religious difference. In *Heirs of Yesterday*, the obstacle to marriage is not Jewish difference—Jean and Philip are both Jews by birth—but different views of Jewishness, familial loyalty, and professional ambition. As a courtship narrative set in a middle-class, Reform milieu, *Heirs of Yesterday* extends the work of British Jewish writer Amy Levy across the Atlantic. Levy's 1888 novel, *Reuben Sachs*—written in response to Eliot's philo-Semitic, romanticized portraits in *Daniel Deronda*—used the marriage trope to explore Jewish life among the upwardly mobile class in late Victorian London and to expose limitations placed on women.[139] Like the connection between Wolf and Zangwill, the commonalities between Wolf's and Levy's works provide evidence of transatlantic networks of exchange among Jewish writers in the late nineteenth century.

Debates in African American literary studies about the uses of domestic fiction in black women's writing also provide a useful comparative framework for evaluating Wolf's work and her obscurity. In *The Coupling Convention: Sex, Text, and Tradition in Black Women's Fiction*, Ann duCille challenges earlier critics who had "marginalized" late nineteenth-century black novelists like Pauline Hopkins and Frances Harper "for their alleged assimilation of so-called white values." As duCille shows through her recuperation of such writers, their use of light-skinned heroines and the bourgeois conventions of the marriage plot functioned as a means to "rebut . . . the racist imaging of black women."[140] *Heirs of Yesterday* makes an especially provocative pairing with Hopkins's class-conscious depictions of family life among black professionals and intellectuals in *Contending Forces: A Romance Illustrative of Negro Life North and South*, also published in 1900. Through her novel's domestic setting and refined female characters, who conform to traditional ideas about femininity, Hopkins mobilized the politics of racial uplift and respectability.[141]

Well-educated and well-mannered characters like Jean and Philip in *Heirs of Yesterday* similarly serve to portray Jews as upright citizens and respectable members of middle-class society, making an argument for equality by emphasizing their shared social mores with gentiles. Wolf makes clear her intent to overturn exoticized images of Jewish women through Jean's encounter with the artist Stephen Forrest. Correctly intuiting his desire to fix her as a "type" and refusing to be hemmed in by romanticized notions of Jewish womanhood, Jean declines to pose for him. Later, without her consent, Forrest transforms his memory of her into a portrait titled "The Jewess" and attempts to further exert his power by claiming the painting as his property rather than putting it up for sale.[142] As a pianist, Jean is an artist in her own right, determined to use her music to control her self-representation and to assert her individualism. Wolf, as a novelist, uses her art in much the same way.

As duCille illustrates, middle-class black protagonists were often juxtaposed with, and seen as less authentic than, dialect-speaking folk characters, like those who inhabit the writings of Zora Neale Hurston, one of the first black women writers to be reclaimed by feminist scholars. Similarly, Wolf's characters provide a sharp contrast to Yezierska's heroines, who were also claimed by early scholars of American women's history and writing. Whereas the poverty, Yiddish-inflected dialect, and sensuality of Yezierska's ghetto folk heighten—and at times exuberantly celebrate—Jewish difference, characters like Jean and Philip, who are "endowed with . . . name[s]" and "features" that "tell . . . no tales" (99), may be viewed as inauthentically whitewashed, scrubbed clean of all outward markers of difference. Yet, much like domestic fiction by black women writers, *Heirs of Yesterday* takes a stance against ethno-racial assimilation, and it does so, interestingly, by incorporating a passing narrative, a genre most often associated with African American literature. Philip's decision to pass for gentile to avoid being "socially handicapped for life" (101) echoes the choices made by light-skinned black protagonists who cross the color line and pass for white in fiction by black women writers such as Nella Larsen and Jessie Fauset, as well as in works by men such as Charles Chesnutt and James Weldon Johnson. While the ease with which Philip sheds his ethno-religious heritage challenges pseudo-scientific notions of Jewish racial difference, it is equally important that *Heirs of Yesterday*—like many of the black passing narratives that have entered the

American and ethnic literary canons—rejects passing as a means of attaining equality. As argued elsewhere, in supplanting the passing narrative with a marriage plot, *Heirs of Yesterday* redefines Jewishness in terms that privilege consent over descent.[143]

Wolf's redefinition of Jewish identity in *Heirs of Yesterday* is further enabled by the novel's Western setting, which positions her depiction of fin-de-siècle Jewish life beyond the confines of the East Coast urban ghetto and within the woman-dominated movement of late nineteenth-century literary regionalism. Wolf, whose novels are all set in her home state and whose final work, *Fulfillment*, was subtitled *A California Novel*, belongs to a group of women writers that includes Helen Hunt Jackson, María Amparo Ruiz de Burton, and Gertrude Atherton, whose writings explore the history and culture of the Golden State. As discussed earlier, Wolf's views on Judaism and Jewishness were very much shaped by the distinctness of the California Reform movement. Sketching the novel's setting with a regionalist's attention to time and place, Wolf links her vision of progressive Judaism to the expansive geography of the American West. The novel opens with Jean "making her way westward along Pacific avenue," walking "swiftly, lightly, the joyous wind of motion in her going," and taking off her jacket in the warm February sun "to enjoy the freedom" (87). This opening image of Jean's westward movement sets the stage for her embrace of Reform tenets later in the novel. In marked contrast to Philip's association of his abandoned religion with the cramped confinement of the ghetto, Jean views Judaism as "singularly free, unhampered, broad, open to the light of day"—a vision that draws upon the language of the frontier and makes within it a space for Jews and for women (162). Due to the specificity of its Northern California setting, this edition of *Heirs of Yesterday* contributes to ongoing efforts to recover nineteenth- and early twentieth-century women authors such as Atherton, Ruiz de Burton, Mary Austin, Sui Sin Far (Edith Maude Eaton), Sarah Winnemucca, and Miriam Michelson, whose work engages with—and often provides alternatives to—white masculinist myths of the West.

Given the specific temporal context of Wolf's novel, whose ending coincides with the Spanish-American War in 1898, *Heirs of Yesterday* offers new opportunities to consider how women writers addressed US expansionism and empire, lending further credence to Amy Kaplan's claims that white, middle-class American women participated in the imperial project through the rhetoric of "manifest domesticity."[144] In considering Wolf's complications of the coupling convention, it is important to keep in mind that the onset of the war interferes with the neat resolution of the marriage plot. At the very moment that Philip reconsiders his renunciation of Judaism through his love for Jean, telling her, "You have become my religion," and asking, "If you are Jewish, must I not too be Jew?," the novel zooms outward from its domestic narrative and the quiet intimacy of the couple's romance (240). Ripping her story straight from bold newspaper headlines, Wolf describes the sinking of the battleship USS *Maine* in Havana Harbor. The historical backdrop of the war thus overtakes the lives of her fictional characters, with Philip deciding to enlist as an army surgeon and Jean devoting herself to volunteer work for the San Francisco Red Cross.

Like so many of Wolf's portrayals, her characters' patriotic responses to the war correlate with the historical narrative. The first man to enlist in the army following the attack on the *Maine* and in the face of the United States' impending declaration of war on Spain was a young Jewish physician, Colonel Joseph M. Heller, whose "fighting spirit" and "eagerness to serve [his] country" roused pride among his co-religionists.[145] Meanwhile, the *San Francisco Call*, in an article titled "Israel's Tithe to America," reported on how Jewish women, including members of Wolf's own Philomath Club, supported the war effort through their involvement in the Red Cross.[146] As historian Jeanne Abrams has shown in her research on the Reform community's investment in the Spanish-American War, military service abroad and Red Cross service at home became a means for Jewish men and women to show the "compatibility of Jewish and American ideals in matters of government and humanitarian diplomacy," to answer anti-Semitic attacks by illustrating "that Jews were just as brave and patriotic as any other group of Americans," and to ensure that Jews would take part in the bounty of manifest destiny.[147] The historical event of the Spanish-American War offered yet another way for Wolf to portray the Americanness of her Jewish characters while also demonstrating, in Kaplan's words, how "the female realm of domesticity and the male realm of Manifest Destiny were not separate spheres . . . but were intimately linked."[148] The novel's final pages depict the departure of the Manila expedition with Philip on board and Jean standing with the crowds in a farewell salute. As in William Dean Howells's classic story "Editha" (1905), which is similarly set during the Spanish-American War, the man's military enlistment disrupts the marriage plot. Rather than resolving with the union of its two main characters, *Heirs of Yesterday* concludes with narrative ambiguity.

While she was in the process of working on *Heirs of Yesterday*, Wolf wrote to Zangwill of her plan to end the novel "happily for love's sake"—a plan that met with the British writer's approval.[149] But as the events of the Spanish-American War unfolded, Wolf apparently altered her course, ultimately deciding to end the narrative on a much more ambiguous note than she initially proposed. Upon reading the finished novel, Zangwill was not wholly satisfied with Wolf's ending. He hypothesized that Wolf was "emulat[ing] the ambiguity of Charlotte Bronte in 'Villette' with an even greater uncertainty," stating, "I don't know if it is a good plan."[150] For today's readers, the ambiguity of Wolf's unconventional ending is likely to add to the novel's richness while also providing evidence of Wolf's increasing commitment to realist aesthetics. Even more so than *Other Things Being Equal*, which concludes with the couple's marriage while hinting at the uncertainty of the future, *Heirs of Yesterday* closes on a note of open-endedness.[151] This uncertainty reflects the sociopolitical and global changes taking hold at the turn of the new century as America's path through modernity became intertwined with its status as an imperial power.[152]

The ending also serves as a potent reminder of the ways that women writers complicated the coupling convention, varying the underlying structure of the marriage plot to serve a range of aesthetic and ideological purposes. The ending may leave us with uncertainty about Philip's fate at sea, but it also reinforces the dominant image of Jean as an unconventional heroine whose identity rests on her individuality rather than matrimony. In this regard, too, Jean may resemble the woman who created her. Relegated to almost a century of obscurity, despite a well-hidden gravestone, and in the absence of a substantial archival record, Emma Wolf's identity resides in the body of fiction she produced.

NOTES

Epigraph quoted in Lillian Ferguson, "Leading Epigrammist in Recent Fiction is a California Girl: Great English Critics Have Given High Praise to Miss. Emma Wolf's Novels," *San Francisco Examiner*, December 1, 1901, 25.

1. One of the few scholarly monographs to consider Wolf's writing is Diane Lichtenstein, *Writing Their Nations: The Tradition of Nineteenth-Century American Jewish Women Writers* (Bloomington: Indiana University Press, 1992). There is some evidence of increasing attention to Wolf's work since Barbara Cantalupo's republication of Wolf's 1892 novel *Other Things Being Equal* in 2002. For an overview of some of the current scholarship on Wolf, see Barbara Cantalupo, "Emma Wolf," in *Oxford Bibliographies*, Oxford University Press, March 30, 2015, www.oxfordbibliographies.com. Nina Baym also includes a brief discussion of Emma Wolf's fiction, as well as the writing of her sister, Alice Wolf, in *Women Writers of the American West, 1833–1927* (Bloomington: University of Illinois Press, 2012), 77–79.

2. "Miss Wolf's New Story," *Jewish Messenger* 88, no. 24 (December 1900): 1.

3. D. J. Myers, "Emma Wolf's Stories," *A Commonplace Blog*, May 30, 2010, http://dgmyers.blogspot.com/2010/05/emma-wolfs-stories.html. This designation has recently been challenged by Jonathan Sarna's recovery of Cora Wilburn's work, especially her novel *Cosella Wayne* (1860). See Jonathan Sarna, "The Forgetting of Cora Wilburn: Historical Amnesia and *The Cambridge History of Jewish American Literature*," *Studies in American Jewish Literature* 37, no. 1 (Spring 2018): 73–87.

4. Review of *Fulfillment: A California Novel* by Emma Wolf, *Overland Monthly, Second Series* 67, no. 5 (1916): ix–x.

5.   "Emma Wolf, Beloved S. F. Author, Dead," *San Francisco Chronicle*, August 31, 1932, 9. In her entry on Wolf in *Jewish American Women Writers*, Cantalupo assumed that Wolf had lived her last fifteen years in Dante Sanitarium, since a letter to the editor of the *San Francisco Chronicle* on August 31, 1932, by Rebekah Godchaux notes that Wolf "rarely left her room," and her obituary in the *San Francisco Chronicle* on August 31, 1932, stated that she died in Dante Sanitarium. Further research revealed that her death certificate stated that Wolf died on August 29, 1932, from a postoperative embolism that occurred after a minor surgery to remove an orbital tumor, and the 1930 census indicates that Wolf resided at 2100 Pacific Avenue with her sister Celestine ("Linnie").

6.   Paula Hyman, *The Emancipation of the Jews of Alsace: Acculturation and Tradition in the Nineteenth Century* (New Haven, CT: Yale University Press, 1991), 20.

7.   Ava Kahn, "Joining the Rush," in *California Jews*, ed. Ava Kahn and Marc Dollinger (Hanover, NH: Brandeis University Press / University Press of New England, 2003), 29.

8.   See Annick Foucrier, ". . . To Divide Their Love': Celebrating Frenchness and Americanization in San Francisco, 1850–1909," in *Celebrating Ethnicity and Nation: American Festive Culture from the Revolution to the Early Twentieth Century*, ed. Jurgen Heideking et al. (New York: Berghahn, 2001), 140–56. An early history of French immigrants in California was written by Daniel Levy, a friend of the Wolf family and a lay leader of Temple Emanu-El; see Daniel Levy, *Les Français en Californie* (San Francisco: Gregoire Tauzy, 1884), and "Letters about the Jews of California, 1855–1858," trans. Marlene Rainman, *Western States Jewish Historical Quarterly* 3 (January 1971): 86–112.

9.   Ava Kahn, "Introduction," in *Jewish Voices of the Gold Rush: A Documentary History, 1849–1880*, ed. Ava Kahn (Detroit, MI: Wayne State University Press, 2002), 38.

10. Marc Dollinger, foreword to *Jewish San Francisco* by Edward Zerin (Charleston, SC: Arcadia, 2006), 7.

11. Levy, "Letters about the Jews," 93.

12. Jackie Krentzman, *American Jerusalem: Jews and the Making of San Francisco*. Waltham, MA: National Center for Jewish Film, 2013, DVD.

13. Fred Rosenbaum, *Visions of Reform: Congregation Emanu-El and the Jews of San Francisco, 1849–1999* (Berkeley, CA: Judah L. Magnes Museum, 2000), 4. Originally noted in Peter Decker, *Fortunes and Failures: White Collar Mobility in Nineteenth-Century San Francisco* (Cambridge, MA: Harvard University Press, 1978), 21.

14. Levy, "Letters about the Jews," 100.

15. Emma Wolf, "Social Life in American Cities: San Francisco," *Delineator*, September 1897, 343.

16. Edward Zerin, *Jewish San Francisco* (Charleston, SC: Arcadia, 2009), 19.

17. Wolf, "Social Life in American Cities: San Francisco," 343.

18. Kahn, "Introduction," 39–40.

19. See "Cleveland Assembly of 1855," *Encyclopedia of Cleveland History*, Case Western Reserve University, https://case.edu/ech/articles/c/cleveland-assembly-1855.

20. Rosenbaum, *Visions of Reform*, 29. San Francisco Jews took the Reform movement further than many of their co-religionists. For instance, Emanu-El instituted various innovations to the musical component of its religious services, bringing in a Catholic opera singer for the high holidays in the 1860s, introducing a choir of non-Jews because they wanted to have the best voices possible, and replacing the shofar with a trumpet played by a member of the symphony. That Wolf admired Levy is evident from the tribute she wrote in the March 4, 1910, issue of *Emanu-El*:

> Once upon a time, there lived a very good man, and he was much beloved. And when he was very old, a great nation pinned a ribbon upon his breast and called him Chevalier of the Legion of Honor, because he had been a loyal and loving son to his adored country. But all the while he had been marching with another legion as well. And the men who march with this legion wear no ribbon upon their

breasts that men may gaze upon, but deep down and hidden within their hearts there lies a wondrous Decoration. And though we may not see it, we know when it is there. For wherever one of his sweet legion passes, that place is made the better and happier thereby. And to whomsoever one of this sweet legion speaks, that person has known something beautiful that cannot be taken away. And though, perhaps, you may never have heard of this legion, and may not believe what I have told you of it, yet it is true,—you may be very sure that it is true. Because Daniel Levy belonged. Daniel Levy, nobleman—chevalier of the legion of the honor of God.

Dena Mandel suggests that Wolf modeled the character of Daniel Willard in *Heirs of Yesterday* on Daniel Levy. See Dena Mandel, "A World of Difference: Emma Wolf, A Jewish-American Writer on the American Frontier," PhD diss., University of Alaska, 2008, 136–37.

21. Shari Rabin, *Jews on the Frontier: Religion and Mobility in Nineteenth-Century America* (New York: New York University Press, 2017), 7.

22. Moses Rischin, "The Jewish Experience in America: A View from the West," in *Jews in the American West*, ed. Moses Rischin and John Livingston (Detroit, MI: Wayne State University Press, 1991), 32.

23. Rischin, "Jewish Experience in America," 34.

24. Ibid., 36.

25. Judith Pinnolis, "'Cantor Soprano' Julie Rosewald: The Musical Career of a Jewish American 'New Woman,'" *American Jewish Archives Journal* 62, no. 2 (2010): 2.

26. "Simon Wolf & Associates, Master Pioneer Jewish Merchants of Contra Costa County, California," Jewish Museum of the American West, www. jmaw.org.

27. "Death of Simon Wolf," *Weekly Antioch Ledger*, September 14, 1878, 3.

28. See "City Dwellers Make Their Summer Holidays by Mountain, by Stream and by Sea: Santa Cruz, San Mateo, San

Jose, Ben Lomond . . . ," *San Francisco Chronicle*, July 12, 1896, 3.

29. See Nicholas C. Polos, "A Yankee Patriot: John Swett, the Horace Mann of the Pacific," *History of Education Quarterly* 41 (March 1964): 17–32.

30. John Swett, *Public Education in California: Its Origin and Development with Personal Reminiscences of Half a Century* (New York: American Book Company, 1911), 222.

31. John Swett, *Methods of Teaching: A Hand-Book of Principles, Directions, and Working Models for Common-School Teachers* (New York: American Book Company, 1880), 35.

32. Ibid., 51.

33. Ferguson, "Leading Epigrammist," 25.

34. Swett, *Methods of Teaching*, 296.

35. Charlene Akers, introduction to Harriet Lane Levy, *920 O'Farrell Street: A Jewish Girlhood in Old San Francisco* (Berkeley, CA: Heyday, 1996), ix.

36. Rebekah Bettelheim Kohut, *My Portion: An Autobiography* (New York: A. & C. Boni, 1925), 60–62.

37. Ibid.

38. Rebekah Kohut, *More Yesterdays: An Autobiography (1925–49), A Sequel to My Portion* (New York: Bloch, 1950), 38, 40. Readers who are interested in drawing comparisons between Wolf's and Kohut's differing religious trajectories can consult Joyce Antler, *The Journey Home: Jewish Women in the American Century* (New York: Free Press, 1997), 40–54, in addition to Kohut's autobiographies.

39. Emma Wolf, *Other Things Being Equal*, ed. and with an introduction by Barbara Cantalupo (Detroit, MI: Wayne State University Press, 2002), 66.

40. "Pittsburgh Platform," *Encyclopaedia Judaica*, ed. Michael Berenbaum and Fred Skolnik, 2nd ed., vol. 16 (New York: Macmillan Reference, 2007), 190–91.

41. On *The Chosen People*, see Adam Sol, " 'I Shan't Let You Shirk!': Sidney Nyburg's *The Chosen People* and Reform Judaism of the Early Twentieth Century," *Studies in American Jewish Literature* 27 (2007): 56–64.

42. Rosenbaum, *Visions of Reform*, 16.

43. Ibid., 46. For more on women and Reform Judaism, see Karla Goldman, "The Ambivalence of Reform Judaism: Kaufman Kohler and the Ideal Jewish Woman," *American Jewish History* 79, no. 4 (1990): 477–99.

44. Marc Lee Raphael, "Rabbi Jacob Voorsanger of San Francisco on Jews and Judaism: The Implications of the Pittsburgh Platform," *American Jewish Historical Quarterly* 63, no. 2 (1973): 191, 192, 203.

45. Frances Bransten Rothmann, *The Haas Sisters of Franklin Street: A Look Back with Love* (Berkeley, CA: Judah Magnes Museum, 1979), 70.

46. Ibid., 11.

47. Courtesy of Donald Auslen's private collection.

48. Lori Harrison-Kahan, "Ghetto Realism—and Beyond," in *The Oxford Handbook to American Literary Realism*, ed. Keith Newlin (Oxford: Oxford University Press, 2019), 201–18.

49. Kahn, *Jewish Voices*, 36.

50. On the history of the Concordia Club, see *House of Harmony: Concordia-Argonaut's First 130 Years* (Berkeley, CA: Judah L. Magnes, 1983).

51. All citations from *Heirs of Yesterday* refer to the page numbers in this edition and will be indicated parenthetically.

52. "Philomath Club," in *Who's Who Among the Women of California: An Annual Devoted to the Representative Women of California, with an Authoritative Review of Their Activities in Civic, Social, Athletic, Philanthropic, Art and Music, Literary and Dramatic Circles*, ed. Louis S. Lyons and Josephine Wilson (San Francisco: Security Publishing Company, 1922), 199.

53. Anne Ruggles Gere, *Intimate Practices: Literacy and Cultural Work in U.S. Women's Clubs, 1880–1920* (Champaign: University of Illinois Press, 1997), 80.

54. "Affairs in Society. Preparing for the Murphy Ball. Several Recent Engagements and Weddings—Interesting Notes," *San Francisco Chronicle*, January 21, 1895, 5. See also "The

Philomath Club: Its First Open Meeting at the Palace Yesterday," *San Francisco Call*, January 15, 1895, 12.

55. See "An Anti-Suffrage Club," *San Francisco Call*, November 25, 1895, 16.

56. See Karen Blair, *The Clubwoman as Feminist: True Womanhood Redefined, 1868–1914* (London: Holmes and Meier, 1980).

57. Although Levy was well known in San Francisco in the 1890s as a contributor to *The Wave*, the journal that also gave Frank Norris his start, her most significant role in literary history occurred in the early twentieth century when she and Alice B. Toklas, her O'Farrell Street neighbor, traveled together to Paris following the 1906 earthquake and became part of the Stein circle. When Levy returned to San Francisco, Toklas stayed on to make a life with Stein.

58. "Emma Wolf," *American Jewess* 1, no. 6 (1895): 295.

59. Helen Piper, "Interview with Emma Wolf," *San Francisco News*, December 2, 1930, 5. In previous publications on Wolf, when this article was quoted, it was inaccurately cited as from the *San Francisco Examiner* on December 3, 1930.

60. Emma Wolf, "Brissac's Little Debt," *The Wave: A Journal of Nineteenth-Century San Francisco*, February 27, 1892, 13.

61. Naomi Seidman's *The Marriage Plot: Or, How Jews Fell in Love with Love, and with Literature* (Stanford, CA: Stanford University Press, 2016) demonstrates that nineteenth- and twentieth-century Jewish literary works that took up questions of erotic love, courtship, and marriage played an important role in "constitut[ing] the cultural character of Jewish modernity" (82). Seidman's argument that Jewish "literature . . . created new social practices" (4) might be fruitfully extended to Wolf's work, with its depictions of couples negotiating secularization and modern marriage. As Seidman suggests, readers received a "sentimental education" through literary representations of marriage, learning new rituals for love and courtship while also maintaining aspects of Jewish tradition.

62. For more on the reviews of *Other Things Being Equal* and its positive reception in the American press, see Cantalupo's introduction to *Other Things Being Equal*, 33–34.

63. "Spoke on 'Apostasy': Rabbi Hecht Discusses Intermarriage of Jews and Christians," *Los Angeles Herald*, March 6, 1904, 6.

64. Emma Wolf, foreword to *Other Things Being Equal*, 61.

65. Emma Wolf, "The Author's Purpose by the Author," *Book News* 15, no. 175 (March 1897): 342.

66. It is possible that Wolf did not completely abandon *Dreamer of Dreams* and that *The Joy of Life* was a revision that stripped the text of Jewish content. We suggest this possibility based on the publication timeline and the fact that references to the biblical phrase "dreamer of dreams" appear throughout the novel. The JPS publication committee rejected *Dreamer of Dreams* in November 1894, and *The Joy of Life* was published in 1896. In the published edition of *The Joy of Life*, the third-person narrator notes that "the dreamer was left to his dreams" (250) when one of the brothers, Cyril, dies. Furthermore, the novel concludes with these lines: "Thus Antony Trent emerged from his short excursion into the Gardens of Paradise, where after all only they who 'know' not—Youth and dreamers of dreams—may tarry; and the man, touched with knowledge and sorrow, came again into the tangible world of Fact, and bowed once more before its ancient sovereign, Mammon, called The Great. The gods, in their love for him, had flung him the Philosopher's Stone,—a hope" (253). A review of the novel in the *San Francisco Call* on October 25, 1896, titled "New Novel Full of Human Interest by a Clever Young San Francisco Girl," describes the two main characters as follows: "Antony possesses, in addition to his money-getting ideas, something of a soul. His brother, Cyril, must be assisted through the world, and here is the difficulty. In sharp contrast to his brother, Cyril is a philosopher, a thinker, a 'dreamer of dreams'" (21).

67. In Jonathan Sarna's *JPS: The Americanization of Jewish Culture, 1888-1988* (Philadelphia, PA: Jewish Publication

Society, 1989), the author reveals that the JPS was first
instituted in Philadelphia in 1845 with the following aims:
"self-defense against Christian proselytization and the
furtherance of Jewish literature" (2). For many reasons, by
1851, the society was dismantled. It was reconstituted in
1871, although the members of its board were mostly New
Yorkers with the exception of a couple of Philadelphians
and Simon Wolf of Washington, DC. In the late 1870s, the
organization dissolved again. According to Jonathan Sarna,
the third iteration of the JPS, founded in 1888, survived and
experienced its "golden years" between 1888 and 1893: "For
most publishers, the first five years are critical ones—the
years in which they set forth their aims, find their niche,
establish their reputation, and seek to become financially
secure. For the Jewish Publication Society these turned
out to be golden years, filled with excitement and success.
The books it published achieved widespread notice, won
considerable critical acclaim, and secured for the Society a
respected position in the field of Jewish publishing" (Sarna,
JPS, 29).

68. Deuteronomy 13:1.

69. Letter from Emma Wolf dated May 8, 1893, written from
1711 Geary Street, San Francisco, to Mayer Sulzberger,
chairman of the publication committee of the Jewish Publication Society of Philadelphia. Held by the National Library
of Israel's Schwadron Autograph Collection.

70. Martin Meyer, *Western Jewry: An Account of the Achievements of the Jews and Judaism in California, Including Eulogies
and Biographies* (San Francisco: Emanu-El Press, 1916), 14.

71. Letter from Emma Wolf dated November 14, 1893, written
from 1711 Geary Street, San Francisco, to Mayer Sulzberger,
chairman of the publication committee of the Jewish Publication Society of Philadelphia. Held by the National Library
of Israel's Schwadron Autograph Collection. Wolf ends her
letter with the following: "Awaiting an acknowledgement
of receipt, in which I wish you would kindly inform about
when I may expect your decision."

72.   Henrietta Szold, *Manuscript Book, Jewish Publication Society of America, November 20, 1890—July 24, 1911,* Jewish Publication Society Archives, Temple University Libraries Special Collections Research Center, 21. Since it appears that most JPS manuscripts were reviewed by three readers, it is unclear why Wolf's manuscript was sent to five different people. Perhaps the JPS enlisted extra readers to ensure that Wolf's novel would be given serious consideration.

73.   Henrietta Szold, *Minutes of the Publication Committee of the Jewish Publication Society of America, 1888–1905,* Jewish Publication Society Archives, Temple University Libraries Special Collections Research Center, 37.

74.   Alan Silverstein, *Alternatives to Assimilation: The Response of Reform Judaism to American Culture* (Hanover, NH: Brandeis University Press, 1994).

75.   Sarna, *JPS,* 20.

76.   See Ibid., 53.

77.   Szold, *Minutes,* 39.

78.   Quoted in Ferguson, "Leading Epigrammist," 25.

79.   The minutes read,

> A regular meeting of the Publication Committee of the Jewish Publication Society of America was held Sunday, October 24, 1897, at 8 P.M., in the office of the Society, 1015 Arch Street, Philadelphia, Pa., the Hon Mayer Sulzberger in the chair, and Messrs. Adler, Amram, Cohen, Jastrow, and Stern of the Committee present.
>
> . . . .
>
> The written reports of Messrs. Adler, Krauskopf, Landsberg, Philipson, Stern, and Straus, and the verbal report of Mr. Amram recommended the awarding of the $1000 Prize, if awarded at all, to Miss Emma Wolf for "Little Jaffa." The written reports of Messrs. Cohen, Eisenthal, Gross, and Liepziger, and the verbal reports of Messrs. Jastrow and Sulzberger recommended the awarding of same, if awarded at all, to Mr. Louis H. Pendleton, for "Little Prince Almon."

> By the vote of the members present, it was decided not to
> award the prize. (Szold, *Minutes*, 100)

80. Sarna, *JPS*, 86.
81. Szold, *Minutes*, 100.
82. See Cantalupo, "Letters," 121–38.
83. Lori Harrison-Kahan, "'A Grave Experiment': Emma Wolf's Marriage Plots and the Deghettoization of American Jewish Fiction," *American Jewish History* 101, no. 1 (January 2017): 21.
84. Israel Zangwill, "A New Jewish Novelist," *Jewish Chronicle* 1.453 (February 5, 1897): 19.
85. Zangwill to Wolf in Cantalupo, "Letters," 128–29. Letter dated December 2, 1896, from 24 Oxford Road, Kilburn, N.W.
86. Zangwill to Wolf in Cantalupo, "Letters," 129, 130. Letter dated February 5, 1897, from 24 Oxford Road, N.W., and letter dated July 2, 1897, from 24 Oxford Road, Kilburn, N.W.
87. Edna Nahshon, *From the Ghetto to the Melting Pot: Israel Zangwill's Jewish Plays* (Detroit, MI: Wayne State University Press, 2006), 20.
88. Zangwill to Wolf in Cantalupo, "Letters," 129. Letter dated February 5, 1897, from 24 Oxford Road, Kilburn, N.W.
89. Szold, *Minutes*, 136.
90. Sarna, *JPS*, 79.
91. Nancy Huston Banks, "New York Ghetto," *Bookman*, October 1896, 157–58. For a fuller discussion of this debate, see Harrison-Kahan, "Ghetto Realism—and Beyond."
92. Cited in Sarna, *JPS*, 80.
93. Sarna, *JPS*, 235, 81.
94. Ibid., 82.
95. Emma Wolf, Review *of Idyls of the Gass* by Martha Wolfenstein, *Jewish Comment*, December 6, 1901, 2–3.
96. Ibid.
97. Sarna, *JPS*, 207.

98. Allen Lesser, "Life with Mother Too: Review of Harriet Levy's *920 O'Farrell Street*," *Menorah Journal* 35 (1947): 322. On Levy's submission for the JPS award, see Sarna, *JPS*, 207–8 and 337n72.

99. Gere, *Intimate Practices*, 220-221.

100. Sarna, *JPS*, 53.

101. Lucas Dietrich, "'At the Dawning of the Twentieth Century': W E. B. Du Bois, A. C. McClurg & Co., and the Early Circulation of *The Souls of Black Folk*," *Book History* 20 (2017): 315.

102. Israel Zangwill, *Dreamers of the Ghetto* (Philadelphia, PA: Jewish Publication Society, 1898), 20.

103. Dietrich, "'At the Dawning of the Twentieth Century,'" 310.

104. Review of *Heirs of Yesterday*, *Current Literature: A Magazine of Record and Review* 30 (January–June 1901): 122.

105. Ibid.

106. "Books and Authors," Review of *Heirs of Yesterday*, *The Living Age*, December 22, 1900, 792.

107. "Miss Emma Wolf," *Mechanics' Institute Library Bulletin*, September–October 1901, 1, 5.

108. "Miss Wolf's New Story," 1.

109. "The Library Table," *The Menorah Journal*, Vol. xxxiii, no. 5 (1902), 350.

110. Joseph Lebowich, "Contemporary American Jewish Writers," *American Hebrew and Jewish Messenger*, December 2, 1904, 15.

111. Zangwill to Wolf in Cantalupo, "Letters," 134. Letter dated December 12, 1900, from 5 Elm Tree Road, St. John's Wood, N.W.

112. See Harrison-Kahan, "'A Grave Experiment.'"

113. Wolf's relationship with the monthly New York magazine the *Smart Set* began in 1902 when they published two of her stories: "A Study in Suggestion" in March and "A Still Small Voice" in October. Her stories and novellas appeared in the magazine under four different editors. The other stories in the *Smart Set* include "The Courting of Drusilla

West" (February 1903), "The End of the Story" (December 1904), "Tryst" (July 1905), "Farquhar's Masterpiece" (March 1906), "The Conflict" (November 1906), "Louis d'Or" (August 1907), and "Father of Her Children" (June 1911). Throughout the seven years that Wolf published in the *Smart Set*, she addressed the intimate struggles of upper-class life and supplied the "cleverness" the magazine promised its readers while maintaining the integrity of her beliefs about the power of love and the importance of family life. In February 1909, the *Century Magazine* published Wolf's short story "The Critical Miss Devine" in its memorial issue honoring Richard Watson Gilder, poet and long-time editor of that magazine.

114. Barbara Cantalupo, introduction to *Emma Wolf's Short Stories in "The Smart Set"* (New York: AMS, 2010), xiv.

115. Harry Levi, *Jewish Characters in Fiction: English Literature* (Philadelphia, PA: Jewish Chautauqua Society, 1911), 142.

116. Ferguson, "Leading Epigrammist," 25. In a review of *The Joy of Life* (1896), a *New York Times* reviewer echoes Ferguson's praise, noting Wolf's "want of pretentiousness" and describing her method as "singularly unassuming" and "highly philosophical." See Review of *The Joy of Life*, *New York Times*, June 5, 1897, 18.

117. *American Hebrew*, July 30, 1920, 275.

118. The *American Jewess*, the journal founded and edited by Rosa Sonneschein and published from April 1895 to August 1899, did attempt to fill this gap by appealing to an audience of middle-class Jewish American women. Unsurprisingly, then, the journal not only published some of Wolf's writing but also profiled her in its September 1895 issue and featured her on the cover of the March 1896 issue. For more on the *American Jewess*, see Jack Porter, "Rosa Sonnenshein [*sic*] and the *American Jewess*, the First Independent English Language Jewish Women's Journal in the United States," *American Jewish History* 68, no. 1 (September 1978): 57–63.

119. Decker, *Fortunes and Failures*, 117–18. For further discussion of anti-Semitism in the United States and particularly

in San Francisco, see Tony Fels, "Religious Assimilation in a Fraternal Organization: Jews and Freemasonry in Gilded-Age San Francisco," *American Jewish History* 74, no. 4 (1985): 369–403; Naomi Cohen, *Encounter with Emancipation: The German Jews in the United States, 1830–1914* (Philadelphia: JPS, 1984), 224–31; Naomi Cohen, "Anti-Semitism in the Gilded Age: The Jewish View," in *Essential Papers on Jewish-Christian Relations in the United States*, ed. Naomi Cohen (New York: New York University Press, 1990); Leonard Dinnerstein, *Anti-Semitism in America* (New York: Oxford University Press, 1994); Ralph Mann, "Frontier Opportunity and the New Social History," *Pacific Historical Review* 53, no. 4 (1984): 463–91; and Michael Dobkowski, *The Tarnished Dream: The Basis of American Anti-Semitism* (Westport, CT: Greenwood Press, 1979).

120.   Decker, *Fortunes and Failures*, 100. For further discussion of such prejudice, see Peter Decker, "Jewish Merchants in San Francisco: Social Mobility on the Urban Frontier," *American Jewish History* 68, no. 4 (1979): 396–407.

121.   See Harley Erdman, *Staging the Jew: The Performance of an American Ethnicity, 1860–1920* (New Brunswick, NJ: Rutgers University Press, 1997). In a pivotal scene in Wolf's first novel, *Other Things Being Equal*, the characters attend a performance of *The Merchant of Venice*, starring Edwin Booth as Shylock. This episode in the novel was based on Booth's famous 1889 performance as Shylock at the California Theater, which Wolf attended.

122.   See Donald Pizer, *American Naturalism and the Jews: Garland, Norris, Dreiser, Wharton, and Cather* (Urbana: University of Illinois Press, 2008).

123.   Frank Norris, *McTeague: A Story of San Francisco* (New York: Signet, 1981), 37–38.

124.   Elisa New, "My Favorite Anti-Semite: Frank Norris and the Most Horrifying Jew in American Literature," *Tablet*, October 24, 2013, https://www.tabletmag.com/sections/arts-letters/articles/mcteague-frank-norris.

125. Matthew Baigell, *The Implacable Urge to Defame: Cartoon Jews in the American Press, 1877–1935* (Syracuse, NY: Syracuse University Press, 2017), 3.

126. "No Means of Support," *Puck*, January 17, 1894, 379.

127. "Unprejudiced," *Puck*, May 2, 1894, 166.

128. "Strictly Orthodox," *Puck*, October 17, 1894, 131. For more on *Puck*, including on the magazine's treatment of race and religion, see Michael Alexander Kahn and Richard Samuel West, *What Fools These Mortals Be! The Story of Puck: America's First and Most Influential Magazine of Color Political Cartoons* (San Diego, CA: IDW, 2014).

129. Kahn and West, *What Fools These Mortals Be!*, 207.

130. Quoted in Ferguson, "Leading Epigrammist," 25.

131. It is worth noting that other early Jewish American novels depicting genteel, acculturated Jews are similarly understudied. Wolf's work makes for a compelling comparison, for example, with Nathan Mayer's novel *Differences* (1867), which is set during the Civil War and features a prosperous Jewish family who lives on a Southern plantation and owns slaves. Mayer's plot, too, depends upon courtship and marriage, including Jewish-Christian intermarriage.

132. Lori Harrison-Kahan and Josh Lambert, "Finding Home: The Future of Jewish American Literary Studies," *MELUS: Multi-Ethnic Literature of the U.S.* 37, no. 2 (2012): 13.

133. "Library Table," 350.

134. Emma Wolf, "One-Eye, Two-Eye, Three-Eye," *American Jewess* 2, no. 6 (1896): 279–90.

135. Wolf's short story "The Courting of Drusilla West," published in the February 1903 issue of the *Smart Set*, is another strong example of this tendency. As Cantalupo discusses in the introduction to *Emma Wolf's Short Stories in "The Smart Set,"* "The main character is a determined, single, professional woman who rejects all social expectations placed on her, especially marriage. . . . The story confronts the feminist call to the 'New Woman' to free herself from the bonds of marriage yet provides an alternative, if not altogether conventional, conclusion" (xi).

136. See Clare Virginia Eby, *Until Choice Do Us Part: Marriage Reform in the Progressive Era* (Chicago: University of Chicago Press, 2014).

137. See Harrison-Kahan, "'A Grave Experiment.'"

138. Elizabeth Ammons, "Edith Wharton and Race," in *The Cambridge Companion to Edith Wharton*, ed. Millicent Bell (Cambridge: Cambridge University Press, 1995), 80.

139. Levy's *Reuben Sachs* also puts an interesting twist on the intermarriage plot. When the novel forecloses marriage between the Jewish couple Reuben Sachs and Judith Quixano due to differences of class, Judith ends up married to Bertie Lee-Harrison, a convert to Judaism.

140. Ann duCille, *The Coupling Convention: Sex, Text, and Tradition in Black Women's Fiction* (Oxford: Oxford University Press, 1993), 33, 31.

141. On the politics of respectability, see, for example, Evelyn Brooks Higginbotham, *Righteous Discontent: The Women's Movement in the Black Baptist Church, 1880–1920* (Cambridge, MA: Harvard University Press, 1994).

142. The depiction of Forrest, who is lame in one foot, is one of several, often subtle representations of physical disability in Wolf's oeuvre. Given the ways that her own physical disability contributed to her career as a writer, Wolf's work offers intriguing source material for scholarship in disability studies.

143. See Harrison-Kahan, "'A Grave Experiment.'"

144. See Amy Kaplan, *The Anarchy of Empire in the Making of U.S. Culture* (Cambridge, MA: Harvard University Press, 2002), especially chapter 1.

145. Joseph M. Heller, "Forty Years Ago," *Jewish Veteran*, June 1939, 15. On Heller as a source of pride in the Jewish community, see Seymour Brody, *Jewish Heroes and Heroines of America* (Hollywood, FL: Frederick Fell, 2004), 104; and "Col. Joseph M. Heller Dies," *Washington Post*, October 12, 1943, 8.

146. "Israel's Tithe to America," *San Francisco Call*, July 24, 1898, 19.

147. Jeanne Abrams, "Remembering the Maine: The Jewish Attitude toward the Spanish-American War as Reflected in *The American Israelite*," *American Jewish History* 76, no. 4 (June 1987), 440, 444. In *Jews on the Frontier*, Shari Rabin notes a similar impulse among nineteenth-century Jews, especially in the West, who "benefited from Manifest Destiny and . . . applied its language and concepts towards their own religious ends, mixing and matching it with Jewish diasporic and messianic traditions" (124).

148. Kaplan, *Anarchy of Empire*, 18–19.

149. Zangwill to Wolf in Cantalupo, "Letters," 133. Letter dated May 14, 1898, from 24 Oxford Road, Kilburn, N.W.

150. Zangwill to Wolf in Cantalupo, "Letters," 134.

151. It is worth noting that when Wolf published the revised edition of *Other Things Being Equal* in 1916, she added a final line: "And so the future took them." This change from the first edition leaves readers with an even greater sense of uncertainty about the couple's future.

152. For more on the ending of *Heirs of Yesterday* in relation to realism, see Harrison-Kahan, "Ghetto Realism—and Beyond."

A NOTE ON THE TEXT

The novel was transcribed from the first edition of *Heirs of Yesterday*, which was copyrighted in 1900 by A. C. McClurg & Co. of Chicago. In making editing decisions, we have prioritized readability and fidelity to the original text. We silently corrected obvious typographical errors. Otherwise, spelling, punctuation, and capitalization are as they appear in the original text. All notes are by the editors.

Heirs of Yesterday

by Emma Wolf

CHICAGO

A. C. McCLURG & CO.

1900

For something larger had come into his life, a sense of a vaster universe without, and its spaciousness and strangeness filled his soul with a nameless trouble and a vague unrest. He was no longer a child of the Ghetto.—ZANGWILL.

FOREWORD

The tide of social culture sweeps literally upward with the grade in San Francisco, dropping inadequacies on the way. The tide of Jewish social culture runs its mimic parallel alongside of it, mounting hill for hill, matching inadequacy with inadequacy. Yet science proves that, this side infinity, parallels never meet.

And thereby hangs the comedy.

"If it takes six generations from the hod, or pick and shovel, to make a gentleman of an ordinary American," asked the wag, "how many generations from the Ghetto does it take to make a gentleman of a Jew?"[1]

"Bah!" said Philip May, contemptuously, "what have I to do with Ghettoes!"

And thereby also hangs the comedy, or—what you will—according to your light.

CHAPTER I

At sunset of a certain exquisite day toward the close of February, a young girl might have been seen making her way westward along Pacific avenue. She walked swiftly, lightly, the joyous wind of motion in her going. The waning afternoon was warm, and she had slipped off her jacket, carrying it under her arm, her slender shirt-waisted figure seeming to enjoy the freedom. The breath of violets was in the air, a marvelous sky of tender rose-shot gold before her—the spirit of the beauty of the hour had passed into her face.

In the serene light the houses rose, now stately, now picturesque, among velvety lawns and palms and rose-trees, here and there a red-stone mansion showing vivid and princely among the general scheme of perishable wooden architecture. Glimpses of the lovely island-dotted, hill-encircled bay smiled up to her as she passed the corners along the heights. She was in the midst of the fairest residence environs of the town.

Turning southward, she came abruptly upon two unpretentious little houses standing snugly together near the corner.

She ran up the steps of the nearer and rang the bell, scarcely conscious that she was happily humming a song while she waited.

The door was opened by a buxom, clean-aproned Irishwoman.

"Well, Katie," asked the girl, entering quickly, "how is everything getting along? Has any one been near the table since I left?" She did not pause; she moved as she spoke toward the dining-room.

"There it is, Miss Jean, beautiful as a picter, same as you left it. What would the likes of my clumsy hands have to do wid anything you touches? And there's nobody else."

"And the kitchen, Katie?"

"Come and take a smell."

She tripped after her into the shining room steaming with importance and good savors.

"It smells like—like your kitchen, and that means it makes me
hungry," the girl assured her, critically approving.

"Ah, go long wid the blarney eyes and tongue of you," laughed the
privileged old cook and house-keeper, in pleased excitement. "Who
wouldn't have the best dinner in the land when her boy as was her
baby is coming home to-night after ten long, lonesome years widout
a sight of him. Laws, Miss Jean! when Mr. Mays stood and looked at
that table two hours ago, his hands just trembled wid joy, even if his
face did look like it did the day poor young Madame Mays died, and
he sat and shivered for her."[2]

"Sat and *what*, Katie?"

"Shivered. That's what all them old Jews does when some one
dies as is dear to 'em. Leastways that's what your own poor mother
says to me when I see him sitting on a footstool and wanted to give
the poor dear man a comfortable chair wid a back. 'Let him alone,
Katie,' says she. 'He has to sit low and shiver,' says she. 'It's the Jewish custom.'"

The girl's laugh rang out unrestrainedly.

"For shame, Miss Jean, to laugh over a poor young thing's death;
and she just a mother," reproved the old woman, in shocked
solemnity.

The laugh died lingeringly on Jean's lips. "I was not laughing
at what you said, Katie," she explained, with a vanishing ripple of
mirth; "it was the way you said it. Probably my mother said he was
sitting *Shivah* for her, which is—"[3]

"It's haythen English, then. Well, Miss Jean, all I hope is that
Phily'll like his dinner."

"Dr. May now, Katie. Remember he's a grown man past thirty, and
a physician besides. Of course he'll like his old Katie's dinner. Did
you say Mr. May is at home?"

"Home and dressed these two hours. He's in the sitting-room
waiting."

The girl slipped out, tiptoed softly through the hall, knocked gently, and then immediately opened the door in furtive, mischievous
noiselessness.

Joseph May stood before the glass, absorbed in his own reflection. His deep-set eyes looked out from the brown, furrowed face set in its framework of grizzled hair and beard, taking stock of the over-hanging brow, the long, thick nose, the straight, close-set lips—the upper one shaven; his eyes measured the thick-set, stooping figure, slightly below medium height. An eager anxiety dominated the whole attitude and aspect of the man.

"Oh, vanity of vanities," murmured the girl, her hand still upon the door-knob. "Vanity of vanities, Uncle Joseph!" She shook her head in tender mockery at him as he veered around.

He laughed sheepishly up into the dancing light of her dark gray eyes. "Well, Jean," he returned, with a helpless shrug, his palms turned upward and outward, "what can a man do when he is such a dood like me?"

"Dude! I should think you are a dude. Come here and turn around, sir, and let me admire you."[4]

He revolved in slow, solemn delight under her hand placed lightly upon his shoulder.

"Who ever heard of a man's making such a beauty of himself just for another man," she observed, severely. "And a man of your years, too!"

"Then you think I will do, Jean?" he asked, in serious anxiety. "You think he won't be ashamed from his old father?" The man, although an American citizen of more than forty years standing, spoke with a marked foreign accent, composite of Jewish and German.[5]

"I wouldn't give a penny for his taste if he were," she returned, with a loyal uplift of her head, "even if you do think he's the Grand Mogul in person."

"*Chutspah ponim!*"[6] murmured Joseph, lovingly. "*Chutspah ponim*—as if you don't know he is yourself!"

The girl's alert senses—more alert than usual this evening—winced secretly under the familiar jargon.[7]

"Old man," she said, gently, argumentatively, "do you happen to have a picture of a certain illustrious young surgeon about you? If you do, we might settle that point at once and for always."

He clapped his hand to his breast-pocket, a look of comical surprise crossing his face as he felt its emptiness.

"So you've forgotten it at last," she laughed. "How your friends will miss it! There, don't mind my teasing, Uncle Joseph—you will have the original with you in just about an hour or two, and can pilot the man himself around to your old cronies. Now sit down in that easy-chair so as not to disarrange your beauteous attire before the grand moment arrives. And remember, dear, you are not to get excited. You know Dr. Thallman—"

"Yes, yes, I know, Jean—I got my son to live for now. See how quiet I am." He held up a trembling hand.

She stooped impulsively, pressing her lips to his bald forehead.

"I'm going home now," she said, moving toward the door. "Greet the prodigal for me—without words."

"To-morrow night you and Daniel," he called huskily after her.

"Uncle Daniel, surely," she replied, turning back. "And, Uncle Joseph!"

"Yes, dear child?"

"Please don't take two plates of soup!"

He chuckled softly after her entreating voice and retreating figure.

Shadows gathered in the quiet room. The old man sat motionless in his great chair. . . . .

"I tell you, boys, she's a bonanza for one of you. A little princess, *junge,*[8] mit hair what comes most to the floor down!"

Out of what dim corner of his brain had the words sprung?—words scarcely noticed when spoken almost forty years before. Was it the suggestion of Jean Willard's creamy girl-face with its shadowy eyes and her mass of shadowy dark hair? Was it the spirit-presence of one whose memory never left him in such silent moments as this? Was it the strange joy of calling her son—scarce known, grown to a man—*his* son? Was it—. He lost the links of thought.

He was back again in the office behind Simon Alexander's store, one of "the boys" crowded round the glowing stove, and Simon Alexander himself was making the announcement which caused them all to start with openly expressed interest over the pleasing thought that another fair young girl was coming into their rough lives.

That was the night young Goldschmitt, without an English word in his vocabulary or a cent in his pocket, had come staggering in, his pack on his back, and demanded explanation of the cruel treatment he had received from the women he had approached with his wares. Whereupon they discovered that a certain wit, one Samuel Weiss by name, had written for the ignorant immigrant a list of questions to be asked, each one prefaced with a dainty oath, such as, "Dam you, lady, here's a dimity that will make your eyes water!"

Young Goldschmitt wept tears of boyish grief over the unfolding, the others swore mysterious vengeance on the witless wit, and while Daniel Willard, the scribe, sat quietly down and wrote up an elegant text for the sale of his textures—"just like a book—just like a book," they all agreed—Charlie Stein trolled out:

> "With a stone for a pillow and a sky for a sheet,
> Oh, a peddler's life, my dear ones, is a hard one to beat."

To the truth of which sentiment several of those present could offer personal testimony.

But they were all chafing to get up and away to the home old Arnheim had prepared for his wife and daughter just arrived on the steamer from New Orleans, and when Simon, who gave all "the boys" wide credit—which bore wider interest—had made a bed for poor Goldschmitt on the counter—for they were no sybarites in those days—they started in a body out into the raw night air.

He remembered their passing the historic gambling palace at the corner of Washington and Kearney streets, ablaze with lights, radiant with luxury and vice, glorious, sensuous music floating out above the noise of jingling gold, above the tragic shot of a pistol, above the monotonous cry of the croupier—a Frenchwoman this night—chanting persuasively, "Make-a your bets, gentlemans—gentlemans, make-a your bets." Some one was for stopping, but Daniel said, sternly, "Boys, that is hell." Yet a moment later, when they reached Arnheim's house, the young Frenchman lifted his hat, and said, half quizzically, half reverentially, "But now, boys, we go to heaven."

So they went to heaven through a pair of brown eyes, and many there were who gazed through thereat. And the way was long and sweet to Joseph May.

He remembered the night before the Eureka ball, when, after a long, silent walk under the stars with Daniel, his beloved friend, he had said, suddenly, "Daniel, when you have no objection, to-morrow night at the ball, I will ask Jeannette Arnheim to marry me." Such was Joseph's way, short and direct. And Daniel, after a moment, had said, tenderly, "if it is for your happiness, Joseph, and for hers, what objections can I, a poor occasional journalist, have to offer?"

And the next night—at that ball, whither she had gone with him in her simple, unadorned white silk gown cut low in the neck, a string of pearl beads around her lovely throat, her hands in small white silk gloves drawn tight with a dangling tassel—at that memorable Eureka ball, with all the boys fighting for a dance with her, he, Joseph May, the quietest of them all, had asked her for her hand—and won it.

And behold there was light divine for the quiet man on that long-ago wedding day, when all the boys had kissed the bride—except Daniel Willard, who had only kissed her hand—and they had gone away to live happily together forever after. Forever after—

She brought success with her—everything he touched prospered. But five years passed before the promise of the long-awaited little one came to them, bringing with his glory—

Nay, why this mist of tears? Their plans? Had he not executed them—without her? Had not the long empty years—

"My dear father," broke in Philip May's virile voice, "I am glad to be with you again."

The next minute the room was flooded with light, while, through mist-blinded eyes, the little old Jew felt his hand caught in a powerful grip, and looked up at his son's broad-shouldered manhood.

CHAPTER II

As he followed his father into the dining-room, the wheel of time seemed to Philip May to leap back to the starting-point of memory. The past fifteen years, which had plunged him far beyond on the sea of life and thought, slipped from him and left him stranded on a shore which alone, in all the moving flux of things, seemed to have stood still. How much of this sensation was due to outward fact—the old-fashioned familiar furniture, the ancient Sabbath lamp[9]—an heirloom—burning this Friday night with accustomed holy brilliancy, the square-set old man himself, whose hoar-touched hair and beard but faintly suggested the silent passage of the years—he did not consider. He felt a sudden mental stooping, a bending to the cavern of a childhood which had been covered over, almost forgotten in the background of his experience.

From the farther doorway, Katie, the faithful housemaid, his quondam nurse, radiant, rosy, and rejoicing, courtesied to them as they entered.

His scrutinizing eyes fell instantly upon her, and with a flash of recognition of a different nature, he went toward her with hands outstretched.

"Well, Katie," he said, "do you recognize the old plague of your life?"

Covered with confusion over the mastery of his voice and personality, she laid a rough, trembling hand in his, all the contemplated welcome of ecstatic words and embracing arms shrinking shame-facedly out of the back-door.

"Thankee, Mr. Philip," she stammered. "I'm very well, thankee. You've growed some, sir, but I'd 'a' knowed you was Phily anywhere."

His laugh rang out heartily as he pressed her hand between both his. The lingering laugh startled the old woman—it was as an echo of something loved and lost. When she returned to her kitchen two unaccountable tears rolled down her cheeks.

"Shall I take my old place?" he asked, standing at the foot of the table.

"For sure, Philip, for sure," said Joseph, vainly endeavoring to keep the army of overpowering emotions from his voice and limbs. In the church of the old man's soul there was an intoning of prayer and thanksgiving, the while he ladled soup—the while the dominant face opposite was engraving itself upon his intoxicated senses. It was a strong, intent face rather than a handsome one—a face with little room in it for frivolity, its very reticence proclaiming that strength, or narrowness, of purpose which bespeaks "business ahead." True, the brow, broad and thoughtful, beneath the wave of thick dark hair, might have belonged to an artist, a dreamer, but whatever the temperament of heredity it bespoke, the suggestion was overpowered by the doggedness of will of the individual as evidenced in the cool, discriminating hazel eyes and assertive mouth and jaw.

"It's hard to realize that so many years have passed since we dined together," the younger man observed, picking up his napkin, grimly amused over a mellowing representation of Moses with the Decalogue benignly regarding him from the opposite wall.[10] "I don't know whether it is a trick of the gods," he continued, lightly, "or of Katie's unrivaled soup, but I'm inclined to think I have never been away."

"I can tell you how long. You were away—leaving out vacations—just fifteen years, three months, twenty-three days and one-half."

The ghost of a frown gathered into the doctor's quiet regard. "Perhaps," he began, in the tranquil, sonorous voice which most of all seemed to measure an insurmountable distance between them, "perhaps I staid too long. My duty, I know—"

"No, no," interrupted the father, eagerly, apologetically. "It was just like it should be. When you asked, didn't I say yes? Didn't I tell you I want you shall know everything money can buy when it will make you a better doctor—and a more happier? And besides, there was your friend—your poor sick friend."

"Yes."

"And you could not leave him. So I told to all who said, 'But why he don't come home to his father—maybe he, too, needs him.'

Didn't I always say to Daniel and Jean, 'Is it not fine a man shall stay by his friend so long he wants him?'"

Philip protested swiftly with his hand. "Who is Jean?" he asked, abruptly.

"Jean? Oh, you don't know who is Jean," laughed the old man, delightedly, as though upon familiar ground. "Well, you will know her soon—to-morrow night. You see, I said to Daniel, 'You and Jean and Philip and me will have a nice little dinner together, and while we have a little game, the children can make a little music and get acquainted.' And Jean says, 'But, Uncle Joseph'—she calls me Uncle Joseph for short, because I too am short—'who do you think this Dr. Philip May is that Jean Willard should come to call on him?' And then she goes on, 'Now don't tell me he is a prince—all the young Jews are princes to the old ones—tell me *what* he is, if you can.' But she don't mean one word—she's just a little *lachachlis ponim*—you know what that means?[11] No? It means mischief-faced one—one who says things just out of spite. Oh, by'm-bye you'll learn Yiddish all over again when you stay long with me. But you don't know who is Jean—. Wait. Will you take some more of Katie's good soup?"

"It *is* good," Philip acquiesced, cordially. "But I always limit myself to one plate."

"Just like Jean. She always makes fun of me. Why? Is it more healthy? But when I learn you to speak Yiddish you will learn me what I must not eat. Of course Dr. Thallman is a fine doctor, but now when I have a doctor in the family, he don't expect I will stay by him, I guess. Well, I will ring so Katie takes the plates out. You must not laugh when I make mistakes—I have seldom company for dinner—only Daniel and Jean sometimes, and then Jean does it all, and all me and Daniel has to do is to eat. But Jean knows better how it shall be done. To-night she wanted to order oysters and frogs and—*ich weiss viel*;[12] but I said to her, 'No, Jean, better we have a good old-time dinner so Philip feels more to home: a good noodle soup—'" here he began to intone like a cantor—"fish *à la Yitt*,[13] like Daniel calls it, some nice green peas and fried potatoes, a fine young roast duck, and salad—and for dessert, well, I compromised with her on a frozen something—but with coffee and cigars, I guess you'll pull through, hey, Philip?"

It was a long speech for Joseph May to make, but the excitement and happiness of this long-anticipated, intimate moment had loosened the reserve of half a lifetime.

"It could not suit me better," returned Philip, the edge of his fine teeth showing in a suspicion of a smile, as he gave his attention to the fish. "But who is this oracle of your manners and menus? Who is Jean?"

"I will tell you," said Joseph seriously, holding up his fork in one hand and a bit of bread in the other. "Help yourself to wine, Philip—Thallman says I mustn't—I can guarantee you can get no better Sauterne nowhere—I paid a big price the case for it, years ago. Good? I knew you would like it. Well, what I was telling you? Oh, yes, about Jean. Jean is the chile of Daniel's brother David, who lived in Los Angeles. Well, his wife died long before him, and when David died—now about ten years ago—there was no one to look after the little girl, who was about fourteen years, except an old aunt in New York. So Daniel comes to me—he always asks me what he shall do when it is business, just like I always ask him when it ain't business—and he says, 'Joseph, you think I am good enough to take care of that young girl?' And I said, 'And when she was a young angel, and when she was a young devil, there is no one who can better take care of her as you.' So Daniel went down and brought her up, and when once you see her, Philip—. Well, I won't say no more about it now. You know I bought these two houses for an investment, account the view and location, but when Daniel brought the chile to the city he wanted to keep house, so I thought why not rent one to Daniel and keep one for myself, for when Philip comes home? And so you have it. And about Jean, there is not much to say. Only she looks after her two old men—like she calls us—and she says she has her hands full. All I know is she leads Daniel and me round by the nose and, *schtiegen!*[14] I'll tell you something—we make believe we don't know it—because we like it!"

As he glowed and expanded, enumerating all his homely loves under the pleasantly interested gaze of his son, it seemed to Joseph May—to his own surprise—that, despite the strong grief of his youth, life still held in reserve for him a bright spot into which he was now entering. And so, while they ate the savory dishes and drank the golden wine, he drew nearer the knowledge of his son, telling, with his unconquerable Jewish rhythm and accent, in quaint choice of English, now quite correct, now ridiculously faulty, occasionally mixed with the Yiddish jargon—the story of his simple life: the few hours passed in the downtown office, his fingers ever on the realty and stock market, with Daniel for his amanuensis; the sunny afternoons when he and Daniel would take the car and ride to the Park, where, sitting among the trees and flowers, they reviewed past and present through the medium of a good cigar; of the rainy or foggy evenings when Daniel or he would step across the connecting porch at the back and pass an hour or two together over a little game of picquet.[15]

"And sometimes we go to the the-ay-ter," he concluded, with an air of reminiscent joy. "Generally Jean gets the tickets for us, because she knows the good places and what Daniel and me will like. Daniel, he likes somethings sometimes what I wouldn't like, so he and Jean goes alone. Say, Philip, you know about the time Daniel bought the tickets?" He bent a laughing face upon him, his very nose seeming to scent the memory of the joke.

"No; what was that?" questioned Philip, the feeling that he was at some variety performance growing with the speeding minutes.

With a wave of the hand Joseph swept plate and glasses out of his way, and leaned his arms upon the table in an abandonment of enjoyment, his bushy eyebrows appearing to wink at Philip as he bent forward in confidential confab.

"You know," he said, speaking in a somewhat lower voice, as though fearful of being overhead, "Daniel isn't the man who gets the best of a bargain. He's a little too good, you know. Where he has to do with business he is like a little chile. You know what the young people call him?—the Chevalier.[16] Because, Jean explained to me, he is like some man who once lived who was 'without reproach.' Well, he goes to the telephone, and takes off his hat, because he thought at first a lady's voice answered him, and he asks for two good seats; 'the first seats, please,' he says—I give you my word—I heard him. And what do you think? When we come to our seats, sure enough we have the first seats—the first seats from the door! Daniel gets red

in the face like fire, but he only lifts up his head and says, 'There was
some misunderstanding'—and could I tell him it was a joke? But
that ain't all. Now comes the joke on me. You know it's a piece about
a man what escapes from prison, and when they go running after
him, somehow, in the excitement, they catch the wrong man, and
I too got so excited I jump up and holler out, 'You've got the wrong
man! You've got the wrong man!' And Daniel pulls me by the coat
and says, 'Sit down, Joseph, sit down; they've got the right man—it's
that way in the play'—and he drags me into my seat. Gott! I thought
I should die a-laughing."

He wiped his eyes now, and as the appreciative response died from
Philip May's lips, the distance between them had widened as star
from star.

"I am not of this world," thought the scion of cultured modernity,
even as, centuries before, another young Jew said of another world
and found—Golgotha.[17] But he continued to smile pleasantly upon
his father.

"Oh, we can tell you lots of little stories like that," Joseph promised, tilting back his chair in order to reach the box of cigars on the
side-table. "But—I guess you won't want to be sitting nights with an
old stick-in-the-mud like me. Lots of young men they like to come
and sit or talk with Daniel, but me, I guess I ain't much company. Of
course when you begin to practice you won't have much time"—he
leaned across to light his cigar at Philip's—"but—"

He noticed that his companion's attention had wandered, and
presently realized that the room was filled with distant music.

"Who is that?" demanded Philip, briefly.

"That is Jean. You can always hear it like it was in the next room.
What you think of that?" He looked at him in placid triumph.

The music thrilled gloriously through the dividing-walls. Philip
listened in artistic wonderment and enjoyment.

"She knows how to play," he returned, with the last note.

"Yah. So every one says. There she goes again."

But in the midst of the mounting Schubert ecstasy there was a
sudden crash of chords—and silence.

"She often does like that," said Joseph, as though relieved. "But
I was saying about the way you will pass your time. Of course you

will join a club; I was thinking I will have your name put up at the Concordia, and Louis Waterman says he wants you in the Verein."[18]

Dr. May meditatively flicked the ash from his cigar. He had a singularly well-formed hand, and Joseph was attracted by its perfect control. Suddenly the cool hazel eyes looked up and met his father's.

"I may as well tell you at once," he said, in pleasant brevity, with a gentle intonation, as he might have used in addressing a woman or a patient, "that I shall not join any Jewish club."

The blood surged darkly over Joseph's face as if in response to a blow. "Why not?" he managed to ask.

"Frankly," explained Philip, lightly, "beyond the blood I was born with, pretty nearly all the Jew has been knocked out of me."

"So," said Joseph May.

"I rather think it got its first blow the day when, a little shaver, I ran howling to Katie demanding to know what the fellows in the street meant by calling me a 'Christ-killer'—they did such things here in the early seventies, you know. 'Sure,' said Katie—I remember her word for word—'that's what you be, I guess, my lamb.' 'And who was Christ?' I asked. You remember the name was taboo on Jewish lips in those same broad-minded days. 'Bless the little haythen,' said Katie, 'don't he know that Christ was the Lord?' 'And when did I kill him?' I asked, deeply interested in my forgotten crime. 'Oh, centuries ago,' replied the girl, 'hundreds of centuries ago.' 'Before I was born?' I asked, in astonishment. And, pityingly, she answered, yes. It was a curious conundrum to start a child with on the road of investigation. I unraveled it as I went—knocked the meaning out of it against the bars, vague, yet ever discernible to a sensitive nature, which ever and again rose between my playmates, my schoolmates, my teachers, and myself, and huddled me into my inherited confines. It was not a pretty inheritance. It proscribed me here even in my boyhood. I was an American—with a difference. I hated the difference. I wanted to be successful—successful socially as well as professionally. I resolved to override every obstacle to obtain that perfect success.

"The opening came at Harvard. Thanks to you I have been endowed with a name which tells no tales, thanks to my mother my features are equally silent. I was thrown in with a crowd of young

Bostonians—Harleigh was one of them—who, through the fact that I had been seen in the Unitarian church, took me for one of their own persuasion. It was a suggested evasion of an unfit shackle. There was no preconceived deception. I simply filled the bill. No doubt was ever evinced and no chance of an explanation ever offered itself. There was no need to drag in an uncongenial fact when the nature of our intimacy never called for one."

"No," said Joseph May.

"After that came Leipsic, and still I was bound by the closest ties of friendship to Harleigh, who was just then beginning to show symptoms of the disease which eventually—. But about my backsliding from Judaism. You know Germany is scarcely the soil one would select for fostering the ancient seed, the body Judaic being held there, for the most part, in manifest social disfavor. I once saw a curious exhibition of conflicting forces in a beer-hall in Berlin. A party of students, musicians, were seated at a table near me, drinking, making merry, and talking freely, when one of them ventured the sentiment that what the Jewish composers couldn't borrow they stole, in conformity to Jacobian precept and tradition.[19] Thereupon, a young fellow, with Hebrew characters written all over his face, struggled to his feet, was about to vent his indignation, but, upon second thought, laughed confusedly, and sat down again. Discretion had conquered valor. It was an interesting psychic display. Here's another incident in point which may amuse you. I was seated one night in Paris at a fashionable table d'hôte,[20] when there entered a number of English parvenu Jews, glaringly and aggressively attired, and evidently dazzled by the unaccustomed importance and luster of their own jewels and satins. I had just become disinterestedly conscious of their entrance, when a *grande dame*[21] seated near me leaned quickly forward and said, 'Pardon, monsieur, but would you mind taking the seat next to me? I shudder to think of one of those Jews being placed beside me.' It was highly diverting, but I moved up, and trust she was more comfortable. But so the fashion goes the world over. The question—if it is a question—is no better in England, where a noted English litterateur, himself a Jew, has summed up the situation by saying that the great middle class, at least, hung between the Ghetto it has outlived and the Christian society it can neither live with nor without, presents the miserable picture of a people astray. And judging by my incognito visits behind the scenes, in intercourse with my own countrymen, I should say that the Jew, *per se*, has never been given the latch-key to the American Christian heart. At best he is received with a mental reservation. Apparently, practically, we present the magnificent spectacle of a country without racial prejudices. Individually, morally, as the French say, we are very wide of the mark. Why, the mere fact of the restrictions against them at many of the summer resorts throughout the country openly bears me out.[22] In short, I have discovered that to be a Jew, turn wheresoever you will, is to be socially handicapped for life."

He paused to relight his cigar. His father sat with his elbows on the table, his hand partly shading his face. He had laid down his half-smoked cigar. The doctor, after a few thoughtful puffs toward the ceiling, resumed his quietly serious monologue.

"I don't know whether I wrote you, but among my personal treasures I value nothing more highly than the friendship formed while abroad with the family of Dr. Otis of this city, an uncle of Harleigh, who, in anticipation of my coming, has named me for the lately vacated chair of clinical surgery at C— College.

"I am not at all anxious to disclose to him, just at present at least, that I am not what I have appeared to him to be—a Christian born. You see I should be making a move in the wrong direction were I to identify myself unnecessarily with any Jewish club, Jewish anything, or Jewish anybody. Dr. Otis's son wrote me some weeks before I left Edinburgh that, with my consent, he would be glad to put my name up at his club. I accepted, not that I am particularly anxious to get into this or any Christian club, but feel quite sure that is all that I shall have time or inclination for. And from the nature of the life I have led, I am certain that Otis's club will prove more congenial than would a club composed entirely of Jews, from whom I have become estranged both socially and sympathetically."

He threw down his cigar, having fully analyzed his position. "Religiously," he concluded, with a smile of indifference, "from the meager memory I have of it, I consider Judaism a dead letter, a monument to the past. If it advances, it does so crab-like—as its followers read their prayer-books—backward. Only professionally have I any use for graveyards, and for ceremonies—the meaningless yearly shams and shows and protestations—not that!" He snapped his fingers in the air. "Well, father," he asked, with a pleasant laugh, bringing his hand down upon the table in mark of finality, "do you understand my stand? Are you wid me or agin me?"

He glanced toward the silent figure opposite, sitting with hand on brow. The hand was slowly lowered and the old man turned his face upon his son. His mouth was curiously twisted, as though a smile had been contorted into a sneer. He leaned across the table, vainly endeavoring to speak, the dark blood rushing thickly over his neck and face.

The doctor was beside him on the instant. "Lean back," he commanded, his arm about his shoulders, his hand at his cravat.

The old man hurled him off with intolerant violence. "Let go," he articulated, in an unrecognizable voice, "let go—you—you—*meshumad!*"[23]

The barbarous-sounding word held no meaning for Philip May. Scarcely understanding the cataclysmal effect of his words, conscious only of the urgent need of help, he summoned the housekeeper on the instant.

"My father needs assistance," he said, briefly; "see what you can do for him—and quickly, please."

The bewildered woman came forward wringing her hands. "The drops, sir," she said, "the drops; Miss Jean said they was—Lord o' mercy, Mr. May, where did she say they was?"

"Run—ask," gasped the old man, struggling with pain, his eyes turned completely from the pale, frowning man standing frustrate beside him. "Ask—but say—she shall not come—nor Mr. Willard. Say I am—very happy—only this—"

"Go, Katie," commanded Dr. May, sharply.

The woman opened the door and fled across the back porch. Her wild ringing was immediately answered, Daniel Willard's tall figure appearing holding wide the door.

"Where's Miss Jean?" she implored, half sobbingly; and as at that moment the girl herself approached, she stepped over the threshold.

"Oh, Miss Jean," she cried, distractedly, "where did you say you left the drops the doctor—"

"In the upper drawer of the sideboard. Run back at once, Katie, if Mr. May is ill."

"Yes, yes, Miss Jean—the top drawer. Oh, no, he's not sick. Him sick! Nary a bit—he's just billin' and cooin' wid Mr. Philip same's a pair of turtle-doves." Her voice was lost in the distance.

Daniel Willard turned a pair of startled eyes upon his niece.

CHAPTER III

The words came in a cry of bitter agony.

"I am so ashamed, Daniel—I am so ashamed."

The two old men sat in the Park on a bench facing the Scott Key monument.[24] It was an ideal end-of-February day; grass and flowers were deluged with spring sunshine; from the distance came the clamor of happy birds; children ran by, the springtime spell in their cheeks, their eyes, their joyous limbs. A serene, cloudless sky, transparent as a jewel, overtopped it all.

They had wandered up to and through the aviary to the grand court of the Midwinter Fair grounds, past the reminiscent Museum and Japanese village, and now, after a detour through shaded and unshaded walks, had been sitting here for almost an hour, Joseph gazing dumbly before him, only relaxing when a perfunctory "yah" or "no" was dragged from him by Daniel's tender garrulity.[25] The Frenchman himself had been silent for several seconds when the irresistible cry came.

He turned his gently strong face toward his friend. "Don't speak about it—if it hurts, Joseph," he said, in loving solicitude, yet with controlled curiosity.

"Hurts! I wish I could close my eyes forever." The straight lips shut against each other as if for mutual support.

"No, no. It is not so bad. It cannot be. We must not judge so quickly."

"My son is a *meshumad*."

"Ah, he is no criminal. He is only in style."

"Tell me, is it too the style that a man shall be ashamed from his father?"

"Bah! You speak banalities, Joseph."

"I know from what I speak. I can read under his fine English of it. I wish I had no more to speak."

"Will you break my heart, Joseph?"

"What is that—when a heart breaks?"

"Come, come. Are you a man?"

"No. I am a dog—a Jew—an ignorant, uneducated Jew. The son is ashamed from his father."

"Joseph, if you talk any more such nonsense, I will go home. I give you my word I cannot bear it. Come—what was it all about? Tell me—if you care to."

The heavy, darkened eyes looked straight ahead. He began to speak in slow, biting sarcasm, turning the knife in his own heart. "My son is so educated. You don't know how fine he is. We—me—not you—yes, you too, perhaps—you are a Jew, I think? Well, we will go some day and ask him if we can black his boots. You never knowed how mean and low and stupid you and me always was, Daniel. Well, I know—my son told me last night. Jews is what the niggers down South used to call po' white trash. My son told me so last night. It ain't good to be a Jew because then the Christians don't like you. It ain't good to be a Jew, because when the Christians don't like you, you can't get along in this world. So it is better you turn round and be something else. My son told me so last night. And if you have a Jew for a father, you must not say he is your father, because then you will be found out, and then how all would laugh! And for a religion—that is the funniest thing of all—the Jews have for a religion a dead body, but they make believe it is alive! Yes, it is true. Didn't my son told me so last night?" The sneering voice ended in a miserable groan.

Daniel laid his gloved hand heavily upon Joseph's, but Joseph threw it off fiercely.

"Don't," he said, roughly. "What do I care what he thinks about any religion. When he can live better without it—let him. But you—you cannot know what a father knows when his chile is ashamed to look him in the face. I tell you I *know*, Daniel." He turned his eyes passionately upon the protest of the other, his mouth setting bull-doggedly. "And I'll tell you how I answered him." His tone changed suddenly to heart-bursting suavity. "I made out a new will this morning, according. I sent for Paul Stein. A fine will, like you talk so much about—with University Scholarships and Hospitals in, and *ich weiss viel!* So well he can go alone and has no more use for his father, so well he has no use for his father's money. I put it all in the will, and it sounds kind and grand the way Stein wrote it—and nobody will understand—because I fooled even Stein. But whenever it is read, you'll know—and he'll know, just what it means. I left him a dollar—that's the law, Stein says—and he can make *Shabos* with it, or put it in a crepe band on his hat when it is still the style to make believe you care.[26] But it won't make me nothing out. For me—I will be silent in my grave."

Daniel could not speak for grief. His own face was eloquent with repression. But, "I will speak to him," he said, finally.

"Speak to him! Speak to that stone." He pointed his cane toward the glistening marble of the monument. "Will you tell him—nicely—because you always speak nicely—will you tell him, 'Philip, you must love your father'? And will he come and give me his arm? Ach, Daniel, *lass mich gehen.*"[27]

"You go too quickly, Joseph. Me, I do not jump like you. No; I will go to him and tell him *why* he should love his father and—his religion."

Joseph's laugh rang out jeeringly. "You always did tell yourself pretty *moshelich*," he said, gruffly. "Did they never end bad—your pretty *moshelich?*"[28]

"Once. But that was a foolish one."

"And you think you can move a rock?"

"I know from where the rock springs. You, too, are a rock, Joseph—but you are only his father."

"Be still," commanded Joseph, flashing a pair of resentful eyes upon him. Then he continued more calmly. "You remember how he used to plant his little legs and say, 'I won't!'—and nobody could whip him? You remember? Well, he has only grown up."

"What a fine little fellow he was," mused Daniel. "You remember, Joseph?"

Perhaps in all the vocabulary there is nothing wider in its yearning tenderness, sooner calculated to find the rift in the rough wall of sorrow, than the word spoken as Daniel spoke it.

"*Ach Gott!*"[29] said Joseph, brokenly.

"Listen. I think I know your boy. The more you oppose him or combat him, the more he will set his face against you. I know the type. But seem to give in to him, while, without his knowing, you gently lead him around your way, and, sooner or later, he will give in."

"I am not smart enough."

"It is not smart you must be—it requires only a little tact." He raised a suggestive, deeply experienced eyebrow.

"That is the same thing," said Joseph, bluntly. "Do you expect I will take my hat under my arm and make him a deep bow, and say, 'Good son, kind son, I am sorry that my father was not rich like yours—because if he was you would not be ashamed of me—but I made a fool of myself last night. Forgive me—I will not do it again.'"

Daniel turned from him in pain.

"Well, what do you want I shall do?" demanded the other, savagely.

"Me? What do I know?"

"You know you know better than me. Why are you so stubborn, Daniel?"

Daniel flashed a radiant face upon him. "When he comes home to-night—" he began.

"He will not come home to-night," said Joseph.

"You mean—"

"He did not stay last night; I did not ask him."

"Then you have not seen him since?"

"He came this morning. I would not see him."

"Ah."

"He left a card."

"Where is it?"

"I threw it away."

"Then you do not know where he is stopping?"

"I looked before I threw it away."

"Do you remember his address?"

"I think it was the Palace Hotel."[30]

"You are not sure?"

"Yes; I am quite sure."

"Joseph, do you want me to go for you?"

"You think it will pay, Daniel?"

"We can risk a little visit. It will not cost much. Is it not proper that I should welcome my young friend home?"

"What will you say?"

"Will you leave it to me?"

"And, Daniel?"

"Yes."

"No one will know about it? Not Jean?"

"Not from me, Joseph."

"Daniel?"

"Joseph?"

"*Nix.*[31] Shall we smoke a little before we go home, Daniel?"

CHAPTER IV

Toward the eighth hour of the evening of the same day, Daniel and Jean Willard were seated together, as they generally sat directly after dining, when socially disengaged. The girl was at the piano, flooding the room with music. The man sat in a glow of lamplight, having drawn his chair close to the table, and his fine leonine head was thrown into strong relief; his eyes were on his book. It was a pleasant room at any time, expressive of its inmates, cozy with love of physical comfort, unpretentiously interesting in artistic and intellectual enthusiasms happily confessed.

They had been sitting thus for nearly an hour, each lost in his and her own occupation, each only sub-consciously awake to the other's presence, when Daniel Willard looked at his watch, laid his pencil within his book, and rising, softly left the room. The girl played on until the quietude of the background stealing to her senses, she turned her head and found herself alone. She lingered a moment, then strayed over to the table.

An interested, puzzled light passed into her eyes as they fell upon the open book, attracted there by the penciled annotations. She was smiling perplexedly over them when her uncle reappeared in the doorway. He wore a handsome dark overcoat; his top-hat was in his gloved hand.

"Going out, uncle?" she asked, absently, scarcely glancing up. "Well, before you go—tell me what m-e-s-h-u-m-a-d means." She spelled it carefully, looking up at him as she finished.

He started perceptibly, coming farther into the room. "Are you studying Hebrew, dear child?" he asked, with smiling restraint.

"Not I," laughed the girl. "There are so many more useful and ornamental things to learn. But you have written the word here all over the margins of these two pages and—"

"I!" His startled exclamation was accompanied by his swift approach. "Let me see," he said, laying down his hat and taking the book from her. As he adjusted his eyeglass he colored deeply.

"It is strange," he observed, finally, "how unconsciously one's thought will pass into one's pencil and father the word. It is very strange." He laid down the book and picked up his hat.

"But what does the word mean, uncle?" the girl insisted.

"Oh, yes, yes. Let me see—" reflected the scholar. "The root is *shomad* or *shamad*, which means to destroy—hence, *meshumad*, as ordinarily pronounced, means one who is destroyed; but as generally accepted, it means the destroying spirit, or one who is destructive or inimical to his religion. Hence, an apostate."

Her gray eyes opened wide, a dull, intuitive flush creeping to her cheek. "And what has Philip May to do with apostates?" she asked.

"Philip May? Why do you speak of him?"

"Why, dear, your page is as black with his name as with the other word."

He gave an ejaculation of annoyance, but immediately recovered his naive equanimity. "Ah," he smiled, placing his hand under her uplifted chin, and kissing her good night, "did I not tell you that the conscious thought is father to the written act?—I am going to call upon Philip May at his hotel to-night."

"At his hotel? Uncle, you are keeping something from me." Her lifted face was stern and pleading.

A sudden fear shook Daniel Willard's conscience. "Why, it is nothing, *chérie*," he said, gently.[32] "But—you must know that Joseph and his son are—what shall I call it?—at the two Jewish social extremes—esthetically speaking."

"Oh, vile!" breathed the girl on impulse, understanding instinctively.

"No, only products of different ages. And this, of which Philip May is a product, is a very artificial age, my dear—one in which even ideals have become artificial. Society is a matter of tastes, not of opinions. Appearances are the only arguments for or against a man—all the heaven in the human soul becoming pulled down, hedged round, slaved in by the tyrant Good Form—the shibboleth of modern social pharisaism. But, being of this age," he smiled, "one must subscribe to the age's requirements, or fall out of line, *n'est-ce pas?*[33]—The right coat—the right manner—when the Jew will have regained these—especially the latter—he will have arrived at his renaissance. I speak in all simplicity and without bitterness," said Daniel Willard, moving into the hall.

She followed him silently to the door. "I saw him this morning," she said, with apparent irrelevance.

"And?"

"He was going up his father's steps when I came out here. And he saw me."

"That was pleasant for him."

She laughed angrily, and again a sense of fear, not unmixed with guilt, assailed Daniel's conscience as he went down the steps.

Jean returned to the sitting-room. She picked up a magazine and threw herself into her uncle's great chair. She made no pretense at reading. A vague sense of exclusion, of being out in the cold, was upon her, and she shivered as though an open door whither she had been approaching unawares had been suddenly slammed in her face. She stood still, in quivering, girlish shame and confusion.

If Jean Willard had a fad, it was for things of the mind; if she had a passion it was for people with minds. She had, theoretically, an enthusiastic sympathy with the Hegelian concept of Beauty's being Spirit shining through matter—though you might easily have doubted this, judging from her outspoken worship of all beauties seen of the eye. Yet it was on the former basis that she had made her own atmosphere and chosen or discarded her associates. She therefore belonged to none and to all of the finely demarcated circles which go to make Jewish society. Morally free and independent, never rich, but always provided with the necessities and a few of the comparative luxuries of life, sought after for her talent and seeking others for theirs, frankly amused or disgusted over the strenuous climbing up the social ladder of those who had not yet arrived, or of those little Alexanders, who, having conquered their own, look around for more worlds to conquer—she held an individual position.

Society, so called, had a bowing, not an intimate, acquaintance with her. Among those she loved she was a magnetic, an imperious power. To most people she was a sealed book, but once known she was known by heart. Of high enthusiasms, bravely loyal and optimistic, hating narrow-minded hypocrisy as she loved broad-shouldered dauntlessness, she had reached her twenty-fifth year, one of those modern anachronisms, a woman with ideals. Had she ever expressed herself to the rank and file upon certain subjects, she would have been as one speaking a dead, hence ridiculed, language. But she never expressed herself—fully—upon certain subjects—to any one.

Nevertheless, a delicate sympathy had always existed between herself and her uncle—they understood each other as most high-minded people, dwelling together, must understand one another. In all probability she could have been no more confidential to a mother or a sister, had she had either, than she was to him. He, imagining her, loved her,—chivalrously; she, knowing him, loved him reverentially. They were the best of good comrades.

And thus it was that, from the beginning, Daniel Willard had discoursed to her upon what, to him, was the wonder, past and to be, of Philip May. Thus she, with her passion for perfection, began to burn her candles. Thus, as his coming drew near, and the two old men, nourishing a tender hope, waxed warm and eloquent over his loyalty to his friend, his professional success, his goodly appearance as evidenced in his portraits, his love of music and of all things artistic, the girl's imagination was loosed. And thus we come to the anomaly of a woman's loving an idea, an unknown quantity.

In the reaction caused by her uncle's veiled explanation, her intuitive grasp caught at the unadorned facts of the situation: the coldly ambitious man whom culture had estranged from, made lost to sympathy with the illiterate old Jew, his father. She had the faculty of putting herself in his place, could understand the shock to his refined ear and tastes, could gauge the shudder of his *amour propre*[34] when confronted by his origin. Yet, knowing Joseph May's unworldly worth, his limitless generosity and good-nature, his yearning tenderness for this same gifted son upon whom he had showered all the advantages which had been denied him,—accepting unquestioningly and unconditionally the wisdom of the fifth commandment—for having known neither father nor mother since maturing, she had never been troubled by the cynicism of the "choice of parents"—her gentle womanhood set its face against her colder, keener estimate of the man.[35] Woman-like—she understood the ugly truth, but could not excuse.

As she sat there, her bitter knowledge of the snarl of things growing hopelessly wider and deeper, she heard the door-bell ring, and rose mechanically to the convention of the moment.

A slight young man with a sensitive, delicate face, limped into the room.

"Why, Mr. Forrest," exclaimed Jean, hastening forward, both hands outheld, "what a charming surprise!"

"Is it?" he asked eagerly, holding her hands close, and looking with almost brutal effrontery into her eyes. "I was not sure that you would not consider it an intrusion. You have never asked me to call upon you."

"No," she conceded, drawing her hands from his and pushing a chair forward. "But do sit down."

He frowned quickly in answer. "I am able to stand a minute," he said roughly. "Why not sit down yourself?" He turned the chair peremptorily toward her, and, with a laugh of assumed carelessness, she complied. She was diffident about combating Stephen Forrest's vagaries.

"I can only stay a second," he said, leaning against the table near her. "I dropped in to let you know that the workmen have left my studio, and it and I are in readiness for that sitting you promised me. When will you come?"

"Do you still cherish that fantastic Judith notion?[36] I assure you I am much too slight a creature."

"Not with your coloring—inner, I mean. Outwardly, I know, you're just a study in black and white. To-night, especially, your eyes—for whom are they in mourning?"

She craned her neck for a view of them in the glass. "For their sins, I suppose," she laughed.

"The desire of the eyes?"

"Ah, that's another story," she said lightly. "How is Kate?"

"She's all right. When will you come? Monday?"

"You seem in a dreadful hurry. Think it over again—about my fitness as a model, I mean. There are any number of girls in the city better suited to the rôle."

"Don't. Of course I know the streets are full of Jews of all descriptions—if that's what you mean—you knock against them at every corner, in every car. They're a bit of local coloring—a prominent feature—the nose, in short,"—he laughed genially—"on the landscape, which our artists have forgotten to work up. But, speaking of Jews, reminds me. Do you happen to know a fellow named May—Dr. Philip May who has just returned from Europe—fellow with thick black hair, cocksure eyes, and proud lift to his head?"

In an agony of self-consciousness, Jean felt the disgraceful, uncontrollable blood rush to her brow—felt herself a victim of the peculiar insight of Stephen Forrest's gaze. "Not personally," she answered quietly.

The artist turned inconsistently and seated himself upon the couch directly opposite her.

"He's a Jew, isn't he?" he demanded insolently, with a sudden ugly gleam in his eye.

"Yes—by birth."

"The birth-sentence is life-sentence—isn't it?" he laughed daringly. "Then I wonder why he is trying to sneak into our Club with that disbarment."

"What disbarment?"

"Why, being a Jew."

"Do you belong to such a Club? What narrow doors you build! And is being a Jew a fault or a crime?"

"It's a misfortune—it keeps the unfortunates out of our Club." He laughed airily, yet with deliberation.

"Why?"

"*Quién sabe?*[37] he shrugged. "The reason's beyond me. It's one of those inherited reasons passed down, like a title, from father to son. Oh, it's a very aristocratic prejudice, I assure you."

"You mean bigotry."

"Now don't be clannish—and pray don't grow argumentative."

"I suppose you know you are saying rather extraordinary things to me—or have you forgotten that I am a Jewess?"

"Oh, you," he said, his brilliant eyes recording his valuation of her—"you are a woman. Your sex unsects you."

She raised her head arrogantly. "One always allows you great latitude, Mr. Forrest," she vouchsafed icily. "I did not think you would make capital of my indulgence."

He leaned impulsively toward her. "Don't indulge me," he commanded angrily. "And don't pity me. Hate me, rather. That, at least, implies no weakness in the object thought of."

She was startled by the full display of feeling, although she had had, time and again, ample proof of his total lack of self-control. She had always pitied him as a potentially strong character warped, through affliction, into an ungovernable, selfish temperament. But his present insolence had aroused a sense stronger than any sentiment she could even bear for him—a defensive sense which only announced itself when assailed.

"You are not worth hating," she returned, slowly, distantly, her eyes traveling from his feet to his head and away.

He turned a dull, dark red. "Why, what is Philip May to you?" he asked, all regard for the sound of things swept out of him by a sudden unreasoning jealousy.

"What he is probably to you—a Jew," she returned calmly, her eyes down-glancing at him.

"Bah! Even half-closed, your eyes can't lie. And as for myself—he isn't worth the lying about—as I am not worth the hating. But I'll tell you what he is to me. I went to school with him. He started out to be clever, and when a Jew starts out to be clever there's no telling how far his cleverness will take him—which sentiment you may interpret according to your own lights and—prejudices. Well, I always hated him. I had that hate for him that the fellow who always comes in second has for him who always comes in first. Can you understand that kind of hate? Things came to him; I had to go to them. He strolled—I struggled; he came in victor, laughing—I came in beaten, panting. We both had brains—he just more than I; we both were artistic—I just more than he. But he had money and was launched—while I had none and was stranded—here." The girl trembled under the corroding envy which left him pallid.

"But what's that the poet says about the first being last, and all that rot?" he laughed sneeringly. "Well,"—he sprang up—"teach it to Philip May—candidate for membership in the Omar Club of San Francisco.[38] Oh, I've been making a display of myself again, I know," he added with studied carelessness, "but you have such 'divine tenderness,' as my sister Kate says in describing some of your playing, that I know you'll forgive—and shake hands?" He held his hand out with a feint at contrition.

"Oh, no," she returned playfully, holding her own hand behind her, "what are you thinking of, Mr. Forrest? Mine is a Jewish hand, you know. It wouldn't dream of putting itself where it would not be given the honor due its ancient lineage."

"Oh, come now," he pleaded, "let's not split straws. Whatever I have suggested or said with that confounded loose tongue of mine doesn't concern you. And—when are you coming to sit for me?"

"Why, never, Mr. Forrest."

"Good heavens, you would not be so childish—you would not destroy a conception that has taken fast possession of me ever since that twilight when I came upon you playing that Beethoven adagio. Oh, impossible, Miss Willard, impossible!" He spoke in imploring eagerness.

"You don't know my possibilities," she returned with iron gentleness. "I am a Jewess—Jew rather, when it comes to my people's being insulted by those who know nothing about them. Now, I'm going to give you a little gratuitous lesson: Every one of us carries the blood, the history of all of us in his veins, no matter how different we may appear, and when you sneer at one of us, you sneer, by implication, at all of us—a communal sentiment, not always comfortable, or commendable, or justifiable, I know. But there it is. So you see I could not cross your threshold without bringing all those shocking old Ghettites and their diversified grandchildren with me—and I could not allow them to be coldly treated."

"You have a very mixed identity," he admitted sarcastically.

"Yes. Droll, isn't it?" she returned as though suddenly struck by the thought.

"And you won't come?"

"No," she looked him straight between the eyes.

He set his teeth over his futile plea. "And all this wasted race-valor for a—Philip May," he said derisively with raised brows. "Well,

I never could compete with him on any proposition. I might as well say good-night." He bowed, waited a moment for her to give some response, but as she made no movement, he turned and limped from the room.

She did not follow him. She heard the front door close behind him with a sigh of mingled relief and pain. It seemed to her as though he had made his disagreeable visit in a flash of time.

Once before she had heard a rumor pointing to the fact that the Forrests were, had always been, Jew-haters, but she generally gave "they say"—gossip's Mrs. Harris—the benefit of the doubt, and when she met Kate Forrest for the first time in the studio of their mutual music-master, had met her gracefully half-way. The musical friendship, thus begun, had never been troubled by the rumored cloven-foot,[39] Kate Forrest keeping it well-hidden—if it existed—while she knelt in homage to her artist superior. And Stephen Forrest, the painter, lamed through an accident in childhood, hovering between his attic-studio and the family living-rooms, had, in his passionate love of beauty, drawn, like a moth to the flame, toward this music-souled Jewish girl with her lovely countenance.

As for Jean, to speak truly, her religion had always lain lightly upon her. It slept in the suburbs of her soul, out of the track and traffic of her life's uses. She could not have recited the Thirteen Articles of faith[40] at the point of a sword, but she might have said there was something in them about the glory of the Ineffable to which she unhesitatingly subscribed. She might even have stumbled over the Ten Commandments, having been told by her uncle when she was years younger that the First was as the whole of which the rest were but elucidation; and, being a lazy little thing, glad of any chance for concentration of energy, she had never troubled herself to review them. However, she could remember a few stories of the Talmud and a number of beautiful quotations from the same, through having lived so long with that same gentle scholar, her uncle. But she knew her Bible—that is, she knew it literarily—its music and imagery having found instinctive response in her being long before she had the power to discern the good within the song. She could not have defined her religion by a dogma, and that was because she also read the daily papers and other current literature,—and, from the life-point view, a dogma only proves how truth may be a lie. And, nevertheless, she was a Jewess—having been born one.[41]

But of late, as mentioned before, she had made for herself a secret breviary which ran somewhat in this wise: "In all Israel there was none to be so much praised as one Unnamed, for his beauty: from the sole of his foot even to the crown of his head there was no blemish in him."[42]

It seemed to her now, as the house-door closed after Stephen Forrest, that all the hitherto straight rays of her life were being deflected, focused toward one isolated figure—the challenging figure of Philip May.

CHAPTER V

D r. May hesitated on the curb before the Chronicle Building at the corner of Market and Kearney streets.[43] The hesitancy involved the trivial choice between paying a visit to the Otises, and receiving one from young Otis. Yet it was big with chance.

As he stood illumined in the white flicker of the electric light, a party of young men came down Kearney Street. Noticing the tall figure under the tall light, one of them gave an exclamation of surprise and murmured a word to his companions, who crossed, waiting for him on the farther side of Lotta's fountain.[44]

The other moved briskly toward the man hesitating on the edge of the sidewalk. "Well, Phil," he cried clapping him heartily upon the shoulder and holding out a hand, "shake, old fellow!"

Dr. May's courteously distant eyes looked through the keen, acquisitive face, as through a pane of glass. "Ah, Mr.—Mr.—Weiss, I believe?" he said politely, vaguely, as though asking a strange patient what might be the trouble to-day.

Weiss took his cue; his hand slid easily into his trouser pocket. "Well," he drawled, chuckling as with great amusement, "I'm glad to see my old schoolmate back. Town's grown a little, you'll find. Which reminds me of an incident which took place in the Sunday-school of the Temple Emanuel on Sutter Street when you and I were kids there.[45] Teacher asked class, 'What did Moses do before he wrote the Ten Commandments?' Class nonplused until an embryo wit raised his hand and said, 'Please, teacher, he kept a cloding-store!' Remember? Droll analogy, wasn't it? How's your father?"

Without waiting for a reply, he sauntered jauntily over to his companions, and passed on.

Philip crossed the street, his excluding eyes fixed upon the brilliantly lighted hotel. He walked through the gleaming marble corridor with a frowning gratitude over the fact that no one knew him there, the idlers about, the elevator boy who gave him a passing glance, taking him at his own apparent valuation and dubbing him some visiting aristocrat.

He entered his room and lit the gas. His deliberate movements as he drew off his overcoat and seated himself before the table strewn with writing paraphernalia, betokened a quiet, undisturbed mental state. He opened the evening paper. But the printed words did not seem to hold his attention. Instead, a musing smile of cold disgust lit his fine eyes. The vulgar familiarity of the contretemps might have filled him only with amusement if it had not carried with it a baffling sense of defeat.

He shook himself, as though to shake from his person and memory the tang—the Ghetto tang—which lay so unmistakably in the voice, the accent, the motions, the very cast of mind as of feature of these people who had stood still. It all spoke out so aggressively to his finely attuned senses, to his sensitive ear, to his inflexible social standards and requirements, to his nice discrimination between presumptuous intrusiveness and that self-respecting unobtrusiveness which respects the unseen individuality of every other. It was the old sad story over again of the disillusioning effect of light.

For of course it was ugly—as everything pointing to ignorance and oppression is ugly.

"We Jews!"

His jaw set hard as though some one had accosted him. What had he to do with Jewry? He stood off, examining himself, giving himself full value. He huddled the rest together in a heap. Yet even as he huddled them, the face and form of his father escaped, smiting him accusingly. Yet why? He had desired to live in amity with him—he had never gulled himself with the idea that they would be mentally companionable. But he was not an ingrate, and had never questioned the urgency of his duty toward him though he had returned to him only at this late day. True, he had developed contrary to his father's expectations and tastes and could never return to his limitations. He pictured himself introducing Joseph May as his father to certain high-bred friends—to the Otises—to Lilian Otis, for instance. His lips set in a grim smile over the imagined bewildering denouement. He laughed aloud, a stinging laugh, over her blue-book limitations frightened out of their sweet serenity by the alien touch upon her life.

He closed his eyes in sign of denial to the grotesque, obtruding contingency. But with the closing of his eyes, the clutch of the past, like a hand upon his shoulder, renewed its hold with impish malice. That there were Jews and Jews, Philip knew well—one sort mumbling and shaking out its prayers as at so many words a minute, keeping to the letter its minor fasts and great fasts, still happily believing themselves princes in Israel as soon as the praying-shawl went around their shoulders, the other erect, cool, skeptical to the top bent of the age, scanning the pages of prayer-book and life with the discriminating eye of intellect, but retaining, for all that, Ghetto ghosts and echoes in mien, or voice, or mentality. And he who had cultivated an unconquerable distaste for all these symptoms, knew that his greatest folly lay in his cheating himself with the philosophy of the ostrich. Fifteen years of absence were as a day to these Jews, with their ridiculous claim of kinship, their petty village curiosity in whoever or whatever bore the remotest identification with their race. Oh, the trail of the Ghetto was over them all.

He threw down his paper, passed his hand across his brow, and, with a sharp shrug of dismissal, turned to the writing-table, just as a knock sounded upon the door. A card was handed him.

A moment later, Daniel Willard, tall, elegant, dignified, a debonair carnation in his buttonhole, a charming light illumining his countenance, came toward him with outheld hand.

"Ah, Dr. May," said the old gentleman, pressing his hand warmly, "this is a great pleasure for me."

"As for me," returned Philip, the vivid color shooting up his clear, dark cheek. He wheeled a chair round toward him. "You are looking well, sir. One would not be extravagant in thinking you had found the secret of eternal youth."

"You think so?" said Daniel, wistfully, putting down his hat and seating himself. "But no. The truth came out in the car to-day when a young girl rose and offered me her seat. But of course I did not take it."

"Of course not," returned Philip, decidedly, conscious of keeping himself well in hand under the tender regard of the soft brown eyes opposite him which seemed to pass like a gentle hand over his soul, measuring its height. "No doubt she caught a glimpse of your mustache and let that signify the rest."

"Perhaps," he acquiesced, passing his hand over that silver military adjunct. "You see, I use no hair-dye, and so fill no one with illusion—except myself. I confess to that." His curly eyebrow went up, seeming to knock off his eyeglass, which he caught dangling. "So you see, after all, I stand admittedly a back number—a man with illusions."

"Yes? Then you're out of the procession. The trend of all modern aim is to be without illusions."

"But what shall one do when one is born with them?"

"Suit your appetite to your dinner—the cost of all idealism."

"Your advice comes just about six thousand years too late, I am afraid."

"You have heard of the Roentgen ray?"[46]

"Assuredly. It is the symbol of the age. It would seem as though a very stylish wit had discovered it. But me—I have another idea."

"Let's have it."

"Oh, it is nothing. But I have thought that to see more—will be, perhaps, to see more that is admirable—beautiful. It is a purely material device, your Roentgen ray, and can no more convert me than your Darwinian theory can alter my belief in the divine origin of man—though I will confess that sometimes the divinity seems as far distant as the monkey does always. But what has all this to do with your home-coming! Tell me, you must speak French like a native now. You remember those abominable verbs and what headaches they gave us? Come, show off a little for your old teacher."

Philip, laughing, drifted into gossip of the Parisian world of art, Daniel Willard's fine old face flushing slowly, as with wine, while the life with which he had always kept himself in touch was charmingly, graphically unfolded for him. His glasses came off enthusiastically, were pointed argumentatively, were closed excitedly, were adjusted decidedly, as he agreed or questioned his companion, lending him finally his old experience, his minute encyclopedic knowledge, his personal acquaintance with some of the great, delightful men of his day whom he had met when, for a brief space of years, he had returned to Paris.

"Ah," he exclaimed, with a sigh, "it is like living the old charm over again. I read my old Paris in your young one, as—as I read your mother's features in your face, my dear Philip. It is wonderful—the resemblance."

It came out naturally, uncontrollably, a trifle tremulously. He removed his glasses, polishing them solicitously.

The slow color rose to Philip May's brow. He bent a trifle forward. "You knew my mother, I believe," he said, swiftly. "Tell me about her."

And Daniel Willard, gentle-eyed dreamer that he seemed, understood the whole harsh tragedy of the demand. It was as though the son of Joseph May had said, "Account for me!"

And Daniel the diplomat, Daniel the lover, Daniel the friend, answered.

"Often I tried to account to myself for her perfect loveliness," he said, softly, reminiscently, "and the only answer I could find was that she was an inspiration of God. There are many such inspirations, I believe, but I doubt if he has been just so inspired since. I take off my hat to the thought of her." He flushed tenderly up to the roots of his silvery hair, with a wistful smile toward her son.

A silence followed his words. Philip recovered himself with a quick, indrawn breath. "Thank you," he said, laconically.

Daniel arose, picking up his hat. "I have enjoyed my little tête-à-tête with you very much," he said, holding out his hand. "I am glad I came—as some of my young friends express it—although your father has asked me to dine with you and him Monday night, and the pleasure will be so soon renewed."

"Monday night?" repeated Philip, questioningly.

"Certainly; so I understood him to say to-day in the Park." He said it lightly, as though deciding, perhaps, a point in rhetoric. "We spent a few sunny hours in the Park this afternoon. I have not seen him since, but I hope he is not lonesome. You see, nearly every night we have a little game of picquet—it is the only game I know—but one must have some plaything when one has a friend. But before I go, Jean—my niece who lives with me and who plays the piano a little—she plays like an angel, though I say it who should not—Jean will play perhaps for an hour for me, and during that time Joseph reads the evening paper. It is then he likes to have some one come in. A *lundi*, then!"[47] He held out his hand again.

"You are very intimate with my father," remarked Philip, constrainedly, as he took his hand.

"Oh, yes. It is a very old intimacy. But of course you have heard that story."

"I think not."

"No? Then I will tell it to you. I am as amusing as a lady's postscript, am I not? However—. Many years ago when I was a lad of twenty earning a precarious living in New Orleans and the neighboring villages by giving lessons in French and German, I was traveling one morning from the city to Biloxi, and was suddenly taken with the most excruciating cramps it has ever been my fortune to endure. I was in the depths of the woods, with no habitation in sight but a forsaken cabin. To this I crawled, thankful for the shelter from the blazing sun. There I lay in feverish agony the live-long day, begging for water from every passer-by, but at sight of me they all fled, crying, "The fever!" as they ran. And they were quite right to run— quite right, for the yellow fever was then raging. But just at nightfall I heard strong, heavy foot-steps, and a rough, kind voice exclaimed out of the darkness, '*Gott im himmel!*'[48] and there stood a little Jewish peddler. Well, he staid with me, and twenty-four hours after, I arose a well man. I have told you I take off my hat to do your mother's memory reverence, but I would take off my coat to fight for Joseph May. Good night." He held out his hand again.

Philip watched him walk down the gallery, lightly, joyously, as one having glad, free thoughts. Then he shut the door.

Was the man an emissary, a *poseur*,[49] or only a rare specimen of human simplicity? At any rate, he found the sands sliding perilously under his feet, found himself clutching at the vanishing land-marks of his journey hitherto, only to have them glide mockingly from his grasp. He flushed uncomfortably, as though some one had laughed at him. He frowned again upon his impotency, upon the intruding memory of the man with his manifest refinements of aspect and thought and manner; he wondered why he suddenly remembered the girl whose shadowy, glad gray eyes had startled his prejudices that morning.

But a second imperative knock again interrupted his thought. The lines fled from his brow at sight of the jovial-faced young fellow before him.

"Hello, Doctor," the latter cried, coming into the room and depositing a violin case upon the floor as he sank into a chair. "Thought I'd knock you up on my way to my apartments up above and see whether you'd settled upon an office yet. Didn't I see the Prince of Courtesy come out of here just now?"[50]

"I suppose you mean Mr. Willard."

"Yes. Old friend of yours? Great old gentleman, isn't he? One always looks for a decoration in his coat when speaking to him. He is quite out of the regulation run of people with his stately, exquisite manner,—and the surprising thing about him is that he's a Jew. You knew that, didn't you?"

"Perfectly."

"Exactly," laughed the other. "He has the habit of always reminding one of the fact by some manner of means, as though he were afraid one might forget it or think he was ashamed of it. Queer infatuation for the inevitable, eh? But to get back to Gentile-ity—what about the office?"

"I've about decided on the one on Sutter Street," he responded, bringing his galloping thought to rest upon his visitor. "But what do you mean by apartments up above? Don't you live at the family home?"

"Did, but the workmen are all over the place, and I never could stand a mess. So I've pitched my tent here meanwhile, although my mother has me tied to her by a string. By the way, she sends you her love, and Lil—her respects."

"Thanks," laughed Philip. "I shall call upon them as soon as I get in calling spirit."

"By Jove, I was almost forgetting! They want you to dine with them Monday night—without ceremony. They told me to secure you to-night, and they'll ring you up in the morning."

"Too bad," returned Philip, with polite regret. "I have an appointment for Monday night." He was surprised over his own decision, and stopped abruptly.

"Already! Our old sawbones said you had a neat little ovation at the college to-day. But I don't suppose your date is with the medical department of your life."

"No. With my father. These rooms were just a makeshift until now, when he finds himself ready to take me in."

"A stranger, eh? But I can't imagine any one's taking you in—there's something too cool and practical about you—businesslike, one might say. But about your father. Queer we don't know him. May—May? John May, the newspaper man?"

"No," said Philip, suppressing an internal grin. "Joseph May—a retired merchant—in fact, a retired man in every sense. He has cared little for the world since my mother's death."

"That accounts for our ignorance then of his personality. I should like to meet the father of Philip May."

"Some day," promised Philip, in careless dismissal.

"All right. And I want you to dine with me a month from to-day, April 1st, or 2d, will you?"

"What's the occasion so long anticipated?"

"Well, the Omars meet for re-election of officers—and new members—March 31st, and I want to have a jollification in my rooms the night following—to celebrate your becoming one of us. You still play?—the piano, I mean, not cards."

"I can take a hand at either on occasion," laughed Philip. "My accomplishments are promiscuous, if nothing else."

"It's all art—or science," returned Otis, rising. "And anything under those elastic heads goes with us. We're not specialists in the art of life—we're for the all together, as Stephen Forrest might put it."

"Stephen Forrest? Surely I know that name."

"Artist, lame. Devilish clever."

"I think I knew the man a little—we went to school together."

"I'm glad of that. It's better having Stephen Forrest with you than agin you. He has all the attraction of a danger signal."

Philip smiled. Being a San Franciscan born, and possessed of an excellent memory, the aristocratic prejudice of the Forrest family was not unknown to him. Besides which, he dimly remembered that between himself and this particular Forrest there had been, in the old days, little love lost or regretted.

Left to himself, he set his brow against the hostile thought, as he set the judgment of his senses against the obtruding argument of Daniel Willard's personality. Suddenly a light flared up about the memory of the fleeting glimpse of those wonderful, glad gray eyes of the morning—his father's insinuating words and tone, the diplomat's careless allusion.

"Faugh!" he thought, disgustedly, "they're all alike—shrewd, persuasive, crafty."

Which goes to prove how a name may carry its own judgment with it.

CHAPTER VI

"Jean, Jean! Hurry a little, my dear," called Daniel Willard from the foot of the stairs.

"But it's early yet, uncle. Why, I believe you've actually put on your overcoat, and I haven't even got into my gown and—"

"Sh—!" The tall figure below disappeared through the door of the living-room and the girl retreated in surprise from the balustrade.

But perhaps he was going farther after escorting her to Laura Brookman's, she thought, and she had better not detain him unnecessarily—she held his stately disapproval in much too wholesome respect. The preliminaries to her toilet being accomplished, it took her but a few minutes to complete it with the donning of the simple white gown which had seen much pleasant service, and presently she was running downstairs, carrying her gloves and wrap, and pinning on her hat in her descent.

"Here I am," she announced, coming into the flood of gaslight, still intent upon jabbing in a refractory hat-pin. "It's ridiculously early, but I don't mind with Lau—"

She stopped abruptly, her hands dropping from their task, at sight of the stranger standing tall and easy under the chandelier.

"Dr. May, Jean. My niece, Doctor."

The girl acknowledged the introduction as he received it, with calm grace, reflecting the reserve in the glance from his hazel eyes, the distant smile upon his reticent lips, unprepared though she was for the meeting.

"Shall we not sit down?" she asked undecidedly, noticing that both gentlemen held their hats in their hands.

Her uncle quickly undeceived her. "No; if you are ready, we will go. We are going to drop you on the way. Dr. May has an hour to spare and is coming with me to the French Hospital[51] to visit Bonnat,—you know poor old Bonnat, Jean?"

"Your dear, ladylike old man who wears his pride like a last year's bonnet? Well?"

"My dear, you know you like him," reproved Daniel. "But I have told the doctor he will find him a hard case."

"An interesting one, from all accounts," observed Philip, moving toward the door as if to hurry them. "Nothing arouses my egotism more than the hope of overcoming other people's failures—or Bonnats."

Daniel helped his niece with her wrap. "But," hesitated the girl, distantly, "I really don't care to inconvenience Dr. May. Mollie will walk to Laura's with me."

"It will be no inconvenience," he assured her, in surprise, holding the portière aside. "Although my hurrying you off in this fashion robs your uncle of his usual concert."

"Your father has been telling tales," she returned, pleasantly formal, walking with him to the door.

"No—the walls."

"I forgot I had a critic on the other side. Next time I shall play pianissimo."

"Wouldn't that be selfish?"

"But everybody is selfish."

"In degrees."

"And with exceptions. Witness somebody waiting out here on the steps for me. Ugh, how dark and cold it is!"

The bitter fog drove straight in their faces on the icy breath of the keen March wind as he closed the door behind them. They joined Daniel Willard waiting for them at the foot of the steps. Jean slipped her hand through her uncle's arm, and they turned southward, down the hill. They walked briskly, their steps ringing sharp on the asphalt. The gas in the street lamps flared wildly, making grotesque shadows of the tall, hurrying figures with the fluttering drapery of the girl between.

"I like it," she laughed, when Philip protested against the tug of war between hill and wind. "I've been raised on it. It's like getting on in spite of things—and I'd think it lots of fun if it didn't take uncle's breath away."

"Not at all," repudiated Daniel, drawing himself up to a straighter perpendicular. "I have not been speaking because it is foolish to fill one's lungs with the fog. Am I not right, Doctor?"

The latter met the girl's merry eye with a twinkle of his own before assuring the old gentleman of the wisdom of his caution. "Although," he added. "I've been told it is accountable for the famous complexions of the women of the city. So it compensates itself gallantly."

"Yes, we're all radiant," said Jean, turning up her own creamy colorlessness for his inspection, "and all wild and woolly. Please take notice that, despite her fearlessness, a girl with only two blocks to walk at night is punctiliously provided with an escort. But, with due exaggeration admitted for art's sake, surely only the blind would fail to remark our beautiful women."

"Everything is in the eye of the observer," laughed Philip, equivocally, glancing down at her. "Some people are beauty-blind, you know. And standards differ—and no one is the measure of all things. Remember the ass who preferred his thistle to gold."[52]

"Happy ass," murmured Jean.

"Most asses are happy," he vouchsafed.

"Being stupid?" she suggested.

"Being satisfied," he returned, shortly. Then suddenly remembering that he detested any display of self through word or tone, he drew rein, surprised at his slight lapse under the girl's lovely eyes.

They stopped presently before an imposing house.

"Good night," she said, putting up both hands to turn up her uncle's coat-collar. "Don't bother to come up the steps, dear." She held out a frank hand to Dr. May. "I'm glad Uncle Joseph has you back," she said, swiftly.

"Good night," he returned, courteously, taking her hand and raising his hat.

The next minute she had run up the steps and rung the bell. As they waited while she stood just beneath the flickering lantern, holding her long gray wrap about her, her face showing fitfully in the wavering light, Philip's critical eye paid reluctant homage to her personality. She disappeared abruptly as in a well of light, and the two men turned toward the Sacramento Street cars.

A delicious sense of warm luxury greeted her. She walked slowly through the stately hall and up the broad, familiar staircase, as directed, oblivious for once to the harmony of rugs and hangings and deep-toned walls. Pained over the vague yet indubitable reserve with which Philip May had met her, scorning herself for what she had expected merely on the score of her friendship with his father, glad of the thought that he was kind—spreading the glow of his going to poor old Bonnat into a sort of halo over his coldly intellectual aspect—"for kindness," she argued, as though apologizing for his apostasy, "is as good a working creed as any in this hungry, workaday world"—lost in her chaotic abstractions, she reached her friend's boudoir before she realized it.

A tall, handsome young woman, crowned with a mass of golden hair, absorbed in applying the last daub of powder to her nose, threw down her hand-glass at her approach and came gayly toward her.

"Oh," she said, delightedly, "I'm so glad you've come early—now we can have a few words together before we go down. How do you look? What have you on?" She was hurriedly unfastening the girl's wrap while she spoke.

"Just the old white thing," replied Jean, in surprise. "You said no one would be here but Paul Stein, and that we three would have a good old talk together, your lord being due at his club."

"Yes, I know. But I was afraid you had come in a shirt-waist, or something of that sort."

"Suppose I had? Paul doesn't count—but I felt like looking nice to-night, hence my festive appearance in this old rag."

"The old rag was an inspiration, and you look lovely. Don't stare at me as if I were daft. The fact is, Jean—would you have come to dine with us to-night if I had rung you up rather late?"

"I don't know. Why?"

"Well, Charlie sent me word he was going to bring some one home to dinner, but as I wasn't in—. Sit down there." She pressed her into a chair.

"I believe you are positively excited over something," murmured Jean, eying her with curiosity.

Laura laughed and seated herself near her. "To tell the truth," she began, half jestingly, half judicially, the color sweeping over her rose-tinted cheeks—then she stopped. "Jean," she essayed again, wholly earnest now, "do you think I care for you?"

"Laura," repeated Jean, in exaggerated solemnity, "do you think I care for you? You are beginning to frighten me."

"Because you frighten me. I don't know how to begin—you are so different on some points from other girls. Well, then, Ted Hart is down in the billiard-room with Charlie."

"Indeed! One of the gold-incrusted Harts?"

"Yes; the bachelor."

"I thought he lived in the East, or abroad, or somewhere."

"He does, but he is visiting his business interests on this coast and, incidentally, his brothers."

"Well, what do you want me to do about it? Does he threaten your peace? Is that why you ran upstairs?"

"No; I was waiting for you. I wanted to ask you to be—amiable to him."

"What a libel! Am I not always amiable?"

"No; and you know you're not. If a man doesn't just happen to come up to your demands you can freeze him into an icicle."

"Thanks. It doesn't sound pretty, but it isn't true. I only treat a man according to his pretensions. But what is the matter with poor Mr. Hart?"

"There! You are going to be difficult to-night. I know it—I feel it."

Jean laughed softly, amusedly. "You have no idea how hard and ordinary those violet eyes of yours look just now," she said, slowly. "Just let that match burn out of them, Laura—and drop it."

"There are millions in it, Jean."

"That sounds like an echo of your husband."

"Yes," Laura agreed, with a slight laugh. "Charlie is rather blunt. Perhaps you prefer the more poetic. Then why not 'take the cash and let the credit go'[53]—although—"

"Don't get any deeper in the mire of figures, I beg of you. Think of calling a man Cash!"

"I was thinking more of the credit, Miss Independence."

"And what is that, pray? My beggarly little bank-book?"

"No—the even smaller one, the invisible account we all hold against Fate, the banker of dreams, who loses all we have in mad speculation, and when we come clamoring for our own—behold closed doors."

"Listen, Laura. Don't I hear the children's voices?" The quiet tone restored Laura Brook-man to a sudden consciousness of undue intensity. They were both pale, but the older woman laughed the emotion away.

"I was actually reading you a sermon, wasn't I?" she said, rising with the girl. "Yes, the children are waiting to kiss you good night."

Whatever the cause of her agitation, Mrs. Brookman was happiness incarnate when they left the nursery a few minutes later. When the two friends went downstairs together she was pleased to turn her little venture at matchmaking into a merry jest.

"They have gone into the library," she said, as the sound of men's voices reached them.

"Is that the voice of Cash?" whispered Jean. "Its sound is unfamiliar to me. I recognize Paul's and—"

"Wait a minute—who is that? Why, it's that Vic Davis. He must have come in with Paul." Each favored the other with a little grimace of distaste.

They entered through the drawing-room. As Mr. Brookman caught sight of them from his position among the group before the blazing open fire-place, he lounged good-naturedly toward them. Good nature seemed the keynote to the man—it exuded, as it were, from every inch of his prosperous-looking, lazy figure and stout, florid face. He called his wife's friend "Jeanie" in loud-voiced jocularity, and at any time would have gladly played at making love to her; but she called him "Mr. Brookman," in pleasant friendliness, and he never got any further than a foolish killing glance or two.

Jean was introduced to the stranger, a quiet-mannered man, whose keen yet kindly eyes were the only good feature in a face marked with the wear and tear of opportunity enjoyed.

"The *bonne bouche* last," said Paul Stein, a tall, slender man of thirty-five or thereabout, upon whose plain, thin, clever features the rough hand of life had left harsh manuscript.[54] He put out an imperious hand to Jean. "Here's a warm place—come and share it."

"No, I see my favorite chair in that corner. But you can talk to me just as comfortably from a distance."

"I am never distant with you if I can help it," he said, pushing a hassock toward her, but pausing to shake hands with Mrs. Brookman before seating himself. "Vic been making his apologies for coming?" he asked, glancing good-humoredly at the vivid-faced, eagle-nosed young fellow behind her.

"She refuses to accept them," the latter retorted, extending a deferential hand to Jean, "although I assured her I never would have ventured in if the wind hadn't been so pressing."

"Mr. Davis has not called upon me since the day I refused to give him my hand," laughed Laura, sinking upon the couch and inviting the unexpected guest to the place beside her.

"What's that?" exclaimed Brookman, in mock suspicion, from the depths of the great arm-chair, where he had gulfed himself into a shapeless heap. "Is there a skeleton in my closet?"

"I only asked for her palm," soothed Davis, "thinking it might make good reading matter. But she was too superstitious to let me see it."

"Superstitious! If I had been superstitious I would have begged you to read it at once. There isn't a suspicion of superstition in me."

"But," drawled her husband, "she won't make one of thirteen at table or—"

"That's a good Christian superstition," observed Paul, indulgently.[55]

"I know a man," retorted Laura, glancing toward her husband, "who, every morning before going downtown to earn his children's bread and butter, prays, 'Lord, deliver me from the evil eye of a yellow dog.'"

"All Jews are superstitious," quietly remarked Hart, from where he stood toasting himself before the blazing log.

"Every one is," supplemented Paul, "and every one denies it. The Jews, if anything, are less so than any other race. We're too material, you know, too practical—we've had the dream knocked out of us."

"Why, there, Paul, you and my uncle are altogether at outs. He says, 'While the Jew stands, his dream stands.'"

"Oh, when the Chevalier says that, Jean, he is arguing from the Messianic hypothesis.[56] He's romantic. We evolutionists have got over that—evolutions, like millenniums, being slow work."

"Exactly. That is just what he says—we haven't outgrown all our weaknesses yet. Although he doesn't call dreaming a weakness."

"Of course he doesn't—for every Jewish weakness he has an excuse. He is loyal as he is learned."

"Once a Jew always a Jew," remarked Brookman, as though settling the question.

"That's where you're dead off, Brookman," exclaimed young Davis, with a knowing laugh. "Do any of you happen to know Phil May—or, rather, Philip May, M. D., Ph. D.—and any other D in the alphabet you happen to think of?"

"Do you mean the English artist, or the young American physician, Dr. Philip May?" asked Hart, with interest.[57]

"The American. But surgeon suits him better, I understand."

"Yes, I believe it does. He treated me last year at Baden Baden.[58] A fine-looking man—wears a short, dark, pointed beard. But I didn't take him for a Jew."

"Ha, ha! that last hits him off capitally. He has made quite a record for himself in the cutting business since his return here."

"I met Dr. May to-night," Jean hastened to inform them. "He is the son of my uncle's old friend, Mr. Joseph May. I had not heard of any wonderful operation of his in this town."

Davis threw back his head in a paroxysm of laughter. "That's one on you, Miss Willard," he cried. "What! You haven't heard of that already celebrated cutting affray of his on Kearney Street last Saturday night?"

"Cutting affray?"

"Let's have it, Vic," exclaimed Brookman, voicing the contagion of the young fellow's evident excitement.

"It's not a long story. You know Sam Weiss?"

"Yes." The affirmation was unanimous—they all knew the song-and-dance amateur.

"Do you agree with me that he's an all-round good fellow—give the coat off his back for a friend—and all the rest of the cardinal virtues?"

"Sure," said Brookman, seriously. He was apt to indorse all Davis's tastes and sentiments. The women were silent.

"Well, it seems he and Phil May were schoolmates once upon a time, and as intimate as May's peculiar oysterdom and royal loneliness permitted. Sam has always taken great stock in May's success—felt as though he had had a hand in it in some occult way, and was delighted over the thought that his old chum was coming to settle here. Well, last Saturday night, as you can imagine, he was tickled to death to come upon him at the corner of Market and Kearney streets."

By some inexplicable attraction, the animated dark eyes had come to rest upon Jean Willard's attentive face, and to her he addressed the story of the short encounter in his own terse, slangy expressiveness. "Gave him the glassy eye, you understand," he concluded, with a shrug, "in the full electric light and gaze of two of Weiss's friends."

"Yes," said Jean, quickly, before the disgusted expressions on the faces of the others could find vent in words. "But that remark about Moses—wasn't it rather far-fetched?"

Davis looked at her pityingly. "Joseph May kept a clothing store in days of gold," he explained, concisely. "But Weiss is only a case in point. Dr. May has been pleased to state his attitude in unmistakable terms of frost to several other Jews of former acquaintance—and—mark my words—he won't have to wait till the long run to hear from them in return. I don't happen to be honored with his acquaintance, but just as an expression of opinion, I'd like to—kick—kick—him—from—here—to—Jerusalem!" The clan spirit was up in arms. His loud, frank voice had sunk with the last words to a peculiar, slow quietude.

"Save him the trouble of rolling there on resurrection day, eh?"[59] laughed Brookman, approvingly. "But what's the matter with him? Strikes me we're as good as the next ones. What's wanting? Look at me. Look at my wife—look at my children. We've as good as the country affords. Who has a finer home—who's better dressed, better fed, hey? My son will have all the education he's fit for and my daughter all the accomplishments going—if she wants 'em. We help support the theaters and operas, and help liberally, by Jove! We travel, enjoy our money and ourselves—and let others enjoy our money as well. Where's the kick?"

He basked broadly in the sun of his prosperity. A great, genial satisfaction shone from him as he spread his hands on the arms of his handsome chair. A bright spot of flame sprang to his wife's cheek. Her eyes and lips smiled non-committally—she made no comment.

"Oh, you forgot," laughed Paul, "that when Jeshurun waxes fat, he kicks.[60] Dr. May is only a modern example. He has evidently weighed the pros and cons of the situation, and given himself over to the heavy-weight. Taking a Dreyfus on Devil's Island as a basis for action—who can blame him?"[61]

"By God!" exclaimed Brookman, raising his fist to heaven. The exclamation had no bearing upon Philip May—it was but the suffocated protest against the crime of a nation over which the heart of every reading Jew was bursting with bitter indignation.

"Of course, I don't know your Mr. Weiss," interposed Mr. Hart, after an eloquent pause, "but I do know Dr. May, and I can readily imagine his not relishing being slapped on the shoulder by certain people—to say nothing, figuratively speaking, of a certain style of voice. But that doesn't prove he has drawn the line at all Jews. He is far too sensible."

"And one swallow does not make a summer," suggested Laura, gently.

"I told you Weiss is only one of many," reiterated Davis, hotly. "And, among other tales, I have heard that old man May told some fellow that it will be impossible for his son to join the Verein, or any other club, for that matter."

"*Nebbich*," murmured Brookman, with a sorrowful shake of the head.[62]

"Don't you think," began Jean, very quietly, "that we judge too quickly where our proverbial sensitiveness is concerned? If Philip May has seen fit to act as Mr. Davis says he has, how do we know what he has in view? How do we know what ambition or ambitions are leading him, and how old ties may hamper him? His social standards and tastes are not necessarily the same as ours. His accomplishments and wit may have traveled beyond a coon-song or an Orpheum joke—they may even fail to see the point in those diverting Jewish stories in Puck and other witty periodicals.[63] Do we know all his life holds? May there not be a passage in his which might explain—excuse—not only a distaste, but a hatred of all Jews? Isn't life full of unthought-of possibilities? Must we still continue not only to judge, but to condemn, everybody according to our own little lights?"

As she made her low-voiced plea for the development of individuality at any cost, Laura eyed her curiously.

"Come, come, Jean," drawled Paul Stein, ironically, "how can you waste so much good interest on a fellow who has such a low opinion of his breeding that he has quit bowing to himself? My dear girl, we don't need Philip May."

"I was speaking in the abstract," lied the girl, glibly. "But as to needing him, Paul—you spoke differently last week. Why, he was to be a sort of representative, an edition de luxe, the Jewish chef-d'oeuvre of San Francisco;[64] you were so anxious to meet him—he was going to be such a stimulus!"

The attorney looked at her musingly. "Yes," he said. "I had read one or two of his articles in medical reviews and was captivated by the virility of the man's style, concluding that the style was the man. It seems I was mistaken. Unfortunately, I have not yet attained the Christian humility of turning the second cheek. I have this minute discovered that there is a rather strong party spirit in me, and I can't, in all consciousness, try as I may, assume the brilliant, disinterested amusement of laughing stars high out of the heart of life. But Philip May is only a result of existing conditions, a sign of the times—set upon a height. He is not a type—he is only one of those inevitable, recurrent figures, dominant and bitter, pitting himself against fate in vain. The thing is, what does he want, will he get it, is the game worth the candle?[65]

"Oh, among ourselves we know that individually, feature for feature, we are all beautiful"—he grinned benignly upon them—"but outside, among others, *en masse*, our *tout-ensemble!*[66]—oh, my children!" He covered his face with his sinewy hand. A laugh of responsive understanding encouraged him further.

"And we can laugh, nevertheless," he granted them, "because we know that, inwardly, we're the right stuff, good backbone stuff, which it would be folly to eliminate from the civic anatomy. How's that for fairness, Mr. Hart?"

"Not bad. Go ahead. Diagnose us."

"Oh, talk, though cheap, is often extravagant," laughed Paul. "But I like to splurge in that line once in a while, and can afford it—if you can afford the listening. Of course, we know the ignominies of the past against which we are still combating: that to-day we excuse ourselves on the score of being descendants, often to the exclusion of the more vital responsibility that to-day will be yesterday to-morrow, and that some day we will be ancestors. But we know, besides, the wheels within wheels—we know there are gradations. We don't judge every rich Jew by the first flamboyant, gold-congested parvenu we happen to meet in his mansion on the heights, nor every poor Jew by the ignorant, sing-songing old clo' man south of Market Street.[67] We even admit that if, now and then, the one on the top were to exchange places with the one at the bottom it would be a good game of puss-in-the-corner.[68] But think of cramming all Jewry—think of cramming one complex Jewish soul into an epigram! Why, we bulge over and out of every part of it. And yet, to some people, Judaism still means an old man who speaks gibberish, wears a beard and a praying-shawl, and whose golden rule is 'Do others or others will do you.'"

"By Jove," cried Davis, approvingly, "we're not such an uninteresting lot, after all."

"Oh, you're the sort that likes to be sugared over and swallowed whole in audible contentment," laughed Paul, sarcastically. "Few Jews can stand adverse criticism, and that's what keeps so many of them from taking on the little outward graces that count for so much. But don't imagine I think we've cornered the brain and virtue market of the world. We're first-rate students because no power on earth can beat us in that intensity of purpose—born of the old-time restriction—of doing the best we can with our only unfilchable property—our brains; we are great financiers through enforced specialization; we are thrifty and industrious because we've had to fight for every right of possession inch by inch; we care for our poor as no other poor are cared for, because we were once one in misery, because we can't climb effectually without pulling our weaker ones up with us, and because it was only on the condition that the Jewish poor would not become a burden on the community that the Jews were first granted settlement in the New World. I can laugh

good-naturedly enough, Jean, over the wit of Puck's stories when
our shrewdness, or features, or mannerisms are the point of ridicule.
I'm not like the cultured Irishman who sets his teeth at the sight of
printed brogue—but when it comes to libeling our honesty and la-
beling the race with certain low-down propensities, I draw the line.
We've had enough of tradition. Yet, you see, all our civic virtues lie
rooted in some hard, grim, ugly fact, and I agree with Dr. May—the
looking-back vision is not pretty—the harking-back accent is not
musical. But though I too would cover it over, would say 'hush' to it,
the very knowledge of the *cause* of its ugliness would make me say
it in another tone than that of shame." He paused with quivering
nostril and compressed lip.

"I did not think you cared so much for your religion," said Jean, a
great wave of emotion thrilling her voice strangely.

"Neither did I." He smiled wearily. "But it's no longer a matter
of religion—think of a man's religious thoughts having anything
to do with his success or non-success in this material age! No, it's
something more tragic—it's a matter of race—and there is no way
out of that except by the slow honeymoon route of intermarriage.
Well? Queer how these forces lie silent in one, covered over by the
day's battle."

"That's no fairy-tale," agreed Davis, in hearty seriousness. "For
my part, being a Jew doesn't bother me much the year round, except
when New Year's or Atonement Day comes along, and we have to
close up shop."

"But there's one little cynicism of yours I wish you would qualify,
Paul," interposed Jean, earnestly, "and that is your remark about the
virtue of the race. Surely you know there are no happier homes in
the world than Jewish homes, and that fact usually bespeaks virtue."

"There's that sweet tooth again," Paul returned, reproachfully.
"Of course we're a temperate lot—even at the lowest pitch we don't
drink, or beat our wives. But omitting the many love-matches—
God bless 'em!—when you come to think of the many others, the
mercenary and manufactured ones, in which the girls are supposed
to love the men they're told to love—surely you don't still cherish
that beautiful, primitive dream of universal peace, happiness and
fidelity?"

"That sounds interesting," said Hart, pulling up a chair finally, and seating himself in a leaning attitude of rapt attention.

"But the insinuation is not true," combated Jean, flashing round upon him, overwhelming him in the sudden passion of her eyes. "Ninety-nine and a half Jewish marriages out of a hundred *are* happy and—and honorable."

"Bravo! But how about that half case?" questioned Paul, quietly.

"Something keeps it from becoming a whole case" was the swift, fearless, pure-eyed response.

"Indeed? What?" murmured Paul, smiling gently.

"Ask Mr. and Mrs. Brookman," cried Davis. "They should make pretty reliable witnesses."

Brookman shook a reproving finger at him. "We belong to the God bless 'em crowd," he said, comfortably.

Mrs. Brookman laughed lightly.

"However, Mr. Brookman," broke in Jean, playfully, feeling a certain tension in the turn of subject, "tell us why a Jewess, even without the grand passion as a nucleus, always loves the man she marries."

"Because her mamma tells her to," laughed the great, good-natured fellow, with supreme satisfaction.

"And, Laura, how about the man? Why does a Jew always love his wife?"

"From an inherited, unconquerable sense of duty." The caustic flippancy drew a laugh. Brookman gallantly returned her a military salute.

"Not bad, so far as they go," remarked Stein, abruptly. "But, merely as a looker-on, might I say, supposing your conclusions to be true—she loves him, finally, because he is the father of her children, and he loves her because she is his—his property, I mean."

The brutal words stilled the air.

"Jean, will you play for us?" Laura Brookman's light voice broke the scarcely perceptible awkwardness.

The girl arose at once, Stein following her leisurely to the piano.

"You are hateful to-night," she vouchsafed him in a low voice as she seated herself and he leaned against the instrument.

"You are inharmonious to-night," he retorted. "I detected it as soon as you came in."

She ceased to look at his provoking face. Her fingers ran over the keys.

"I can't play," she said after a minute, letting her hands fall into her lap.

"You can't, but you will," he said.

"What do you mean?"

"I mean you always do—you always believe, even—in spite of things. Isn't that your herculean motto? Then play."

She began, her eyes upon his thin, plain face. Then she forgot him and played on.

"What is it?" he murmured, when her hands rested, carried away, despite his disturbed mood, by the exquisite grace and mystery of the music.

"A poem of Macdowell's.[69] Perhaps afterward, Laura," she said, turning her head in answer. "Ask Mr. Davis to sing a coon-song for us, will you, Paul?"

"What! after your little flip at the coon-singing genus?"

"I didn't." The girl flushed distressfully. "I couldn't—besides I like them—the songs—too much."

"You could and you did. On impulse you can do anything, friend o' mine. But don't torture your sensitive conscience—you haven't hurt him. He belongs to the breed that always thinks you're pointing to the fellow behind. Ask him, and prove me."

He came delightedly, flattered by the request, singing song after song to her swinging accompaniment with all the jubilant rhythm, the peculiar darky joy, which make the coon-song so unmistakably a song of color, not omitting several inimitable cake-walk steps, as though his feet must, perforce, respond to the charm.

He swung off finally, and Jean found Theodore Hart leaning on the piano in Paul Stein's place. He spoke of music—he had heard much—tentatively watching her face. Jean questioned him carelessly, unaccountably annoyed over the fact that the man's eyes and ears were frankly absorbed in her. She knew that Charlie Brookman and Vic Davis were holding a laughing chat in the corner, that Laura and Paul Stein were seated together on the couch, evidently talking fitfully, the former gazing before her, her elbow crushed in the pillow behind, the latter bent upon disentangling a piece of cord fantastically twisted about his fingers. Their attitudes disturbed her indefinably. The evident admiration of the man near her irritated her.

"You are a champion worth having," he was saying. "Your views are broad—broader than most women's."

Broad! When she had been narrowing them to fit the case of one man! She stared at him coldly. Yes, Paul was right—she appeared and felt inharmonious.

She was glad, a little later, to find herself on the street alone with Stein, glad of his uncompromising silence. The wind had abated, the fog was dissipated, the air was crisp and bracing, the stars twinkled in cold brilliance. The two friends climbed the hills with long, quick strides, intimately still.

CHAPTER VII

Thus did Philip May set about defying and humbugging tradition, the present—and himself. He was young, he was strong, he was free—he acknowledged no overlord but his own will and inclination. The adverse past he simply kicked off as a man might a pair of shoes grown shabby or uncomfortable, the only apparent obstacle to his consequent comfort being his frequent stumblings against the discarded in unconsidered places.

During the first two weeks following the memorable evening of his return and the anti-climax of the wordless reconciliation between his father and himself, he found little time for introspection or politic forethought. His professional reputation had preceded him through his writings, and chance, in the form of mischance for others, came to greet him. Dr. Otis, succumbing to a contingency of the grip, was forced to put his patients and himself in other hands—whereby two of the most critical operations of his experience fell to Philip May's account. The fortunate victims happened to be men prominent in the city's doings, and the fame of the newcomer's hand of steel might have spread sensationally, had not the young physician's professional reticence saved him from that indignity of popular quackery. He was used to success, and dismissed it with matter-of-fact brevity.

Virtually, however, it was not to be thus dismissed. The personal attraction of the man brought his name too easily to the lips of those with whom he came in contact. Lilian Otis, welcoming him, not only as the devoted friend and attendant of her cousin, John Harleigh, but as one of the most abiding memories of her last European jaunt, gladly added these later credentials after presenting him or his name to the inner court of her charming and influential set.

Within a month he felt his grasp firm upon the life upon which he had entered.

With a single exception: he had effectually barred himself out of the proud, silent heart of his father. Nominally drawn together under the same roof, they were more grimly estranged than they had been when divided by a continent and sea. Any effort toward the simplest converse was strained and painful. Philip felt the lack of intimacy, but recognized it as another insurmountable proof of their being kindred only through accident of birth. Joseph May, exponent of the most intense and sensitive race under the sun in the matter of family ties, crushed his knowledge into the bitter pill of lovelessness, and chewed it, folding his lips close over the bitterness in that wildest of all misery—misery which keeps its mouth shut. Even Daniel Willard heard no further word of complaint or reproach. His talk of him was full of boast and bluster.

"Never he gives himself any rest," he said, with a helpless shrug of indulgent pride. "When he don't go nights to the hospital, he writes or studies, and when he don't write nor study he has a call to make, or something like that. Last night he wanted I should take a walk with him. But what for? I was tired, and better he goes with younger men. But he likes it when Jean plays. One night he most broke his appointment because he waited till she finished."

"I shall ask him to dine with us *Sedar* night," said Daniel, dealing the cards in absent fashion.[70] "I have not seen so much of him as I should like, and that will be a good chance. We shall have no one but Mr. and Mrs. Brookman and Paul Stein, and you two. Then he can ask Jean to play whatever he likes—after the singing is over. Do you think he will come, Joseph?"

"You can ask him.—Forty kings—a tierce to the jack.[71]—Jean is a *nix-nuts*.[72] Never she comes to see me no more."

"No?" said Daniel, discarding as if in deep thought. "She is a little busy with the Boys' Club.[73] Particularly with one of the boys—little Joel Slinsky. You should see some of the drawings he makes of the people of his neighborhood—unconscious caricatures of the Russian Jew. But to me it is not all funny. Jean does not mean to neglect you; she asks how you are feeling every day."

"So," commented Joseph. But in some manner, too subtle for his defining, he knew that the sudden ceasing of the girl's unceremonious comings and goings had coincided with the advent of his son. And another dream was laid aside with his broken potsherds.

And Jean, during the two or three weeks following her evening with the Brookmans, had been quietly, though uncertainly, divorcing herself from the same romance. Final proof of his positive alienation was still wanting, and a loyal spirit breaks its idols slowly. But her days were occupied with her customary obligations and pleasures, many self-imposed, many necessary, and she allowed herself no quarter for a morbid sentiment. Stephen Forrest was harassing her with importunate letters, so passionately pleading against her dogged stand, so ironically bitter against his limited opportunities, so humorously humble, that sympathy was playing ball with her resolution.

Besides, the gods were with her, for the moment, in giving her another Nemesis to contend with. Theodore Hart, who, before meeting her, had lived all things but a pure passion, had been suddenly, surprisingly, overwhelmed by that novelty and given himself wholly to its influence. With all his intentions written openly in his attentions, in the good, old-fashioned Jewish way, he had come to tempt her from her moorings. He represented the carnival, the luxe of life—he represented to her clear-eyed, end-of-the-nineteenth-century knowledge, all gifts—save one. And in the material sunlight of the end of the century he easily stood for a temptation.

In withdrawing from her pretty old-time intimacy with Joseph May, she had not forgotten that it would hurt and astonish him, but she was determined to risk no running against Philip May's courteous surprise should he happen upon her innocent familiarity with his household.

However, pulling down a blind one morning before setting out for town, she espied her old friend pacing the safe back porch in smoking-jacket and velvet skull-cap, and she was down upon him in a minute.

"Good morning, Uncle Joseph," she sang out, blithely; "why aren't you down at your office this sunny morning?"

The stocky figure stopped short. "Good morning, Miss Willard," he returned, with biting dignity. "I am surprised you still know me."

"Miss Willard, indeed, old humbug! Aren't you ashamed of yourself? Kiss me and tell me why you are still at home at half-past ten?"

He submitted his forehead to her imperious caress. "I have a little headache," he explained, with an unintentional sigh, "and my son said better I don't go to the office. I telephoned your uncle when there is any important mail he shall come up with it."

"Is there anything I can do for you in town? I have some shopping to do and—. But there is Uncle Daniel now."

He came hurriedly out of Joseph's doorway, a look of concern furrowing his brow.

"Feeling a little lazy this morning, Joseph?" he asked, brightly, laying his arm across the stooping shoulders.

"Oh, so-so. Nothing to speak about, but when you have a doctor in the house always you can find a little pain. What you got there, Daniel?"

"Only a catalogue of the sale of the Powers estate." He handed him the booklet. "Well, Jean, have you and Joseph been making up?"

"He calls me Miss Willard," she answered, in mock despair, "and is altogether very proud and haughty. But if he doesn't behave, he can't come to our dinner party, can he, Uncle Daniel?"

"What dinner party?" asked the old man, smoothing her hand as it lay upon his arm. "You know I don't go to dinner parties."

"But considering that you come every year to—"

"Oh, you mean the *Sedar*. When it is, Daniel?"

At that moment the door giving upon the porch was again hastily opened and Philip May appeared upon the threshold.

"Don't let me startle you," he laughed, coming out, as his father rose nervously from the settee. "Nothing is wrong, father. I have just remembered that I forgot to tell Katie about a box of books that is coming for me. How is your head?" He stood beside him, an attractive, manly figure, hat in hand. Jean leaned against the box of mignonette on the rail, clasping her gloves.

"It is still a little heavy," returned Joseph, reseating himself. "But that will go soon."

"With the morning—if you keep quiet. By the way, Mr. Willard, I have intended dropping in upon you some evening, but have not yet found the opportunity. I'm glad of the chance of telling you I'm coming, just the same." He smiled, winningly holding out a hand.

"I understand," returned Daniel, without a trace of resentment. "But we were just asking your father to dine with us on the second of next month in the hope that you would come too."

"The second—second—. I should be delighted, but it seems to me something was said about that date." He pressed his hand to his brow. "Ah, yes," his eyes lightened. "Otis—an engagement made a month ago. Well, I am truly sorry, but if I can break away, I'll drop in upon you during the evening. Next Tuesday, isn't it? I shall not forget. Good morning. Good morning, Miss Willard." The next minute he had passed through the doorway, an utter stranger to the girl.

"You did not say whether I could get anything for you in town, Uncle Joseph," she resumed, coming toward the two old gentlemen, the pretty note of her voice slightly strained. And then she noticed that the catalogue in the dark-veined hands was waving as if in a violent wind, that the heavy eyes were raised apologetically to her, seeking to cry down some unspeakable pain.

"Will you ask Katie?" he returned, slowly, speaking correctly, as he sometimes did when under stress of a relentless spur. "She said something to me to-day about curtains. Will you ask her, please? And, Jean, my dear, you know Philip is very busy—and he has many invitations—and he cannot always arrange his time. I hope you will not think it is anything else." He did not look toward Daniel—he addressed his half-plea, half-apology, away from the eyes of his friend.

The girl flushed under the old man's ponderous artlessness as she would not have done in a more worldly atmosphere. But her uncle saved her an evasion.

"Surely, Joseph," came the brisk, cheery rebuke, "you cannot think we would doubt his sincerity. It is only surprising that a man like Dr. May has not always a previous engagement"; and he laughed over his little conceit, meeting Joseph's eyes with frank cloudlessness.

Jean went in to consult the housekeeper.

"Oh, no, Katie," she answered, decidedly, when that functionary had made known her wants. "Let Dr. May furnish his own study. Is that all?"

"But, Miss Jean, you always does choose them things for us, and how can you ask a man to know anything about it?" She was following her persuasively through the hall.

"I have told you, Katie, that it is impossible," she reiterated, turning quietly upon her. "No doubt Dr. May has every intention of choosing his own carpet or rugs." Her sentence halted—a footfall upon the stairs apprising her that Dr. May was still in the house. She wished herself well out of the door—in Jericho—anywhere but there.

"Well, there now, I'll just ask him," exclaimed the woman, planting her hands triumphantly upon her hips as he came down the stairs at the foot of which they were standing. "I've been asking Miss Jean, Dr. Philip, to get them things for your study, and she says as you knows more about it than she do and will be wanting to be doing of it all yourself. Is that true, now?"

Philip, standing on the last step, smiled amusedly, glancing down at the distant dignity of the girl in her dark tailor-gown. The black velvet of her hat cast a soft shadow upon the creamy whiteness of her face. She made a charming figure in the dim light of the hall.

"Her pleading is quite thrown away," she hastened to say, with pleasant carelessness, turning toward the door. "Your father often used to ask me to relieve him of such household nuisances, but this, of course, is different."

The housekeeper moved reluctantly away. He put out his hand to take the book from within her arm.

"What are you reading?" he asked, prolonging the grace of the short moment. "What! Carlyle?[74] You don't pretend to like the old growler?"

"I love him. He is a fire-god—all shams come to his stake. And as for me—I'd like to be his fuel-bearer!"

Her intensities set the healthy blood in his young veins stirring. At least—at any rate her eyes were irresistibly lovely. He was forced to put the book back into her hand as she turned the doorknob with the other. "And such violent cures attract you? But—one moment— why is this different?"

"Different?"

"Isn't my room part of my father's house?"

"Oh, I had forgotten that. Why should I inflict my provincial tastes upon you? Surely, you have cultivated your own, in all things, in all these long years and experiences." She had the door open, was half way down the steps, before he could decide whether in her words or in the nonchalant lift to her little head had lain a dim suggestion of contempt. He knew nothing of her but her music and the mutable gleams of thought fleeting over her expressive face. He raised his brows in amusement over the contempt, vaguely surmising its origin.

A half hour later, making his daily call upon his bed-ridden friend, Dr. Otis, flattered by gentle, white-haired Mrs. Otis, coquetted with by golden-haired Miss Otis—in that atmosphere of accustomed high breeding which had become his own—their nature having grown his habit—he quite forgot the scarcely grasped attraction of Jean Willard. Young Otis had been haunting him like a shadow. Weeks before the coming of Dr. May, his enthusiasm had aroused the interest of the quietly cynical "Omars" almost to lionizing pitch, but their curiosity was forced to suspend judgment owing to the jealous attention the doctor gave the unexpected practice which had absorbed him almost from the day of his arrival. He had, however, met several of the members casually, and judging from these glimpses, he was contemplating with pleasure his introduction to the modest little circle.

Nevertheless, he was forced to break his dinner engagement with Otis when the appointed evening arrived. "An unforeseen consultation detains me," his message ran, "so be reasonable, dine without me, and I shall be at your rooms as near 7:30 as will be possible, that you may coach me in regard to those club matters, individualities, etc., which are bothering your conscientious ciceroneship."

Near the hour named, Otis admitted him. The room bore a company expectancy in the open piano, the cards and counters upon the table, the wine cooling in the corner beside the genially appointed buffet.

"This looks promising," remarked Philip, putting down his hat and topcoat, and coming forward to the full light. With a faint motion, as of weariness satisfied, he threw himself upon the couch near the center of the room and glanced approvingly about him. "I regretted having to send that message, Otis, but you know a physician's time is always half-mortgaged."

"Yes, I was sorry," returned his host, shortly, nervously throwing one leg over the other as he lounged opposite in the deep-cushioned easy chair.

The doctor's quick ear detected an unfamiliar restraint.

His expressive eyebrows met in a fleeting question. "You had something to tell me?" he asked, pleasantly.

"Well—yes. But of course—now that you are here—" He smiled a vague conclusion to his sentence. Philip noticed that, despite his easy attitude, the young fellow's supple hand was twitching the heavy tassel on the chair arm, his glance roving unsteadily about the room.

"You would perhaps have asked me not to come, had we met earlier in the evening—is that it?" he asked, with amused interest. "Out with it. You are expecting somebody whom it would be pleasanter for me not to meet?"

"Oh, no, no. Not at all, not at all," reiterated Otis, with extravagant politeness. "No one is coming but Taylor, and Griswold, and Stephen Forrest. You have met them all, I believe."

"All but Forrest—and he and I used to be daily neighbors—at least, bodily."

"So I understand. Were you—were you at all—friendly during those school days?" The frank, clear-eyed face was uncomfortably flushed, the voice distant and cold.

Philip's fine hand closed involuntarily upon itself. His intuition was on the alert. "There was no friendship between us," he returned, candidly. "I believe he considered me his rival—he was very seriously ambitious."

Otis drew in a deep, uneasy breath. "As you were. I—that may account for his antagonism—although, of course, as our electing is conducted—one never knows who drops the dissenting ball."

"You mean," questioned Philip, with reassuring gentleness, "that my name has been discredited?"

"Oh, confound it!" burst forth the other, apoplectically. "The man has it bruited that you are a Jew.[75] But, of course, I am only waiting for your denial of the damned preposterous libel."

"Why damned—why preposterous?" He was leaning forward as though to study his vis-à-vis more closely. His eyes were steady, his mouth half smiled. A slight, warm flush tinged his cheek.

"But—but you're not," combated Otis, lamely, sitting up in consternation.

"But I am," asserted the other in calm conclusiveness. "Don't you see that I am, now that you look at me?" He spoke kindly, as a superior might lead a child he desired to teach.

"Surely you never said—" began Otis, icily.

"You never asked."

"But there are means of apprisal."

"I saw no necessity. The gates were nominally down. You required no passport proclaiming the contrary."

"Did Harleigh know?"

"No. And if he had?"

"By Jove—he hated a hypocrite!" The word came in resistless passion.

"Which more—that or a Jew?"

"I must judge him by myself. We out here are still unregenerate enough to damn the hypocrite with the lowest of criminals."

"You mean you could have forgiven—cared for—the avowed Jew?"

"Before the hypocrite."

"Bosh!"

The cool comment acted like a probe. Otis's hot young eyes met his skeptical challenge with prompt reply. "I admire—respect many Jews," he returned defiantly.

"At a distance."

"You are a stranger to your own birth-place," Otis returned, quietly. "Otherwise you would know that here and there one meets a young fellow who is frankly Jewish, yet welcome in any set."

"Here and there. How did the exceptions come to be tolerated? Was the card of admission heavily tipped with gold, promising prodigal spending—or with the fame of talent, promising rare entertainment? You imply some excuse for the open door."

Otis met his gaze directly, uncontrolledly now. "You are a man of the world," he replied, without more ado. "You know from what center all social circles are drawn. You know equality rounds them all. You also know—although you may choose to ignore it—that not only equality of individuality, but coincidence of family tradition, is the barbed wire fence hemming all round—and out."

"And there we naturally separate," supplemented the apt pupil, thoughtfully. "But inform me further—I own to a hitherto unsuspected myopia—what becomes then of our grand scheme of democracy? What becomes of the glory of the self-made man?"

"A shibboleth. There are no self-made men—in society. Nor elsewhere."

Dr. May studied him. "I think I understand your reservation," he answered, slowly. "Then it is true—the age of miracles is past. The gods no longer conceive—we are all essentially fellow-made. What a responsibility!" He leaned forward in an attitude of the deepest musing. Then, as with a sudden start of self-consciousness, he said quickly, "But don't let us trouble ourselves with the analysis—it requires delicate handling. My little venture was just one of those operations, as it were, which we call successful when the patient does not die under the knife, although he may succumb later to nature's weakness or unforeseen complications. Queer how a man incognito may meet all requirements—and how, with just a birthmark exposed, is the same man never again."

Otis eyed him closely, with a sudden sharp pain at heart, thinking to find in the face the sarcasm so dangerously absent from the voice. But the face was quite as quietly intent—it wore the expression of one engaged in reading an interesting, impersonal phase of life.

However, after a moment, "Confess," laughed Philip abruptly, "you feel as though you had been made game of by a clever rogue."

"You were under false colors," Otis flashed back through set teeth.

"What! Under the Stars and Stripes? Think a moment, my countryman."

"By heavens!" exclaimed the young man, springing to his feet. "Do you think we can forget the man you stood for? There's the torturing inconsistency of it—the honorable man of brains, the perfect, worshiped friend, but—"

"Yet a Jew. It is strange. No, don't torture yourself. Perhaps even Harleigh would have drawn back from the ugly revelation. If Harleigh had known, there might never have been a friendship—if there had been no friendship, there might never have been a deception to unveil. Who knows? The premises are too hypothetical. There is someone knocking at your door."

In fact, a chorus of knocks was in progress.

"You will stay, of course," said Otis, quickly. "I—I trust you will not impute any narrow prejudice to my attitude. But in my surprise—. I hope you will stay."

"Thank you. It will be rather interesting meeting Stephen Forrest." His perfect repose, judged in the new light seemed merely a refined impudence. Otis turned from him as from a stranger. A new, subtle mystery emanated from him—the mystery of ghostly ages.

The three men entered hilariously, Stephen Forrest limping in last. At sight of Dr. May, who had risen, a perceptible embarrassment fell restrainingly upon them. They had counted upon Otis's averting his coming.

"You have all met Dr. May, I think," said Otis, off-handedly, as Taylor and Griswold bowed. Forrest, with a curt nod, seated himself at the table and began laying out the cards in a game of solitaire.

"I scarcely think Mr. Forrest remembers me," suggested Philip, leaning his strong, well-knit figure against the piano, his eyes deliberately fixed upon the delicate face of the artist. "Yet we ran each other rather close when we were youngsters."

"I remember you distinctly. But I never ran," returned the artist, absorbed in the careful placing of his cards. "You will remember that you always got in first. Success and you ran hand in hand. Always have, I hear."

"I have been most successful in hiding my failures. How else?"

"Otis can enlighten you. I have also heard somewhat of you from—er—our mutual friend—the lovely Jewess—Miss Jean Willard." The cards required all his attention. Philip treated the insolent face and tone to a speculative regard.

"Do you mean Daniel Willard's niece?" broke in Otis, hurriedly assuming the office of sentinel. "What a glorious pianist she is! I heard her play last week at the benefit for the Children's Hospital. Taylor, you ought to know her."

"Miss Willard? Certainly. She is one of the finest amateurs in town, in my estimation," returned the 'cellist, sincerely wishing the uncomfortable moment over.

Philip's eyes still held the feignedly nonchalant face of the artist. He resented the unnecessary introduction of Jean Willard's name in the hostile assemblage—he could not understand the introduction, nor yet his own resentment.

Forrest lifted his eyes from his play with a provoking sneer into the steady hazel eyes still covering him. Then he passed his glance on to his host. "I thought we were going to play," he said, impatiently.

"You're in a hurry, but I suppose we'll have to humor your proverbial restlessness. Of course, doctor, you'll take a hand."

"What is your game?"

"Poker, in plain American—what the English call Bluff," said Forrest, swiftly. "You know it, I presume."

"That is another of my successes," returned Philip, with smiling imperturbability, from his position at the piano.

"Ah, but before we begin," drawled Griswold, striving against the discord, "won't you play something for us, Dr. May? We have been hearing marvelous eulogiums of your skill with the keys."

"It is merely a race propensity," said Philip pleasantly, seating himself and running his fingers over the keyboard. "I have not touched the piano in months, so you will excuse my undisciplined fingers. I believe the last time I played was on the last night of January of this year." The piano was turned so that he faced them. His eyes, grown strangely brilliant, were raised to Otis standing pale and disturbed behind Stephen Forrest's chair. Otis knew the date as that of John Harleigh's death, but his senses had grown confused under the spirit of aloofness breathed by the magnetic figure at the piano, under the probing gaze compelling him like a confessional the while the harmonious fingers ran a haunting, incessant accompaniment of sombre, pursuing chords. Years before, in a German gallery he had met just such a gaze from a head of the Christ, and the resemblance before him now was a bewildering revelation. But his thronging thoughts were submerged in a sudden mad rush of melody, rhapsodic, barbaric, fierce, uncontrolled, yet melody throughout, which swept out to them.

"My Bedouin ancestry," smiled the player out of the storm beating, retreating, engulfing itself. But presently the tones mourned into quiet, crept out, climbed, soared like a soul out of materiality.

"A Mosaic flight," annotated the doctor's voice through the profound majesty. "Or, rather, Beethoven. But what odds? They're both god-heads."

And then, pursuing the same flight he merged into the Lohengrin prelude, the swelling spiritual strains increasing, diminishing, choiring toward—a brutal crash.[76]

"There's a Heine-esque finale for you," he laughed, as he rose in the throbbing silence. "I never hear that prelude without thinking of the story Catulle Mendes tells of the Jew who possessed an exquisite bust of Wagner, about the brows of which he had placed a laurel wreath, and about the throat—a cord.[77] But enough of revelation—let's get down to reality and bluff."

His face was deeply flushed as he crossed the room to the table. They felt his mastery of the moment, of themselves. But he was no longer master of himself—and he knew it: knew that the Jew, crushed to earth within him, had defied him throughout his playing, was defying his strong control now.

He seated himself and, with imperious assertiveness, picked up the cards. A cork popped, cards were dealt. The game proceeded. The players 'passed,' 'bet,' 'stood,' 'called,'—the terms ringing out with the chink of money, while from the beginning Philip May kept up a constant hum of song,—snatches of opera, popular airs, costermonger[78] and coon songs, never pausing, never allowing it to interfere with his own cool, fortunate play, but driving Stephen Forrest to the verge of frenzy.

"Quit that confounded singing," he ordered finally, quite beside himself as his vis-à-vis drew in the pool with careless ease.

Philip bent his head in profound acquiescence. The next minute he was whistling, softly, clearly, charmingly, as though it were impossible to be still. The excitement had brought out the bravado. It was a phase of reversion—the rich, strong emotiveness of primal nature showing through the veneer of culture. And in that moment when he stood alone, revealed, he seemed more the man, more the individual, than he had ever seemed before, and Otis almost feared him—his unknowableness. And all the while the winnings piled up about him, and he smiled between his whistling, and the hours flew, and Stephen Forrest's breathing grew quicker as he felt the man opposite him winning his slender means with the ease and indifference of an experienced gambler with whom the gods were in league.

"One," said Griswold, discarding.

"Pat," said Forrest.

"Pass," said Otis.

"Two," said Taylor.

"Three," announced Philip, the dealer.

The betting began with Griswold, rose with Forrest. Taylor dropped out. Philip raised Forrest two-fold. Griswold laid down his hand.

"I call you," said Stephen, hoarsely, throwing down his last gold piece, his face white and shaken as he leaned across the table.

"Think twice," admonished the winner pleasantly.

Stephen half rose from his chair, "I have called you," he said, incoherently, glaring at his opponent.

Philip took up his interrupted whistling, laid open his cards—the highest possible hand.

Forrest bent forward to look. An unutterable hate flared into the face he lifted to Philip's. "You dealt," he ground out—"you dealt—you damned whistling Jew—you've been—"

There was a flashing movement, a chair was overturned—the singularly well-shaped hand had gripped the slender throat.

But before the protest could be voiced as the others sprang to their feet, the hand relaxed. Forrest sank back livid and speechless.

"I beg your pardon," said Philip, standing pale and haughty before his host. "I am sorry to have spoiled your evening. You had better look to your friend."

He did not offer his hand. Another moment and the door clicked behind him.

CHAPTER VIII

Leaning upon silken pillows, his strong, silvered head and fine features in a glow of soft light, Daniel Willard led the yearly songs of praise and thanksgiving over the deliverance from bondage of the children of Israel. It was the sanctification feast of the Passover.[79] High above the joyous sonorousness of the men's voices, rose the sweet treble of the women. The wine gleamed ruby-red in crystal glasses and in the two ancient silver goblets, Willard heirlooms, always used upon this occasion, one by Daniel, one by his close, time-tested friend, Joseph May.[80] Upon the satin damask before the master of the festival, was placed the little cluster of mementoes indicative of the burdens and victories of the band of God's chosen: the unleavened bread, the bone of the paschal lamb, the bitter herb, the parsley and vinegar, the almonds—and—apples figuring as mortar.[81]

Usually, with good-natured placidity, Daniel hastened with the historic significances and observations, in order to hurry forward the dinner. But to-night Joseph, in his new velvet house-cap, in new, sternly serious exactitude, had allowed nothing to be omitted; every passage was given in its entirety.[82] And Daniel had submitted indulgently, striving to relieve the intoning with an occasional whimsical turn or trill, arresting any unseemly laughter by a quickly raised finger or eyebrow of admonition, and then continuing gravely on over his delightfully familiar way. But despite their earnestness, Elijah had not appeared with tidings of the long awaited Prince of Peace, and his filled glass and set chair, the door left invitingly open for his coming, had served only to elicit a gay cynicism from Paul Stein.[83]

But the prelude was all conscientiously chanted, the fragments of unleavened bread removed, and, dinner being served, their half-restrained holiday gayety bubbled forth with the sumptuous good cheer. Dinner over, the cloth was again cleared of all but the wine, glasses, and quaintly illustrated books, and then began the Hallel, the triumphant, soul-stirring hallelujahs.[84]

They waxed hilarious. Soft-voiced Laura Brookman, beautiful in shimmering gala attire, looked flushed and merry, sharing her book with Paul Stein, pretending to be shocked over his low-voiced, modern elucidation of the ancient Hebraic text. Brookman, comfortably doubled over his Hagaddah, sang out like a cantor, with all his lungs, and wondrous attempts at improvising. Daniel and Joseph accompanied softly, somewhat quaveringly, as though lost in old memories of home and kindred, breaking now and then into louder ecstasy when some particular refrain carried them from their feet with reminiscences of lost loves and voices. Jean, radiant in diaphanous white, sang along in smiling abstraction, one ear given to her surroundings, the other to the possible ringing of the door-bell. But eight o'clock came, and still Elijah delayed.

It was during the full flood of the paean on the Building of the Temple that the faint peal, almost lost in the mounting, lusty singing, was heard by the listening girl, and she arose starry-eyed.[85]

"The Prince at last?" asked Stein, while the others looked up questioningly.

"Throw wide the door, my dear," cried Daniel, with flushed cheeks, "and go forth to greet him."

Joseph shaded his face with a trembling hand while the girl hostess moved into the hall.

"I came to meet Elijah," she laughed, with winsome grace, making him a deep obeisance as they met within a foot of the dining-room.

"Did you expect him?" Philip asked, her words, herself, seeming but to bear out, to plunge him deeper into the vision of the power of the past which had opened out the night before to reabsorb him.

"We always expect him—traditionally—this night," she smiled. "It is the Sedar night." She pulled the portière aside, and the Past, in truth, engulfed him.

He had not expected it—the grim coincidence struck him as full of subjective, dramatic possibilities. He smiled, under his mustache, over the thought while he stood with his hand upon his father's shoulder and Daniel Willard presented him to the other guests.

He seemed to bring with him an air of philistinism, of worldly alienation, yet of polished criticism. The sweet comfort of the moment was lost. But he begged them to continue the singing.

"Don't let me feel that I have stopped the music," he said, seating himself beside Jean. "That chorus sounded particularly triumphant as the door was opened for me."

"Mr. Brookman will sing the last verse for us," said Daniel. "He is a whole choir in himself."

Brookman laughed. "All right. Laura, you hum along with me and divide my blushes."

While his voice rose and swelled in the grand old air, its virile resonance toned down, yet sustained, by Laura's liquid lilting, the wonder of it all flashed through Philip's disturbed being. He seemed to have stepped into some strange side-show out of the grand-court of life. Yet in how many homes throughout the universe was the ancient custom being celebrated that night! To endure after so many ages, nay, in spite of so many ages, of hate, oppression—progress! It was marvelous, well-nigh supernatural.

His practiced eye measured the mien and faces of those about him. Joseph May, squat, sturdy, stubborn, symboling an impregnable foundation, defying time through an immovable, inherited bigotry rather than through any studied conviction. Daniel Willard, dreamer, idealist, joying in his own interpretation of the spirit of the law, reading life and men through his own halo—a dreamer in Israel who dreamed he was awake! Charles Brookman, calm, happy in his materiality, product of "enforced specialization"[86] in his success, product of a sternly simple domestic morality in his negative goodness. Laura Brookman filling beautifully her costly frame, quick-witted, quick-cultured, consciously conventional, full of unsounded reserves. Paul Stein, deftly observant, keenly alert, strong-hearted, carrying no superfluous sentiment, frankly Semitic on his face value, heartily of his race through nature and love, intellectually above it in being able to judge it—without prejudice. Jean Willard,—but here his cool analysis paused before the dreamy power of a loveliness more of spiritual suggestiveness than of beauty of feature—for here, he thought, lay, perhaps, the answer to all the mystery, to all the poetry of passion and endurance of the race. A representative group whose blended characteristics would scarcely have produced that legendary composite—the "typical" Jew.

The song ended, Daniel cried "bravo!" and Jean clapped her hands. Her satiny white skin was stained now with a faint rosy underglow—she was happy—forgetful of all rumor, of all suspicion. Was he not there, beside her? The unconscious coquetry of joy helped unconscious nature. Conversation drifted easily into tête-à-têtes.[87]

Philip admired the wealth of eschscholtzias, the glorious golden California wild poppies, glowing upon the table and about the room, and Jean explained how she had kept them all day in a darkened room, only bringing them into the candle-light at the hour when she wished to awaken their satiny splendor.[88]

"Counterfeiting daylight for the beautiful stupids," she said. "The only fault they have is that they fall to pieces so quickly." The long golden petals already strewed the table-cloth.

"But nothing is permanent," he suggested lightly. "Nothing ever is—it is only a becoming."

"You mean evolutionally?"

"Anciently speaking—yes."

"Nothing is—it is only a becoming," she repeated musingly, fastening the poppy she had been toying with in her bosom. "Then there is hope for all of us. For of course that remark refers most of all to us poor dots of humanity."

"Oh, man—man is only a passing thought in the mind of the Creator," he teased, trying to forget himself in gauging her, and noticing how the poppy seemed to glow up into her eyes.

"What a skeptical thought! Besides it is blasphemous. According to that, how many more low thoughts He must have than great ones." They were laughing into each other's eyes. "And what a lot of vain sophistry and red-tape cant we Jews escape by making our God a glorious abstraction." She was speaking in the serious strain most natural to her.

"'We Jews!'" He drew a hard breath. "But what of Sinai?" he questioned.

"You are speaking anciently again."

"How?"

" 'Nothing is—it is only a becoming'—nothing more so than the Jew and Jewish commentary."[89]

"But—this." His eye swept the symbols of the festivity. If she was minded to teach, why not? Surely she had the most beautiful eyes in the world! And there was a certain cadence to her pretty young voice—

"Oh, this is a picture—" she was saying, "part of our ancestral gallery—which we unveil every year for the sake of auld lang syne.[90] If you could have heard our rabbi at the Congress of Religions you would understand what I mean—how we move—how singularly free, unhampered, broad, open to the light of every day, Jewish thought is.[91] Oh, I was so proud of him. He seemed to overtop them all. I wish I could tell you how—but I am so densely ignorant, I never get anything but the spirit out of things."

"May you not have judged through instinctive racial sympathy—prejudice?" he murmured, enjoying her swift enthusiasms, the music of her voice making dim the meaning of her words.

"Perhaps. But how else does one judge—honestly. One cannot detach oneself from oneself, can one?" She questioned him with her eyes, not waiting for his answer. "Wait a minute—I do remember something. Our other rabbi, our younger, beautiful-voiced one, said, at the time, that when we pray we do not pray to the divinity above us, but to the divinity within us.[92] Well?"

"Truly? And you pray so? And is it efficacious?"

"Thereby hangs a tale."

"Tellable?"

"Oh, yes; if I am willable."

"Well?"

"It's another proof of that 'becoming' theory of yours. When I was a little girl I used to say a Hebrew prayer of which I understood not one word—recited it like a poll-parrot. I could repeat it now word for word, straight from the beginning, if—"[93]

"How did it go?" He spoke impulsively, the color springing up his cheek.

"Oh such gibberish!" She ran through it laughingly.

He could have repeated in unison—they were linked by a 'coincidence of family tradition.'

"But I renounced that as soon as I was allowed the silence of prayer. I remember at that stage I was very confidential to my God, told him all my little vanities and ambitions, begged him to make me successful in my examinations, to make my teachers love me, to give me certain pretty frocks, and all the other desires of childhood. Then, as I grew older, and life grew shorter and more sacred, I ceased to itemize—I adopted a sort of cipher—a shorthand mode of communication. And then I discovered that my God was not listening to me—that I was blasphemous in thus addressing him—and so I ceased to pray."

A silence fell between them.

"And yet," she looked up with a flash of radiance, "the primitive notion is there just the same. Because in *very* happy moments I do pray—instinctively."

"What do you pray?" What a child she was, still full of the wonder of her own growth.

Her mouth dimpled merrily. "My uncle says it's the whole of religion in a nut-shell." [94]

"Well, teach me."

"Oh, no," she answered very quietly.

"Oh, but you must."

She raised her eyes to his insistent gaze. What! repeat to this self-constituted critic, this cold-eyed man of the world her fragmentary rhapsody of joy and gratitude for life, her childish "God bless everybody, and make me be a good little girl"! "Little" girl, forsooth!

Yet he could feel the family bent through her blushing reticence. She was a girlish Daniel Willard—and he told her so.

"Then diagnose Uncle Daniel—and I'll prescribe for myself."

He looked down at her, noticed inconsequently a tendril of dark hair caressing her tiny ear—struggled a moment against her physical charm—and submitted.

She was no longer Jean Willard, the Jewess. She was only a beautiful girl sitting close beside him, whom it lay within his possibilities to attract. He turned more directly to her. . . . There rushed over

Jean the full sway of a brilliant man throwing aside his accustomed reticences for her sake. The murmur of the other voices died out of her consciousness. Whether it was only the briefest span of time or a cycle in which they spoke together she could not have told. She only felt that she had traveled deep and far alone with him.

"Come," he said, half rising from his chair. "Where's your piano? I'll play you a strain—two strains—three—more eloquent of these different phases of the grand passion in different types of humanity than I could or would describe to you in words. The music to you—" He paused, resuming his seat as the maid presented a card to her mistress.

Jean's foot tapped the floor impatiently. "Oh dear," she murmured, with frank annoyance, and, with a fleeting pout lost in a smile, she murmured a word of excuse, and left the room.

Could Stephen Forrest have guessed she was on the point of relenting? Else how account for his assurance in again crossing her threshold, she wondered impatiently, hurrying through the hall. How could she get rid of him without hurting his dangerous sensitiveness, without letting him know that he was an intrusion upon a moment so superlatively happy she had wished it without end?

But her impatience fled at sight of his weary pallor. "Let us both sit down," she said in an impulse of compassion, all party spirit and inclination lost through the woman. "You look tired to death."

"I am," he said, following her example and sinking into a chair, surprise over her gentle acceptance of his being there giving his conscience a leap of shame. "And I can give no excuse for my daring—after our last meeting—except—"

"The picture?" She prompted kindly as he paused.

His little scheme of vengeance looked mean and petty beside her broad forbearance. He had never seen her as she seemed revealed to-night—his impressionable senses took in her full value for love and art.

"You are going out," he said with quickened breath, his eye sweeping over her unusual radiance.

"No. I am staying in." She spoke gently, but shortly.

"Then I am intruding—you expect others."

"Oh no. No one else is coming."

He chafed under her courteous curtness. He fully appreciated her spiritual absence, her reluctance to being there with him. He could feel her resolving his visit into a business interview, nothing more. And he could not, in all decency, force it into anything longer.

"And so," she added, breaking in upon his reflection, "what is that long thought?"

"Yes, I am going. No, don't trouble to speak the little social fib— you know I always understood what was passing behind your face. But as for our last set-to, I believe, yes, I feel sure you are going to relent."

"Perhaps. If you promise to be good." The playful words were charged with a warning meaning, which he grasped at once. Unfortunately, however, they only served to recall the real object of his being there.

"Good? Oh, I'll be good enough," he laughed with a contemptuous snort. "I'll paint a picture that will be a picture, never fear— but it will be you—only you—and I'll be romantic and call it—'the Jewess'—but remember, it will be only you. And then when it's quite finished, and I've put it away, out of the reach of memory, I'll paint its companion. Want to hear what that will be like?"

"I am listening to you."

"It won't be so much to your taste, because, I promise you, it will belong utterly to the realistic school—and you don't like naked truths, do you?"

"Not ugly ones. I mean I shouldn't choose them—for companions. And what will you call my 'companion'?"

" 'The Jew.' "

"Indeed. And you think you can find nothing but an ugly model?"

"Oh, he has stood for me already. But you mistake my meaning—he is most inconsistently good to look at in conventional attire. We were speaking about naked truths."

"And where did you discover this interesting sham?"

"In Dr. May."

"Yes?" The rising inflection was sweetly, stilly dangerous.

" 'Pon honor. He stood unconscious model for me last night. Oh, it was rich, rich!" He threw up his arms in an ecstasy of false delight, but hurried on, goaded by, trampling ruthlessly over, the protest in her proud face. "I'll paint him," he continued, leaning toward her in smiling, low-voiced confidence, "as he never chose to be painted before—full face, not profile—at the moment when his counterfeit bit of pasteboard was torn to shreds by a set of finical young Christians who politely shut their club-door in his face. I could throw a good deal of quiet drama into that. I think you would prefer it to the more sensational pose of clutching the throat of the man who dared to call him Jew?"

His still smiling face was ghastly, his nostrils quivering; he scarcely saw the features of the girl before him. "He has a hand of steel, that mutual friend of ours. Look!" He threw back his head disclosing to her battling senses the still plainly discernible red marks upon his delicate throat. "Philip May—his mark—at your service," he presented with mock courtesy. "What spicy reading the press could make of it if placed at their clever interpretation."

An icy hand pressed upon her heart; she strove vainly to answer his waiting pause.

"Pshaw!" he laughed roughly, "you're deathly pale. Don't take it so seriously. Let me assure you it will have a tame enough ending. I should only need to offer him this alternative—publicity, or apology before witnesses—and flop! the Jew would be in character—upon his knees."

She sprang to her feet, a flood of released blood rushing madly from her throat to her brow. "You lie!" she flamed, in imperious suffocation. "You lie Stephen Forrest!"

He laughed somewhat dazedly at the passion he had evoked.

"Why," she repeated more slowly, measuring his ironic insolence, "I'll prove that you lie."

Acting impetuously upon the impetuous thought, she was out of the room before either of them could take count.

Somewhat surprised over her low-voiced summons, Dr. May followed her through the hall. She did not turn to him until they were both well in the room, and Stephen Forrest, hiding his astonishment over her summary retort under a gracious suavity, stood up. He looked deferentially toward her while she spoke.

"You must pardon my calling you so impulsively, Dr. May," she laughed, still tremulously, "but I have challenged Mr. Forrest to prove his boast that you would sooner go on your knees to him than see your name—attached to some vile story of his concoction—in print. Will you second me?"

He smiled reassuringly into her beautiful eyes, turning from her to Forrest and looking him over as a mastiff might a terrier. "Is that your proposition?" he asked quietly, with a raised eyebrow.

A light, the quick light of jealous insight, flashed in upon the artist's confused consciousness: her intensified loveliness, her dress, her unexpected gentleness toward him, her passionate umbrage, Philip May's presence. "Decidedly you have me at a disadvantage," he said softly, turning to the girl, a mad pain at his heart. "Surely you must know I never should have expressed myself as I have, had I known that the love you felt for Dr. May, so naïvely, yet plainly expressed to me not long ago, had this consummation in view—had come to this. Was it quite fair to me?" He held out a hand of truce.

She looked down at it, white, impassive. Something indescribable in her face smote into his pity. "Ah well, I've made a mess of it, as usual," he confessed sharply, "and the only way out of it is through the door. Good-night." He brushed past Philip as he limped his way out.

Philip turned hurriedly to Jean. "I'm sorry you have been drawn into this unpleasant affair," he said in a matter-of-fact, impersonal manner, a scowling light in his eyes, "and sorry my pleasant evening has been spoiled. Mr. Forrest and I will settle this little discussion outside. Excuse me to Mr. Willard, will you?" He took her hand gently, pressed it strongly, scarcely glanced at her, and caught the front door just as it was closing behind Stephen Forrest.

CHAPTER IX

Several of the personages concerned in the incidents herein detailed, enjoyed their next morning's breakfast with a peculiar relish.

Among them, Paul Stein, seated in the restaurant he usually frequented, after opening his crackling newspaper and glancing over the foreign dispatches, turned idly to the local news. In a moment the gleam of interest in his eyes burst into amazement, radiated into keen amusement. He folded the paper comfortably to the desired columns, propped it up against the cream pitcher and prepared to enjoy his berries and his news, his whole head snapping with absorbed pleasure while his eyes ran down the lines.

"Well done, by George!" was his continuous commentary as he proceeded. "Wonder who wrote it up. Smacks of high comedy. Good subject—confoundedly, disgustingly good."

The waiter came with his coffee. He carelessly turned the page to the stock and bond reports. He drank his coffee without reading. "How did it get out?" he queried. "Bell-boy called in the row, no doubt—a hundred outlets in a hotel like that. Found by someone who knew its literary value. What an ass it makes of him. Pity. In spite of rumor he seemed every inch a man. Nothing of the Malvolio in his outside make-up.[95] Dear me, what a pity! A derisive thing like that fixes his reputation. Can't live it down or fame it down. If his father sees it, he will eat his heart out. And the Chevalier. And Jean—wonder what she'll have to say now. Well," he travestied, "you can't fool all the people all the time. Poor little Jean with her heights!" He rose with a love-laugh in his eyes.

His was a solitary breakfast—a silent commentary. Elsewhere tongues, and eyes, and thoughts were busy tearing the man and his motives to shreds. Much talk, many sneers, some indignation of two sorts, and over all the ready laugh, followed the reading of the clever skit.

Jean had untwisted the tightly spiraled newspaper and placed it beside her uncle's plate. Generally, he supplied her with occasional tid-bits from his perusal, often passing her the paper when he had read through an item of unusual interest. It was the first morning of the Passover—both leavened and unleavened bread were upon the table.[96] Daniel, who was very fond of the whitey-brown crisps had been forbidden them by his physician, but he always buttered and ate a mouthful as if in excuse for his untimely toast.

He failed to notice that Jean, despite her cheery demeanor, was eating as though under compulsion. Presently she saw him hurriedly put down his cup and half turn from her, his absorbed gaze traveling over the printed page held close in his trembling grasp. His color mounted steadily, hotly, to his temples.

"What is it?"

She stood behind his chair, leaning over his shoulder, her hand upon his to steady the fluttering paper. There was a moment's breathless, absorbed silence.

"An abominable lie, my dear," pronounced Daniel finally, his voice crushing huskily over the words. "Abominable. Some rival's cowardly thrust."

The girl still leaned over his shoulder. Irritated by her silence, he turned his face so suddenly that it struck against her cheek. He was startled by the icy touch.

"I am just finishing," she explained, taking the paper, and drawing from him so as to effectually conceal her countenance.

"You will have already discovered the falsity of it," he laughed angrily.

Jean laid the paper beside him upon the table. A chill smile touched her lips. "The writer is witty," she remarked lightly. "What diverting copy the story makes." She laughed curiously. "It really makes a very funny story."

"The story! But there is no story. What are you talking about?"

She laughed softly, indulgently, in bitter knowledge.

Daniel's face turned fiery. "You must be prejudiced, my dear," he said slowly, putting the brake upon his anger, "to believe so readily in the vile cowardice and buffoonery of an apparent gentleman—and my friend."

She looked straight, and pale, and unswervingly into his eyes. Daniel shook off his glasses. "You can believe it then," he exclaimed, catching them as they fell dangling.

Her close-pressed lips refused to answer. Her uncle arose from the table. They were as near a quarrel as circumstances had ever drawn them.

"I am going to the Temple this morning," he said distantly, comparing his watch with the clock.

"It is too early yet, isn't it?" remarked Jean. She had turned from him to throw open the window.

"I will go over to Joseph—now—before he has a chance to read that—calumny." He had not yet driven the emotion from his voice.

Jean's heart gave a leap at the name. "Poor Uncle Joseph!" she murmured musingly, and then she started to feel her uncle's heavy hand upon her shoulder.

"As long as you live with me, my dear," he said quietly, "never look or speak distrust in my presence of Philip May. Do you understand?"

Her eyes were suddenly blinded with tears. "Yes," she whispered indistinctly, turning her head from him.

And meanwhile, over next door, Joseph May had been enjoying his Passover breakfast. Into a bowl-like cup he had broken a quantity of the *matzos* and poured over all the rich, creamy coffee.[97] As the aroma of the delicious beverage steamed up and about him, he lost himself in its delectable consumption. Only when half finished could he sufficiently withdraw himself from his thraldom to unfold the messenger of malice which lay so innocently beside his plate.

In a flash the world was lost to him, the devil had him in his clutch. But not wholly. He had had his experience and, with a stealthy glance around, as though innumerable eyes were upon him, he crept to the sideboard and poured three careful drops from the tiny vial down his throat. He stood a moment while the drug, taking effect, deadened limbs and faculties. Then he crept back to his place at the table, pushed aside his half-finished cup, picked up his half-finished newspaper article. He sat with furrowed, leathery skin and glazed eyes, reading in the ridicule. The clock ticked audibly from the mantelpiece.

A springing footfall was heard upon the porch outside. An intimate hand was on the door. There was a sharp, swift rustling as of paper being fiercely crushed.

"Come in," cried Joseph May.

When Daniel entered there was no sign of newspaper or disturbance. The former lay close-hidden against the drugged breast.

"Good *yuntoff*,"[98] said Daniel cheerily, searching the whole room with a glance.

"Good *yuntoff*," returned Joseph, putting down his lifted cup. "What news this morning?"

"Have you not read the news as usual?"

"No. My paper was stole this morning. You can tell me all what you know while we go."

Out of the Ghetto, out of the bitter oppression and its consequent suppression, came to the children of the Book a peculiar power—the baffling, triumphant power of Silence at need.

But long before and after his father sat in the synagogue striving to straighten the snarl out of his soul, Dr. May was busy bandaging broken bones that three or four men might walk straight. The day proved a very busy one for him. Before dawn he had been called in consultation over the broken ribs and limbs of a woman inmate of a sanitarium, who had discovered that happiness was to be found only "in the long run," and had tried to compass the stretch—through the window—only to make a failure of death as she had of life,—and the hours following his grim task with her afforded him little leisure.

It was a very jaded memory which recalled the events of the two preceding nights while he stood waiting to be shaved by his barber before going home to dine. He remembered them then, out of the press of the day's work, more in connection with the fact that he felt small inclination to keep his promise to take Lilian Otis to the private view of some late acquisition at the Hopkins Art Institute.[99] He had, it is true, noticed an insubordinate demeanor among his students during the clinic of the afternoon, but, in his innocence, had referred it to the tense state of his own nerves, and let it pass without rebuke.

It was only now, at this last hour of daylight, while he stood indifferently scanning the morning's paper, that the truth laughed in upon him through a staring, jocose headline.

He read it to the end. The article, for all its kindly humor, was degrading from first to last word. To be held up to the ridicule of the public gaze as if in the very act of crawling into a place placarded with "No admittance" for such as he, was an indignity utterly confounding to his proud reserve. Moreover he was dumfounded. When he left Stephen Forrest the night before, he had felt assured that his insolent threat had been but an ill-humored jest without intention. The last glimpse of Jean Willard's face had brought the inflamed artist to a brutal straightforwardness which left no room for doubt.

"Enough has been said," he had flung in response to the physician's command to halt. "A scene is a bore, but a rehashing of it in any form is abhorrent. A dash of a saving sense of humor would have saved all of us from an awkward leave-taking—and I think we both understand that the case is closed, Dr. May. Good night."

Philip's dogged sense of justice acquitted Forrest fully and freely of any complicity in this literary thrust, while quickly snatching at the possibility that it had leaked out through one of the countless, uncounted exits for such an occurrence in such a place.

His father found him curiously silent. He found his father curiously loquacious. After two minutes together each had fathomed the other without an explanatory word, and Philip, looking into the flushed, excited old face, locked his conscience into deeper dungeons.

"You had better go to bed early," he brought himself to say as he rose from the table. "You seem nervous. I'm sorry I have an engagement."

But once upon the street on the way to the Otis mansion, calm in his worldly, non-committalism, he was conscious of a peculiar duality of personality—as though he, Philip May, were criticising the manner in which Philip May was about to play his rôle under Miss Otis's enlightened eyes. They had been very flattering eyes, very gentle and womanly when looking into his but two days back—they had half-revealed, half-withheld a story, the reading of which Philip May had been idly postponing, but which he promised himself he would glance into to-night, though he suddenly realized, with a sense of surprise, that he was more curious than concerned.

He was admitted directly into her presence. He was not quite clear as to what he had expected in regard to her attire, but there was something about hers as she came toward him which caught his attention.

"Are you quite well?" he asked, taking the tips of her fingers in his hand.

"Dear me—why so professional?" she smiled from the edge of her lips, the baffling brilliancy of her eyes clouding for an instant as she looked up into his strong, quiet face. She was affecting an unfamiliar little drawl which brought an amused gleam to his eyes. "Or is it merely courtesy. Because I'm not very well to-night. You see I am dressed to stay at home. It was too late to send you word when I felt the headache coming on."

She had used this device before to keep him alone with her. But to-night neither her attitude nor her eyes asked him to stay. She stood, apparently careless of covering over the awkwardness of her cold, waiting laugh which his keen ear interpreted as a polite dismissal.

He smiled in disconcerting comprehension.

"Then I shall have to go down alone," he said. "Don't let me keep you any longer than necessary. I am sorry."

"Yes, it is too bad."

"Good night."

"Good night."

Well! That was neatly dispatched. He drew a breath of admiration when he stood again without in the night, and almost laughed aloud.

Unmistakably well done—clearly, concisely, and without ado.

But upon what verdict had the order for his social quarantining been issued? Jew—or hypocrite?

Hypocrite? How? In presenting his credentials of simple manhood without an irrelevant pedigree, without the "And Abraham begat Isaac—and Isaac begat Jacob"—etc., etc.

—And Joseph begat Philip.

Now Philip was a Jew—?

Jew? How?

Christ-killer.

The child's incomprehensibility was at last answered in the mocking irony of the man.

Yet deep within, beneath his bitterly flippant scoring, he could feel the clamor and tumult in his breast apprising him that not only had he a rôle to play, but a life to live. And the possibility of an unsought isolation laughed grimly and sickeningly before him. He was too young, too healthy, too full of unproven powers, too much in love with his fellows and their approbation, to view the prospect with equanimity. Lilian Otis, he knew, was nothing more to him than a pleasant part of his social plan, but for several interminable moments his soul felt homeless and seedy—a veritable tramp of a soul that longed to vanish for a space out of the eye of a former high estate.

Yet he reached his own door hating the thought that, for a second, it should appear to him as a refuge. What had happened to him? Bah! he was still Philip May—the man. He felt the quiet smile of conscious power upon his lips. The incident—folly, perhaps—was closed. Life, strong, earnest, lay all before him. He walked quietly upstairs, abstractedly conscious of his father's voice escaping through the closed door of the sitting-room, and made his way toward his own apartments at the back of the house.

His study was cloaked in darkness, its windows thrown wide to the night. As he entered the room, he stopped short just over the threshold.

At the farther window of the other house, just facing his, sat Jean Willard, her face peculiarly softened by the night, by a strange pale sadness shadowing it.

His pulses gave a happy bound toward her. The wild, surmising words of the painter swept blindly through his memory—as though, in one flash, God had said, "Let there be light," and there was— Jean. And in one flash, here, beyond the dazzling vanity of his social pretensions, in this back-window of his life, he saw that she was perfect for love. Saw himself closer to her than the arm's breadth dividing her window from his. What if—. He was facing her.

She neither saw nor heard him; she sat looking away, her elbows on the sill, her chin resting on her clasped hands.

He leaned against the casement, bent nearer to her, and whispered through the night:

"Jean—sweet!" His voice reached her in a music of overpowering yearning.

She started violently, sprang to her feet, her low rocking-chair swinging wildly back into the shadowy room.

She stood upright and stiff before him, yet with every nerve a-quiver. There would be no feigning here, no lip-service to the conventions from this daughter of an intense, a tragic people. And he understood her with that same dim sense of kinship which had assailed him before—kinship with a nature in its depths direct and stern and serious.

"No," he said swiftly, "do not misjudge me. If the light of the words spoken last night has—"

But he had not gauged her wholly. He realized it as her white, fierce face struck through the night, silencing him.

"You would not dare," she breathed, all her passionate soul flaming to her eyes, her romantic little head thrown back intolerantly, "you would not dare to imagine you *owe* me something on the score of that outrage. I credited you at least with the surface delicacy of a gentleman. But—but since you have gone so far, I will not evade its unspeakableness. I want you to understand just what that man meant, lest you gull yourself with another supreme pretension"— she rushed on heedlessly, her words tumbling pell-mell upon each other—"under the fallacy of a distorted report. Don't misunderstand me—I am neither ashamed nor afraid of the truth—for there was some truth in that man's charge, but not as your egotism must interpret it. Let me make clear to you the bond between your house and mine. You—you know what those two old men down there are to each other—you know the God they worship and which you ignore—but possibly you do not know the household god of clay they had set up for themselves through all the years of your strange, unnatural absence—you do not know that they had made your name the watchword and hope and pride of their wistful lives—you did not know with what fanatic joy they had waited for your return. And I am linked to them, I followed their lead, I accepted their fetiches—I bowed to their idea of you, and it was this *idea* of a man captaining his own life through his own honest, splendid powers that I loved—not you—never you—and even you, in the slight knowledge you have of me, must know that for you, Philip May in the flesh, you whose loyalty to a dying friend I sentimentally weighed in your favor against the needs of an old father, for you who dare to despise your people of whom you know nothing whatsoever, for you, Philip May, coward, egoist, and snob, I have nothing but utter detestation and contempt."

She paused, trembling, ashen to the lips, over-mastered by the storm of her contention, overleaping all bounds in her desperate self-defense. She met his gaze intolerantly.

He was studying her quietly. How her little rushlight knowledge, her drawing-room ethics, her pulpit-broad judgments, glowed through and transfigured her! But her passion had stirred something elemental, overwhelming him as the other girl's controlled evasion never could have done. She stood before him, lovely and forbidding—at once his conscience and despair.

"You are mistaken in my motive," he answered, gently. "But at any rate, in your grand sum total of me, we are, for this moment, quite at one."

She turned from him into the dark.

And downstairs, as though above the cackle of the disinterested, Joseph May was holding forth, against all the world. "I tell you, Daniel," he cried, pounding the table in his emphasis, "all the doctors in the city is talking about him. You know what Thallman says to me yesterday? 'Mr. May,' he says, 'we'll all be breaking our necks just to see Dr. May get in some of his clever work.' And, by Gott! he meant it. He's young, but he's on the top already. Say, Daniel, what did I always tell you? a prince, a *vahre* prince!"[100] He swaggered, he strutted, with expanded chest and dangerously flushed cheeks. The cards lay in disorder upon the table. The old man measured the floor with restless feet, talking Daniel down and out of all confidence. There was no shame to be found here, no knuckling down under the world's coarse thumb. He had played his part of know-nothing throughout the day even to the deceiving of his friend, but at the last hour he was overdoing it, and Daniel saw through the fierce pride of it. He longed to tell him to hush, he had tried to leave him, hoping the excited heart might find rest in sleep, but Joseph's insistence forbade it, Joseph's bravado demanded he sit there silent, and blind, and deaf to the truth.

"Do you know, Joseph," he ventured, finally, "I feel a little tired? And you, don't you think it time for two little children like you and me to be in bed? Me, I am a little tired."

"So? I never felt younger in all my life. But then, you see, my son he is my tonic." He laughed boisterously.

"It may be. I hope so. I was glad he came in, even for a little while, last night."

"And why he shouldn't come in? You make me sick sometimes, Daniel, when you speak about nothing like if it was something wonderful." He glared a moment, then laughed weakly. "Well, my boy, when you are sleepy you can go home. For me, I think I will wait a little for Philip."

"Well, good night, Joseph. Sleep well."

"Good night, Daniel. To-morrow afternoon I think I'll go me a little to the club. I don't know when I had a game at the club. You can tell Jean—when there is something good at the the-ay-ter this week—she can get seats for you and me. I don't know when I was to the the-ay-ter."

CHAPTER X

Philip May stepped out of his peculiar social fiasco into the work of the next day. Released from his vain, guarded intimacy with the Otises, unfettered by any other distracting personal ties, he was free to apply all his thought and strength to the chosen field in which he felt himself master. And making his rounds from patient to patient, from hospital to office, often passing half the night in the operating-room, there was little left to recall him to the memory or regret of a trivial social defeat, save the figure of a girl passing him with averted gaze, and the furrow-browed old man who had drawn so close to him in his social seclusion that his bearing might have been called tenderness in a more demonstrative nature. His total aloofness from club and drawing-room life soon carried the story of his derided self-valuation beyond the gabble and concern of current gossip.

Even Jean Willard, after her first fierce sobbing regret had spent itself, striving to shrug down the painful memory of her impetuous part in it, asked herself wearily what it would matter—to anyone—a hundred years hence! Not much, truly. Infinity is wide and the gods do exquisitely fine work. But to Jean—then—much. It is never a question of a hundred years, or months, or weeks, or days hence— it is always a question of now, of to-day, with its storm and stress, its laughter and tears, its mistakes and achievements, its hopes and despairs. That alone concerns us. We cannot shift our burdens and responsibilities with a shrug. To earnest minds like Jean Willard's, there is no such thing as resignation or indifference. Humanity climbs upward with a groan, and the history of individuals, as of nations, is the record of a few passionate moments of striving—of love or hate, of defeat or victory.

Who, questioned Jean, in her self-scourging, had constituted her his judge? Who was she that she had dared to hold the mirror to his face? In her bitter self-prosecution she forgot her instigating excuses; in trying to be just, she beat herself into seeing through his eyes. But quite oblivious to her mental captivity or the loss of her old independence of opinion, she began to think, to speak, through Philip May's intuitively surmised tastes and distastes. Her friends found her changed, intolerant, hypercritical. She thought she was piercing through the familiar face of things down to their truth in relation to the whole world—and growing sadder in her knowledge. The dream being knocked from under her, the plunge into reality left her in that state of despairing pessimism common to all young people until they get their bearings, when they find that *another* view is never the whole view.

Everything and everybody within her range of observation, from the idiosyncrasies of her nearest to those of the scarcely noticeable Jewish passer-by, revealed another justifiable peg to hand Philip's social apostasy upon. Nothing was too sacred or too low to escape her half-frightened scrutiny—and presently she found herself contorted into Philip May's ally, a spy to all her own and her friends' movements and motives. Formerly, she told herself cynically, she saw as through a glass—rosily; now, face to face. And she called it Revelation. But there was one phase of her stand which she fully appreciated. Where Philip May had found his excuse for withdrawal, she had found only another claim upon her loyalty. Philip May had taken a snap-shot at the unattractive face turned up to him, and looked away from it with frank and frigid disfavor. But the snap-shot being passed on to Jean, though she recognized the lineaments, she stood immovable beside it, passing over it her tender, protecting hand.

"I hate him," she told herself when in this attitude of defiance.

But closer, more poignant than these impersonal inconsistencies battling within her, was the memory of his voice whispering to her across the night. It hushed all her old high voices, it crushed through the idealist to her imperfect humanity, it drew her as the pole the star, it made all else as the writing in the sand, and she followed, followed—till, setting her teeth in imagination, she saw the possible chivalrous motive behind his act, and turned intolerantly from its insufferable suggestion.

Moreover, her most strenuous effort to dismiss him from thought was wasted through the nature of their propinquity. If, in passing from his sight that night, she had put him out of her life, she might have laid the ghost of the memory. This, however, was denied her. Day after day they met on the doorstep as both were coming in or going out, day after day their eyes might have met as he stepped from his carriage and she came out of her front door. But, as if by mutual consent, they avoided the visual encounter, though Jean knew distinctly enough that his eyes had held her. And there was a charm of misery about these avoided encounters, which she, in another inconsistency, realized with relentless self-contempt. Though she gave herself up to the gospel of constant occupation, she could not separate herself from warring thought of him. The very walls of the house next door held a sinister attraction for her, as though his association with them had imbued them with something of his personality.

But the interior of the walls knew her no more—she had effectually barred herself out of them. The two old men, her friends, were cognizant of this, each in his own degree. Her uncle viewed her changed attitude with stern sadness, but in Joseph May's silent heart a bitter animosity had arisen against the girl. *He* knew the kernel of justice within that garbled newspaper jeer, but how could she have known? And since this alone, this shadow of an alien hand, had been enough for her to condemn—then enough of her! He held her at arm's length now, the girl who had been the darling of those long since forsaken hopes. In the beginning Jean had striven to bridge over the hiatus in her attentions by an added warmth of tenderness when they met, but, with a curious dignity of reticence, Joseph May chilled her into a stranger. He stood so close to his son in his part-deliberate, part-inevitable retirement, that a contemptuous thought in the latter's direction included the old man in its sting. He declined to accompany them on their summer trip through the beautiful southern part of the State, although Daniel reminded him that he was breaking a promise.

"What I shall do there?" he asked, with a shrug. "I did enough traveling when I had to, with my pack on—." The father of his son interrupted the reminiscence.

Upon the return of the Willards, the former relations between the two old friends were resumed, and almost nightly they might have been seen taking their stroll in the lingering light of the lovely summer evenings, sometimes accompanied by the slender girl, who often willfully shut her eyes to Joseph's uncompromising distance of manner, conducting herself as though nothing had ever come between them. Thus a woman loiters on between the seen and the unseen, though only the seen, unbroken line is called her life.

That the flashing confusion of that Passover evening had left an ineffaceable impression in another conscience, Jean discovered one golden morning in early September while out shopping with Laura Brookman. They had about completed some order at Vickery's when the salesman, knowing their artistic proclivities, asked them to step for a minute into the little picture-gallery at the back of the shop.

"Mr. Stephen Forrest has a few canvases on exhibition, and I think his work will interest you," he said. "He is going abroad next week, and it's a pleasure to see him at last getting the appreciation he deserves. Most of the pictures have been sold." He ushered them into the soft glow of light, and left them.

There were not many, and all were studies of heads, but the peculiar power of character-insight displayed was smiting. Jean, lost in unbiased admiration before a subtle Chinese face, was abruptly dragged from her place by a compelling hand upon her arm.

"Come over here," murmured Mrs. Brookman, excitedly, leading her before a tiny painting almost lost among the others. "When did you sit—or stand—for this? What does that expression mean?"

Jean stood before the proud, sad protest of her own face as Stephen Forrest's inward light had seen fit to transfer her.

"What are you defying—what is it called? I must have that," Laura declared, enthusiastically. "It is you in one of your most charming, unapproachable phases. I wonder if it is sold."

"The picture is not for sale," said a sudden cool, low voice behind them. Jean, recognizing it at once, did not turn, but Laura veered eagerly upon the delicate-visaged artist standing near.

"Are you sure?" she asked, doubtingly.

"Quite. It is mine."

"Do you—then you can tell me what it is called?"

" 'The Jewess.' "

"Oh!" Laura's eyes scanned it again with lightening vision. "And the attitude—I was wondering what she was defying."

"Prejudice."

"Ah!" Laura raised her lorgnon again.

Jean turned swiftly about. "I congratulate you," she said, abruptly.

The blood surged to his brow. "For this?" he pleaded, indistinctly, designating the picture before them.

"I thank you for that. I congratulate you on the others. I wish you all success. Are you coming, Laura?"

Mrs. Brookman followed her into the street.

"Was that Stephen Forrest?" she asked, curiously, as they turned westward.

"Yes."

"When did you pose for him—whose idea was it? Tell me about it."

"There's nothing to tell. It was done from memory."

"How curt you are! What is the matter with you?"

"Nothing—only I'm dead tired."

"Jean—I mean, perhaps we had better take the car."

"No. You said you wanted to walk—to keep your figure within decent dimensions." Her eyes traveled over her friend's well-corseted form. "How stiffly you lace yourself in," she observed, absently, as they walked on at a rapid pace.

"I haven't your willowy ease, dear, I know, and I have to keep my weight and my hips down—or your eyes will be calling me 'Jewess,' from another light."

Jean laughed shortly.

Laura stole a swift glance at her.

"What is the matter with you, Jean?" she begged, finally. "You have grown so moody of late I scarcely recognize you."

Jean forgot to answer.

"Dear, I want to ask you something," Mrs. Brookman began presently, a ring of stubborn purpose in her voice.

"Ask away, Laura."

"You met a man at my house one night—"

"And that's all."

"No, it isn't. And now that I've begun, you're not going to silence me with your 'that's all'—it is difficult enough broaching a subject of this kind with you. What are you going to do with Theodore

Hart? Oh, wouldn't I like to shake you with that indifferent look on your face!"

"How can you feel so violent and talk so much—on such a warm day?"

"Very well. If you can no longer be direct with me—"

"I told you—I met a man at your house, and that's all."

"Not according to his view. What do you object to in him?"

"Him."

"What can you see against him?"

"His face."

"Oh, I know he's not Apollo, but you have managed to care for some homelier people in your life—Paul Stein, for instance."

"Paul is beautiful—to me. Don't put his face in the same category with Theodore Hart's."

"What is so repugnant to you in Theodore Hart's face?"

"The past."

"Bosh! Every man has a past or two. Were you raised in a nunnery?"

"No. A man—my uncle, you know, raised me."

"Too high, sweet, for comfort. And you know the best posterity is being made now from the power of riches. That is where the philosophy—the religion of mammonism comes in."[101]

"Do you think so?"

"Great God, there you persist—"

"Don't be so exaggerated in your exclamations; it's blasphemous to begin with, and dreadfully Jewish to end with."

Mrs. Brookman regarded the girl with a smile of curiosity. "Do you know you have said such things to me very often lately? What is it? Another effect of Philip May's ridiculous act of disdain?"

Silence gathered around Jean's heart and lips.

"You look exactly like that picture now. But to come back to our discussion. Leaving out what you choose to call his past, will you admit his desirability from every other point of view?"

"According to society's valuation—yes."

"Don't forget that his connections are irreproachable, and in the matter of connections, esthetically speaking, a Jew or Jewess generally takes risks when she marries. And do you know the power of great wealth?"

"I have never tested it—I can imagine it, however. I admit it is a very tempting vision."

"At last we come to the point. And you know it is yours—for a word."

Jean slowly turned her eyes upon her friend. There was something so quietly hopeless in her gaze that the older woman felt the dew spring to her brow. "So you too are an advocate of these legalized prostitutions," the girl said, wearily.

Mrs. Brookman's burning cheek turned quietly gray. "How naïve," she returned, with a forced laugh. "At that rate, half the young women of your acquaintance are—that's a hateful word, Jean."

"More hateful than the thing itself? Do let us call things by their right names, Laura. Oh, don't imagine I condemn them in the gross. Some of them walk into it innocently enough—they know nothing different or better, poor, dear, little, happy things. It is only those who do know about whom I feel rather contemptuous."

"Still hitching your wagon to a higher star!"

"I was born that way—brought up that way," resisted Jean, passionlessly. "The copy-books used to say it was a good way."

"Oh, the copy-books. But aren't you afraid you may finally choose a falling star—and have a tumble—and get hurt?"

"Yes," answered Jean, her lips closing like a seal over the word.

"It is better to choose a post—it is safer."

"No," answered Jean, quietly.

The spot of color burned up again in Mrs. Brookman's cheek. "You put yourself above the plane of life," she said, harshly. "You will come down—some day."

"I hope not."

"Oh, you hope not. Do you know what hope is?"

"I forget—it used to be in those stupid copy-books. It's out of print now."

"Heavens—pardon, that's Jewish—but what a thing to say!"

"Well, what is hope?"

"Hope, Jean, is only winged, or, rather, blind desire. It has neither feet nor eyes. Use a more tangible argument."

"Well, then, I *will* not. Is that enough?" Her quick, hot temper blazed momentarily in a flash of her eyes.

"Many fools have said that," persisted Laura Brookman.

"Then I am one of many. Let me alone."

"But they all came down—by and by," the ironical voice pursued. "They started out glorious and free—as you—those fool girls. They said—as you are saying to yourself—somewhere in the world I shall meet some one who shall be all in all to me, who shall king it over me as I shall queen it over him—and all that romantic stuff—whose thoughts and hopes and aspirations and loves and desires shall be like unto mine as flowers sprung from the same seed are like unto each other—and we shall be one, as the Lord God is one, comprising all things. They went as far as to think the thing sacred—poor imbeciles. And some of them never met the other, and some of them found it all a delusion, and some of them found—just life."

"And then?" Something clutched Jean by the throat as she listened—something passionately personal, unspoken, beneath the dreary generality of the spoken.

"And then they took the next best that came along—some soon, some later, some fighting it out to the vain end, but they all gave in finally. And some of them found it was best, not second best, but best."

"Why?"

"Because there are other sides to a woman's soul which need fulfilling—and fate proved kinder to them than it once seemed it ever meant to be. It's not all a giving and having, this bundle of emotions called womanhood—it's a being, too, and every woman is potentially other things besides a lover—a mother, for instance. And the sentimental regret is forgotten when she presses her cheek to her child's, and she finds she has nothing to regret when she has provided her child with the wherewithal for all the complex needs of life, including a good father, who is also a good and loving husband, for whom, through a wise provision in the virtuous feminine make-up, she feels nothing but tenderness and loyalty. And then she understands that perhaps her dream went wrong for the sake of a wider plan." Gradually the intense vibration in the voice had subsided till the sound was like a peaceful, monotonous lilt. She was gazing impassively ahead.

Suddenly she felt the girl's distended eyes upon her. "For heaven's sake, Jean," she laughed, "don't stare at me with that tragic face. Has the bottom fallen out of your sky? I was just talking highfalutin' for the occasion—letting you know that there is generally some nameless first affair lying among the *hic jacets*[102] of most hearts, so as to give you the courage of a sense of companionship—just giving you a little impromptu on the eternal theme—love with variations." She laughed merrily. "Are you ready for the wedding to-morrow? My gown is a dream. I may send the carriage around for you first so as to give my lazy man a few minutes' grace. What will you wear? Which hat did you choose?"

"My tan cloth. I took the black velvet hat with the plumes. Who will be there worth dressing for—Paul?"

"Paul? I suppose so—he and Dr. Thallman have grown quite intimate. I suppose some of the doctor's confreres will be there, but I'm sorry, for your sake, that Theodore Hart is not acquainted." She laughed a teasing laugh.

Jean carried an aching sense of its artificiality into the house with her. She carried it with her the next day to Dr. Thallman's wedding, where they found Paul Stein waiting for them at the foot of the stairs before entering the already crowded, rose-breathing drawing-room. She found herself twisting the memory of his and Laura's old college friendship and his long grind against poverty into the golden glamour which Charles Brookman had so successfully flung around her. The materiality of it all sickened Jean, even while she listened to the simple, earnest service which "maketh the bridegroom to rejoice with the bride."[103] She scarcely noticed when the ring was placed, the beautiful blessing spoken, the binding kiss given.

She was brought to earth by a sudden buzz of joyousness and the merry pressing forward to congratulate the smiling pair under the canopy of roses.

"Oh, Mrs. Weiss," she laughed, stepping back. "I almost threw you. Won't you stand in my place? I am going to wait with the less intimate. How well you are looking." She slipped aside to let the pudgy old lady wedge herself in.

Mrs. Weiss grasped her arm. "You like my bonnet?" confided the fat, coaxing voice, while the fat, comfortable hands folded themselves in white-gloved comfort over the fat, comfortable stomach. "You see, I got no daughter to tell me, and my Sam—what he knows about bonnets? He says, 'Ma, you're a peach,' and he kisses me, and that settles it. I only bought it yesterday—on aggravation. I told my milliner to put regrets in it, but she used her own conveyance and put a feather in instead. And you really think I look nice in it so, Miss Willard?"

A girl behind Jean giggled and the latter had some ado to keep her own lips in order. "It is truly a very pretty bonnet," Jean pleasantly assured her.

"And you got good taste, too," nodded Mrs. Weiss, approvingly, her eyes traveling over the exquisite grace of the girl's toilet. "Wait a minute—I want to tell you that that baker Schwab is out of work again. The Sisterhood is tired of finding places for him what he don't keep. But say, Miss Willard, four little children, and that *schlemiel-ich*[104] wife of his who is too proud to work because she was educated in a cemetery!"

"We'll have to find something for him," said Jean, lightly. "You and I'll take a tramp among the bakers to-morrow morning."

"Oh, yes, take a tramp! You know how old my legs is, my dear? Seventy-two yesterday. They don't go like they used to, but I guess they're always good for one tramp more. All right, you come get me to-morrow morning then. Ain't it the bride looks sweet?"

The cooing, contented voice moved on.

Jean met the merry eyes of a tall, slender young woman, unmistakably a Gentile, whom she recognized as Miss Goyne, an old classmate and intimate friend of the bride.

"Wasn't she quaint?" laughed Miss Goyne, in low-voiced delight.

Jean thought Miss Goyne's euphemism delicious, and laughed responsively. "She's a dear old soul," she said.

"It is so interesting," the girl babbled on, with bright eyes. "You know Cecile and I are old schoolmates, but after we left school our social ways separated somewhat, though Cecile and I would not give each other up for the world. And I am always so interested in everything she tells me about her friends."

Unconsciously, there was that in her tone which suggested the "citizen" speaking of the "stranger." Jean felt it, and a little amused smile, born of a memory of just such a smile on Philip May's lips, showed a tiny edge of her teeth. Miss Goyne thought her quiet. But she also found hers the most attractive personality present, and being slightly acquainted with her, decided to attach herself to her during the "interesting" occasion.

"Oh," exclaimed the girl below her breath, "there is Dr. May. Do you know him? I think—" She paused to bow. "He is looking straight at us. I think he is so distinguished-looking, don't you? I met him at the Otises'—Dr. Otis, you know—and we all thought him so charming until that horrid newspaper article appeared."

"And then you ceased to find him charming?"

"Well, you know how it is. We think very little of a man who is ashamed of his religion, of course. We all respect you so much and think it is lovely of you when you keep up the forms and everything."

"That is nice of you," said Jean, pleasantly. She knew that "condescending" or "consistent" would have better expressed her acknowledgment of the girl's estimate, but graciously chose the more gracious epithet.

"We were so surprised," confided Miss Goyne, gently. "You see he has none of the characteristics—"

"Caricaturistics," corrected Jean, with a soft laugh in her eyes.

"What? Oh!" She hesitated, smiled vaguely in response to Jean's playful smile, but was saved any further interpretation by a sudden swaying sensation which separated them abruptly.

The next instant the house was shaken like a rat in the clutch of a terrier, chandeliers swung violently from side to side, bells jangled, windows and porcelain rattled, dogs barked wildly in the street. . . . The swaying subsided. It had lasted exactly seventeen seconds—a lifetime of mortal terror, as many of the unconscious appeals to the Great Unknown testified. Jean found herself in the doorway, her hand upon Philip May's arm, his hand over hers.

"You were frightened," he said, quietly, his eyes upon her pale face.

"An earthquake always frightens me," she said, in a trembling voice.

"Come with me," he murmured. "Let me get you something—"

"No, no. Thank you. I am all right." She drew her hand from his and turned away.

"Well," laughed a familiar voice above the hysterical hubbub, while Paul Stein's long arms stretched above several lower heads and drew her into a corner, "that was a close call, friend o' mine."

"They always seem to be," she answered, through pale lips.

"I'm not speaking of the shake-up, but of what would have proven a shake-down on your head of that bust over the door if Dr. May hadn't caught it in time. Come, get some color into your face again; it's all over, and everybody's safe. Listen, the musicians are triumphing over our fear. Shall I get you something to drink?"

"No; please don't notice me, Paul. Talk away, there's a dear fellow."

"I was just wondering what was the reason of his, Dr. May's being here, and had about concluded it was mere professional etiquette, Thallman being, or having been, his father's physician—but now I see it was only to save your precious head. Some one behind me—I think it was that delightfully ubiquitous Sam Weiss—was pointing him out to some girl as 'the Jew who would be Gentile,' quite in the spirit in which the Gentiles flogged him through the press, and so saved Weiss his vengeance—I hope. If you'd turn your head, Jean, you'd see how he seems to outman every other man present. Candidly, my inclinations yearn toward him. I'm ashamed to say it, in that he hath done what he hath done—because, though, in the eye of the world, when a man sins he punishes himself only, yet when a Jew steps aside he drags the whole race after him, and we are always answered with our own old clan cry, 'Responsible one for the other.' There, I've talked you back into some likeness of yourself. Now our distinguished subject of conversation and Dr. Sutherland, I believe, are offering their congratulations and—actually taking leave, after a necessary attendance of half an hour. Shall we speak to the Thallmans now?"

As they moved forward, Jean was startled by Philip May's flashing, deliberate gaze straight into her eyes. It mastered her completely. She could not regain her old attitude of defiance toward him. She tried to tell herself that her womanish yielding to its magnetism was due to the fact that he had put out his hand to save her head from a possibly ugly blow.

"I should have gone back and thanked him after Paul told me," she said to herself, hours afterward, when alone. "Now it is awkward.

And then we're not on speaking terms. Besides, he would have done it for any one else. Yes, but that doesn't alter the fact that he did it for me. It's stupid and gauche not to acknowledge it. I must. I will. Still, perhaps there's no necessity—he doesn't know that I know. But I do know. Oh, dear, I hate to be in his debt, and a mere 'thank you' would have—. I—I could write him a note."

She hid her eyes, trembling at the thought of putting herself in communication with him, not realizing the longing at the bottom of her reluctance.

"One can be as short and formal as one wishes in a note," she assured herself, and seated herself before her desk. She began at once:

DR. PHILIP MAY,

DEAR SIR,—

"That's ridiculous," she said, bluntly, with flushed cheeks and stern brows. "What then? Dear Dr. May? That need not mean that he is 'dear' to me—not at all. It is only the usual impersonal address to an acquaintance."

She began again:

DEAR DR. MAY,

I did not know until later that you had saved me from what might have proven a serious accident. I wish to thank you for it now.

Yours truly,

Thursday.   JEAN WILLARD.

"Nasty little thing," she apostrophized, reading it over, and her eyes filled. Nevertheless she sent it.

He received it the following day as he was about to leave his office. He smiled gently over its simplicity.

"Poor little girl, she thought she had to—and it was a wrench," he reflected, appreciating to the full the girlish dignity of the few cold phrases. "Not a superfluous word. Shall I answer it? Certainly."

But it was not so easy a matter as he supposed. An honest answer would have proven a virtual avowal of love—a mad, grotesque proceeding which only flashed through his brain. To answer her in her own spirit was impossible. He chose a non-committal mean, and wrote:

DEAR MISS WILLARD,

Your thanks were unnecessary. I merely put up my hand. It is always ready to do you a service.

Yours truly,

Friday. PHILIP MAY.

Jean read it in dreary hopelessness. And the long autumn days went by.

CHAPTER XI

Two days of rain at the end of January had lessened the community's fears of the dreaded drought—and kept Joseph May a house-prisoner.

"If it clears off this afternoon, I'll go me a little to the club," he said to his son the morning of the third day, as the latter stood drawing on his gloves in the hall.

Philip opened the door and glanced up at the gray, fleeing clouds. "The wind is veering," he said. "But if it stays dry till noon you might bundle up and go down for a while. I suppose Mr. Willard will go with you."

"Daniel? He goes a little to the French Club, but he's got no use for any club much—he don't play cards."

Dr. May's eyes, traveling over his horses' sleek backs, smiled innumerable things. "Well," he said, briskly, and ran down the steps to his carriage.

Joseph watched till he had stooped to the small door which he closed upon himself, till he had waved to him from the window, and the horses started off. Then, all unknown to himself, he smiled reassuringly over the vanishing vision and the memory of the quiet, capable face.

He felt an old-time impulse of good-fellowship toward the world this morning. The world, after all, was not so merciless as he had thought—it had proven itself rather generous toward Philip. Generous? Thought of Philip laughed in the word's face. What did he need of its generosity? Simply by ignoring it and moving straight on had he not put his foot on its low-brought neck? Joseph rejoiced in the man's complete triumph this morning, as a god might rejoice in the strength of his creature's limbs.

He rubbed his hands together mightily, looking out of the sitting-room window. "Yes, I think I'll go me a little to the club this afternoon," he decided, condescendingly.

He had not been to his club since almost a year—how long was it anyhow? Since—he put the date and its contingent memory from him. A patch of blue peeped mischievously out at him from the gray sky like a child's eye at peep-bo. He shook his finger at it, and then laughed over his own nonsense.

Jean came down the steps of the house next door and, seeing him, threw him a kiss, talking pantomime with him about her umbrella and the sky. He shrugged, and spread his palms broadly over his ignorance of the weather-man's purposes and as she reached the foot of the steps he threw her a kiss in turn. Dear chile! He had not been very nice to Jean, he admitted, and he could afford to throw her a kiss. He was minded to open the window and command her to deliver the caress sealed. How long was it since he had kissed Jean? Since—but Jean had disappeared around the corner.

"She goes like the wind," he thought, admiring her fleetness with proudly pursed-up lips.

A moment later Daniel came out and shook his stick at him. Joseph opened the window.

"It smells good, the air. You think the rain is over, Daniel?" he asked.

"The weather-man says no," returned Daniel, doubtfully, buttoning his overcoat.

"Then sure it is over," laughed Joseph. "His word is almost so good as carrying an umbrella when it looks like rain—it keeps it off. The poor weather-man, with this *überzwerich* climate![105] Say, Daniel, the farmers ought to hire him to say no when they want it and yes when they don't. It would be most so good as praying."

Daniel had not seen him so jovial in a year. He felt a glow of curiosity as to the cause.

"Has Philip gone?" he asked, gropingly.

"When he is gone! Never you saw a man what takes so little rest. Last night he was called up at two o'clock. You know Steinman is so sick they—"

"Steinman? Which Steinman?"

"What Steinman! Why, Arnhold Steinman, the banker. He's got appendicitis, and the doctors called Philip quick to operate on him."

He spoke with careless importance. Back of his simple announcement lay a world of late-won victory; at last the influential Jews had been forced to acknowledge Philip's supremacy. What had he, Joseph, cared for the others? It was his own, the people of his race, the people of a past and present common with his own, whose cool ignoring of the man had been like a nail in the father's heart.

"Is he going to die?" asked Daniel, with radiant inconsistency.

"You ask me that when I tell you he's got Philip for a doctor?" said the old man, softly, with a quietly raised eyebrow and shoulder.

Daniel laughed, putting down his foot to the next step. "I don't think I shall see you again to-day," he reflected. "After I finish at the office it will be time for luncheon, and after luncheon there is a meeting of the directors of the French library, and to-night—"

"Well, I guess I got to live without you for one day. Anyway, I think I'll go me a little to the club."

"Yes?" cried Daniel, gladly, his curly upraised eyebrow shooting off his eyeglass. "It is long—I hope you will have a pleasant game. Give my love to any of the old ones you see there. Good by, Joseph. You had better shut that window."

"Good by, Daniel. Better you turn up your coat-collar."

The window was closed. The morning wore itself away, interrupted by three conversations over the telephone—two with Daniel, and a short colloquy with his attorney, Paul Stein. After luncheon, telling Katie he would take "a little snooze," he lay down on the couch in the sitting-room with the newspaper over his face.

It was half-past three, when, refreshed from his sleep, he walked down in the after-rain sweetness, and took the car for his club.

He knew he would find several of the surviving "old ones" there. With Kantian precision, every afternoon at that hour old Alexander, and Houssman, and Frank, and Goldschmitt, formerly joined now and then by Joseph May, found themselves in a certain corner of the spacious card-rooms and gave themselves up to cards and reminiscences. Their stories were known by every frequenter of the clubhouse, and they, as well as the story-tellers, were tenderly cherished as heirlooms by the younger generation. There was a jest current among the latter, as the survivals began dropping off quietly and were gathered to their respective corners in the more spacious Home of Peace,[106] that, in the quiet of the night, they would find one another, and over some grassy table play their "little game," and tell their "little stories."

As Joseph entered now, the graybeards shot questioning glances at one another, and stretched forth curious yet hearty hands toward him.

"Hello, May. *Wie geht's?*[107] What's up?" cried Alexander, pushing a chair round for him.

"Me," beamed May, expansively, sinking into a chair after disposing of his hat and cane and overcoat. "Me—and the sun—and lots."

"You always had a good nose for lots," said Frank, facetiously, his small, keen eyes searching the furrowed face for the tracings of his unpublished chapter. "You remember the time you bought sand-hills for a song where Van Ness Avenue stands now?[108] We said you were *verrückt.*[109] And now you have a corner in lots!"

"No, only seven," returned Joseph, lighting a cigar. "And one is just round the block from yours, Frank, in what my son calls—what you think he calls it?"

He had spoken the name of his Ineffable with deliberate purpose.

"What he calls it?" asked Alexander, with a grin. These old inheritors of a religion without a hereafter could, nevertheless, enjoy a joke upon this, their so imminent sojourning.

"He calls it 'The Common,'" replied Joseph. It was not quite what Alexander had expected; in truth he did not quite understand.

"Yes, it is the common way," interrupted Goldschmitt, who, through a misadventure in his pioneering days, had learned his English more thoroughly than his companions, and kept himself up to date. "Too common. What will he and the other swells do when they get there—hey?" The comment smacked of maliciousness.

"They'll be dead swells then and can't kick," laughed Houssman, shaking over his own wit. "But tell us, May, how Steinman is to-day?"

Then they knew!

"Oh, my son says there is no danger now," said Joseph, with superb carelessness. "He fixed him."

How? What? Steinman? Dr. May? There was agitation among the beards.

"What are you talking about, Houssman?"

Houssman looked at them with disgust. "You didn't know Banker Steinman was so sick they gave him up last night—till they thought of Dr. May? And you hear—his father says he fixed him."

A celebrity sat among them—Joseph, father of Philip. Every Jew kneels to the god Success—the old ones knelt to the reflected glory. Joseph was again one of them.

Cards were dealt, the game began. Cigars were smoked, but Joseph wished he had been in the habit of singing under his breath like Frank—it would have been such a vent. Instead, he played like a magnate, throwing money away with lavish unconcern. It had been his wont to play as he had worked, earnestly, silently, and the others watched him now somewhat uneasily.

"You play like a fool, May," protested Alexander, finally, his sense of economy exasperated.

May laughed. "I got a license to play like I want, so long I don't cheat," he said.

The word sent Houssman back to other days. "You remember in the old days when you and me was partners down in Mississippi, and how we slept one whole night in the swamp because the sheriff found out I didn't had no license?" he asked, with raised chin.

"Well, we were fools—afraid from our own shadows. Didn't I had a license, and wasn't you my partner?"

"But say, May, what a night! Do you like to think about it now?"

"It's a wonder we didn't die from malaria," returned the doctor's father. "You remember when they caught me they said I stole the horse, but wasn't it the judge's daughter what told me to take her horse and run, and tie it to the tree on the bank before I went into the swamp? You said she did it account the bargain she made with that blue-striped taffeta, but I knowed it was account my good looks."

They laughed over the old boy's conceit, hitching their chairs closer together, their beards commingling in a maze of teeming recollection—sons of toil, enjoying the fruit of their labors—toil past.

"I could sit forever talking it over," sighed Frank at last, looking at his watch. "But, *junge*, you know what time it is? Ten minutes past six."

"*Gott im himmel,*" cried Goldschmitt, bustling up. "My wife will think I was kidnapped. Come along, boys."

But Houssman had another card up his sleeve, and before they toddled to the door he flung it down before Joseph.

"I hear your son is going to join the club, May," he said, buttoning up his overcoat, while Joseph did the same.

"You said?" questioned the other, the blood rushing thickly to his face.

"I see your son's name is up for membership, now two weeks. They vote to-night, you know. Dr. Philip May. That's him, ain't it?"

"Yah," said Joseph, a film over his eyes and voice.

"I hope he gets in," said Houssman, tendering his hand.

"I hope he gets in," said Alexander, tendering his.

"I hope he gets in," said Frank, with a slap on the shoulder.

"I hope he gets in," cried Goldschmitt from the door.

Joseph's cup was full and threatened to brim over through his eyes. He wanted a quiet place in which to sing, or cry, perhaps even to pray a little.

Fortunately joy does not kill. When he found himself alone, walking unconsciously toward home, his heart was beating dangerously high. So! He had done it quietly to surprise him! And some night he would say, "Old man,"—they had grown intimate enough even for that endearment, he thought—"old man, shall we go to the club together? You know I am a member now." Steal a march on the old man, eh, steal a march on his old father!

And it was a good move—a shrewd move to get in with those moneyed men. Not that he needed them, oh, no. But—well, he was a chip of the old block. . . . . .

What! already at Clay Street? How had he got there? Verily, Joseph, by thine own peculiar little knock-kneed old Jew's trot and the aid of thy fine gold-topped cane, and by no miracle of wings whatsoever. At Clay Street, then, and yonder in the evening light the row of smug-faced houses which he called his—one of the finest residence corners in the city—and what a city! What a picture! What a place to live in—what a view—what a corner for a doctor! Worth— Oh, down with the smug-faced houses, and behold the lordly mansion in the midst of billowy lawns. There, in the doorway, who is the girl who throws him a kiss? He has seen that girl before, caught such kisses before. Why not?—since Philip had joined the club. And had he not watched a certain quiet face in the evenings while Jean played? Ah, Philip, my son! And it would be, "Good morning, Grandfather Joseph; did you sleep well last night?"

And, "Good morning—" Alas, poor Daniel, never to know the joy of grandfatherhood. Well, well, it would be almost the same, not quite, of course, but almost.

And no doubt that old scheme of showing "a fine public spirit," which he had evidenced in that crazy will which Paul Stein was going to change in the morning—no doubt it was very grand, Daniel, my friend, but was it—human? Alas again, could Daniel put himself in a father's place? Could a bachelor judge? Well, it was all right now.

And Philip would find how much better it was to stand in with your own people—people who cared for you, just like the members of one great family, the big ones for the little ones, the young ones for the—oh, it was going to be all right, all right, all—

"Well, you *are* late," cried a voice above him, and Joseph looked up to find himself at his own doorstep, Philip standing bareheaded in the doorway. "I was beginning to think of sending scouts out to find you."

"No danger I get lost," laughed Joseph, panting up the steps, his eyes on the somewhat care-worn face above him. "A bad penny, you know. I had so good a time I forgot to come home. Was you waiting for me?" He stammered as a girl might, while putting his cane in the stand.

"I'm hungry," returned Philip, helping him out of his overcoat. "And you seem rather fagged."

"Me? No," derided Joseph; "what shall I be tired about? Wait, I'll go in and wash my hands a little before dinner."

"You're all right," commented Philip, noting the excited light in the old man's eyes. "Come in—Katie and her dinner are about boiling over."

It was an uncommonly good dinner, Joseph decided, especially as to the wing of chicken Philip carved for him—and Katie was a good cook and a good girl, and to-morrow Stein would fix *her* all right.

"Why not lie on the couch a while?" suggested Philip, when they had repaired to the sitting-room.

"No; I must read the paper," said Joseph, plumping himself into the easy-chair at the farther end of the massive library table, and, setting his eyeglasses on his nose, he drew the evening paper toward him with a lazy grunt of satisfaction. "Better you lay down, Philip," he added, glancing benignly at him over his spectacles. "I bet you didn't sleep more as two hours last night."

"Something like that," assented Philip, with a laugh, as he seated himself at the other end and drew the writing materials toward him. "I don't require much sleep, you know. Read your paper now; I have an article to finish."

CHAPTER XII

For some little while there was nothing heard in the room save the continuous scratch of the doctor's pen and the occasional crackling of the newspaper as Joseph turned the page. Then, as was expected, awaited, longed for by one of them, the music stealing through the friendly dividing-walls.

"Jean sings to-night," remarked Joseph softly, scarcely looking up.

His voice startled his companion. "I have never heard her sing before," he returned, without glancing up, and then cleared his throat as though it had been rasped by something physical.

"It is some of those old French songs what Daniel likes so much to hear," explained Joseph, his luminous eyes seeking his paper again as though caught poaching.

There were only two in her repertoire, but Jean sang verse after verse, never omitting the refrain of "Lisette's" so proud, so sad regret for the day's lost joy:

> "Si vous saviez, enfants,
> Quand j' étais jeune fille,
> Comme j' étais gentille—
> Je parle de longtemps—
> Teint frais, regard qui brille,
> Sourire aux blanches dents,
> Alors, ô mes enfants,
> Alors, ô mes enfants,
> Grisette de quinze ans,
> Ah! que j'étais gentille."[110]

The pen snailed across the paper. Almost, one might say, it kept time to the throb of smiling, coquettish tears beneath the quaint old ballad. And then came "Madame la Marquise," beginning and ending with a bravura.[111] They could hear the faint clapping of Daniel's hands, and immediately after, the sound of the sweet, sonorous voice of the piano.

Philip laid down his pen—picked up a book. It was his hour of exquisite torture. The girl and her music had, in truth, become his conscience, seeking through his coats of vanity down to the hidden depths of the man, finding within him strange, potential heroisms, mute eloquences, mad, irresistible desires, which, changing with the changing soul of the music, made him, as in mockery, now her knight and hero, now a suppliant poet, now her compelling lover. Her music had thrown down the gates between them—had assumed a face and form—her face and form, and she came to meet him thus, a Child of the Book, with the dream of the Book in her eyes, and though he could not know that through his own distorted dream he had helped to the distorting of hers, he knew that now and forevermore he must read life and himself through her beautiful, denouncing eyes. He was still analyst enough, however, to know that the beauty of those eyes added fuel to the flame of her scorching scoring, satirist enough to say to himself, with grim humor, "For punishment, thou shalt love, without hope, this scorning Jewish maiden whom once thou scornedst." In a world of artificiality and servile flunkyism she alone, through the echo of her girlish, impetuous, "Egoist, coward, snob," seemed the one real—and unattainable—thing to him. Translating now her estimate of him and his blind dream of individualism into the vernacular, he called himself "a dam fool!" and when a man arrives at that stage of self-realization, he may be accounted on a fair road to recovery. The words wrenched wide the arms of his love. Often if he could have stopped the music with a blow he would have done so—and regretted it the moment after. But the words sang on in his memory and stooped his soul in reply. The valuation of this firebrand of an inexperienced girl hung like a price-mark upon him, and the price was bitterly low. And still, to-night, as night after night, he found himself engaged in this dumb, unheard, futile wooing, which, as the music ceased, left him looking into space with blank, haggard eyes.

Gradually the mists cleared and he realized that he was gazing at his father's face.

Joseph was reading, his cigar in the corner of his mouth. Philip's book lay open before him, his hand supported his head—a trick of habit. His eyes were riveted upon the absorbed face opposite. It seemed as though for the first time he saw it—knew it—the leathery skin, the protruding, bony, wrinkled brow, the long, thick nose, the straight, thin lips. His gaze fell from the grizzled beard to the heavily veined brown hands holding the newspaper—sped again to the quiet face above. Mute testimony of a life—the handwriting on the wall! Between the lines his history lay revealed—and Philip read. Time and space slipped away, the struggle, the yearning, the broken pitchers remained. By a strange fantasy he seemed to see the figure of a man moving alone upon an endless, lonely road—put there, how? Back of him lay the years, the centuries, stretching gigantic arms outward, beyond the man, beyond the horizon, beyond all space, beyond all time. The road of Infinity lay between. And the man? Galley-slave of the Past, lugging forever the memory of a Chain—sport of the ages, auto-da-fes, and yellow patch, hate, and prejudice, and jealous venom, plundered, reviled, stoned, and spat upon—heir of all the ages—unconquerable still—yearning ever toward the wide peace of promise![112] Heart-bound, the threads spread out, caught at the gazer, clutched him close.

"I am his—he is mine," said his soul. "Amen."

With an effort toward actuality, he sprang to his feet, and looked at his watch.

"I must be going," he said hurriedly, his hand falling upon his father's shoulder. "I have an operation at St. Luke's—and you are going to bed now."[113]

Joseph looked up, taking off his spectacles. "Yes," he decided, slowly, shoving the glasses into their case. "Perhaps I'm a little tired. What time is it?"

"Just nine. Are you going now?" Joseph was following him.

"I'll go with you to the door. You say it is an important case? What is it, Philip?"

The doctor shrugged himself into his overcoat, the old man standing by the newel-post, watching him. Philip smiled down at him, giving him certain details which brought a look of wisdom into his father's face.

"Oh, it's only an experiment," Philip concluded, feeling in his pockets for his gloves. "My old friends, the authorities in Europe, have been discussing its practicability for the past ten years. I'm only going to put some of their theories into practice—risking one life for many—but I have strong hopes. Ah, here they are." He began drawing on his gloves, waiting for the further question fumbling for exit in his father's agitated countenance. "Well, good night." He picked up his hat as a spur.

"Oh—hold on, Philip. You know I was to the club to-day."

"Yes, so our late dinner proved."

"And—and I heard some news—good news."

Philip felt his pulse give a leap of premonition, and then lie cold. For no definable reason but for dread of it, and the natural possibility of it, he daily awaited the announcement of Jean Willard's engagement.

"Ah," he said, impassively.

"Yes. That was a good idea—waiting till I couldn't go down and find out, but you can't hide it from me no more—Houssman told me your name is on the board—for membership."

His son turned upon him more directly, blank surprise written in his eyes. This suddenly passed, leaving a heavy frown.

"There is some mistake," he said, shortly. "I have never given any one such a right—never spoken to any one of such a desire. I know no one belonging to your club—intimately." The arrogant, masterful voice spoke again.

"It is no mistake," returned Joseph, thickly, uncertainly. "Houssman said it—he saw it plain—and Frank—and—"

"Then it is the horseplay of some practical joker," broke in Philip, gruffly. "One of those gentlemanly means of getting even, I suppose. I—my dear sir—father—why should it trouble you?" He caught the old man by the shoulders, the egoist held again in leash by the look of agony quivering over the blanched features—conscious now, with all Jean Willard's conscience, of his lack of consideration.

"Me?" agonized Joseph, hoarsely, lifting his head in pride. "Me? You think that troubles me? They can go to hell, the whole dam lot of 'em, for all I care! Dam 'em, Philip, dam 'em!"

Philip's hand still pressed upon the trembling shoulders, his calm eyes gradually cooling the blazing ones beneath his.

"It really isn't worth speaking about," he said, lightly, at last. "But I'm glad you heard about it; to-morrow morning I can set them right with a note. I heard Katie go out, I think. Come, let me see you to your room."

"Nonsense. Good night, Philip; I'm all right—you go to your work." His voice dragged. He tried to move from the detaining hold. He seemed suddenly little and weak. Philip lifted him summarily and carried him upstairs. It was the work of but a few quick minutes to get him tucked between the sheets.

For a few seconds after the front door closed behind him, a great stillness lay upon the house. Then Joseph May, huddled in his dressing-gown, shuffling in his slippers, made his stumbling way down the stairs up which the adored strong arms had but just carried him.

Huddling, shuffling, groping, he reached the foot at last, and raised his head for breath. To-morrow morning! God in heaven, what was going to happen to-morrow morning? But the meeting—the meeting took place to-night—and the telephone miles away at the end of the passage. Making fun of them, eh? Making fun of both of them. "I hope he gets in," chuckles Houssman. "I hope he gets in," grins Frank. "I—" God, God, all of them laughing at him—he could hear them now— and surely the telephone used to be nearer the dining-room door. Ah!

He took down the receiver; the connection was made.

"Hello," went the strange, hoarse voice over the wire. "Is Alt-schul there?"

"Who? I don't understand you."

"Altschul—the president—Altschul."

"Got a bad cold, eh? Spell it."

" A-l-t-s-c-h—"

"Oh, Altschul. Yes. Want him? Wait a minute." . . . . .

"Hello. Who is this?"

"May. Joseph May. Is that Altschul?"

"Yes. Whom am I talking to?"

"May. Joseph May."

"Oh—ah—yes. Your voice is somewhat husky, May. How goes it?"

"I want you—I want to say there is a mistake about my son's name. He never gave no one the right to put it up. You understand, Altschul?"

"But my dear sir—"

"I want you to say it's a damned low trick—and I want you to take his name off. You understand, Altschul?"

"But my dear sir—"

"I want you to say that Joseph May resigns from your club, now—to-night. You understand, Altschul?"

"But my dear sir, you, a charter member! Nonsense, May, nonsense. Reconsider it. If that regretable matter of Dr. May's name—you know it has been on the board for full three weeks—if it had come to light in time—"

"Then—the—the meeting is over?"

"I regret exceedingly, but—"

"Then—he—is—"

"A little louder, May. What? I can't understand you. You know it takes only two balls, and—but we shall sift this to the bottom. Say, May, come down and have a little game, won't you? It's a fine night. Say, May?"

He received no answer.

"We've been disconnected," murmured Altschul, turning from the telephone room with threatening gaze.

It was a fine night, warm, soft, balmy, with overhead a cloudless, starry sky. Shortly before midnight, as Dr. May came out of St. Luke's Hospital, two of his colleagues close upon his heels, it occurred to him that, in all his experience, he could recollect none finer. At the corner of Valencia Street, Dr. Otis grasped his hand for the third time.

"Young man," he said, "I wish I had your career to live. Or my own over again—with just that added bit of power you taught us to-night."

Philip laughed. He felt the slight intoxication visible in the brilliancy of his eyes, but his voice was quite steady. "It saves bungling," he said. "And I believe she's going to stand it."

"No doubt of it. Well, sir, I envy you." The distinguished old physician made as if to add something further, turned fiery under the lamplight, and took off his hat, as he strode toward the car.

Philip strolled on with the young interne, giving him an out-of-class lesson in the joy of his success. At that moment he would have readily staked his life on the truth of the statement that the nearest approach to earthly happiness is the knowledge of perfect success. He felt his powers strong within him, knew that he could leap mountains of untold difficulties.

His brain was still busy with analogous complications as he boarded his car, taking a seat on the side of the dummy where he could best enjoy his cigar. At the corner where transfers were given, two men stepped on, seating themselves close beside the tall, silent figure in the corner. They seemed to be talking confidentially, and Philip, absorbed in his own thoughts, took small notice of them, till just within a block of his stepping-off place, when he was attracted by the mention of his father's name.

"Don't tell *me*. I tell you I'm sorry for Joseph May; and if you'd have heard his poor, shaky old voice over the 'phone two or three hours ago, you'd fully understand this feeling. I hated to have to tell him that the meeting had already taken place and that the black-balling was accomplished. Now, the fellow who conceived the original and brilliant idea of using the club's roster as a means of canceling some real personal debt or of perpetuating his vulgar joke, is going to suffer for this. Oh, I know the man deserved some sort of drubbing, but the club isn't a hall of justice—"

The tall, quiet man in the corner swung off, and Altschul spread himself more comfortably while the car spun on. Dr. May's footsteps rang out sharply on the pavement as he walked toward his home.

He had flung his cigar away. His face was inscrutable as he put his key in the latch.

He noticed that the gas was still burning in the sitting-room as he had left it. Katie had not come home then, he supposed, with a passing sense of surprise, while moving toward the room to turn off the light. Something far down the hall near the telephone caught his attention. He went curiously toward it. He stooped over the dark, huddled mass—straightened himself a moment before looking further.

Then he turned up his father's face. But it was cold in death.

CHAPTER XIII

There are prayers—or something—said in the evening, aren't there?"[114] Philip demanded, laconically, on the afternoon of the funeral, when he stood again with Daniel Willard in the May dining-room. Recollections of old ceremonies were pressing in upon him.

"It is customary—yes. But to-night being Friday, there are services in the Temple—and one goes there."[115]

"At what hour?"

"A quarter to eight during the winter."

"Shall I find a seat?"

"Yes, yes; everybody is welcome. Besides, there is your father's seat. Mine is with his. I too am going down to-night. Shall we go together?"

"Thank you."

"I am going home now. Perhaps you will lie down a little." He looked imploringly into the stern, gray face. His own was weary and tear-stained, but he did not know it.

"Perhaps," returned Philip, stifling argument.

Daniel turned away. There was nothing to be gathered from the baffling wall of rigidity behind which the man had intrenched himself. Throughout the day of necessary publicity and ceremony, standing cynosure for the crowd of curiosity-seekers and gossips among the large host of the dead man's time-proven friends, looking for the last time upon the features cowled in peace, beside the narrow bed in which they laid Joseph May next the love of his youth, the son had presented a blankness of aspect as unreflecting as the sheeted mirror in the sitting-room, symboling the vanities of life.

"You are tired," said Jean, when her uncle entered. She helped him out of his overcoat and pressed him to eat something.

"Thank you. I have no appetite for eating." He spoke in distant courtesy.

"Won't you—aren't you going to rest a while?"

He kept his hand upon the knob of the door, waiting to close it upon her. It was a house divided against itself. But the situation had become intolerable to Jean, and she suddenly threw her arms about his neck.

"I'm sorry for—for what I said yesterday morning," she sobbed against his shoulder. "But I couldn't stand near him at the funeral—as you asked me—feeling as I do—as everybody feels—that if it weren't for him—directly—or indirectly—Uncle Joseph wouldn't be where he is now."

"At any rate," said Daniel Willard, coldly, "there is no occasion for this repetition of the remark, is there? I do not like the sound of it."

She drew from him with drooping head. Something in her heavy eyes and white face gave him an uneasy start.

He put his hand out to her. "My dear, are you well?" he asked, gently.

She nodded her head in assent.

"Then perhaps—what was I going to say? Perhaps a glass of wine would taste good if you would bring it to me."

She threw him a look of gratitude and hurried off for the refreshment.

But the shadow of Philip May stood between their usual confidences, nor would it let Daniel Willard take his much-needed rest. He was thinking of certain bitter words spoken almost a year before under a beautiful February sky:

"And I made a new will according, Daniel. A fine will like you talk so much about, with Universities, and Hospitals, and—*ich weiss viel!*—in it. So well he can go alone and has no use for his father, so well he has no use for his father's money.—I left him a dollar—that's the law, Stein says—and he can make *Shabos* with it, or put it in a crêpe band on his hat—if it is still the style to make believe you care. But it will make me nothing out. For me—I will be silent in my grave."

What if the vindictive testament still existed, with nothing to repudiate its revengeful spirit in the eyes of a keen world—and the conscience of the disinherited? If so, then, Joseph, alas, not silent!

Jean, in her incomprehensibility, begged him to dine with Philip May, but it was a silent meal which he partook with him. It was as silent a going forth to the place of prayer afterward.

As they stood on the back platform of the car, approaching the dark pile of the Temple, Daniel noticed that the street was filled with hurrying groups of people who were lost in the shadows of the two great flights of steps leading to the arched portico. It looked as though there were going to be an unusual attendance. As they mounted the outer steps, Daniel glanced at his companion's face, questioning what effect this unexpected crowd might have upon him in his reclusive mood. But, quite oblivious to this feature of the moment, Philip walked in after him to their seats somewhere toward the middle of the nave.

A subdued light from many bulbs pervaded the interior. At either side the richly carved chancel glowed the great seven-branched lamps. At the farther end, above the heavy ruby velvet curtains concealing the ark, rose the gleaming pipes of the organ.[116] The swing-doors at the back opened and shut to a constant flow of softly moving people; stooped, slow-moving, long-nosed, grizzled Jews—those who had paved the way; portly, important, keen-faced Jews—those who had profited by the paving; young, alert Jews of the hour—those who were inheriting;—here smug and self-satisfied, there dignified by the culture, though new, of a far-reaching cosmopolitanism;—broad-bosomed, middle-aged Jewesses in spiritualizing griefs and crêpe veils; graceful, piquant-faced, well-dressed young Jewesses, the light of the world in their eyes. And not one among all these diverse faces, not omitting the most self-approving, the most joyous, or the most empty-souled, but bore evidence of a racial potentiality which falls easily to the line of tragedy. But the Jews formed only a minor proportion of the immense gathering this evening.

"I see one of the professors of Stanford in the pulpit," murmured Daniel. "I could not understand the crush."

Philip received the explanation in silence. There was a numbness possessing his faculties which gave him a sense of being put passively, through no desire of his own, by some resurrectionary process, back into a long-deserted life.

And this was the approach: music which was prayer, prayer which was music, soaring, sonorous, sublime, whether through the voice of the organ, the marvelous intoning of the cantor, or both together blending in vast, deep harmonies, which rose as out of the immensities of the past, reaching the climax in the trumpet glory of the "*Shemah*,"[117] the hope-cry and star of a People through æons of misunderstanding, of exultation, and despair—"Hear, O Israel, the Lord our God, the Lord is One"—which they, having escaped from out their fastnesses, shall some day change to, "Hear, O Humanity, the Lord our God, the Lord is One."[118]

Presently the echoes were hushed, and soft words of comfort were spoken, gentle as a loving touch on throbbing wounds; the music trembled a faint whisper, and the mourners arose in their places, while the "Kadesh"—the glorification of Him who gives and takes in love and wisdom—was quietly chanted to them.[119]

Philip resumed his seat, mechanically, as he had risen, swayed by the simple, compelling services. But during the hour in which the professor of Stanford gave one of his ethically broad, yet bluntly sincere, lectures—this night on the state of the Cubans starving on the country's borders—of which he, Philip, heard only the murmur, as of the rumble of a distant life—he seemed to be listening, stony, incapable of response, before a grave, chiding Power.[120] That some day he might grasp it, bow down before it, he felt with impotent grimness, but to-night, though the mighty voice of the music had stirred him as a voice from afar, it upbore before him only the quiet old face of his father as he had seen it last in death. Stern-browed, tall, commanding, he had attracted many curious eyes when he had risen among the other mourners, but down to the moment when, the benediction said, the throng began to move slowly toward the exits, he had remained unconscious of the public among whom he sat or stood.

The rush of buzzing voices brought him back to his surroundings. He knew that Daniel Willard was returning bows and salutations and that he himself had acknowledged several such recognitions. A tall, thin man, cutting his way through with extended arm, cornered them for a moment near the door.

"Isn't Jean here?" he demanded, with pleasant abruptness.

"No, she did not come," murmured Daniel. "Did you expect her?"

"Well, not by agreement—I only supposed so. I thought I'd use the occasion as a medium for lending her a book we had been speaking about."

"What brings you here, Paul? The professor?"

"He might have, but he didn't. No, I have *Yahrzeit*[121] for my mother—never miss coming if I can help it. Hadn't we better be moving?"

They found themselves in the tail of the vanishing crowd. The sweet night air struck their faces.

"Have you ever noticed," asked Paul, as they approached the portico, "how, coming out here at night, these arches let in the stars and sky exactly as though continuing the roof-scheme of the Temple within? I don't know whether it was an architectural design or divine accident, but it actually makes us carry heaven with us at least a moment beyond the threshold. You ride, of course?"[122]

"Well—what do you say, Philip?"

"Isn't the distance rather too great for you to—"

"No; and the walk will do us both good. Well, Paul, why not bring the book to Jean now?"

"Exactly. I decided to do that when you decided to walk—if you don't mind my company."

"We shall be glad of it," said Philip, unexpectedly, and they veered around. There was something irresistibly attractive to him in the personality of this rough-visaged son of Judah. The old gentleman walked between, briskly, intrepidly, his young companions thought, but in the silent intimacy of his own bones, he knew he was very tired.

"What did you think of the lecturer's flat-footed expressions of opinion, Dr. May?" asked Paul, as they strode out Sutter Street, with long, steady strides.

Philip started. "The lecture? I'm afraid I lost most of it. I was still absorbed in the echo of the services. But—was it Jewish?" He felt a sudden desire to set Paul Stein talking—for diversion; he liked the suspicion of reserve strength in his manner, the twinkle in the corner of his bright eye.

"Was what Jewish?"

"All of it—the simple prayers with most of the Hebrew omitted— the superb organ music—the non-Jew in the pulpit."

"It was all Judaism—robbed of provincialisms and anachronisms." The words came from Daniel Willard. "Why do you question it, Philip?"

"It seemed heretical—to the ancient idea."

"The ancient idea is the new idea. It is long since you have been in a synagogue."

"Yes."

"Not that it would have been told you there in so many words. But the ancient idea of which you speak—the Talmudic idea—was that the Law was never to be a sealed matter—that it was always to remain open to the interpretation of the search-light of progress."[123]

"In other words, we evolve," put in Paul, lightly.

"That is your word—mine is progress," held the gentle Pharisee.[124] "But perhaps it all means the same in the end—perhaps we all mean the same in the end. I hope so. Yet it seems to me I can hear the silent, continuous, unhampered stride of the Jew, keeping step with Time. As though he, the freeman, were moving on to the brink of the Universal—the Messianic religion which was meant by the first and shall be the last—though we may then call it by another name. For, one by one, the superstructures of Judaism, having fulfilled their mission of promulgation, will crumble away—one by one, her messengers, having fulfilled their time and office, shall lay them down to rest and pass into a tale that is told—while she, ever with her hand at the brain of Life, stands imperturbable, immortal, gazing down the ages. And when the great moment of coalition takes place, the Jew will be found in the van and waiting."

"In short," said Paul, in the ensuing pause, "we shall be to the manner born—the others will be the parvenus."[125]

"No, Paul; I do not like the spirit of that remark," reproved Daniel. "Youth is always a little vindictive, it seems to me. The eyes of age are more humble—having seen. But I was not always old. Time was when I too thought that to be of the Chosen People was to be of God's elect—his darling, a peculiar treasure unto Him. But time has taught me the mockery of any divine nepotism. We *were* elect— through Abraham—who, myth or man, stands forth the great intermediary, the mouthpiece between God who is God—and Man. That is all for which we were elect—all for which we are 'to the manner born.' But since that moment of Revelation, most men—deny it though they may—believe in a Something which we have given them—and which we call God."[126]

"What do you mean by belief in God?" asked Paul.

"The sense of an existent Ideality," replied Daniel, quietly, "an ideality—a perfectability—whither the potentiality, the growth of man tends—and which still, as we advance, retreats like the horizon, beckoning us ever onward. A gray abstraction to some, perhaps, but which alone makes for and marks our religion."[127]

"And, as a race, what are we?" questioned Philip May.

"Let the Christians answer that."

The words were Paul's. An oppressive silence gigantic with Titanic powers and gruesome memories hung like a weight upon their senses at this retort courteous.

But Daniel Willard interposed. "No, Paul—not as a race; only—and that again only in part—as a social figure among the nations. As a race we are what our religion has made us. There is a something in the roots of every one of us, a something which has got implacably mixed with our blood and is inseparable from it, which had made us what we are long before oppression came near us. We cannot separate ourselves from this ancient heredity. The Ghettoes were only the great storehouses in which this racial germ was preserved and forced to exotic intensity. Our ethics are our birthright. And whenever a Jew fails to be proud of this birthright it is through cowardice, or ignorance, or both. And whenever a Christian is unjust to a Jew, it is through cowardice, or ignorance, or both. But what I meant to say was, that a Jew can only deny himself by word of mouth."

"And that generally gives him away," added Paul, feeling that the old gentleman had inadvertently approached delicate ground, "and then all his perjury is in vain. Then—what atonement can he make for his folly, Mr. Willard?"

"'God is regained in a moment of repentance,'" quoted the scholar, quietly.[128]

"Not through a death-bed repentance, I hope," laughed Stein. "That should be as theologically impossible as we have made death-bed bequests illegal. In the other world—"

"What *is* the other world?" demanded Daniel, sternly.

"The world of the immortal soul."

"And what is this immortal soul of which you speak so glibly?"

"That which aspires—here and now, as the mortal is that which desires—here and now." He spoke rapidly, delighting in the Socratic cross-questioning upon a subject for which most thinking Jews are generally ready with some independent opinion. "According to which," he added, lightly, "in heaven, as yet—the here-and-now heaven—the gathering is small and select. Now that, I grant you, is not an idea borrowed from the seers and prophets, who kindly left all speculation upon the future state to our own ingenuity—and needs; but it agrees with my idea of a religion which, robbed of its wrappings, has for its standard of judgment only a man's conduct—and has nothing to do with this or that bowing or kneeling acquaintance with dogmatic theology. No, I'll wager that what the patriarchs did give us, Mr. Willard, was not the religious characteristic at all—it was rather one of economics. Why, even in the beginning, they found only one God necessary."

"You are pleased to jest, Paul."

"No, mon Chevalier. I only wished to relieve the oppressive sense of diving in waters too deep. I visited the Deaf and Dumb Asylum the other day and was sadly impressed by the deaf children speaking of those who can hear as 'the hearing ones,' as though they possessed a royal gift.[129] I was beginning to fear I was speaking as though I thought my people and myself the 'hearing ones.'"

"You are, my dear Paul. And yet, for all your nonsense, I believe you to be a good Jew."

"A Jew surely—but a good one?—save the mark! I am a composite of all that I have known—a child of to-day as well as of yesterday—and, come to think of it, I'm not sure I'm not—under that scoring—a pretty good Christian, as well."

"Why not?" returned Daniel, quietly.

Paul cocked his ears. Philip was diverted, awaiting the next move.

"Surely you do not think that a challenge to me, Paul. Surely you must know that I do not forget that Christianity sprang from beneath the very heart of the stern-browed, eternal Mother—a beautiful, graceful youth—or, as John puts it, 'Moses made the Law, but grace and truth came by Jesus Christ.' Which, I take it, is an admission that, without Judaism as a basis, Christianity would be only a beautiful dream signifying nothing. Was not Christ a Jew—a Talmudist?[130] Are not all his preachings, nay, his very phraseology, Talmudic? Only he is tenderer than the ironclad Law—necessarily ironclad for its time and surroundings. He speaks down to the masses always—the subtlety of Christianity lies in this world-tenderness. Judaism addressed itself to the strength of man, Christianity to its weakness. Therefore Judaism was for the few, Christianity for the many. The outside world was pressing too close, its own world growing too varied for the reticences of Judaism. Judaism speaks to the reason, Christianity to the heart. Judaism controls—Christianity consoles. We all have hearts and emotions; we have not all brains and the power of standing alone. The inadequacy of Judaism lay in ignoring the heart till the reason was satisfied, or, rather, it sought to satisfy the heart through the reason. A stern religion truly—but it endures. Why? Why? Why? Because in the eternal flux and vanity of all things, forms, and ceremony, and dogma, God remains. God is the keystone of Judaism. While God stands, the Jew stands."

"And that is all that is necessary?"

"All, Philip—to the enlightened. Just as the 'I am!' of the first commandment comprises—to the enlightened—all of the others. 'I am!'—What?—Justice. And what is Justice? In patois—Love."

"Yes—the greatest Brotherly Love—in the long run," supplemented Paul. They stood to let a car go by. When they had reached the opposite pavement, "And after all," he continued, "what does all the cant and quibbling amount to? To my understanding, just this: Christianity teaches one to bear life for the after-heaven's sake, Judaism to live life for life's sake. No setting aside of this wonderful perfectible or damnable physical being, but that stern, far-reaching principle of atavism which, for the good of man, made Moses the first Board of Health, and which, in pointing out the visiting of the sins of the parents, physical and psychic, on the children unto the third and fourth generations, pronounced for that great religion of Humanity whither all sane minds are bound. And now that I have patted myself back to self-complacency, to revert to your antitheses, Mr. Willard, in what lies the inadequacy of Christianity?"

"In making Jesus a God," returned Daniel. "Make Christ a God and you absolve man from attempting to follow in his altitudes. Leave him a man, and you establish the divine precept of example—what Man has done Man may do."

"Oh, the Christ myth, as men who do their own thinking call Christ's divinity, is being gently put away with other leading-strings and swaddling-thoughts," said Paul, earnestly. "It was and is still a device for leading childish souls. But there are few children left in this era of newspaperdom, and Christ remains the great ethical teacher, the great young Radical of a hidebound theocracy, but still a Jew, who, having uttered his thought a span above the specified height, found, as Heine says, Golgotha.[131] Strange that when the Christians are beginning to disclaim him as a God, the Jews are beginning to claim him as a man."

"Showing that all light tends to a focus," observed Daniel.

"No, showing still that we are nothing if not clannish. I am peculiarly in sympathy with all his teachings, and haven't a particle of doubt that I should have been of his party had I lived in his day. Christ's party, mind you—not Christianity's. To me, Jesus has always been the Raphael of religions—as Moses is the Michel Angelo—a comparison which, no doubt, would sound blasphemous in Christian ears—but I mean it in all reverence.[132] Do you understand me, Dr. May?"

"I think you are—what did you call it?—rather a radical Jew," said Philip, with a half smile.

"If that means rational—perhaps. But I'm only one of many, especially in this feeling about Christ. Why, I know a little girl," and here a merry, deep-seated tenderness came into his voice, "who feels her kinship with him so strongly that she cannot bear to think of the crucifixion. 'No, I will not look,' she said to me once, angrily. 'And if there had been any women there—I said women,' she repeated, pointedly—'they would have died in their helplessness while that Roman brutishness was being perpetrated. Think, Paul, only thirty-three.' And when at the end of the nineteenth century a Jewish maiden falls to weeping over the self-willed death of Christ, for which and in whose divine name the most unspeakable crimes of a world were perpetrated against her ancestry without even the excuse of the youth of that world, I think we may be said to be beginning to see straight."

"Oh, Jean always goes the full length," murmured Daniel, recognizing the picture. "And I think you are inclined to follow after, Paul."

Paul laughed softly, and a sudden cold distaste for the man attacked Philip May. He resented the laugh, resented his right to that outspoken inflection of tenderness. He shook hands with both of them when they stopped before his door.

"I—I shall see you to-morrow," hesitated Paul Stein,—"about your father's will."

"The will? I had forgotten about that. It will have to be to-morrow night, then." He spoke shortly. Had he been able to see in the dark, he might have noticed the swarthy color in Paul Stein's high cheekbones, and the troubled setting of Daniel Willard's tired face. The appointment made, he bade them good night, letting himself into his own house as the other two entered the one next door.

The oppression which had petrified him throughout the long day was disturbed—the usual nice balance of his nerves overthrown. He walked hastily from the dimly lit hall into the sitting-room, but out of its shadows rose the long black shape of that which had claimed it for two days, and he wheeled about, walking toward the less haunted dining-room. Midway he seemed to come upon a horror of memory, for he stopped short as though fearful of stepping upon something. The next minute, however, with a rough shake of the shoulders, he went forward. But the stiff order of the room, with its straight-backed chairs, was not what he sought, and retracing his steps, his brow drawn in deep, impatient furrows, he walked upstairs to his study. The room was at the back of the house, and he entered its wide darkness with a sense of passionate thankfulness for its quiet remoteness. His leather easy-chair was pushed near the open window, and he threw himself into it with a hard-drawn breath of relief.

The dread day was over. In the first moment after the calamity, when he could take thought of what had happened, he had wished, with elemental savagery, for carriage and spade that he might take and bury his dead in quiet and alone—that the carping, peering world might be forced aside and left unaided to make its own inferences, which must necessarily be beside the mark. That he and his father had parted in something deeper than reconciliation, something stronger, in its silent recognition of mutual need and growing custom, he had not the morbidity to put aside. In truth, he kept the knowledge beside him as he would have kept his father, had he had the power. Besides, during the eight or nine months following his withdrawal from all interests in the power called society, he had become almost a world, a law, and a judge unto himself—immune to the power's approval or condemnation. If he was living down the derision, he was accomplishing it unconcernedly, immersed as he was in his profession. His old habit of success was his again in the sphere in which he had now concentrated all his energies and ambitions, and he had thought himself content to go on—although a girl next door held for him in the depths of her beautiful eyes nothing but a corroding contempt and detestation. And now—what?

The echo of the two quiet-souled, thinking men he had just left acted like a rasp to his deliberate equanimity. They had met the guns of fate with an unquestioning "right about face!" and come out calm, unscathed, self-approved from the fire. What were the narrow prejudices of the world to them? They were happy in their life, happy in their circle—independent. He alone—. His nostrils dilated in his sneer at self. But it was not a cold, superior sneer—it was hot, and miserable, and jealous—not over the well-deserved spirit of peace which encompassed those two, his mental equals, but because one, the younger of the two, had the right to meet "a little girl" he knew, on equal terms—had the right to speak of her—. He ground his teeth over the thought, stifling the groan which rose to his lips as the sound of a raised window drew his eyes to the wall of the other house just facing him.

The white figure of Jean Willard placing a glass with violets upon the broad outer ledge, leaned for a moment against the casement, then she put up her hand to close the window, her head thrown back and up, her eyes arrested by the young moon, which, drawing her out of the dark, made her own face a shadowy, slender moon of beauty.

All a lover's vocabulary surged from Philip's soul to his lips as she appeared thus again to him in his second hour of need. He sprang recklessly to his feet, and stood—wordless—facing her. Then—

"Jean, will you not speak to me?" his voice crushed out, hoarsely.

She drew back, startled by the second summons, crossing her wrists instinctively over her bare white throat, her eyes, her lips forbidding him utterance.

"Good night," he challenged, desperately.

For a fleeting second a bewildering, bewildered softness mutinied over her countenance, gone before he could grasp it. Then, "Good night," she answered, distantly, faintly. And window and blind fell between them, while, on either side, two souls stood struggling, the girl against, the man in the toils of a master-spirit common to humankind.

CHAPTER XIV

T here will be no contest," he said again, after Stein had laid before him all his rights and powers.

"But it would be mere child's play. You owe it to yourself to take into account the fact that he intended altering it—that he called me up that very morning with that intention."

"You owe it to your father," added Daniel Willard, in a low voice.

Philip met his gaze intently. "I owe it to my father to have the will probated exactly as it stands, without comment or contest. So far as I can judge, it is a very excellent and just will."

"Except to yourself," interposed Stein.

"How so?"

"It is virtually an affirmation of disinheritance."

"You misinterpret. The document merely indorses a tacit mutual understanding. I have been independent of my father's pecuniary assistance for many years, and he did me the honor to consider me capable of always standing alone. That is all. We were the best of friends."

"So I interpret—interpreted—when drawing it up, but—"

"It is the only interpretation. To contest the will would be to assume the contrary, which would be preposterous. He has made me, you must also remember, his executor along with Mr. Willard."

Both pairs of eyes were directed upon his countenance, endeavoring to discover just what amount of feeling lay behind his disconcerting calm, Paul looking for a trace of justifiable disappointment, Daniel for a glance of bitterness to show he understood. But the unperturbed business-like coolness of his whole head and figure afforded them no food for speculation.

"I shall enter upon my duties as executor with the most interested co-operation, Mr. Willard," he added, leaning back as with the intention of prolonging the interview. "Especially the hospital endowment. I have acquired some knowledge of the subject in my varied experiences, and it may enable me to ride one or two of the hobbies of which my father often heard me speak. But as to the scholarships—now that, I suppose, was an idea upon which you and he must have had some conversation."

"It was a theory of mine—I often spoke about it to him—yes," admitted Daniel.

"Then with Mr. Stein's advice, after he has probated the will and adjusted the several legacies, we'll know 'where we're at,' and proceed accordingly. Both the hospital suggested and the other are to be self-supporting and non-sectarian as—the sky—I believe?"

He bent his eyes in pleasant questioning upon his father's friend. He turned the painful occasion into an interesting business proposition.

Finally, with his knowledge of life, his thorough training, his wide outlook, his calm grasp of the struggling whole, he laid before them the result of his experiences and observations, Paul Stein, with the frank, unstinted praise of absorbed attention, leading him on with quick, intelligent eyes and questions. If, thought Paul, one could separate the strength of a man from his vanities, what a prize were here in the perfectly developed intellect thus disclosed—what education of the faculties, what culture of expression, carrying him, Stein, bodily and mentally, into the atmosphere where his own true self glowed and expanded in its just element. He remembered telling Jean Willard long before, that he awaited Dr. May's coming as one awaits the appearance of an author's chef d'œuvre, and how she had twitted him afterward with his easy change of opinion. But to-night, after emerging from the charm of his individuality, he found it in his heart to condone much, to acknowledge that an "all-round" gifted man, such as he undoubtedly was, had some excuse for seeking a circle other than that which he had accepted as representative of all Jewry.

When Philip returned to the sitting-room after seeing the attorney out, he found Daniel Willard standing hat in hand.

"It has been a very interesting evening to me," the old gentleman began, hurriedly, with flushed cheek and appealing eye. "But my—my dear Philip"; his voice quavered, his hand went out imploringly.

Philip pressed it, waiting courteously.

"Ah!" Daniel exclaimed, with an effort of despair. "It is all my fault. If I had not spoken of these—these theories—which had no personal bearing upon him—none, I assure you, Philip—he might have hesitated over the distribution—it might never have been written. As it was, the idea—my idea—lay ready at his hand at the fatal moment."

"What fatal moment?" Philip spoke in gentle sincerity.

"But no, Philip," murmured Daniel in stifled determination, drawing his hand away, "but no. Let there be no more feigning between us. Surely, surely, you noticed the date upon which the will was drawn?"

"Certainly. February 28th of last year—the day after my return. What then?"

"Ah, you *will* lock yourself away from every one. Can you not come out a moment for me?"

"I think," said Philip, in a low voice, "that I have made it quite clear that I thoroughly approve of my father's will and shall lend my best efforts toward the execution of it. I am glad he has remembered you as he has. What more is to be said at present?"

Daniel turned from him with a sigh.

"Oh—one moment, Mr. Willard," called the detaining voice. "About this house. I hope to leave it almost immediately. I suppose arrangements can be made as to Katie's legacy without delay—I can arrange with her—and the furniture—"

"You have no desire to stay on?"

"No. I shall take chambers in the building where I have my office." He stood by the table, idly rasping the leaves of a book. To Daniel it seemed like the sawing into the last cord binding him to the strongest tie of this being.

"Me—I can have nothing to object," he said, a trifle uncertainly, with great dignity of mien. "There is Paul, your attorney, to consult. We—I shall miss you."

"You will always be my most welcome guest," returned Philip, somewhat dully.

Daniel's eyes were traveling over the familiar furniture as if in farewell. Suddenly he made an excited movement toward the heavy old writing-desk in the corner.

"Of—of what are we all thinking?" he stammered, incoherently. "There—there—he often made business memoranda for me. Will you permit me, Philip—will you permit me to search the desk?"

"Anything you wish, Mr. Willard." He walked across the room and opened the desk for him, only partly understanding the old gentleman's disturbance. Daniel sat down, pulling out an inner drawer. Philip turned away.

He sat down at the table, and, gradually, even the sound of rustling paper was lost to him. He felt cut adrift from his surroundings, like a man ready and waiting to travel forth upon a lonely journey. Resentment or self-pity held no part in his mental attitude. He felt himself utterly devoid of the power of any sentiment for or against anybody. People—Daniel Willard, his niece Jean, as he remembered her with her last verdict of "patricide" written mercilessly in her accusing eyes—were as so many separated entities who could have no possible concern in the cold scheme of life which lay just before him.

A heavy hand upon his shoulder caused him to look up into the pallid joy of Daniel Willard's face.

"I have found something—I knew I would," said Daniel, agitatedly, laying a slip of fluttering paper upon the table before Philip, but keeping tight hold of it and of the shoulder upon which he leaned. "It is only the fragment of a letter written to me when I was away last summer, but never sent. It is not much. We cannot convince the outside world with it—but for you—read it."

It was almost illegible. It lay looking up at him in helpless exposure, and he deciphered it slowly.

MY DEAR DANIEL,

Sometimes it is good when a frend goes away so you can rite him what you cannot say—Daniel I thout to myself that day when she died never I could laugh agen, but now when I look at my son my belovid only chile, Gott knows I am proud and happy—Daniel tell Jean he saved the life of a poor girl last night what evrybody said was going to die—tell Jean never was a son better to his father as my Philip to me—tell Jean

The soft breathing of the gas overhead was distinctly heard in the wide stillness.

"I am looking at it too," came Daniel Willard's voice in strange quietude. "It is very bad spelling."

The face beneath gave no sign of hearing.

"And bad writing," continued the gentle voice. "I can just make it out—even the good, loving heart."

The fine hand beside his made as if to cover the paper. Daniel's fingers closed vise-like over the hand.

"What! Ashamed still? See, Philip, let us examine it together and let it speak for itself and for him. He cannot speak for himself—he never could. He had no eloquence—and very poor English. He was just what the elect call 'a little old Jew'—'Jew-man,' as lips that call themselves refined sometimes put it. I will paraphrase that epithet for you: Often, his voice in speaking dropped into sing-song, his speech into jargon. Sometimes he used his hands for punctuation-marks—they were the only marks of expression he knew; and—God have mercy on his memory!—I have known him, in moments of reversion, to mistake his knife for a fork. He who ran could read his faults; they were written so plain on top. But just with a short pause, the runner could have read that Joseph May never drank his manhood away; he never betrayed a friend; he never wronged another man's wife; he never slandered a good name; he never lied himself into fortune or favor. Yet his life was not all a negation, seeing his hand was always glad to follow the promptings of his good heart. His soul was as faultless as this perfect, well-kept hand of yours over which mine rests. All his life he lived true, but he wrote and spoke in a way to make the angels of culture weep. Now weigh him."

The gas breathed on monotonously.

"It is more bitter than death for me to have to speak in this way to you," went on the low voice in strong intensity, "but he was my friend—and I am old, and you are young, and so you will listen to me. For when a son comes to measure his father, he must bring with him something greater than the pretty, petty scale of a conventional estheticism. The cry of blood is such a far, wistful cry, Philip. It ties us heart to heart—it understands so much. If we had not that to rely on, how many of us would be alone, lonely with an awful soul-loneliness, within this hurrying, misjudging world. There is a verse which I have read which always occurs to me as something very beautiful—always it seems to me it should be set to the most beautiful music the world can produce. It is that scene in which Bathsheba comes with a petition to her son, the great and wise King Solomon, clad then in the purple of his worldly glory. The Book says: 'And the king rose up to meet her, and bowed himself unto her, and sat down on his throne, and caused a seat to be set for the king's mother; and she sat on his right hand'—ah, forgive me."[133]

A woman might have been speaking to him for gentleness. Philip raised his eyes, bitter and glooming from his still white face. He cleared his throat.

"Thank you," he said, hoarsely, and stood up.

Daniel turned for his hat. "You will present this—justification—to Paul Stein to-morrow?" he asked, his finger on the paper.

Philip's face set like steel. "Nonsense," he said, lightly. "There is no justification necessary to any one." He put his hand over the paper with an excluding gesture of possession.

Daniel moved aside.

"And—you are still determined to leave this house?" he asked.

"Quite. To-morrow possibly."

"Well, good night, Philip."

"Good night, Mr. Willard."

He accompanied him to the porch-door. He stood listening to his footsteps long after they had died away.

CHAPTER XV

But whatever Philip May, or any other, was battling with in silence of heart, was presently lost, swallowed up, in the shock which shook the whole nation to its foundations, when, on a night of February, two hundred and fifty American seamen were hurled, without herald, out of a friendly port into the port of the silent Unknown.[134]

The calamity brought the nation as one man to its feet. A great shout for revenge reverberated from ocean to ocean; and while the conservatives frantically begged the yelling mob to keep still—for God's sake—others as frantically shrieked to them to keep on—for man's—for humanity's sake, in the shape of Spanish-starved Cubans. A strong people felt its great, untried sinews swelling, the young giant felt its unmatched muscles straining and pulling, and spoiling for a fight. "Manifest destiny" was at work with its hideous means—life went between a hurrah and a sob—there was no longer any individual life—it was all national.

And amid the passing of ultimatums and resolutions of Congress demanding the immediate evacuation of Cuba by the inimical Spanish, and the haughty responses of the proud Dons to the "Yankee pigs,"[135] the latter, with characteristic directness, sent their troops marching to the front. On a gray afternoon in April the gallant First Regiment, to the patter of roses, and clanging of bells, and booming and whistling, and cheering and bugling, and waving of banners, marched out and away from the soldiers' paradise, the Presidio of San Francisco.[136] But the ranks were soon filled in to overflowing by the call for volunteers, California answering mightily with ten times her quota—men, incapacitated by years, or physical inadequacies, or family obligations, weeping with disappointment because their country refused to accept their mort-gaged lives. During those days women's lips took on that close-pressed look which comes to them in time of war, despite the brave cheer of their words.

Suddenly the tension broke. On the 1st of May occurred—Dewey! And any little shaver, from ocean to ocean, could tell you, with the pride of a veteran, the story of that famous little ante-breakfast sail of the Asiatic squadron into the beautiful bay of Manila where Com-modore George Dewey so gallantly and gracefully led the gallant Dons their piteous dance to death, wiping, within seven hours, the entire Spanish fleet off the face of the Pacific Ocean.[137]

All hearts turned breathlessly westward toward the island spoil of war.[138] The rendezvousing at San Francisco of the troops destined for the Manila expedition went picturesquely on, the great military camps at the Presidio and Bay District track grew into white-tented cities, the streets were alive with blue-coats and fluttering flags. Down at the ferries the women were receiving the incoming sol-diers with luncheons and roses. Everywhere, singly and in bands, women were cutting and sewing abdominal bandages and comfort-bags—and love knows what!—for some—any—dear life. Out at the camps they fluttered to and fro bearing hampers of eatables—and uneatables—and shoes and underclothing, for the boys of varied and, ofttimes, piteous fortunes. There was not a moment left in Jean Willard's life in those memorable days to justify any regret or self-despair—she had found, for the time being, an absorbing interest beyond self, and she gave herself to it with fanatic zeal.

And her face began to wear the white, spiritual light of a devo-tee. And Daniel Willard, looking at her, felt his heart contract with anxiety.

"You will wear yourself out with those boys," he ventured to expostulate.

"It's all in a good cause," she laughed, gathering up a heap of mag-azines, and dropping them into a box ready for delivery at camp.

"Yes—but you are robbing—"

"Daniel to pay Paul? I know, dear, but it is only for a little while, you know. And, speaking of Paul—our tin-soldier, Sergeant Stein, I mean—I promised to bring him something good to eat this evening. Will you go with me to the Presidio after dinner?"

"Certainly—since you have promised. But it seems to me a little rest—"

"Rest!" echoed the girl blithely, stretching her arms high in air. "Why, I've been resting all my life. Besides, I'm perfectly happy doing these things. No rest—to be happy, uncle mine."

The fleeting, haunted look in the eyes above the laughing mouth robbed his own of light.

They left the car at Lombard Street, walking westward out the broad boulevard, under the sweet, still peace of the early evening sky. A bugle floated out from the distant trees of the Reservation, rousing the sleeping echoes. A cavalryman, trotting by on his black charger, turned to look again at the fleetly moving, pale-faced girl with the wondrous uplifted eyes. For to Jean the beauty of the evening, the environment, the call of the bugle, were full of an unspeakable, exquisite harmony.

They entered the Reservation gates, moving with the crowd of visiting sightseers through the white-tented, sentry-guarded camp streets, till they found their guardsman, Sergeant Stein, standing in his blue army-coat outside his tent-door. He took, with exaggerated thanks, the box of dainties he had jestingly demanded, and strolled about with them searching out their young Jewish and other acquaintances among the volunteers. Lights began to gleam opalescently through tentings, the sentries continued their monotonous pacing in the sands among the curious throng.

A superior officer accosted Paul Stein and, with a military salute, he bade his friends good night, while they continued on to the car terminus at the foot of the grounds. They stood still on the elevation among a group of soldiers, and faced the strangely impressive scene before them—the ghostly illuminated tents stretching north, east, and west to the firs and pines shadowing the long foot-bridge leading barrackward—thousands of strong, soldierly men looming up darkly, big with destiny, against the serene sky flushed now with the last rose-streaks of a lingering sunset; beyond the waters rose the eternal, watching hills. Two tall, bearded civilians sprang from an approaching car, stood a moment in consultation, and passed perforce before them. The nearer one bent a quick, recognizing regard upon them, and hats were raised in salutation.

"Ah, Philip," murmured Daniel, noting the glance pausing for a second time over his niece's face as they passed hurriedly on.

"That was the Governor with him," he remarked. "I hear they are on very friendly terms."

He received no answer.

He turned to look at her. "My dear," he said, with startled tenderness, "let us go home at once."

"We were going to wait for 'taps,'" she reminded him in surprise.

"Yes. But I think I have changed my mind. Let us take this car."

The next day he presented himself at Dr. May's office.

"You are surprised to see me," he suggested, when he was admitted, and the doctor motioned him to be seated.

"Yes—but very glad," returned Philip, seating himself opposite his visitor.

"Of course you cannot know. Yet last night—at the Presidio—I believe I was not mistaken—it occurred to me afterward that you had regarded strangely, had noticed—"

"Your niece?"

"Yes."

"She is not well—is that what you have come to say?" He spoke hurriedly, peremptorily.

"But you are mistaken," faltered Daniel, putting up a trembling hand. "That is the strangeness of it—she is very well. But you noticed how she looks? She is fading."

"She looked paler—and thinner, I thought," he acquiesced, roughly. "Does she complain?"

"No, she laughs. All day she is occupied from morning till night with Red Cross work and looking after those friendless soldiers at the hospital. She gives herself no rest."

"Her music?"

"She plays patriotic airs. She does not sing."

Philip smiled with bitter intuition. "There is—some one in the army, perhaps," he began.

"Oh, no, no," interrupted Daniel, positively. "There is no one, but—" He stopped, struck abruptly with a possible idea.

Philip laughed shortly, as though he had been answered. "Take her away," he said, coldly. "She is too intense. That sort of strain would break down the calmest."

"Where shall I take her?"

"Oh, 'any old place,' as the soldiers in camp say, only don't keep her here." The even edge of his handsome teeth gleamed in a smile.

"You advise it—seriously?"

"Yes."

"But she will not go. She will laugh at me and say she is quite well."

"Use a subterfuge. Say your physician has ordered—the mountains—for your health."

Daniel flushed. After a pause, "You seem to understand her," he murmured.

"Yes," Philip smiled.

CHAPTER XVI

Jean toiled up Laura Brookman's broad stairway. She stood for a moment at the top, uncertain in which direction to go, when the sound of a child's voice reached her and she went toward it, pushing open the door of the children's bedroom.

"May I come in?" she asked from the threshold.

"Why, it's Jean," cried Mrs. Brookman, dropping the brush with which she was curling her little daughter's hair, and going quickly to meet the girl. "Draw up a comfortable chair for Jean, Elsie. Tired, dear?"

"Tired? Me? Yes, I believe I am—I can't imagine why," echoed Jean, opening her eyes wide, and sinking into the low rocking-chair Elsie dragged toward her. "But one would think I were ill or dying by the way you look at me. You're getting me mixed up with Uncle Daniel, aren't you? He is the one on whose account we are going away—that dreadful insomnia, you know. No, don't unbutton my jacket, Elsie; I've only dropped in for a minute to say good by. We are going to-morrow morning at eight and—oh, Elsie, why are you having your hair curled, and what may the gorgeous array on the bed portend?" She leaned back, pale, but animatedly interested.

"Mrs. Baker is giving a tea this afternoon for the benefit of the Red Cross Society," explained Elsie's mother, resuming her task, "and Elsie has been asked to sing. Where have you been, Jean? Doing a lot of walking?"

"Oh, no. I've just made a few good-by calls—I wanted to see some of the soldier boys' mothers before I leave. I heard that Mrs. Levison has grown so downcast, now that the troops are about to go. You can't draw a smile from her, although the girls are doing their best to cheer her with patriotic orations. 'Talk away,' she snapped, grimly, this afternoon. 'For me, I'd rather have a live coward every day than a dead hero any day.' But we finally got her to admit she didn't mean exactly that, although, through her tears, we couldn't just make out what she did mean. Out at Mrs. Arnstein's, who has been a brave Spartan mother all along, they told me how she began to cry last night during dinner when the dessert was brought on, because Ben couldn't have any—and it was his favorite pudding! Think of it, Elsie! Isn't that shocking?"

"I wouldn't cry about an old pudding," answered the child, con-temptuously, her cheeks and eyes glowing.

"You and Jean would make good drummer-boys," said Laura Brookman, letting a heavy silky spiral droop to her daughter's waist. "And all this patriotism in the abstract, Miss Willard, is very high and brave, and unselfish, but I doubt if you would sing the same song if some one dearer to you than—"

"You don't believe that, Laura," returned Jean, gently. "You know if I had any one very close to me, which I haven't, who could, and didn't want to, join the army, I'd be ashamed to claim him as my own."

"Nonsense. You have sung that song to the echoes," said Laura, harshly. "I should think the responsibility would make an eloquent girl like you hesitate once in a while from expressing herself so care-lessly. You have influenced quite enough young recruits."

Her eyes flashed for a moment upon her friend.

The girl put her hands to her temples. "Do you know, I really think I have a headache," she said, surprisedly. "Or was it your hor-rid words, Laura, that sent such a throb—dear me; how everything swings! There, it's gone. What do you think happened to me last night? I almost fainted when I was saying good by to Paul, and if that—why, Elsie, sweetheart, what is the matter?"

"Mamma pulled my hair," sobbed the little one, putting her head down on her knees.

Mrs. Brookman had the little face against hers in a minute. "Hush," she whispered, imperatively. "As though mamma wouldn't rather hurt herself than you."

A rush of miserable understanding thrilled through Jean. "Don't be a cry-baby, Elsie," she said, coming to the rescue, "and I'll tell you what Charlie Taylor did night before last to help his country. You know Charlie Taylor, the boy who lives across the street from me? Well, his brother, Lieutenant Taylor, has gone to the front, and Charlie promised to look after the ladies for him while he is at the war—a real squire of dames is he, like those they used to have years ago, you know. Now, Lieutenant Taylor has a young wife who isn't very well, and she is living with her mother away out on Scott Street, and the last command the lieutenant gave Charlie was that his wife, Edith, was not to be frightened about him. Well, night before last, one of those fake-extra newsboys began suddenly to make night hideous with his war-cry, and just as I ran to the door to hear what he was saying, there was a sudden silence, and a moment later Charlie Taylor, hatless, with golden hair flying in the breeze, appeared around the corner like a beautiful young St. Michael. 'Why, Charlie,' I called, 'what have you in your arms?' 'All that fellow's extras,' he shouted back. 'I bought 'em. Now he can't frighten Edith.' So he's my Captain Charlie."

The child forgot her tears, listening to the bright, enthusiastic voice, and Laura Brookman regained her composure. But the girl sprang restlessly to her feet. "I must go," she said, looking at her watch. "Don't forget you are to be my squire at the Boys' Club, Laura, while I'm gone, and don't forget my soldier boys. Oh, how I hate to go away—now."

She kissed them good by, and was soon out in the sunshiny, windy street, where every house was bright with flags. Now and then a soldier passed, Jean nodding to each in the camaraderie born of the hour, which was never misunderstood or abused. A rag-tag regiment of tots was having a council of war in a sand-lot, as to whether it should be a land or naval battle that day; two solemn-looking youngsters in infantry-striped overalls were bearing a wounded comrade off the field of battle. The starry-eyed girl passed along among this toy war, her thoughts wistful and far away from it all. Two schoolgirls, holding hands, came by, softly singing "Tenting To-night." She had passed these same singing schoolgirls before, and now she smiled absently into their eyes, while almost running into a tall, lanky bluecoat at the corner.

"Why, Paul!" She held his hand while he lifted his gray campaign hat. "Once again, for luck."

"I hope so. Where are you bound for?"

"Just around the corner, home. And you'll come and dine with us."

"Not to-night. But I'll walk down to the house with you." They strolled along together.

"How many subscriptions did you get up to-day?" he asked, looking fondly down into her deeply shadowed eyes. "How many more Jewish volunteers did you count—how many hungry souls did you feed and how many soleless souls did you console? How many romantic hearts did you—"

"Silly fellow, keep still. I haven't accomplished a thing to-day. Oh, yes, I attended a meeting this morning—and thereby hangs a tale." She laughed a short, embittered laugh.

"Well?"

"Well, a vote of thanks was offered to all the ladies who had given assistance to the soldiers, especially for the splendid patriotism shown by the Jewish and colored ladies." Her eyes flashed in her pale face.

Paul smiled. "Evidently you don't like fine distinctions," he mused, amusedly.

"They're not fine—under that," she said, swiftly, nodding toward a flag which fluttered out in the breeze.

"But it was meant most kindly. Jean, Jean, don't be forever butting your head against a stone wall. It's no use. The long and short of it is—well, there's that," he indicated the flying colors, "and here we are—answering; with no spread-eagleism, only in common decency, wiping out, perhaps, an old-time unjust accusation—with our lives. On the battlefield all blood flows red." He took both her hands in his, having reached her doorstep.

"I won't tell you to be brave, Paul," she said, looking into his strong, kind eyes. "But oh, my dear, take care of yourself."

He threw back his head, laughing aloud. "That reminds me of a popular song we sang long before your day:

> " 'Mother, may I go out to swim?
>   Yes, my dearest daughter;
> Hang your clothes on the hickory limb,
>   But don't go near the water.'

Which is all very loving and foolish, and therefore human. Well, friend o' mine, once again, good by. Be good to yourself—and to all our own." His hands gripped hers tensely.

"I will, Paul," she responded, truly. "Now I'll stand here and watch you to the corner."

"That's like you," he returned, gayly, swinging off. But the next minute he was back again.

"It seems as though I couldn't leave you," he laughed, hurriedly. "But it just occurred to me that some news I heard at camp might lessen your solicitude for yours truly. Colonel Smith told me this morning that our eminent friend, your quondam neighbor, Dr. May, has offered his services, been appointed, through his friend, the Governor, an acting assistant surgeon, and sails with us on Wednesday for Manila—so——. What, Jean, you're not going to faint again!" He put out a startled hand.

"I never do more than make a feint at it," she reassured him, smiling through her pallor. "It must be the sun in my eyes. Yes, you'll be in skillful hands."

"No doubt of it. Well—so long!"

At the corner he turned. The great flag on the staff fluttered out in the stiff breeze toward him. The westering sun illumined him as he raised his hat high. It was thus that Jean ever after remembered him.

"I am not going in," she thought, dazedly. "But what was I going to do? Oh, it doesn't matter—I'll just walk down the street—perhaps I'll meet uncle."

She strolled away.

CHAPTER XVII

But she turned down the first side street, dully conscious that she did not wish to meet her uncle, or any one—that, for a little space, all she desired was to be quite alone, that she might have time to forget the dread vision Paul Stein's words had brought to her—the vision of a lonely form, of a bearded face, dead and upturned to a cold, white moonlight.

For several minutes, long as infinity, her darkened senses could hold nothing else, and it only faded when the gripping, never wholly absent memory of Philip May's voice, calling her as out of the whole world, resumed its despotic sway. Over and again she had striven to banish from her life the memory of its passionate longing, though, at the same moment, came the recollection of how she had responded to it. It confounded reason. Had he had no provocation? Were not existing circumstances extenuating? What right had the Past to him—the Past with its—

Fifth commandment!

She raised her head as to a living voice—answered by the rebuke of Life. The flash of eternal truth smote her relentlessly. Fifth commandment—the far-seeing care of the man-of-God for the old! Heavy tears welled to her eyes at thought of the yearning old father, Joseph May, lying silent with his stilled griefs. The tie of blood—so Titan-strong in the Jew—was *that* the Middle Pillar upon which the House stood?[139] She tried to beat back the swarming, lashing thoughts. And yet—and yet, came the passionate rebuttal, this sentimental care, this forever turning of the eyes backward for fear of treading on some outworn tradition, this tyrannous claim upon free will—was not *that* the power which impeded union, which, first suffocating, would finally stamp out individuality, and hold forever in leash the dream of barriers down, straining at the heart of life?

"I cannot understand it," her tortured soul complained, tossed from sentiment to reason, striving to seize life by the forelock, demanding the answer which is only given when life is slipping through the fingers.

Alas! the answer did not lie with her. She recognized the futility of her struggle, and gave in at last. For her there remained only one comprehensible cry forevermore, and she lifted her woman soul to that, finding the common factor which reduces all to one denomination. She moved on, strong in surrender, prisoner to an unsought love for a man who was presently going out of her life as silently as he had entered it.

And his going away—she did not exalt it to any heroism—it was only, as Paul had said, common decency; but the silence of it, the loneliness of it, these were the smiting, possessive powers of it over a nature and love like Jean Willard's. She ached in her helpless wistfulness. If she could have stretched out her hand to him, have seen him only once, to—

But, the test was granted, as, abruptly turning the corner, she came face to face with Philip May.

She stood still and held out her hand, looking straight and truly into his stern face.

"You were going without saying good by to us," she explained, gently. "Was it quite fair?"

He commanded his bewilderment. "I thought so," he said, quietly.

She tried again. "I—I wanted to ask you to take good care of some of my friends."

"I shall remember. I think I know at least one." His lips parted in a faint smile of understanding.

"And of yourself," she added, in undaunted misery.

"Thank you." He waited for her further pleasure.

She stood looking beyond.

"I shall not forget your order," he repeated, and raised his hat in leave-taking, noticing her uncertainty of manner.

"I—" She raised her saddened eyes suddenly to his. The blood rushed responsively over both their faces.

"Which way are you going?" he demanded, on impulse.

"Anywhere—up this hill, I think."

He turned and walked with her.

"You are very kind," he said, with desperate control.

"No, no."

"I could almost find it in me to speak to you. By heaven, I will—you have given me the chance!" But the leap of hope died down the next minute, leaving an inevitable memory in its stead.

They walked on silently for a space, as though weighted by the stillness of the dying day, removed by its pensive hold from all the world besides, they too alone, mounting the hilly, almost deserted streets.

He spoke abruptly. "Perhaps I misinterpret you," he said. "I don't want you to mistake me. I am still the same derelict you arraigned last year—egoist—"

She turned her head swiftly. "Forget that," she sharply commanded.

"I have not changed," he reiterated, harshly, "in spite of the lesson. I still stand stolidly by my first principles. But this is nothing to you."

"It is very much to me." She looked before her to the hill horizon.

A pale intensity of purpose settled over his features.

"I hated the badge of difference," he gave forth between his teeth, holding back half, explaining, not pleading, according to his nature.

"Yes."

"I had a dream of fusion with—my kind."

Her lips set in sad understanding.

"I considered myself neither fakir nor fool."[140]

"I know."

"I said to myself, I am an individual, not a class."

"I understand."

"I said to myself, 'What have I to do with Ghettoes?'"

She did not answer.

"I felt the warm, free sun of the present burning and quickening within me. I was strong and forward-looking. I decided I would not be fate's social cripple linked by an invisible chain to a slavish past. *I resolved to break the chain.*"

She stood a moment before crossing the street and looked sadly up at him.

"I discovered *you can never break the chain.*"

The passionless words chimed fatally with the perfect stillness about them. They walked on under the weight of their finality, closer together, more apart from the rest of the world, for their stern meaning.

He bent his set, fighting face fully toward her. "I discovered there are other—closer—more binding links riveting us to the chain. For I succeeded in pulling at the chain—till my father fell."

She had always demanded that any wrong-doer be punished— she had always agonized over the pain of any one's punishment. She pressed her quivering lips close, keeping herself doggedly down.

"That is all," he announced.

"Hush." She could not bear his harsh reticence.

"Understand me—it has not made me any gladder to be a Jew than I was before—even though I know that the thought of the unfettered Jew is the same as that of the unfettered Christian, even though I have been taught that breed is stronger than creed—and even though I know that the Jew is no longer a religion apart—only a race apart."

He raised his hat a moment as though it burned his brow. "I have never thanked God that I am different from other men,"[141] he said, grimly, looking beyond her face for a second. Then he came back with a start to its pale beauty.

"I'm not worth thinking about, or troubling you about," he said, thickly. "I had no hope of ever seeing you again—never of speaking to you, surely. This solitude with you has unmanned me. Forgive the intrusion if you can. You have been generosity itself in listening to me."

"I am not generous," she said, bitterly. "I am just a moral prig."

The gleam of a tender smile shot into his eyes. "You are an idealist," he began, gently. "All this apart, I could never reach the sky-line of your requirements, although I can look up to it as other men look up to their heaven." He paused, his eyes lingering upon her; then he continued softly, "I have heard—have seen—much argument—but you—you are the only argument I know which makes me ready to stand by that for which you are the loyal—my only—torch-bearer. I have even thought that perhaps the ancient tyranny which still constrains us has endured—was only love-in-wisdom having you in design. Ah, you see, I cannot help myself—you have become my religion—if you are Jewish, must I not too be Jew?"

He tried to smile away his loss of control. But his hand groped toward her, only stopping, through force of memory, before it touched her.

"Does it pain you very much to know I love you?" he asked, quietly.

The voices of evening seemed suddenly hushed, awaiting her answer. She raised her eyes to his.

They walked on together over the hill.

* * * * *

In all beautifully risen San Francisco there is no prettier view than where she, sitting on her western hills, the sun in her eyes, gazes over the silvery waters of the bay curving out to meet the Golden Gate. In all her history, never did the meeting waters seem more fraught with meaning, and power, and high emprise, than toward five o'clock of the afternoon of May 25, 1898. For hours, the crowds here on the heights, on balconies, on housetops, as on the lower water front, had stood patient, breathless, many thus keeping silent tryst with those whose ship they had promised to watch till it should sink beyond the line of vision.

Just at five the signal came in the booming and banging of guns, the mad shrieking of whistles, the clang and clamor of bells. It brought the heart of the city to its throat in a prolonged sobbing, deafening cheer. Around the cove came the gay dancing flotilla, resplendent in fluttering bunting and flags and pennants, in the midst of which, black with humanity and war-paint, proudly breasting wind and billows, rode the pioneer fleet of invasion—the City of Peking in the lead, closely followed by the Australia and City of Sidney.[142] It was the Peking, however, which carried the California First, and most of the watching eyes grew dim following her. Past volleying Alcatraz sped the inspiring pageant, past Fort Mason and the downs, past the white city of tents and the Presidio sending soldierly farewell, past the old fort, out through the open Gate, and so straight into the sunset.[143] The sun shot down in a silver vapor. The vanishing ships were figures of mist.

In the press of the crowd near the mansion which lifts its terra-cotta beauty to the blue jewel above, two school-girls, standing hand in hand, began softly singing The Battle Hymn of the Republic.[144]

An old gentleman standing near reverently raised his hat. The girl beside him stood gazing after the mist-shapes—that look of yearning in her face which seeing eyes call prayer.

NOTES

1. This is a version of the common proverb "It takes three generations to make a gentleman." The earliest version appears to have come into print in James Fenimore Cooper's *Pioneers* (1823), although the expression predates the specific proverb. See Jennifer Speake, *A Dictionary of Proverbs* (Oxford: Oxford University Press, 2008). Wolf also refers to the proverb in her article, "Social Life in American Cities: San Francisco" (September 1897), in the *Delineator*:

> Farther east tradition has decreed that three generations from the hod are necessary to the making of a gentleman, and, by analogy, three generations from pick and shovel should do as much for the son of the Golden West— providing, of course, that his adventurous father was inconsiderate enough to be a mere child of nature, born, like Adam, without a grandfather worth mentioning. The generation of present importance is only half-way to the pre-scribed goal, but there are vigorous young men now in the field who have brought with them from foreign universities and Eastern association a flavor of manly distinction and cul-ture which promises to bear good fruit. The making of a lady, it goes without saying, is beyond the province of calculation. And, leaving out of the question those off-shoots of some of the best families of the East and South who have grown up with the city, a glance at the fine lineaments and bearing of

many of San Francisco's lovely daughters goes to prove that femininity often attains by a bound of intuition what it takes three generations of the stronger sex to acquire. (343)

2. Kate speaks in Irish American dialect. The term "blarney" typifies representations of Irish speech. The term derives from a stone on the top side of Blarney Castle near Cork City in Ireland, which legendarily gives the person who kisses it "the gift of gab." "Blarney" is used here to refer to flattering or cajoling speech. When Jean compliments the smells of Kate's kitchen, the Irish cook jokingly accuses Jean of flattery.

3. *Shivah* (usually transliterated as *shiva*): the Hebrew word for "seven." In Judaism, it refers to the seven days of mourning that follow a funeral. Joseph May sat on a footstool when his wife died because of a custom during *shiva*; the mourner sits on a low stool or box, rather than a regular chair, as a means of expressing grief.

4. In late nineteenth-century American usage, a "dude" denoted a dandy, or a man unduly concerned with fashion and appearance.

5. In this context, "Jewish" refers to the Yiddish language.

6. *Chutspah ponim*: Yiddish phrase meaning "bold face." "Chutzpah," usually translated into English as "nerve" or "shameless audacity," often has a negative connotation; here, it is being used in a positive and affectionate sense.

7. From the Old French, "jargon" means "jabbering" or "unintelligible speech." The term was imported from the French into German specifically as a pejorative designation for the Yiddish language.

8. *Junge*: German for "boy."

9. The Sabbath lamp, or Judenstern, was a brass, star-shaped, hanging oil lamp, common in Germany and the Netherlands, on which the ceremonial Sabbath lights were kindled.

10. Decalogue: Ten Commandments.

11. In Yiddish, *lachachlis ponim* literally means "spiteful face."

12. *Ich weiss viel*: German for "I know a lot." Note that oysters and frogs are *treyf* (unkosher), forbidden according to traditional Jewish dietary laws.

13. *Yitt*: Jew.

14. *Schtiegen*: may be used here to mean "seriously" in Yiddish.

15. Picquet: a card game. Usually spelled "piquet," the game originated in France and uses French terms.

16. Chevalier: a French term for a knight or chivalrous man.

17. Golgotha: the hill in Jerusalem where Christ was crucified.

18. The Verein Club, or the San Francisco Schuetzen Verein, was a men's paramilitary and social organization founded in 1859 by German Jewish immigrants. The Concordia Club was a men's social club founded in 1864 by German American Jews; Levi Strauss and other members of Temple Emanu-El belonged to the club.

19. Wolf appears to be using the term "Jacobian" to refer to the biblical story of the twins Jacob and Esau. In Genesis, Jacob convinces Esau, who was born first, to sell his birthright for a "mess of pottage." Jacob later tricks their blind father into bestowing upon him the blessing of the firstborn son. In simplified terms, one might say that Jacob "steals" Esau's birthright.

20. Table d'hôte (French): a complete meal of several courses offered at a fixed price.

21. *Grande dame* (French): a great lady.

22. In the nineteenth century and into the twentieth century, many hotels and summer resorts barred their doors to Jews. In 1877, this discriminatory practice provoked a nationwide controversy when banker Joseph Seligman and his family were denied entry to the Grand Union Hotel in Saratoga, New York, by the hotel's owner, Judge Henry Hilton.

23. *Meshumad* (or *meshumed*): Yiddish for "apostate."

24. The Francis Scott Key monument was built in 1888 in Golden Gate Park to commemorate the man who wrote the lyrics of "The Star-Spangled Banner."

25. In 1894, the California Midwinter International Exposition (or Midwinter Fair) was held in San Francisco's Golden

Gate Park. The "Museum" refers to the exposition's fine arts building, which is now the de Young Museum, and the "Japanese village" refers to the ethnological exhibit on Japanese culture that later became the Japanese Tea Garden.

26. *Shabos* (usually *Shabbos*): Yiddish term for the Jewish Sabbath, or day of rest and worship. "Make *Shabos*" refers to preparing for the Sabbath, especially for the Sabbath meal. A band of crepe worn on a hat or a sleeve was a sign of mourning.

27. *Lass mich gehen*: German for "let me go."

28. *Moshelich* (usually transliterated as *mayselekh*): Yiddish for "stories" or "tales."

29. *Ach Gott!*: German for "Oh God!"

30. Palace Hotel: a luxury hotel that opened in San Francisco in 1875. The Philomath Club, the women's club to which Wolf belonged, held its regular meetings at this hotel.

31. *Nix*: German for "nothing."

32. *Chérie*: French for "dear."

33. *N'est-ce pas*: French for "Isn't it?"

34. *Amour propre*: French term meaning "self-respect."

35. Fifth commandment: refers to the fifth of the Ten Commandments in the Jewish tradition, which states, "Honor thy father and thy mother." "Choice of parents" is likely an allusion to Israel Zangwill's story of the same name. See I. Zangwill, "The Choice of Parents," *Cosmopolitan* 20, no. 2 (1895): 209–17. In talking with his friend, the main character of Zangwill's story explains that he is writing for "posterity," and by this term he means that his audience is the unborn. He confronts his incredulous friend, questioning why "retain such an inherent anachronism as compulsory birth, a disability which often cripples a man upon the very threshold of his career? . . . If you are to develop your individuality, it must be your own individuality that you develop, not an individuality thrust upon you by a couple of outsiders" (210).

36. Judith, a Jewish biblical heroine, known for beheading the Assyrian general Holofernes, was a popular subject in Western art.

37. *Quién sabe?:* Spanish for "who knows?"
38. The Omar Club may be a reference to the Omar Khayyam Club of London, which was founded in 1892 by admirers of Khayyam's *Rubaiyat*; the Omar Khayyam Club of America was founded in 1900. For a history of the British club, see *The Book of the Omar Khayyám Club, 1892–1910* (London, 1910).
39. This is a reference to Kate's underlying anti-Semitism. In medieval European culture, Jews were represented as having the cloven foot of the devil.
40. The Thirteen Articles of faith, or the *Shloshah Asar Ikkarim*, recorded by Rabbi Moshe ben Maimon ("Maimonides" or "The Rambam"), are a list of principles of the Jewish religion, as derived from the Torah.
41. The idea of eschewing religious dogma while retaining a belief in an Ineffable God was not unique to Jean but prevalent among religious reformers, including the leadership of Temple Emanu-El in San Francisco. According to the prevailing sentiment of the Reform movement at the time, Judaism was naturally progressing from biblical and postbiblical times toward contemporaneous Reform Judaism and beyond, leaving behind particularistic forms and dogmas and moving toward a universal ethical monotheism. For an explanation of radical Reform Judaism at the turn of the twentieth century that specifically focuses on the theology that Wolf would have encountered at Temple Emanu-El, see Marc Lee Raphael, "Rabbi Jacob Voorsanger of San Francisco on Jews and Judaism: The Implications of the Pittsburgh Platform," *American Jewish Historical Quarterly* 63, no. 2 (1973): 185–203.
42. 2 Samuel 14:25.
43. The Chronicle Building was San Francisco's first skyscraper and housed the offices of the *San Francisco Chronicle*.
44. Lotta's fountain, commissioned by actress Lotta Crabtree in 1875 as a gift to the city of San Francisco, was originally located at the intersection of 3rd, Market, and Kearny Streets.

In 1974, it was relocated to the intersection of Market Street where Geary and Kearny streets connect.

45. As discussed in the introduction, Wolf's family belonged to Temple Emanu-El, which was originally located on Sutter Street and was also known as "The Sutter Street Temple."

46. Roentgen (or Röntgen) ray: a precursor to the X-ray, named for German scientist Wilhelm Röntgen, who discovered the rays around 1895.

47. A *lundi*: French for "see you Monday."

48. *Gott im himmel!*: a Yiddish exclamation meaning "God in heaven!" (or "good heavens!").

49. *Poseur*: a poser or fake, an affectation from the French.

50. Prince of Courtesy: possibly a reference to Alfred, Lord Tennyson's poem "In the Garden at Swainston," which reads, "Still in the house in his coffin the Prince of courtesy lay." The phrase denotes someone of patrician family and emphasizes chivalric virtue.

51. The French Hospital was founded in 1851 as San Francisco's first private hospital.

52. "The ass who preferred his thistle to gold": a reference to Aesop's fable "The Ass Eating Thistles." The moral of the fable is that different people have different tastes or preferences. Wolf uses this same phrase in her novella "The Conflict," published in the *Smart Set* in 1906.

53. "Take the cash and let the credit go": a common proverb, famously used by Edward FitzGerald (1809–83) in *The Rubaiyat of Omar Khayyam*: "Some for the Glories of This World; and some / Sigh for the Prophet's Paradise to come; / Ah, take the Cash, and let the Credit go, / Nor heed the rumble of a distant Drum!"

54. *Bonne bouche*: French for "tasty bite."

55. The superstition against seating thirteen people at a table relates to the thirteen people at the Last Supper.

56. The "Messianic hypothesis" likely refers to the belief that the messiah, or savior, will come to liberate and redeem the Jewish people.

57. Phil May (1864–1903) was a British artist who did illustrations for many British and Australian periodicals,
including *Punch* magazine, where he became a regular
contributor beginning in 1895. The January 1904 *Magazine
of Art* published a tribute to May, recognizing that he "will
always be remembered for his technical perfection, for his
mastery in seeing and realizing his character, for the truth
with which he fitted not only character but expression to
his subjects, for the directness and richness of his humour
and for the beauty of his work. . . . As to character, he has so
far excelled nearly all other draughtsmen in rendering with
remorseless truth every type of low-class Jew, and, moreover,
wrote Hebrew so well, that it has often been surmised that
he sprang from the race himself" (31, 35). However, based
on a biography of Phil May by James Thorpe, this surmise
does not appear to be accurate; see James Thorpe, *The English Masters of Black-and-White: Phil May* (London: Art and
Technics, 1948). Wolf would have been acquainted with
May's work from his illustrations for Zangwill's *The King of
Schnorrers* (1894), if not from other sources.

58. Baden-Baden: a fashionable spa town in southwestern Germany, near the border with France. Tourists often visited for
medicinal purposes since the hot springs were believed to
cure a variety of ailments.

59. A reference to *t'chiyat hameitim*, Hebrew for "the resurrection of the dead," a doctrine of Jewish theology. According
to this doctrine, during the Messianic Age, the Temple
will be rebuilt in Jerusalem, where the Jewish people will
gather from the far corners of the earth and the bodies of
the dead will be brought back to life and reunited with
their souls.

60. This phrase is from Deuteronomy 32:15: "But Jeshurun
waxed fat, and kicked: thou art waxen fat, thou art grown
thick, thou art covered *with fatness*; then he forsook God
which made him, and lightly esteemed the Rock of his
salvation."

61. Dreyfus: French Jewish military officer Captain Alfred Dreyfus was falsely accused and convicted of treason in 1894 and imprisoned in the French penal colony on Devil's Island. The Dreyfus Affair is one of the most infamous historical cases of anti-Semitism.

62. *Nebbich* (or *Nebbish*): Yiddish for "poor thing" or "poor man," often used to indicate an object of pity.

63. Coon song: a musical genre especially popular from the mid-1880s until the early 1900s. Composed by both white and black musicians, coon songs conveyed stereotypical images of African Americans using ragtime rhythms; the word "coon" was a common racial slur in the nineteenth-century United States. "Orpheum joke" refers to a vaudeville joke; the Orpheum Circuit was a chain of vaudeville theaters. *Puck*: a late nineteenth-century American magazine featuring political satire, cartoons, and other humor; as discussed in the introduction, *Puck* regularly printed anti-Semitic caricatures.

64. Edition de luxe (French): limited or rare edition. Chef-d'oeuvre (French): masterpiece.

65. "Is the game worth the candle?": a relatively common expression asking whether the rewards are worth the effort to attain them. It originated as a translation of the French phrase *le jeu n'en vaut la chandelle*.

66. *En masse* (French): in a group. *Tout-ensemble* (French): an assemblage of details forming the whole.

67. Clo' man: clothing seller. For more details regarding the social geography of San Francisco, see Decker, *Fortunes and Failures*, 196–230.

68. Puss-in-the-corner: a children's game for five players, similar to musical chairs. The player nominated to be "puss" stands in the center, and each of the other players stands in a corner. The players in the corners attempt to exchange places as the puss attempts to gain a corner. The player left without a corner becomes the new puss.

69. Edward MacDowell (1860–1908): an American composer and pianist who wrote verses for many of his own musical

compositions. In 1907, MacDowell's wife, Marion Nevins MacDowell, founded the famous MacDowell artists' colony at the site of the New Hampshire farm where he worked in the summers during the last decade of his life.

70. *Sedar* (usually transliterated as *seder*): a Jewish ritual meal held at the beginning of the Passover holiday. In Hebrew, "seder" means "order," referring to the prescribed order of the service that accompanies the meal.

71. Joseph is referencing the game of piquet here.

72. *Nix-nuts*: German for "good for nothing."

73. Daniel is referring to Jean's charitable work with the settlement houses, part of the late nineteenth-century movement in which middle-class volunteers, usually women, provided educational, recreational, and social services to the urban poor. As part of the settlement house movement, the San Francisco Boys' Club was "formed to help the growing boys who haunt the streets become useful citizens instead of roughs" ("Local News in Brief," *San Francisco Call*, March 29, 1894, 7). See also Ann Marie Wilson, "'Neutral Territory': The Politics of Settlement Work in San Francisco, 1894–1906," in *California Women and Politics: From the Gold Rush to the Great Depression*, ed. Robert W. Cherny, Mary Ann Irwin, and Ann Marie Wilson (Lincoln: University of Nebraska Press, 2011), 97–122.

74. The reference is to the Victorian writer Thomas Carlyle (1795–1881).

75. Bruited: rumored (English, of French etymology).

76. Lohengrin: an 1850 opera by Richard Wagner, a German composer and author of "Jewishness in Music" (1850), a controversial essay that attacked Jews for having a negative effect on German culture.

77. Heinrich Heine (1797–1856): a German-Jewish poet whose lyric poetry was often set to music by famous composers. Catulle Mendès (1841–1909): a descendant of Portuguese Jews who was born in France and became a poet, dramatist, and art critic. In his 1886 critical study, *Richard Wagner*, Mendès praised the German composer's work.

78. Costermonger: a boisterous singsong, like that of a street seller.

79. Passover: a Jewish festival commemorating the Exodus of the Jews from Egypt and their liberation from slavery. Participants in the meal will often recline on pillows as a symbol of freedom.

80. During the Passover seder, participants drink four cups of ceremonial wine over the course of the service.

81. Wolf is listing some of the items that appear on the seder plate, which is placed on the table during the meal. These items are symbolic, though interpretations vary. For example, during the holiday, Jews eat unleavened bread (called "matzah" or "matzo") because the Israelites did not have the time to allow their bread to rise in their rush to leave Egypt. The bone of the paschal lamb (z'roa) represents the lamb that was sacrificed on the night the Jews left Egypt. The bitter herb (maror) is a reminder of the bitterness of slavery. Parsley is a symbol of springtime (which is when Passover takes place) and new beginnings; today, it is typically dipped in salt water rather than vinegar to represent the tears shed by the Israelites when they were slaves in Egypt. The almonds and apples refer to the charoset (today, usually a mixture of apples, wine, and walnuts), which represents the mortar of the bricks made by the enslaved Israelites. Charoset derives from the Hebrew word for "clay."

82. Wolf appears to be using the word "house-cap" to refer to the skullcap, or yarmulke, which Jewish men wear on their heads as a sign of respect for God.

83. Elijah: a biblical prophet who, it is said, would arrive on Earth to announce the coming of the Messiah. During the seder, a cup of wine is placed on the table and the door to the house is opened in order to welcome Elijah.

84. "The quaintly illustrated books": a reference to the Passover Haggadah, the text used during the seder. Hallel: a prayer of thanksgiving recited during the Passover service.

85. "The paean on the Building of the Temple" refers to the song "Adir Hu" ("Mighty Is He"), which is sung toward the

end of the seder to express the hope that God will rebuild the Holy Temple.

86. Earlier, Paul Stein uses the term "enforced specialization" to refer to the idea that, historically, Jews became financiers because they were often kept out of other professions due to anti-Semitism.

87. Tête-à-têtes (French): a face-to-face conversation between two people.

88. Wolf published a poem about love titled "Eschscholtzia (California Poppy)" in 1896 in the *American Jewess*.

89. Jean is referring to God as an abstraction in accord with the Reform Jewish understanding of the "God-idea." When Philip references Sinai, he recalls to her a biblical tradition of an immanent and personal God. Jean responds with the assertion that Judaism has progressed over time and the Bible is a record of an earlier form of Judaism suited to its own time but not of the present moment. Jean's position on the nature of God and the relationship of current Judaism to the biblical tradition aligns with the theological commitments laid out in the 1885 Pittsburgh Platform of the Reform movement.

90. A Scots phrase that translates to "days gone by," "Auld Lang Syne" is also a popular folk song based on a poem by Robert Burns and is often sung at midnight on New Year's Eve.

91. Jean is referring to the 1893 World's Parliament of Religions, the largest event among many other congresses at the World's Columbian Exposition in Chicago. The World Congress of Religions was the first formal gathering of representatives of Eastern and Western spiritual traditions. Several Reform rabbis spoke at the gathering. Jean may be referring to Dr. Emil Hirsch's speech "Elements of Universal Religion" or Dr. G. Gotthiel's "Syllabus of a Treatise on the Development of Religious Ideas in Judaism since Moses Mendelsohn."

92. The first proclamation of the 1885 Pittsburgh Platform is that all religions express "the consciousness of the indwelling of God in man."

93. Jean is likely referring to the *Shemah*, the daily prayer. It is the best-known prayer in Judaism, affirming faith in one God.

94. This echoes the classical Reform sentiment that Judaism hides within itself a treasure of ideas and sentiments—a kernel—that can only be reached by shucking the husk of forms and rituals to reach the essence of the religious ideas, freed of ceremony. See, for instance, the 1844 platform of the Berlin Association for the Reform of Judaism, found in W. Gunther Plaut, *The Rise of Reform Judaism: A Sourcebook of Its European Origins* (Lincoln: University of Nebraska Press, 2015).

95. Malvolio: a character from Shakespeare's *Twelfth Night, or What You Will*. The term is used to refer to individuals who like to spoil other people's fun.

96. This is an indication of the particularities of Reform Jewish custom in which the symbol of the holiday—unleavened bread—is present, even though the characters are not adhering to the law of eating only unleavened bread.

97. *Matzos*: unleavened bread.

98. *Yuntoff* (usually transliterated as *yontif*): Yiddish for holiday. Joseph and Daniel are wishing each other a "good holiday."

99. Later renamed the San Francisco Art Institute, the Mark Hopkins Art Institute was San Francisco's first art and cultural center.

100. Gott: God in Yiddish and German. "A *vahre* prince" likely means a real, or true, prince; in German, *wahr* means "true."

101. Mammonism: a greedy devotion to accumulating wealth.

102. *Hic jacet*: Latin for "here lies," a term used to refer to an epitaph.

103. From the *Sheva Brachot* (seven blessings), a component of the Jewish wedding ritual.

104. "Sisterhood" refers specifically to the organization of women at a synagogue. *Schlemielich*, an adjectival form of *schlemiel*, refers to an inept person in Yiddish and is usually used as an insult.

105. *Überzwerich*: Wolf is likely using the German word *überzwerch*, which means crosswise, or not as it should be.

106. "Home of Peace" refers to the Jewish cemetery in Colma, California, where members of Temple Emanu-El were buried. For a discussion of Wolf's gravesite in Home of Peace, see Cantalupo's preface to this edition.

107. *Wie geht's?*: "How are you?" in German.

108. Much of modern San Francisco was built on land made up of sandhills.

109. *Verrückt*: "crazy" or "insane" in German.

110. "La Lisette de Béranger" (1843) was a popular French folk song written by Frédéric Bérat. In English, the lyrics that Jean sings read as follows:

If you only knew, children,
When I was a young girl,
How I was sweet—
I'm talking about a long time ago—
A fresh face, brilliant eyes,
A smile with white teeth,
So then, oh my children,
So then, oh my children,
A poor working girl, fifteen years old,
Oh! was I sweet.

111. "Madame la Marquise" (1868) is a French song by Louis-Albert Bourgault-Ducoudray based on lyrics by poet Alfred de Musset.

112. Chain: likely a reference to *di goldene keyt*, the "golden chain" of Jewish tradition, passing uninterrupted from one generation to the next. "Auto-da-fes" refers to the ritual of public penance of condemned heretics and apostates that took place after a heretic's trial during the Spanish or Portuguese Inquisitions, involving a public procession and reading of their sentences. Artistic renderings usually depict torture and burning at the stake, and the term has become associated with this brutal form of punishment. "Yellow patch" refers to badges that Jews were required to wear in public to identify themselves in medieval Europe, beginning in the 1200s and lasting, in some areas, as late as the 1700s. The

patch was a requirement in medieval England beginning with the 1274 Statute of Jewry.

113. St. Luke's: an Episcopalian charitable hospital that opened in 1871 in San Francisco. It was later replaced by the Mission Bernal campus of California Pacific Medical Center.

114. Philip is referencing the custom of holding a *Shiva minyan* service in the home of the bereaved, a short prayer service that concludes with the recitation of the kaddish to honor the memory of the deceased (see note 119).

115. Friday night is the eve of the Jewish Sabbath.

116. The ark is the cabinet containing the Torah scrolls. The organ indicates that the temple is a Reform synagogue; Reform synagogues in Germany began using organs in the early 1800s, and the instrument continues to be an object of controversy in Judaism since its adoption symbolized an attempt to imitate Christian church music.

117. *Shemah*: daily prayer. The word "*shemah*" translates in Hebrew to "listen."

118. Here Wolf indicates the Reform Jewish theology of an ultimate, millennial moment of universalism, in which all humanity would join together in "brotherhood of man and the Unity of God." See W. Gunther Plaut, "Introduction," in *The Rise of Reform Judaism: A Sourcebook of Its European Origins*, ed. W. Gunther Plaut (New York: World Union for Progressive Judaism, 1963).

119. Kadesh (usually spelled "Kaddish"): Translated as "holy" in Hebrew or "sanctification" in Aramaic (the language of this particular prayer), kaddish is the Jewish mourning prayer. According to Jewish law, a son is obligated to recite the kaddish three times daily in the eleven months following his father's death.

120. The Stanford professor, who appears not to be Jewish, is discussing the humanitarian crisis in Cuba during the Cuban War of Independence (1895–98), which ultimately escalated to become the Spanish-American War.

121. *Yahrzeit*: the anniversary of someone's death on which the bereaved (usually the children of the deceased) recite kaddish.

122. Paul is asking Daniel whether he is willing to ride (presumably a streetcar) on the Jewish Sabbath, an act that, at that moment in history, would be prohibited according to the dictates of Orthodox Judaism but was permissible among Reform Jews.

123. Paul is referencing the idea of progressive revelation, drawn from the neo-Kantian Jewish philosopher Hermann Cohen (1842–1918). This idea, which was embraced by Reformers, was that God did not reveal all of Torah at Mt. Sinai, but that through the use of God-given reason and interpretive abilities, revelation continues to happen as modern Jews study, interpret, reinterpret, and apply the words of the Torah in new contexts. The idea was popularized as Reform theology by Abraham Geiger, one of the founders of the Reform movement.

124. Pharisee: a member of an ancient Jewish sect who observed both the oral law of Moses as well as the written law of the Torah and believed in the afterlife.

125. According to many Reform leaders, the world was naturally progressing toward a universal religion of truth, and Jews had a specific, prophetic role in bringing about that universal moment because of their inheritance of revelation. They saw the future universal religion as a "developed and purified Judaism" and believed Jews as particularly important in this progress toward a universal idea. See Benny Kraut, "Unitarianism on the Reform Mind," *Proceedings of the World Congress of Jewish Studies*, 1981, 91–98, and "Judaism Triumphant: Isaac Mayer Wise on Unitarianism and Liberal Christianity," *AJS Review* 7, no. 8 (1982): 179–230; Annette M. Boeckler, "Monotheism, Mission, and Multiculturalism: Universalism Then and Now," in *All the World: Universalism, Particularism and the High Holy Days*, ed. Rabbi Lawrence A. Hoffman (Nashville, TN: Jewish Lights Publishing, 2014), 30–39.

126. Daniel chides Paul for his belief that Jews are God's Chosen People, which Daniel finds chauvinistic. Daniel, in contrast, believes that Jews are chosen only insofar as they have a

prophetic role to play, not for any innate characteristic. Wolf's characters are debating questions about Reform Jewish theology that were being debated in her time.

127.   The phrase "existent Ideality" comes from Hegel's definition of sentience in his 1847 *Philosophy of Nature*.

128.   The quotation is Solomon Shechter's paraphrasing of the Chasidic master the Ba'al Shem Tov. See Solomon Shechter, "The Chassidim," in *Studies in Judaism* (Philadelphia, PA: Jewish Publication Society of America, 1896).

129.   The Deaf, Dumb, and Blind Asylum, founded in 1860, was located from 1869 until the 1970s in Berkeley, California.

130.   Talmudist: someone who studies ancient rabbinic writings.

131.   This is a reference to Heine's quote, "Wherever a great mind expresses its thought, *there* is Golgotha." Heinrich Heine, "Concerning the History of Religion and Philosophy in Germany," trans. Helen Mustard, in *The Romantic School and Other Essays*, ed. Jost Hermand and Robert C. Holub (New York: Continuum, 1985), 170–76.

132.   Raphael and Michelangelo are Italian Renaissance artists.

133.   1 Kings 2:19.

134.   Wolf is describing the sinking of the USS *Maine* in Havana Harbor. The event marked the beginning of the Spanish-American War in 1898.

135.   Don: a Spanish honorific used to refer to men of the nobility. In the Spanish press, and especially in anti-American political cartoons, America was represented as a "Yankee pig" to indicate its imperial greed in trying to take away Spanish territories.

136.   Presidio: A US Army post located in San Francisco.

137.   Wolf is describing the Battle of Manila, the first major battle of the Spanish-American War, which occurred on May 1, 1898. The battle was a victory for the United States under the leadership of Admiral George Dewey.

138.   The "island spoil of war" refers to the Philippines.

139.   This is a reference to the biblical story of Samson. See Judges 16:29.

140. A fakir, or faqir, derived from *faqr*, is a Sufi Muslim ascetic who has taken vows of poverty and worship, renouncing all relations and possessions.

141. This refers to the Jewish daily blessing, "Blessed are You, Eternal our God, who has not made me a gentile."

142. *The City of Peking, Australia,* and *City of Sidney* were troopships used during the Spanish-American War. These ships left San Francisco for Manila on May 25, 1898. As often is the case, Wolf includes historical events in her fiction.

143. In the late nineteenth century, Alcatraz was used as a military fort and prison; it later became a federal penitentiary. Fort Mason was a military base.

144. "Battle Hymn of the Republic": a patriotic song whose words were written by Julia Ward Howe in 1861 to the music of "John Brown's Body." The lyrics were originally written in support of the Union and the abolitionist cause. "The mansion which lifts its terra-cotta beauty to the blue jewel above" is likely a reference to the Cliff House, which had a dramatic roof with turrets, dormers, spires at the time Wolf was writing. For a history of the Cliff House, see "Cliff House History," National Park Service, nps.gov/goga/learn /historyculture/cliff-house.htm.

ABOUT THE EDITORS

Barbara Cantalupo is professor of English at the Pennsylvania State University and editor of *The Edgar Allan Poe Review*. She is the author of *Poe and the Visual Arts*, which won the Poe Studies Association's Quinn award for a distinguished monograph on Poe, and she is the editor of Emma Wolf's *Other Things Being Equal* (Wayne State University Press, 2002) and *Emma Wolf's Short Stories in the Smart Set*.

Lori Harrison-Kahan is associate professor of the practice of English at Boston College. She is the author of *The White Negress: Literature, Minstrelsy, and the Black-Jewish Imaginary* and the editor of *The Superwoman and Other Writings by Miriam Michelson* (Wayne State University Press, 2019).